SECRETS IN SICILY

PENNY FEENY has lived and worked in Cambridge, London and Rome. Since settling in Liverpool many years ago she has been an arts administrator, editor, radio presenter and advice worker. Her short fiction has been widely published and broadcast and won several awards. Her first novel, *That Summer in Ischia*, was one of the summer of 2011's best selling titles.

GW00649207

SECRETS IN SICILY

Penny Feeny

First published in the United Kingdom in 2018 by Aria, an imprint of
Head of Zeus Ltd

9 7 5 3 1 2 4 6 8

A CIP catalogue record for this book is available from the British
Library.

ISBN 9781788547314

Aria
an imprint of Head of Zeus
First Floor East
5–8 Hardwick Street
London EC1R 4RG

4

Also by Penny Feeny

That Summer in Ischia

The Apartment in Rome

About *Secrets in Sicily*

Sicily, 1977

Ten-year-old Lily and family arrive for their annual summer holiday in Sicily. Adopted as a toddler, Lily's childhood has been idyllic. But a chance encounter with a local woman on the beach changes everything...

10 years later...

Ever since that fateful summer Lily's picture-perfect life, and that of her family, has been in turmoil. The secrets of the baking hot shores of Sicily are calling her back, and Lily knows that the answers she has been so desperately seeking can only be found if she returns to her beloved island once more...

For my family

Part One

1977

1

In Lily's earliest memory of the villa there was no Harry; even her mother was shadowy. She was two, or maybe three. Her father had led her through rooms that seemed huge and dark and cluttered with fascinating curiosities. The pair of them had burst out onto the terrace and on the table, she remembered, lay a bowl of peaches, flushed and downy and warm from the sun. Her father had picked her up and whirled her around his head and then he had lowered her and stroked her cheek with his finger, saying her skin was as soft and silky as a peach. In another summer, baby Harry appeared and she began to dote on him. Six years later, though he could be irritating, she couldn't imagine being without him.

He'd been dozing in the back of the hire car on the way from the airport and she'd had to push him off her shoulder more than once, but now he woke with a jolt to ask if they were nearly there. Lily's insides were tight with anticipation. They were driving along country roads and the scenery enthralled her: silvery groves of olives, golden orchards of oranges and lemons, ranks of vines trooping uphill in formation like sturdy little armies, everything shimmering in a heat haze. The sky was so blue and the air so hot that the road ahead of them was wavy and out-of-focus.

She was excited, but nervous too, because there was always the chance that things would have changed. That they would turn into the bumpy drive that led to Villa Ercole and it wouldn't be there anymore because it had caught fire. Or they wouldn't be able to have their usual rooms because other people were staying. Or the sweet chestnut trees cradling the hammock would have been chopped down. Or the old clanking bicycles thrown out... Lily wanted everything to be exactly the same; she wanted to be able to run across the cool terracotta tiles and find familiar touchstones. This was important to her.

Even her parents were excited to be at the start of their holiday, their mood giddy. 'Shall we have a bet,' Alex said, 'on what colour dress Dolly will be wearing?'

Lily and Harry giggled. Dolly, like many Sicilian women of her generation, would be wearing black, even though she hadn't been widowed; black conferred dignity.

'While Gerald,' said Jess, 'will be in white. Off-white, rather...'

'And a big straw hat,' said Lily.

'Nicotine white,' said Alex. 'With splashes of Nero d'Avola.'

'What's that?'

'It's a type of red wine.'

'Nero means black in Italian.'

'True,' said Alex. 'But the Italians describe grapes as either black or white, whereas we'd say red or green. D'you think they might be colour-blind?'

'Grapes aren't red actually,' said Harry. 'They're purple.'

'Oh, what heaven!' said Jess. 'Look at all those juicy melons.'

Ahead of them a donkey was trundling a cart laden with huge glossy watermelons. With a wave at the carter, Alex accelerated past it. 'Even better,' he said. 'Look down there!' And to their joy Roccamare came into view.

The fishing village huddled in a sheltered cove with a row of palm trees along the shoreline and a forest of boat masts in the harbour. Villa Ercole lay on a spur of land above the beach, screened by oleander bushes. Years ago it had been painted the same pink as the oleander but this had faded in the sun, and Gerald in his nicotine-white trousers and wine-splashed shirt wasn't the sort to bother with redecoration.

Alex had to swerve to avoid the pot-holes and they could hear the suitcases sliding in the boot. They were coming for a month, as usual, but they didn't bring a lot of possessions. Who needed toys when you were running about outside, or several different outfits when you spent all day in a swimsuit? Besides, Gerald had sets of backgammon and chess and packs of cards and old scratched gramophone records for dancing. Jess and Alex thought his record collection antiquated and the sound quality poor, but this was good for Lily and Harry because no one was worried about wrecking them. Villa Ercole was the sort of place where you could run completely wild without getting into trouble and Dolly was the best provider of sweetmeats and pastries that Lily had ever come across.

Harry wound down his window and shouted. Alex played a fanfare on the car horn. Dolly came rushing out in her black dress, though she wore an incongruous flowered overall on top of it, which Lily was pleased to see because it meant she'd been cooking. Jess unwound herself from the passenger seat and spread out her arms, towering over Dolly, who was closer to Lily's height.

Dolly's real name was Addolorata, after Our Lady – not the Madonna with the Christ child, but the grieving mother whose son had died on the cross. Alex had nicknamed her partly because she was small and chunky and full of treats like a bag of dolly mixtures and partly so that he could greet her with: 'Well, hello, Dolly!' as he did now.

'Every year,' she told them, planting kisses on their cheeks, 'I hate it when you go and I think, can I wait until you come back? And here you are again and the year has passed quickly after all!' She had been with

Gerald for so long that her English was good, though her accent was strong.

'It's eleven months actually,' said Harry and she laughed and chucked him under the chin.

Then Alex squeezed her in his bear hug so that her toes were barely touching the ground. 'You smell delicious,' he said.

'Cinnamon cannoli,' said Dolly, blushing because Alex always made her blush. It was a trick he had with people; they would open up to him like a rose unfurling its petals. That was partly why he'd gone into journalism: he could tease out stories. 'For the children,' she added.

'For us too, I hope. Only had a plastic mini-meal on the plane.'

Dolly clucked her tongue and prodded the hollow below his ribs. Both Jess and Alex had supple willowy frames; their clothes hung on them in loose folds. Jess's skirt, made of a patchwork fabric in one of her own designs, drifted from her narrow hips. Lily was plump and sturdy and her stomach growled at the prospect of cannoli.

'Gerald napping as usual?' said Alex.

'Tsk!' exclaimed Dolly. 'I tell him this is special day. Don't have too much wine at lunch. Does he listen to me? *Figurati!*'

Gerald and Dolly were always criticising each other. She despaired because he wouldn't look after himself properly and he complained that it wasn't her job to boss him around. Why didn't she just get on and cook his favourite dishes? And she would shout that he never appreciated her cooking anyway. When he'd been smaller Harry had sometimes been frightened by Gerald and Dolly's quarrelling, but Jess had assured him it wasn't because they didn't like each other. Lily understood that in Sicily it was considered insulting not to join in an argument and give as good as you got. The performance was exhilarating. 'Though you and Alex don't yell,' she'd pointed out and Jess had smiled serenely.

'No? Well, we agree on a lot of things, I suppose. And that's how come we enjoy doing stuff together, isn't it?'

Lily's parents were not like other people's, and it wasn't only because they preferred to be called by their first names. She and Harry weren't parcelled away; they were consulted and included in adult activities. They were allowed to come on demonstrations and wave banners – they even had their photo in the paper supporting the miners. And once, for two whole terms, Lily didn't have to go to school because Jess taught her at home.

Now, anyway, they were on holiday, and a month when you are ten is an eternity and the days stretched ahead: vibrant and scorching and infinite. The previous summer, there'd been a heatwave in England too. The ground became parched and the rivers dried up and the government appointed a 'Minister for Rain' – which Gerald and Dolly thought was a huge joke – but it wasn't the *same*. It could never be as magical as coming to Roccamare.

Harry ran straight through the wide hallway of the villa, through the *salone* with its card table and record player and bits of ancient pottery. The walls were hung with engravings and mirrors freckled with spots so your reflection looked as though you'd come out in a rash. He ran through the open doors onto the terrace, which had statues in each corner and an amazing view of the sea. The statues hadn't come with the villa, which was originally an old farmhouse. Gerald had bought them. He'd bought the farmhouse too, when it was nearly derelict, and with the help of an architect friend in Palermo he had recreated what he called his classical oasis. (That was why the villa was named after Hercules: fixing it up had been such a massive task.)

Gerald was outside, snoozing on a steamer chair, and the ends of his moustache were rising with each breath. His feet, sticking over the end of the chair, were in faded canvas espadrilles that could have dropped off at any moment. Harry scrambled onto his lap and lifted the brim of his straw hat. Gerald took off the hat and squashed it onto Harry so that it swallowed him up. 'Good Lord,' he said, sitting up straight. 'The McKenzie contingent. So soon?'

Gerald's eyes were sunk deep in their sockets, hooded and smudged, but they always brightened, Lily had noticed, at the sight of Harry and Alex. She felt, although she couldn't explain why, that he looked at her in a different way, as if he didn't quite trust her. Which was silly because Harry was far more likely to break one of his records or knock over his drink. Harry might appear to have the grace of an angel but he was awfully clumsy. As it happened, Gerald was already reaching for her, drawing her towards his knee. 'We must measure you both against the post,' he said.

This post, where once horses had been tethered, was notched with marks showing how much they had grown. It was how Lily knew she had visited the villa when she was two and three and four. There'd been a couple of years' gap when Harry was very little, but then Lily'd had her period of home schooling and her parents had decided it was important for her to return. Important for Alex too: he'd been coming to Sicily ever since he was a student and he said the island got under his skin.

The measuring could wait. Lily followed her mother and Dolly into the kitchen. On the table stood a jug of lemonade and a tray of cannoli, brown and crunchy, sprinkled with sugar and filled with creamy ricotta. 'I'll make some tea too,' said Jess. The only things Gerald missed were English breakfast tea and Oxford orange marmalade, which she'd brought in their luggage. She settled the big old kettle on the hob. That was also from England; Italians didn't use kettles.

When it had boiled, Dolly seized the handles of the tray. *'Vieni,'* she said. 'We eat outside.'

Gerald hadn't moved from his chair. Alex was sprawled on one nearby, his arms akimbo, his hands clasped behind his neck and his head thrown back. Gerald was flapping his hat and saying in his dry rasping voice, 'There was a ceremony in Santa Margherita a few days ago. You just missed it.'

'You went?'

'No, but I heard about it. Ribbons cut, balloons fluttering heavenwards with prayers of thanksgiving attached. Some noisy fireworks. Interminable speeches, applause, the usual guff. Politicians taking credit for doing precisely nothing.'

'You mean they've finished the rehousing programme?' said Alex, dropping his hands to his knees and jerking forward. 'The families finally have somewhere to live?'

'Good Lord, no,' said Gerald. 'Long way to go yet. Plenty of people in the prefabs still, but the new town is definitely taking shape alongside the old and it's as good an excuse as any for a celebration.'

'It's nine bloody years since the earthquake,' said Alex. 'Nine years and counting.'

Harry had been chasing after a lizard. He bounced up to the table and said, 'Can I have a cannoli? Do you mean Lily's earthquake?'

They all looked at her and she shuddered. She could feel her body twitch as if it were about to convulse – something that happened rarely these days. Jess came over and Lily buried her face in her patchwork skirt; the warmth of her thigh was comforting through the cotton. 'Don't cry, my precious,' she crooned. 'There's nothing to be frightened of now.'

2

Lily wanted to be first on the beach the following morning, but Dolly had delayed them, filling a hamper with what she insisted were essentials. By the time they arrived, several family groups had already formed their encampments and settled in for the day. Some had even brought Calor gas stoves so they wouldn't miss out on spaghetti for lunch. A gang of youths in tiny luminous swimming trunks were showing off with a beach ball. An audience of teenage girls flickered their cats' tongues over ice-cream cones. Nearly all these people stopped what they were doing and swivelled their heads as Jess in her sundress glided towards them.

Lily was used to this. People often stared at her parents because they were so tall and blond and ethereal like the gilded couples illustrated in her Andrew Lang fairy books. In Sicily they stood out more than ever, but Jess wasn't self-conscious when people gazed at her. She smiled back and said *buon giorno*. After all, Roccamare was a small friendly place, and the McKenzies were known to be regular visitors.

They chose their patch and spread out the towels and Jess drove the stake of the umbrella deep so it wouldn't topple. Then, abandoning all possessions, the three of them ran down to the sea. (Alex had stayed behind to help Gerald polish up a translation.) They frolicked like porpoises until they got thirsty and were tempted out of the water to see what nibbles Dolly had provided. As they wriggled and rummaged through the hamper, Jess rubbed sun lotion into their bodies. It didn't take long for Lily's skin to turn to toffee, but Harry always went through a pink shrimp phase first.

Lily was munching a pear, trying to stop its sweet juice dribbling down her chin, when Harry dived into the bottom of the basket. 'Guess what I found!'

'What?'

'You have to guess.'

'Is it something you can eat?'

He giggled. 'Nope.'

'Is it a toy?'

'It might be.'

'Is it yours?'

'Nope.'

'Is it mine, then?'

'It might be.' He kept his fist closed and looked sly, but his hand wasn't big enough to hide the object completely and part of it poked out, pale and shiny.

'I know!' squealed Lily. 'It's my little statue I found last year. The one that went missing, Give it back.'

'Shan't,' he teased.

She lunged towards him, but Harry was on his feet and running, threading a path through swimmers and sunbathers. He had to keep moving, the sand was so hot it would burn your soles if you lingered. Lily managed to catch up, because her legs were longer, and to bring him down. They tussled together in a heap, but when she prised open his hands they were empty.

'What have you done with it?' she shouted. 'You've lost it!'

'It was lost anyway, till I found it.'

'That doesn't stop it being mine. Where's it gone? Did you drop it?'

Jess was standing over them, blocking out the sun. 'What's going on?'

'It was a silly stone,' said Harry.

'No, it wasn't. It was a precious bit of marble. It's two thousand years old and very valuable.'

Jess crouched down. 'Are you sure, darling?' she said. 'Is that what Gerald told you? Where did you get it from?'

'I found it, when we went to visit the quarry. Don't you remember?'

Jess's memory was really rather poor, Lily felt, whereas she could remember absolutely everything. (Since the age of three, at any rate. Apparently you weren't expected to remember anything much before that because your brain wasn't ready. That was why she had no recollection of the earthquake and only faint images of the nuns floating about in their snowy wimples. And Villa Ercole. And Alex and the bowl of ripe peaches.)

'The quarry,' she went on. 'Where we went for a picnic.' The ancient site had been blissfully deserted. The grass had grown long and golden yellow, butterflies had spangled the bushes. And sections of great stone cylinders had been strewn casually around, as if a giant had dropped a fistful of building blocks.

'Oh, you mean Cave di Cusa?'

'Alex said the piece would have chipped off the rock when they were carving the pillars and probably the slave made it into a figure in his break.'

'Slaves didn't have breaks,' said Jess. 'Is that really what Alex told you?'

'Sort of,' mumbled Lily, trying to recall her father's history lesson: how the slaves had run away when the invaders came, flinging down their tools in the middle of their work – and how the quarry had been untouched ever since. 'Anyway, Harry's gone and lost it and I'll never be able to find it.'

'I buried it,' he said. 'To keep it safe.'

'Liar, you threw it away.'

'Come and finish your snacks,' coaxed Jess. 'Then you can pretend you're archaeologists digging things up, like Toby.' Toby Forrester was Alex's best friend from school. They'd worked on digs together, but Toby was the one who'd become a full-time archaeologist. Gerald was his uncle.

'I don't know where to begin,' complained Lily.

'I don't see how it can be so important if you forgot about it for a year.'

'It just *is*.' Objects became important when you invested them with special powers. Lily hadn't given the carving a thought all the time they'd been at home. But now that they were back in Sicily where votive offerings multiplied at roadside shrines and figurines of patron saints swung from car mirrors and ancient sarcophagi and sacrificial altars littered the countryside, *obviously* a piece of chiselled marble would take on a special and miraculous identity. 'I can't leave the beach without it.'

Jess sighed. 'Do you think you can remember where you buried it, Harry?'

He pointed at a churned-up patch of sand and then darted towards their umbrella before he could be asked to help further.

'I'll have to go after him,' said Jess. 'Will you be all right, darling?'

Lily ignored the question. She plunged her spade to the hilt, so deep and so fiercely that its handle snapped. Then she had to scrabble with her fingers, but all she turned up were old sweet wrappers and cigarette butts. She felt tears gathering and her face reddening with frustration because she had set herself such an impossible task.

The people stretched out on their towels were taking little notice, but a woman, a stranger, picked a way through the bodies and crouched down beside her. She wasn't dressed for the beach. She wore a tight skirt and a sleeveless shirt with the collar turned up to protect her neck. She had dark curling hair and enormous sunglasses that covered most of her face. Her top lip curved over the bottom one in a way that made her look slightly sulky, until she smiled. She smiled now and opened her palm to show Lily. 'Is yours?' she said.

Lily was surprised at being addressed in English and then delighted when she saw what she was offered. 'Yes!' she exclaimed. 'Where did you find it?'

At this the woman shrugged as if she didn't understand the question. She was gazing intently at Lily through her sunglasses but she didn't take them off. 'You stay here in Roccamare?'

Lily gestured behind her. 'Up on the hill, in Villa Ercole.'

The lady nodded, as if it was the answer she was expecting, as if English people never stayed anywhere else. And it was true that most of the visitors to this coastline were Sicilian, that most of them not only knew each other but were related too. Gerald stood out as an eccentric foreigner. Lily scrambled to her feet and said, *'Grazie mille,'* in her best accent.

The lady smiled again and said, *'Piacere.'* She was still kneeling, looking up at Lily. *'Come ti chiama?'*

'My name's Lily.'

'That's pretty. *Arrivederci*, Lily.'

'*Arrivederci, signora,*' said Lily, skipping in triumph to Jess and Harry, who were packing everything up as they couldn't stay on the beach in the full blast of the afternoon.

Lunch at the villa was always followed by a siesta. Lying on her bed, on top of the sheets with an electric fan whirring in the corner, Lily tucked the carving inside her pillowcase to keep it safe, though she'd have to take it out before Dolly changed the bedlinen. When Dolly wasn't cooking, she was washing and cleaning, sweeping and scrubbing. She would put down powder to get rid of the ants and hang up sticky strips of paper to trap the flies. She was waging war against nature, Alex said, trying to stop it from crossing the threshold. As in her dealings with Gerald, she foolishly believed she could win.

*

Lily didn't give much thought to the woman on the beach. It didn't occur to her to wonder how she had known the piece of stone was hers or why she'd taken the trouble to return it. But a couple of days later she reappeared. The bumpy track that passed Villa Ercole was not much used and Lily and Harry, playing in the copse of almond trees, were surprised to see a car park

27

on the verge. When the driver stayed in his seat and his passenger got out, they supposed it was to ask for directions.

At first Lily didn't recognise the woman because she wasn't wearing her sunglasses. Her eyes were brown and oval like the almonds, which gave her a sleepy look. She was carrying a curious device in a grey case. She leant over the wall and called out in Italian. When Lily didn't respond, she said in English: 'You are Lily, yes?'

Lily nodded.

'Do you remember me?'

Lily nodded again and Harry, joining her, said, 'Who's she?'

'She's the person who found my statue after you lost it.'

The lady said, 'The view is so beautiful here I must stop and take a picture.' She undid the zip of the grey case and took out a large oblong camera. 'This is Polaroid. You know it?' They didn't. 'I show you how it works, yes? If you stand together.'

Lily held Harry's hand. The leaves formed dappled shadows on the ground and behind them, she knew, was the glint of blue sea. The lady pointed the viewfinder at them and pressed a button. 'Now,' she said. 'We must wait.'

Generally Jess was the family photographer, fiddling about with the light meter and the lens focus. The film had to be sent away to be developed before Lily could help arrange and label the pictures in an album. She had never seen a photo emerge like magic from the mouth of a camera, the image taking shape before their eyes. She and Harry both squealed.

'You like it?' said the lady. 'You want to keep it?'

'Can we, please?'

There were eight photographs, she told them, on each film, so she would take seven more and share them out. She had bought the camera in America when she'd lived there; it was where she had learned her English. She took some shots of the children, together and apart. Then she asked Harry if he would like to have a go. He took two pictures of Lily and the lady leaning against the wall, not quite touching, and a third one of them with their arms around each other's waists. Lily snapped the lady pretending to pick a nut from the tree and she would have taken another, but the film was used up. The man in the car, who they'd forgotten about, hooted and called: '*Dai*, Carlotta, *sbrigati.*'

'*Arrivo*, Claudio! I have to go,' she said, her voice wistful.

'Will we see you again?' said Lily.

'I hope so.' She shuffled the pictures between her fingers like cards, hesitated a moment and then thrust them at Lily. 'I will keep one,' she said. 'These are for you.' Quickly she turned and got into the car. The man, Claudio, reversed and they drove off in a puff of dust.

Lily and Harry ran indoors and found their parents and Gerald in the *salone*. They were sitting at the table, with a carafe of wine in the centre. The wine in their glasses was a light straw colour; there wasn't much left in the carafe. The needle was sticking on the record player but nobody made any move to take it off. Jess smiled lazily, 'What have you got there, poppet?'

'Photos.'

'Photos? Where did you find them?'

'They're of me and Harry. A lady took them.'

'I suppose she wants paying?' said Alex. 'She should have sent you to ask us first.'

'They're a present,' said Lily. 'She's gone now.'

'A present? That's a bit weird. Are you sure you got the right end of the stick?'

'She spoke English,' said Lily, annoyed that her word was being doubted. 'She said I could keep them, didn't she, Harry?'

Harry nodded. 'They were magic photos.'

'Magic? How?'

Lily handed over one of the snaps of Harry and herself sitting on the stone wall. 'Oh,' said Alex. 'Polaroids.'

'Let me see,' said Jess, and Lily passed her the rest.

The adults gazed at the pictures in an abstracted and bemused sort of way. In the background the record continued to stutter its same irritating phrase. 'Turn that off, will you, darling? Thanks. Who is she anyway, this photographer?'

'I don't know. She didn't tell us.'

'The man called her Carlotta,' said Harry.

'She isn't English?'

'No, she's Italian. She's the lady who found my statue when it was lost on the beach.'

'You mean this is the second time you've seen her?'

'Yes.'

'Curiouser and curiouser,' said Jess and Lily began to think that, like Alice in Wonderland, her parents were getting easily confused. Probably because of the wine. This must have been one of those days when they started drinking as soon as they woke from their siesta. Gerald encouraged it. His prime time was in the morning. If he had any work to do it was always abandoned by lunch. He never exerted himself in the afternoons.

'She was nice,' said Lily.

'Is this her, standing next to you?'

'She let me take it,' said Harry.

Jess examined the snapshot more closely, with a baffled frown. She gave it to Alex, who was peering at it when Dolly came into the room.

Dolly had a way of walking that made her seem bigger than she really was, bustling and puffing and wiggling her bottom like a duck. Gerald was the opposite. He didn't make unnecessary movements, as if he had to conserve all his energy to feed his brain.

'Cosa c'è?' she said, alert at once to the atmosphere.

31

Gerald gave a minimal, elegant wave of his hand towards the scattered pictures.

Dolly pounced. *'Matre santa!'* she yelped. Dolly invoked Matre santa, the sainted Mother of God, several times a day so Lily wasn't surprised at her exclamation. But then the healthy copper of her face faded as if it were being rinsed out of her skin. 'What are these?'

'Apparently someone called Carlotta took them this afternoon,' said Jess. 'And gave them to the children. You know everyone around here. You don't recognise her, do you?'

'No' she said firmly. *'Assolutamente no.* I have never met this woman.'

'Can I have them back, please?' said Lily, holding out her hand. She'd no idea what the fuss was about or why the photos had caused such a stir but, since they'd been given to her specially, she intended to keep control of them.

3

The McKenzies never missed the Sunday *passeggiata*, when families in their smartest outfits strolled along the Roccamare beachfront. Alex swung Harry onto his shoulders so that between them they were double the height of the crowd and Harry had the best view. 'Can you see anyone we know?' asked Lily, skipping alongside. She and Jess were both wearing gored skirts cut from a fabric Jess had designed, paired with white tee shirts. She liked the way they matched, the approving looks from passers-by who could tell they belonged together.

After a while Harry pointed and called to Lily, 'Over there. I can see her.'

'Who?'

'The lady with the camera.' He wriggled his way down Alex's back as if he were a tree he'd been climbing.

'Whoa!' said Alex, bending to rub his shin where Harry had accidentally kicked it. 'What's the hurry?'

No one hurried during the *passeggiata*. The whole point was to saunter, to stop every few minutes to exchange greetings. You could spend as long as you liked choosing your favourite flavours of ice cream and nobody would rush you. But Harry said, 'I want her to take my picture,' and bolted down one of the streets that led to the central piazza.

'Little bugger,' said Alex.

'I'll go after him,' offered Lily.

'We don't want you disappearing too. We should stick together,' said Jess.

But Harry was swift and nimble and it was much harder for the three of them to barge through the knots of people gossiping. When they got to the piazza there was no sign of him. Usually he would head straight for the fountain in the middle to check for coins or fishes, though he never found either; it was more often filled with dirt and dry leaves.

'Little bugger,' said Alex again.

Café chairs and tables were set out beneath two facing rows of ornamental orange trees. On the left-hand side, a band was playing – one man with an accordion and two with fiddles – and people were dancing to the music. They scoured the spectators for a dazzle of white-blond hair until Jess exclaimed, 'There he is!'

Through a gap in the Sunday suits, Harry could be glimpsed hopping up and down, while the dancers waltzed gaily past him, as if he longed to join in. He didn't notice his parents or respond to anyone calling his name until Alex used his masterful voice. 'Harry!

McKenzie! Here! Now!' Begrudgingly he mooched towards them.

'You shouldn't have run off like that, darling,' Jess said. 'Why didn't you wait for us?'

'I wasn't going to get lost,' said Harry. 'And I wanted to see her again.'

The music swelled and died, there was a hearty burst of clapping. One of the couples, Lily saw, included the lady Harry had chased. She'd been dancing with a much older man who had a flat linen cap pulled low over his brow. He kissed her hand and she laughed and waved him goodbye. She started walking in the direction of the McKenzies and then stopped abruptly when she saw them watching her. She had been wearing her sunglasses on the top of her head; now she pulled them down over her eyes, which Lily thought a little odd.

Harry skipped straight up to her so there was no way they couldn't all say *'Ciao'* to each other, though afterwards there was an awkward pause. She had no camera so they couldn't ask for more photographs. Alex began to say something in Italian and the lady said, 'Is okay, you can speak English, I will understand.'

Alex said, 'Are you the person who took the Polaroids?'

Jess said, 'It was very kind of you to give them to the children.'

The lady said, 'You have a beautiful family.'

'But Polaroid film is expensive and we ought to reimburse you.'

'No, please, is my pleasure.'

Some people vacated a table nearby and Alex said, 'Then let us buy you a drink.' He pulled out a chair so the lady had to sit in it and they took up their places.

A waiter appeared to take their order. *'Prego?'*

'Can I have an ice cream?' said Harry.

'What about you, Lily?'

'Orange granita, please.' At home she might choose a Mivvi or an Orange Maid but they weren't as special as granita, which was a treat you couldn't find anywhere else.

The lady, seated opposite Lily at the round table, was gazing at her steadily through her dark lenses. The set of her mouth was serious, not smiling or laughing any more. 'I have learned the names of your children,' she said. 'And I am Carlotta Galetti.'

Jess and Alex introduced themselves and Jess said, 'Do you live here or are you visiting family?'

Even Lily could see that Carlotta was more sophisticated than most of the locals. She was stylish and glamorous, the sort of person who was bound to live in a big city.

'I come from near here,' she said. 'From Santa Margherita, in the Belice valley.'

'Santa Margherita?' said Alex. 'Were you there at the time of the earthquake?'

'Yes.' She shivered and her hands trembled on the table top. The waiter set down their order: an espresso for Carlotta, beers for Jess and Alex, Harry's gelato in a paper tub and Lily's gorgeous glowing granita in a glass with a long-handled spoon.

Alex could soften his voice till it ran like melted butter. 'Did you come for the ceremony? We were told it happened last week.'

'No, not for the ceremony. I am here for holiday in Roccamare only.'

'It's good to hear they're making progress with the new town though,' said Jess. 'Were any of your family affected?'

Carlotta's hands moved from the table into her lap so Lily could no longer see if they were twitching. She could, however, see a tear slide beneath the rim of the sunglasses. Otherwise she sat motionless, completely different from the dancing queen who'd gladdened the heart and taxed the joints of her elderly partner. 'I lost my family,' she said.

'Oh, my goodness! How dreadful!'

'I went away for a long time. Many years. It has been difficult for me to come back.'

Alex said, 'I can imagine. I saw how it was.'

Carlotta dabbed her upper lip with a paper napkin. The single tear wasn't followed by another. She said in surprise, 'You were there?'

'Yes. I'd come out to Sicily to celebrate New Year with a friend. Toby was working on the dig in Mozia – his uncle owns Villa Ercole, which I think you know. Afterwards I stayed on to volunteer with Danilo Dolci. I was impressed with the man's activism, with what he was trying to achieve, and I wanted to be a part of it. And then we heard the call for help and went along to do what we could.'

This, thought Lily, is where he will tell her how he found me. She used to love hearing the story, the dramatic way Alex told it. Tunnelling through the fallen rubble, working by torchlight in the freezing January cold, not letting the chaos and the sobbing and the noise deflect him from his belief that he could hear a cry. A plaintive cheep, a bit like Moses in his basket of rushes, although she had been older than Moses and the reason her cry was so feeble was because she'd been trapped and hidden in a crater for two days and no one knew she was there. The aftershocks had continued and further stones had been dislodged and Alex's ear had picked up the sound of her squawk, which no one else had noticed. And *that* was why she was here today with the father who had saved her life. She was a miracle baby!

For some reason, he didn't say any of this to Carlotta.

'You were one of the rescue workers?' she asked, her voice rising incredulously at the end of the sentence.

He nodded.

'One of the students who came to help?'

'I wasn't even a student any longer. I was a bum, drifting about, looking for a cause. I was glad to find one but I wasn't doing anything more heroic than the next guy.'

'They said I was lucky to be alive,' said Carlotta. 'To survive when so many others didn't. My husband...' This time she didn't try to stop the tears. They rolled down her cheeks and Lily and Harry watched in fascination. Dolly often burst into luxurious sobbing, but hers was noisy and punctuated by invocations to the saints. Carlotta's quiet flood was more troubling.

'Oh, please,' said Jess, reaching out to touch her shoulder. 'We shouldn't be talking about this if it affects you so badly. We'll go and leave you in peace.'

Lily thought that if her parents took Carlotta home to the villa and chatted to her and let Dolly fuss over her, she might begin to cheer up. Instead, she was surprised at the speed with which they both downed their beers and rose to go.

'You coming, kiddies?' said Alex.

'I haven't finished my granita,' said Lily.

'If you should go somewhere I can stay with her,' said Carlotta. 'I need, in any case, to wait here for my friend.'

'I want to stay too,' said Harry.

'I don't know,' said Jess. 'You've already given us kittens once and the town's so busy this evening...'

'I will look after them,' said Carlotta.

'Can I have another ice cream?' said Harry.

Lily started to protest that wasn't fair, but a louder deeper voice drowned hers. Carlotta's friend (Claudio, the driver of the car, not the old man in the cap) was hailing her from the dried-up fountain.

'No, you can't,' said Jess. 'Come on. We have to find Dolly and give her a lift back.'

Dolly would have no problem getting home. Lily knew that her mother was making excuses, but she stopped letting the orange crystals melt slowly on her tongue and shovelled the rest down her throat.

'You know where we are,' Alex said, 'if you're here for a bit longer and want to visit us.' He stared at Carlotta very hard as if he might be able to penetrate her sunglasses.

Carlotta said, 'Yes, thank you.' She rose from the table to greet her boyfriend, who seemed annoyed that she had gone off without him.

Normally the McKenzies would have stayed for introductions because they liked meeting new people, but Alex rapidly propelled them away.

'Why ever did you do that?' said Jess.

'Yes, why?' said Lily.

'Do what?'

'Invite her to come over,' said Jess.

'She'll come anyway if she wants to. She did before. Now she knows she doesn't have to sneak around outside.'

'Why would she sneak?' said Lily.

'Alex, you know something, don't you?'

'What could I possibly know?'

'Surmise, then.'

'What does surmise mean?' said Lily. 'Is it like surprise?'

'That's it!' said Jess brightly. 'I surmise that your dad's going to devise a surprise.'

She was talking in riddles. Lily supposed they would have to wait till they saw Carlotta again to find out why.

4

Jessamy McKenzie lay naked on the bed in a darkened room. The heat enveloped her like a moist blanket. She'd undressed in order to shower but the water was reduced to an erratic dribble – not an uncommon occurrence. Alex had taken the children to cool off in the sea. Sweat was collecting in the hollow of her collarbone, soaking through the cotton sheet into the mattress. It was late afternoon, but she hadn't been able to sleep during the siesta. It was far too hot and anyway her mind had been whirring, reviewing everything she could remember about the past nine years.

From the day she'd met Alex she had entered a different world. The one she'd grown up in was populated with socialite older sisters, school crushes, pony gymkhanas and parents who alternated between indifference and indulgence. Jess was a late, unplanned baby and, as the youngest, she was frequently patronised.

'It's a stage you're going through,' her bossiest sister, Dinah, informed her. 'The need to rebel.'

'You have to kick against the pricks,' said Jess.

'What pricks?' said Dinah suspiciously, as if she might be deliberately insulting her husband. Dinah had been among the last generation of debutantes and the ritual had suited her; she'd accepted Johnnie Winthrop's proposal at a hunt ball. A decade later, at a demonstration against the Vietnam War, Alex had scooped Jess from beneath the hooves of a police horse in Grosvenor Square. The age gap had set her on a different course from her sisters, but the meeting with Alex had yanked her into another stratosphere.

'You don't know anything about him,' Dinah said.

'I know enough.'

Alex contributed scurrilous articles to *Private Eye* and the underground newspaper, *International Times*. He also pulled pints in a pub and helped to organise radical poetry readings in the bar upstairs. Living in his world involved committing to positive activism, attending street rallies or meetings in sleazy back rooms (and, less frequently, sitting around getting stoned to Jimi Hendrix or King Crimson). It required passionate engagement and Jess threw herself into it.

The first time he took her to Sicily he borrowed Gerald's VW and whisked her off on a magical mystery tour. 'There's someone I have to show you,' he said. 'Someone I want you to meet.' And she recalled, with a lurch, Dinah's warning.

Dinah had meant that Jess knew nothing about Alex's family – antecedents were everything in her circle – but it wasn't true. Jess knew that his father had been killed before he was born, in one of the last battles of the war, at Monte Cassino. That he had been brought up by a struggling mother, who was relieved to send him away to school when he won a scholarship. That he considered himself without ties. That his first trip to Italy had been to visit his father's grave. That through his friendship with Toby Forrester he had visited Sicily and kept coming back. But she couldn't imagine the mysterious person he wanted her to meet.

'Who is it?' she said. 'Are you going to tell me or do I have to guess?'

Alex liked springing surprises and he liked the way she reacted to them. He enjoyed an audience. 'Guess away,' he said.

They'd been driving past newly tilled fields; the feathery stems of wild fennel swayed along the verge; the spring air was fresh with promise. As they approached the outskirts of the town a high wall rose ahead of them, shielding a spreading magnolia and the peak of a terracotta roof.

'Okay,' said Jess. 'Someone's locked up here. Someone who needs help. Oh, God, this is an asylum, isn't it? And a perfectly sane person is being incarcerated against their will and you want to set them free.' (She had recently finished reading *One Flew Over The Cuckoo's Nest*.) 'What is this compulsion you have, Alex, always to be rescuing people?'

She was laughing as she spoke, but she was also remembering the horse's forelegs inches from her head when the anti-war placard had been knocked from her grip and she'd lost her balance. She'd been lifted in the rough embrace of a donkey jacket, seen fair hair spilling over a turned-up collar and the worried eyes of a stranger. She'd heard a gentle lilt asking her if she was all right, then saying, 'Quick, we'd better get out of here.' Pulling her to safety, away from the crush and the truncheons, spooning sugar into her tea to counteract the shock. How could she not have fallen in love after such an encounter?

'Congratulations,' he said. 'You're getting warm.'

'Really?' She darted a kiss onto his cheek.

'Really.' He pulled up in front of a pair of elaborate wrought-iron gates and she spotted a statue of the Virgin Mary set into a niche in the wall. 'But it's not an asylum, it's a convent.' He got out of the car and jangled a bell pull.

'Are they expecting us?'

'I got Dolly to ring ahead. She knows the Mother Superior.'

An elderly nun, wimple flapping, trundled down the path holding an enormous key. She unlocked the gate and let them in, on foot. The convent was a low plain white-washed building with no hint of the baroque flamboyance that characterised so many of the local churches. A short flight of steps led up to the main entrance and they were admitted to a tiled hallway with a strong aroma of beeswax – polish, or candles, or maybe both. Another nun led them into an anteroom and spoke to Alex in Italian. Jess couldn't follow, but when she started to ask a question, Alex flashed a grin and said, 'Wait and see. *Pazienza!*'

The nun returned with a child, scarcely more than a toddler, in tow. The child was wearing a navy overall and had cropped hair so Jess wasn't certain whether it was a boy or a girl. Alex held out a hand and the nun gave the child a nudge. '*Dai*, Liliana,' she said.

Alex smiled and said, '*Ciao.*' He took his other hand from behind his back and presented it as a closed fist. '*Sai cos'è?*'

'*Caramelli?*' said the child and squealed when Alex opened his fist to show she had guessed correctly. She took the sweets and he helped her unwrap them.

Jess watched in astonishment. She knew how romantic Alex could be in private and how persuasive when he needed things to go his way. She'd also seen his fury when his view of social justice was challenged. But his tenderness with the little girl was so unexpected it floored her. The girl was now sitting on his knee, sucking her boiled sweets, quite at ease. She reached up and stroked the stubble of his jaw with her palm, as if intrigued by the unfamiliar sensation. In a convent, Jess supposed, she wouldn't come across men, other than priests.

'Who is she?'

'This is Lily. Lily, meet Jessamy. My two flower girls.'

'Is she a secret?'

'No, why should she be a secret?'

'Because I've been going out with you for six months and you haven't mentioned her before. Is she yours?'

'Mine?'

'Don't act dumb, Alex. You know what I mean.'

'Hey, what are you getting at? Do you think I'd leave a kid in an orphanage if I was her father?'

'You might not have known she existed... till afterwards.' It was far worse to be an unmarried mother in Italy than in England – that was why families guarded their daughters like jailors and kept them at home after dark. But the girls must escape sometimes and you could have sex in the afternoon and still keep to your curfew.

'You're way off!' he said, as if he were tickled to have confounded her. 'Now let's get moving. They've said we can take Lily out for the day as a treat. I'll explain everything.'

Jess sat in the back of the VW alongside Lily, wide-eyed and bouncing with excitement. In the driver's seat, Alex spun the steering wheel, spoke nonchalantly. 'It was the story that turned me into a journalist. I never sold it – British newspapers wouldn't have been much interested anyhow – but it felt... pivotal.'

And that was how Jess learned about his part in the post-earthquake debacle. 'Almost as soon as I brought the baby out of the rubble,' he said, 'she was grabbed, passed around in the torchlight. No one could believe she was still breathing. Nearly three days she'd been underground. People wanted to take her into church to give thanks for the miracle but I managed to persuade them she needed a doctor.'

'You knew where to find one?'

'A field hospital had been set up, so we took her there. I didn't stick around but I was as chuffed as anyone when I heard she'd been claimed by relatives.' His voice dropped, though Lily wouldn't have understood the words. 'Trouble was, they got the wrong baby.'

'You're kidding me!' She glanced sideways at the funny little creature in her institutional garb, at the curl on her neck missed by the scissors. 'It isn't possible! How could they not have known?'

'Because they'd seen half their family wiped out and were off their heads with grief and panic. Besides, they were an aunt and uncle and Lily was in a pretty desperate state. It was the grandparents who eventually recognised she wasn't theirs.'

'So they handed her back?'

'What else could they do? There must have been some surviving family somewhere, but no one else came forward. They probably couldn't afford to look after her and anyhow there was nowhere to live. Half the valley was sleeping under canvas. So she ended up with the nuns. That's why I call to see her whenever I'm staying at Gerald's. I feel kind of responsible.'

'You really did this?' She was finding it hard to take in.

'Aye, I did.'

Reaching across the seat to squeeze his shoulder, Jess said solemnly, 'It's a powerful thing to have saved someone's life. Why didn't you tell me?'

He met her eyes in the rear-view mirror. 'I wasn't sure if you'd believe me. I wanted you to meet her first. But I'm telling you now right enough.'

'What happens to them? When they get older?'

'The orphans? They become skivvies probably. Or nuns. Not a great future.'

Jess turned to Lily again and was met with a disarming smile. 'Oh, my God,' she said. 'This is going to take some digesting. What you've done here... and keeping in touch like this, it's fantastic! I mean, it's all very well thinking we can save the world, isn't it? But in practice, if you can do something to make life better for just one person...'

And that was the seed sown, the kernel that grew on their subsequent trips: visiting Lily in the convent, taking her out for the day, buying her toys and ice cream, a pair of shoes, going to the beach, to Villa Ercole, introducing her to the new baby. It was after Harry was born that their vague fuzzy notion bore fruit. Lily was so good with Harry, so attentive, the ready-made older sibling.

Their decision to adopt was taken in a rush of adrenalin and a warm glow of good intentions. The process was complicated and there was plenty of opportunity to change their minds, but the more often they were told they were mad, the more determined they became. Neither of them had ever regretted it.

*

The Polaroids were on the cupboard beside the bed. Jess had winkled them from Lily's possession, promising to keep them safe. She propped herself against the pillows and examined them for the hundredth time. Lily was fully aware of the circumstances of her adoption; she had never been lied to. And hadn't the McKenzies always hoped that a relative might be discovered to link her with her heritage? Wasn't that why they kept returning to Villa Ercole?

Jess stared at the images in the gloom: black and white and indistinct. You couldn't judge the colouring, let alone the features, of the subjects. Anyway, she had seen Carlotta Galetti with her own eyes; she didn't need a photograph to know what she looked like. The woman was sultry and striking, but there was something unnerving about her too. The speed, for instance, with which her manner had changed from vivacious to withdrawn. Yet it was Carlotta who had sought out the

McKenzies – the children at any rate – and not the other way around.

The photographs were sticking to her fingers, so she put them face down in a pile. She was still lying, chewing her lip, in a defeated position when Alex came back from the beach.

'Lazy mare,' he said, swiping a towel at her, stiff with sand and salt. She grabbed the end of it and they tussled briefly. The bedstead was standard metal chain-link, inclined to sag in the middle. 'You haven't moved since we went out.'

'The water hasn't come on yet,' she said.

'Excuses, excuses.'

She knelt in the dip of the bed. Her limbs were slick and slippery as fish. 'And… I've been thinking…'

'Thinking is not what we do on holiday, Jessa-mine.' (He called her this sometimes, referring to the song that had been a chart hit the year they met.) 'Thinking is for the rest of the year. This month is for Being.'

'I know, but… were the kids okay?'

'Fine. They're pestering Dolly now. They spotted some sea urchins on the rocks and wanted to tell her about them.'

'No jellyfish?'

'Not a single one. Is that what's bothering you?'

'You know what's bothering me. You always know. I mean, who *is* she? What does she *want*?'

'Speculation,' he said, 'is not worth the angst.' He dropped his swimming trunks on the floor. 'I'm going to try the shower again.'

'If you strike lucky with the water don't take it all.'

'Then come and join me.'

The bathroom was a primitive space between their bedroom and the children's. Its small high window was shrouded outside by a creeper. It had no shower curtain or cubicle and there was a dank smell of drains. She followed him and they rubbed soap into each other's chests and armpits. A spasmodic trickle of water gradually rinsed away the suds and stuck their eyelashes together. Alex hoisted Jess up so she could wind her legs around his hips and her arms around his neck. For extra support he pinned her against the wall beneath the window and the ceramic tiles sent a blissful chill through her shoulder blades.

'I love you,' he said.

'I know. Me too.'

'Nothing is going to threaten us,' he said. And then stopped speaking because he had to concentrate on his balance, on staying upright and staying inside her. There were moments when they were in danger of sliding apart, but he held on and she gripped more tightly with her knees. She rose and bucked and their bodies rocked together in a taut, exhilarating rhythm.

After he set her down, her legs felt wobbly and uncertain like a new foal's and she pattered giddily into the bedroom to find something to wear. She picked a shift made of cotton lawn, fine as gossamer, but its lightness was not an advantage: humidity soon reduced it to the texture of a dishcloth. Alex stayed in the bathroom to shave. Jess twisted her wet hair onto the top of her head and stuck in a pin. She leaned against the door jamb watching him lather his chin in the mirror over the sink.

'We've always been open,' she said. 'To the idea that someone might show up from Lily's past…'

'Nothing will threaten us,' he repeated.

'But there's a difference, isn't there, between an abstract prospect that may never happen and an actual breathing living person? Because of what you told me about Lily and the wrong grandparents, I expected we might track down somebody from a different generation. Or distant in some other way. But, Christ, I wouldn't be surprised if Carlotta was younger than me!'

He raised an eyebrow, turned to look at her. 'Are you wearing underwear?'

'God, no, too hot.' The dishrag was already clinging to her nipples.

'Dolly's going to disapprove.'

'Dolly? I wonder what's up with her. Did you see how she reacted to the photos?'

Alex pulled his skin tight and drew a path through the shaving foam with his razor. 'Och, she's a drama queen.'

'She wouldn't keep the truth from us, though, would she, if she knew something for certain?'

'No one in this country knows anything for certain. Even if they did, they'd be in the habit of keeping quiet for fear of reprisals. People aren't going to risk speaking out of turn. I told you, Jess, there's no point speculating. We have to wait and see what happens next.'

'If Carlotta Galetti shows up, you mean?'

'Exactly.'

5

The telephone lived in the hallway of Villa Ercole, with a second instrument in Gerald's study. The McKenzies gave out the number warily, only to be used in emergencies. When Jess, sunning herself on the terrace, heard its long insistent ring, she didn't expect the call to be for either of them.

Dolly answered and poked her head outside. 'Alex, *dov'è?*'

'Do you know who wants him?'

Dolly pursed her lips and Jess felt a surge of apprehension.

Alex loped to the phone. Jess hovered nearby, re-buckling her sandal, toying with her hair in the hall mirror. She caught some words and phrases, the gist of a meeting. She knew he'd tell her the details; they were always open and frank with each other. He replaced the receiver and said without turning around, 'Carlotta wants to meet me.'

'Just you?'

'Yes.'

'Not me?'

'No.'

'Nor Lily?'

'She wants to talk to me about my part in… what happened.'

'After the earthquake? Couldn't I come and listen? I won't interrupt. I don't think you should exclude me.'

'It's a preliminary meeting,' he said. 'There'll probably be others.'

'What are you going to tell her?'

'What d'you mean? The truth, of course, as far as I know it.'

'The business with the family who rejected Lily?'

'Look, I won't make anything up.'

She stepped closer, prodded him in the ribs. 'Never believe a journalist who says they don't make anything up.'

'Jess…' He caught her hand and held it. 'This is too important…'

'I know. That's what I'm scared of. When did you agree to see her?'

'Tomorrow morning in the Jolly Bar.'

The Jolly Bar had a flashing pinball machine and well-used table football, with the blue and red paint flaking off the figures, but it wasn't the one they frequented because Lily and Harry preferred the ice-cream flavours in the Caffe Centrale opposite. That was presumably why Alex had nominated it.

'What will I do?'

'What we always do, Jess. Take the kids to the beach. As far as they're concerned I'm staying behind to work with Gerald. They won't be bothered.'

'You will tell me everything,' she said.

'Why wouldn't I?'

'Sorry, I'm being paranoid.' She buried her face in his neck for the comforting scent of him, a tangible reassurance.

Alex was right: the children asked no questions. As soon as they arrived at the beach they were subsumed into the gang of friends they'd made. Jess watched them scarper to the shore and splash in the shallows with a large inflatable beach ball. Against the dazzling reflection of the sea, the group was a blur. The only things that stood out were the vivid stripes of the ball and Harry's white-blond head. He refused to wear a hat. Lily had blended in, indistinguishable from the rest.

Over the past two summers she'd become close friends with a boy her own age called Marcello Campione. They liked to go exploring together, heading for the untamed scrubby area beyond the sand, where the river Belice flowed into the sea. Here they'd created a den out of an old upturned dinghy. Harmless enough, Jess had thought when she learned of it, but now any hiding place was suspect. She fixed her gaze on the group, determined not to let Lily out of her sight.

She knew she was overreacting: there was no shortage of supervision. Mammas all over the beach were springing up and dusting down their offspring, rescuing them from mishaps, bestowing oodles of affection. Children were considered a shared delight. The McKenzies were good at sharing too, often offering a meal or a mattress to someone in need. They weren't possessive. At least, Jess hadn't thought of herself as possessive until two days ago.

It hadn't been easy, transplanting Lily to their London flat. The bedwetting had been a trial – the twin-tub churning with sheets as well as terry-towelling nappies and fabrics for tie-dying – and the home-schooling an effort, but they had coped. And she'd taken root, hadn't she? She was their beautiful contented quirky daughter, unimaginable in any other family but their own.

Lily was running towards her, droplets of water sparkling on her skin like glitter, her eyes lustrous, her perfect mouth grinning, exposing her muddle of teeth, old and new. 'I'm hungry!'

'What's new, darling? You're always hungry!'

'So's Marcello.' The two of them, chatting in a mixture of English, Italian and Sicilian dialect, delved into Dolly's basket. 'We can have a picnic in our den.'

'No!'

Lily jerked her hand back in surprise. Jess never shouted, never forbade anything on a whim. She knew Lily couldn't possibly be at risk from the attentions of Carlotta when the woman was with Alex in the Jolly Bar. But she couldn't explain her anxieties, her worst imaginings. Her mind kept flitting to the scene: the pinball machine juddering and squealing in the background, the cigarette stubs mounting in the ashtray with the imprint of red lipstick on the filters.

'You don't want to spoil your appetite, darling,' she said. 'Why don't we go up to the villa and see what Dolly's making us for lunch?'

Getting back early wasn't helpful. Alex was still absent and the children sat around the table on the terrace impatiently kicking its legs.

Dolly wasn't pleased either. Time in Sicily might be infinitely elastic, but food was sacred. She'd brought the meal forward but there was no Alex to eat it so they all had to wait. When he finally arrived, panting, she greeted him with an emphatic, 'At last!' and set down the tureen of *maccheroni* with a thump of annoyance.

Gerald, in contrast, was in an affable mood. 'Bit of a breakthrough this morning,' he observed.

Alex looked startled. Don't do this now, Jess was about to beg. Not in front of the children.

'Second stanza,' said Gerald. 'Third line. Finally got the scansion spot on.'

'Oh,' said Alex, in some relief. 'Stesichorus.'

'Stegosaurus?' said Harry, alerted. 'Where?'

'Not a dinosaur, old chap! The Greek lyric poet. What do you think your father and I have been working on since you got here?'

Harry's face was blank. 'Dunno.' He siphoned up more pasta.

Gerald ruffled his hair. 'Well, you've got some learning to do. And you can't start too young. I realise Greek translation is rather an arcane pursuit, but scholarship is as much a calling, you know, as religion. Over two thousand years later, the man still speaks to us.'

'The stegosaurus,' said Harry, unimpressed, 'is hundreds of *millions* of years old.'

'Didn't write many poems though, did it?'

Jess surreptitiously slid some of her *maccheroni* onto Lily's plate; she didn't have much appetite. She was grateful for the diversion, for the giggling over dinosaur literacy; nevertheless, the lunch felt like the longest she had ever endured.

Afterwards, Gerald reclined on his sun lounger, smoking one of his gold-tipped Russian Sobranies, bought on the black market, while the children scurried obediently to their bedroom for their siesta. Jess helped Alex to stack the dirty dishes and carry them into the kitchen. Dolly was preparing coffee. When it was ready, she sat them both down and took her place at the head of the table like a presiding magistrate. 'Drink!' she chided them.

'Please, Alex,' Jess said. 'Don't make me wait any longer.' She glanced at Dolly. There was no point in trying to have a discussion in private. 'Tell us what happened.'

He flicked back his hair, cleared his throat. 'Well, it went okay, the meeting. She was charming, sensitive, and so forth, but, Christ, her story was grim. Not that I expected anything different.'

'But who *is* she? Did she explain?'

'According to Carlotta, the Galettis were bakers. She had married into the family and they lived above the shop. When the earthquake struck they were sleeping – it was the middle of the night. Her husband yelled that they should run and he seized their baby daughter. She couldn't keep up and was hit by falling masonry.' His voice was tense, but matter-of-fact. 'Because she'd been knocked unconscious she was in hospital for some time. She didn't find out what had happened until afterwards and she missed the burial. Not surprisingly, she was pretty traumatised.'

'Whose burial?'

'All of them. Her in-laws were killed too.'

Jess gulped. 'Oh, my God, how awful!'

Dolly said in a low ghoulish voice, 'There were many problems to bury the dead. In the winter the ground was very hard. Also the bodies were not always complete.'

'Because they were crushed, you mean?' It was a horrible vision, limbs splintered into fragments, skulls shattered and unrecognisable.

The shutters were closed so the light fell in narrow bars across the room. Alex sought Jess's gaze in the gloom and held it. 'Aye,' he said. 'But there were also wild boar who came out of the woods on the hillside and scavenged among the corpses – which added to the urgency – and many were mutilated. In fact, there wasn't a final death toll, only an estimate. Some bodies were never recovered.'

'Oh, my God! So how could she even be certain…?' Her question trailed away, the answer too unpalatable.

'Anyhow, the upshot of all this…' he picked up the espresso that had been cooling in front of him '… is that when Carlotta came out of her coma and discovered she was a widow, her own mother arranged for them to stay with relatives on the mainland. In a sense she was one of the lucky ones.'

'How do you mean, *lucky*?'

'There was total bedlam afterwards. The *comune* couldn't provide housing for all the survivors or afford to replace what they'd lost. The government's solution was to dole out passports and train tickets so people could batten on family members elsewhere. Paperwork, when you're overstaffed with bureaucrats, doesn't cost much. It may have been unprecedented, but I reckon it was the easy way out. Like printing money. For Carlotta, among others, it was an escape route.'

Dolly was leaning forward to make sure she caught every word. '*Donna fugata,*' she said.

'Running away isn't a crime, Doll,' he protested. 'The crimes came afterwards when the funding was misappropriated. Anyone would be desperate to flee a situation like that.'

Jess felt wrung out, her guts knotted and twisted at a tragedy of such proportions. She tried to speak calmly. 'So what did she want from you?'

'To hear about my part in the rescue operation. She was out of it, remember, and she'd suffered memory loss. All she has to go on are piecemeal bits of information from a load of different sources. I could give her another angle.'

'So you told her how you found Lily?'

'Yes.'

Jess pictured Lily and Harry snoozing on their twin beds. In this heat their limbs would be flung at all angles, though Lily had a habit of burying her face in her pillow so all you could see was the curl of eyelashes on her cheek. 'And she thinks there might be a connection because she'd lost a baby girl herself in the disaster. Is that right? Did she have any other children?'

'She'd not been married long. She was eighteen when her daughter was born.'

'When was that?'

'March, the year before.'

Jess said in triumph, 'Lily's birthday is the middle of April!'

'Sweetheart, we don't know when Lily's birthday is, all we know is the one the nuns gave her.'

'But if she believed her baby was dead, what made her change her mind? And what about the first family, the ones who thought Lily belonged to them? Was their baby ever found?' Dolly was shaking her head and dabbing her eyes. Jess continued, 'Lily was in that orphanage for nearly three years. There was plenty of time for someone to come along and claim her if they really wanted to, if they thought she might be theirs. Carlotta has no proof, does she? No proof of anything!'

Alex said, 'Apparently she was in the States for a while. This is only her second visit to the area since she left. She'd heard about the blond foreign family with the little dark-haired girl, because we stick out, don't we? Everybody round here knows who we are. She says she didn't mean to disturb us. She saw Lily on the beach with Harry and she was curious... she couldn't help herself. She took the photos because it was the best way she could think of to mull things over and get them straight in her head without upsetting us.'

'Do you believe her?'

'I'm keeping an open mind, but it's plausible.'

Jess said, 'It doesn't matter how many photos anyone takes. There's no way we can ever find out for sure who Lily's parents were.'

'No,' he agreed. 'Not for sure.'

'So why has she suddenly materialised like this? What does she expect us to *do*?'

'I suppose she wants to believe her daughter didn't die. Wouldn't you? It's certainly a challenge, but we're in this together Jessa-mine, are we not? We can't ignore the woman now she's appeared.'

'We *could* actually,' said Jess.

'But would it be fair to Lily?'

'It might be better for Lily. This could throw her completely off-keel.' But she knew Alex's curiosity was piqued; he would have to follow the story, wherever it led.

Dolly gathered the coffee cups and took them to the sink. She said, 'I can ask if is possible someone in Santa Margherita can help you.'

'Really, do you think so? Who?'

'I have a friend… I will make telephone call.'

Doing nothing was not going to be an option.

6

Lily could walk on her hands. Not very far and not for very long but it was a skill she was proud of and one she was trying to perfect. On the beach other children tried to join in, but only her friend Marcello was successful. She'd encouraged him by holding onto his ankles until he learned the knack of keeping his back and legs straight. Even so, she intended to stay the champion. She took to practising up at the villa, close to the wall so she could use it for balance. That was how she heard her parents' voices floating through the open window. They seemed to be arguing, which surprised her for they rarely argued with each other.

'I'm not sure whether the kids should come. We don't know what the old woman is going to tell us. She's probably the town gossip.'

'You can't decide you don't want to hear the answers because you might not like them.'

'What answers? Do you suppose we're going to get anywhere near the truth? And if it *is* painful, how do we handle it then? I think you're being insensitive.'

'And you're being overprotective. I was there, Jess. You can't bury your head in the sand about this. At least we'll be in control if we're together.'

'In control, Alex? Do you really think so?'

Lily's feet wavered in the air and dropped quietly to the ground. She didn't know what they were talking about but she didn't like the idea of being left behind so she searched for Harry and told him their parents were plotting to abandon them. Harry ran directly to Jess and sat on her knee and tugged at her hair, which was loosely braided, and said, 'Can we go on a trip? Will you take us fishing?'

'Maybe another time.'

'That's what you always say!'

Jess sighed. 'Okay, your dad will have a chat with the fishermen down at the harbour, won't you, Alex?'

Harry said, 'Do you *promise*? I mean, *really* promise?'

Lily said, 'Will you take us to Mozia instead, then? We haven't been there for *ages*.'

The island of Mozia was one of her favourite excursions, not so much for the excavations where Toby had worked, as for the dinky windmills on the salt pans and the causeway that was barely below the surface of the sea. From the shore you could look as though you were magic, like Jesus walking on the water.

Alex said, 'Actually, kiddies, we were thinking of going to Santa Margherita. Dolly has a friend who's moved into a new house and she wants us to take her some goodies.'

'Is Dolly coming with us?'

'No, she's too busy. That's why we're being her messengers.'

Lily had only visited her birthplace once before and that was by accident. It had been a rainy day a couple of years ago and the outing hadn't been planned. They'd been driving aimlessly around the valley and the windscreen wipers had been having trouble keeping up with the torrents of rainwater, when they'd found themselves on the fringes of the town. They hadn't even got out of the car, but sat and stared at the ruined houses gleaming in the wet. Lily had thought in disbelief; how could I have been born here? Jess and Alex had watched her face carefully as if they were worried she might get distressed or have what they called a meltdown – though that hadn't happened for a while. She would have liked Alex to show her where he had found her, but he'd said he couldn't work it out. He had tunnelled such a long way into the blackness, orientation was impossible, even at the time. There was no point in going and getting soaked just now.

They set off the following day, with a cardboard box full of treats sitting snugly between them and the car windows open to let in a breeze. There wasn't a speck of rain on this occasion; there hadn't been for weeks. The sky was a brilliant blue and the road was a chalky ribbon snaking through ripening fields and olive groves.

The journey wasn't a long one and when they arrived it was evident the town was still in a mess. The streets were riddled with pot-holes. There were small corrugated shacks, with roofs like tin lids that could blow off in a strong wind, and unfinished apartment blocks with gaping windows, imprisoned in scaffolding. Along one side of the town square stood the façade of a grand palace. Jess told Lily this had belonged to a duke who'd written about it in a famous book, *The Leopard*. He had called the palace Donnafugata, which was the name given to the whole valley after the Queen of Naples fled there. In the story two of the characters, a young man and a pretty girl, had played hide-and-seek in its hundred rooms.

Lily found it almost impossible to envisage so many rooms and you couldn't see them now because they had fallen down in the earthquake, like the rest of the town. The grounds were to be turned into a park for the local children. When Lily heard phrases like 'local children' she would gulp and think incredulously: that could have been me. But the leap of imagination required to transpose her from Highbury Fields to the palms and lemon trees of Santa Margherita was even harder than imagining hide-and-seek in a hundred rooms. She simply couldn't do it.

Dolly's friend lived in one of the apartment blocks that had been completed. These were painted in ice-cream shades of strawberry and apricot and pistachio. Signora Agnese Fantoni lived on the ground floor and in the corner of her window pane was a black-edged card announcing she was in mourning for her husband. 'For the rest of her life, poor thing,' whispered Jess. Also in the window was a songbird in a cage hanging from a hook. When they rang the doorbell, it glared at them with its beady eye.

The old lady who came to answer the door wasn't jolly and stout like Dolly. She was bent over, leaning on a stick and the knuckles of her hand, clasping its knob, rose in jagged peaks. Her eyes were sunken under her brows and spidery red lines webbed across her face. '*Avanti,*' she said in a gravelly voice.

They followed her down the entrance hall into a hot and stuffy room. There was one easy chair, which Signora Fantoni, took and the McKenzies sat in a line on the bed by the wall, except for Alex, who held out the box. 'It's very good of you to see us, *signora*,' he said in his best Italian. 'We've brought a present to show our gratitude.'

They'd enjoyed filling it earlier that morning, raiding the kitchen for pickled walnuts and peppers and artichoke hearts. Dolly had baked some almond biscotti and they'd called at the *alimentari* for wafer-thin ham and a pair of *caciocavallo* cheeses, like miniature money-bags. It was a nice gift, but Signora Fantoni scarcely glanced at it. She was peering at Lily, studying every inch of her. Her fingers crabbed as if they wanted to reach out and pinch her arm to see if she was fat enough to eat. Lily didn't want to meet the *signora's* devouring eyes so she stared down at her shoes instead. These were black lace-ups like nuns wore, but they were bulging as if there weren't normal feet inside them at all, but eagle's talons struggling to be released. She nudged Harry; she couldn't help thinking of the story of Hansel and Gretel. Surely the old lady had to be a witch?

'*Quest'è la bambina?*' said Signora Fantoni.

Alex nodded. 'Addolorata said you could help us with some information.'

The *signora* acknowledged this with a sly smile as if she were the keeper of all the secrets of the neighbourhood.

Jess said, 'I think I should take the children outside to play.'

Harry, squashed between them on the bed, was fidgeting; Lily had much better control. She'd invented a game whereby if she darted her eyes and wiggled her nose she could make something happen, like Samantha in the TV show *Bewitched* – who was a good witch, not an evil one.

Alex said something more to Signora Fantoni and then spoke in English. 'We can all go. Agnese will come with us to show us the old town.'

71

'Is that a good idea?' said Jess.

'It's better than being cooped up here, isn't it? The children can run around and we can have the quiet chat we're after.'

'You're after...' muttered Jess, squeezing Lily's hand.

Agnese had to find a headscarf to shield her from the sun and a different walking stick. Then, with her uneven bow-legged gait, she started up the street. There were other black-garbed old ladies sitting on chairs by their doorsteps, flashing their crochet hooks through lace or shelling peas into enamel bowls. They called out greetings to Agnese and curiously eyed the procession she was leading. Two motor scooters whizzed past and a muzzled dog snarled at them. Harry shrank closer to Lily.

Suddenly Agnese changed direction, hobbling beneath an archway and into a dramatic change of scene. They were surrounded by the shells of buildings. No roofs, no glass in the windows, no wooden doors in the doorframes; weeds and scrubby bushes shooting out of the walls; cracked hearths and floor tiles spattered with bird droppings; staircases that mounted towards the sky and stopped in mid-air: this was what a battle zone might look like. And yet the layout of the streets was distinct, criss-crossing backwards and forwards, looking as if people might continue to gather at the intersections for a chat, as if they might lead somewhere.

You couldn't tell one heap of stones from another, but Agnese was pointing at them as though the buildings were still standing and she could see the shutters pinned back and the women clipping their washing onto wires strung between the windows, and the sign for Salt and Tobacco hanging above the entrance to the bar and the knife grinder and the cobbler beavering away in their cubby-holes. These were familiar sights in other towns Lily had visited so she knew that they should have been here too. Here, where her first family had lived and died… And the worst thing was that she couldn't remember anything about them. She gripped her head with both hands. It felt like the inside of a beehive, buzzing and swarming with winged creatures.

Jess said, 'Are you all right, poppet?' Harry started to run off and she called out after him: 'Don't get lost! We're not in Roccamare now.'

'I'll go and fetch him,' said Lily. 'He won't be able to hide from me.'

Agnese pottered another hundred yards ahead, poking her stick at dried clumps of grass, striking the remains of a doorstep. She was talking about the butcher's shop, which must have been nearby. Lily recognised the word *'macelleria'*.

Harry leapt out from behind a gaping hole in the stonework and shouted, 'Boo!'

Lily gave him a pitying smile. She felt infinitely superior and infinitely sad. 'You mustn't do that, Harry,' she said.

'Because I frightened you!'

'You didn't frighten me at all. It's because it's dangerous. If the walls fell down and crushed you, you'd be like a squashed fly, wouldn't you?'

'Can we play terrorists instead?'

'No, we can't.' Peace marches hadn't made as strong an impression on Harry as they had on Lily. She considered for a moment. 'Why don't we have a treasure hunt?' There wasn't much prospect of treasure in this forlorn abandoned site but Harry wouldn't know that.

'What are we looking for?'

She spotted the glint of a chocolate wrapper. 'Gold,' she said. 'Or silver. But you have to find it out on the streets. You're not allowed to go into the houses because it would be cheating.'

'That isn't fair!'

'It's the rules. I'll be kind and give you a clue.' She jerked her head towards the chocolate wrapper and his eyes followed her.

'That's paper.'

'It's silver paper. The person who finds the most wins.'

Harry scuttled about, swooping onto random pieces of litter. Lily felt pleased with herself and expected her parents to be pleased too. But they didn't even notice when she ran up to them. They were listening intently to Agnese and Alex was translating for Jess. Agnese was talking about the baker this time, the *fornaio*. Lily tugged at her mother's hand. 'I found Harry,' she said. Jess whirled around with a look of dismay. Lily said, 'He didn't hurt himself. He's over there, hunting for treasure.'

Jess seemed distracted, but in a different way from normal. She nodded and craned forward to listen to Alex.

'I'm struggling a bit with this,' he was saying. 'There's a lot of Sicilian mixed in with the Italian and I'm not sure I'm following her properly. Who's who and who survived and who didn't.' He turned back to Agnese. '*Anche una sorella?*' *Sorella*, Lily knew, meant sister.

'*Sì sì,*' said Agnese. '*Si chiama Carlotta.*'

'Carlotta?' His voice rose. '*Sicura?*'

Agnese nodded. Yes, she was certain.

'And this sister's still alive?' said Alex. '*Ancora vive?*'

'*Certo,*' said Agnese. '*Abita Palermo.*'

'She lives in Palermo?' Alex gave a low whistle. He said to Jess, 'Did you get that? It was the guy's *sister* who was called Carlotta.'

'Really? It's not what she told you before.'

'In the café? No. But I'm wondering now if she *wanted* me to get the wrong end of the stick.'

And Jess's mouth broke into its prettiest smile.

7

Marcello Campione's family had invited the McKenzies to join them to celebrate Ferragosto. When she was younger, Lily had thought the festival was called Fairy Gusto; to Harry it was Furry Ghosto. They knew better these days, but kept up the joke. It was an event they always looked forward to: a whole day's partying and feasting, the centrepiece of the summer. It made Lily wish (guiltily) that she could live in Sicily all the time because it was so much fun.

The Campiones came to Roccamare every August from their home in Milan and it was another branch of their family who were the hosts. They owned an olive grove near Castelvetrano, which was famous for its succulent green nocellara olives, as mellow and juicy as plums. They threw open the doors of a large barn once used for storage, now quietly crumbling. It had rough stone walls and holes in its roof, but its cavernous fireplace was ideal for roasting and barbecuing, for producing food on a biblical scale.

The McKenzies were among the first to arrive; dozens more guests were expected. Men were setting up benches and trestle tables in the courtyard outside; the women were in the barn, dealing with the food; a group of boys was scuffling with a football. Marcello was among them, but when Lily waved a greeting he ignored her. Piqued, she looked around for someone else she might recognise and spotted his two older sisters lolling against the bonnet of a sporty Lancia.

Marisa and Giovanna were in their early teens and addicted to glamour. They liked reading *fotoromanzi*, photo-strip stories of thwarted love, and they were obsessed with things Lily didn't know much about: fashion, hairstyles, weddings, the Osmonds. She preferred David Cassidy to the Osmonds and had never been a bridesmaid. Her parents hadn't even got married in a church. They'd both worn cream flared trouser suits to the registry office and had a party afterwards in the upstairs room of the pub where Alex organised the poetry readings. Poetry – *poesia* – was the only word to give this event any romance at all.

She wandered over to the Lancia and said, '*Ciao.*'

Giovanna looked up, said casually, '*Ciao, come stai?*' and resumed her conversation with Marisa. Not exactly a rebuff, but not an invitation either. At a loose end, Lily sought refuge in the gloom of the barn, where Dolly and other matrons were trimming artichokes, podding beans, gutting birds. Dolly had brought her own rolling pin and a container full of chickpea dough that she began to roll and cut out for the deep-fried *panelle*. She let Lily help with the cutting, though her fingers got sticky and her shapes weren't nearly as neat.

Marcello ambled through the doorway. He picked up a tomato and tossed it into the air like a tennis ball. He juggled with a second tomato, then a third, before acknowledging Lily. It was the first time they'd not been on an equal footing, in a neutral place. When he offered to show her around the *azienda*, the estate, it was in such a lordly manner she nearly refused to go with him.

'I'm helping Dolly,' she said.

'*Dai,*' said Dolly. 'You should go and play.'

'Don't you need me?'

But her scrappy pile of *panelle* mocked her. And it was clear from the slow smoulder of the wood and the mounds of food yet to be prepared that it would be a long time before they'd get anything to eat. '*Dai,*' said Dolly again and gave Lily a little push.

She followed Marcello outside. He wove through the cluster of parked cars and spurted into the olive grove. 'This way!' he called.

'Wait!'

'Catch me!'

The olive trees had been planted many years ago in long straight lines, but their limbs were bowed and twisted, their trunks sloped at unlikely angles, not quite falling over, so the symmetry was lost. The furrows between the rows were dry and uneven and Lily often stumbled. But she didn't give up the chase. The silver foliage whispered and shimmered in the sunlight and she pretended she was in an enchanted forest as part of the game. When she reached the boundary, Marcello was nowhere to be seen.

'I know you're hiding,' she sang out. In the distance she could see a curl of smoke from the barn chimney and hear the sounds of laughter but the figures were tiny and remote. She was surprised by how far she had come. Above her head the leaves rustled and she heard a strangled wail. They used to do this in their den: blow long screeching whistles to terrify each other. But that was more effective because the dinghy was dark inside; only a few pinpricks of light came through its rotting shell. 'You don't frighten me. Not a bit!'

'*Adesso arrivo!*' Marcello's lithe tanned body catapulted out of the tree and landed with a graceful roll on the ground. Jess had once said he reminded her of Donatello's David and although Lily didn't know anything about Donatello or his David, she understood it was a compliment. He rose and brushed the dirt from his shorts.

Lily said, 'I bet I could find somewhere better to hide.'

'You'd get lost.'

'No, I wouldn't.'

'The *azienda* is too big for you. Is hundreds of hectares.' Then he boasted about his cousins, the owners, about how they made the best olive oil in the region and how it made them rich.

Lily's parents were not interested in money, or so they claimed, though she didn't see the harm of it if it bought you what you wanted. But her aunt Dinah lived in a large country house with velvety carpets and a grand piano and ponies grazing in the paddock.

'My cousins are rich like yours,' she said. 'They have a farm too.'

'What do they grow?'

'Wheat, I think.' She wasn't sure because the land was leased to tenant farmers and her aunt and uncle had little to do with its cultivation. Her uncle went to work on the train and their children were at boarding school.

'*Comunque,*' said Marcello, 'they can't be your real cousins.'

'Why not? Their mother is Jess's sister.'

'But she's not your real mother, is she? It doesn't count.'

Lily was furious. He had never before tried to put her down. 'That's a mean stupid thing to say!'

He shrugged, unrepentant. 'Is true.'

The olive crop wasn't yet ripe, but she spotted some immature fruits that had fallen. She picked up a handful and flung them at him. Marcello ducked, grinning at the challenge, and collected his own ammunition. His throw was more successful than Lily's and a couple of hard bullet-like olives thudded into her shoulder. '*Colpo!*' he shouted. She stalked off. She wasn't going to play a game she couldn't win. He began aiming his shots at a rock instead.

Lily mooched along the border where the trees ended and scrubland began. Buried deep within her were recollections of the convent, of bells ringing for prayers, of the sickly odour of incense, of long rows of iron beds, of lining up on a bench with other children. There was also the sudden shock of being transplanted into a damp English winter, unfamiliar food, a foreign language. But all of this was secondary to the warmth and love she had from Jess and Alex and baby Harry, who was her brother just as much as Marcello was the brother of Marisa and Giovanna. How could the family she lived with not be real, if it was the only one she knew?

By now she was hot and sweaty and irritated and her irritation was always at its most intense and uncontrollable when she was hungry. Marcello shouldn't have said what he did. It would serve him right if she never played with him again. She kicked at some prickly pears lying on the ground. They had dropped, like the olives, but these fruits were crimson and juicy, ripe enough to eat. She picked one up without thinking and squealed at the stinging sensation that was much worse than nettles. She let go of the pear at once but the spiny needles stayed in her palm and fingers. She couldn't pull them out.

Her shriek rang in the still air and put Marcello off his aim. He hurled his final olive into the dust with a decisive thwack. Then he sauntered towards her.

She stayed where she was, biting down on her bottom lip although the new pain didn't lessen the old, which was like dozens of needles jabbing.

'*Cosa c'è?*'

She held out her hand helplessly.

Marcello had bright, piercing blue eyes. He stared at the spines, which were scarcely visible, and then at her face. 'It hurts?'

'Yes. *Molto!*'

'I think I can help.'

'You know what to do?'

'*Però*, you must keep still. *Non ti muovere.*' Don't move.

He took hold of her wrist with one hand and steadied her fingertips with the other so her skin was taut. He bent his head forward as if he was going to nuzzle her palm like a dog. She was afraid he might be teasing her, but she had to trust him. One by one, he drew out the spines with his teeth. The tingling began to subside.

'Oh, thank you!' she said, buoyant with relief. '*Grazie mille!*' And she put her arms around his neck and kissed his cheek.

'*Fa niente,*' said Marcello. It was nothing. Then he said, diffidently, '*Siamo ancora amici?*' We're still friends?

'*Certo.*' And to prove it she gave him a second kiss. 'Shall we go and see if the food is ready yet?'

'If you want.'

'Well, I'm starving, aren't you?' She slipped her hand into his and they stayed stickily together until they got near to the barn, when they edged apart in case anyone should see them.

The gathering had swelled. The guests were drinking and smoking and the ground was littered with spent matchsticks because it was bad luck to light a third cigarette from the same flame. Somebody had brought a portable record player since there was no electricity on the site. The sound was tinny and Lucio Battisti's latest album, '*Io tu noi tutti*', was playing at a slower speed than usual but it didn't matter because the dancing couples seemed happy to have an excuse to sway close together. Lily expected to see her parents among them. Their height made them stand out and Alex was wearing his red tee shirt with Che Guevara on the front. This was very old and Jess had deliberately left it behind at Villa Ercole for Dolly to turn into dusters. A year later it was still there, intact, and he had rediscovered it with glee.

Dolly was standing over the fire with three other women, turning skewers that looked like spindles because they'd been wrapped with tubes of stuffed intestines called *stigghiola*, which Harry thought were disgusting but Lily rather liked. Gerald was in discussion with the young mechanics who fixed his VW when it went wrong and had the pick of the girls because of their fast shiny motorbikes. The mechanics liked working for

Gerald because, being an English gentleman, he didn't try to drive a hard bargain on price. Alex, she finally located in the midst of another football game. Marcello's father was there too and Marcello ran to join them.

Lily was left by herself again, scouring the party for her mother's wide-brimmed straw hat. The sun was fierce overhead so she didn't think she would have taken it off. Then she saw it, dangling on the end of a branch. Jess was sitting in the shade under a tree with her back against the trunk and her legs drawn up, hugging her knees. Her face was turned towards the person sitting nearby. It took Lily a moment to recognise her as the lady with the Polaroid camera.

8

Jess had watched Lily run after Marcello with amusement. She was no longer bothered about the pair of them disappearing from view. Since the visit to Santa Margherita, her attitude had relaxed. After all, Agnese had been adamant that Carlotta was the name of the young baker's sister. She'd even given them her address in Palermo, though they didn't see much use for it while the woman was in Roccamare. And even if she *was* related to Lily, an aunt didn't have the same degree of attachment as a mother.

She drifted into the barn to offer help and when her offer was rejected she drifted out to check on Harry. A gang of boys was jostling for position in a game of leapfrog. They'd found a handy tree stump, the right height for their legs to straddle. Harry leapt and landed neatly but stumbled over his shoelaces; she tied them up for him and he too brushed her away. She topped up her wine glass and leant against the warm stone wall of the barn.

She narrowed her eyes so that the outlines of the boys and the trees and the people setting up the gramophone blurred into a pattern punctuated by bright shafts of sun. Inside her head she visualised a new design, vivid and curvaceous, a world away from the floral Laura Ashley sprigging that had dominated fabrics for so long. (Her second sister, Rosalind, often decked herself in violets and forget-me-nots, but she was exiled with her husband in Hong Kong and presumably wanted to be reminded of an English spring.) She sensed, rather than saw, a person approaching, a person in a swingy skirt that clung to her hips and high wedge sandals. She blinked and took a few seconds to focus on the form in front of her.

'*Ciao,*' said Carlotta, leaning forward to kiss her on both cheeks, a light perfumed kiss, barely making contact with skin, no need to rub away any smudge of lipstick. 'I have heard your family will be here for Ferragosto.'

'Oh, do you know the Campiones too?' She didn't need to. This was Sicily; no guest would be turned away. Did they even have a word for gate-crasher?

Carlotta waved a hand vaguely towards the men shifting the trestle tables. 'I come with my friend, Claudio,' she said. 'I hoped to see you.'

'I could have met you with Alex,' said Jess, still chafing at being excluded. 'Anything you say to him you can say to me, you know.'

'But he has told you of our meeting? I wanted to talk to him about his experience and now...' She brushed her fingertips along Jess's arm and her touch was transient like the kiss. 'I must speak with you. Woman to woman, yes?'

'About Lily?'

'Also about myself.' She gave an appealing smile. 'You know nothing about me, is true?'

Nothing about me is true? Jess moved from the wall to the shade of a tree. She took off her hat and hung it on a branch. She wanted to look at Carlotta directly, oblige her to be frank. 'So tell me, then,' she said.

'What do you like to know?'

Start with something neutral, she decided. 'Well... um... What do you do?'

'You mean my job? I work in a shop. We sell leather goods, mostly to tourists. I would like very much one day to have my own shop, selling handbags.' She cast a glance at Jess's crumpled canvas tote. 'I think I have a good eye. I can recognise good quality, good design. This is my dream. Rome, *però*, is an expensive place to live.'

'Rome?' said Jess sharply. 'Not Palermo?'

Carlotta ignored the interruption. 'It is hard to be all day on your feet but I don't mind the long hours if there is possibility of advancement. That is the difference on the mainland, you see. There are not so many fingers in your till. On this island we have many problems with corruption. Also we are very vulnerable. We live on one of the earth's fault lines. For us, it is always a struggle to keep our families alive.'

Jess took a long swallow of wine, boldly tried another tack. 'It must have been terrible what you went through, what happened in the earthquake.'

A pattern of shadows cast by the olive leaves danced across Carlotta's face. She spoke in a soft low tone that was almost hypnotic. 'For a long time I thought it would be better if I had died with my husband and baby. I had no wish to continue without them. We loved each other so much, Francesco and I. We were childhood sweethearts. He was always tender, he never beat me.'

'Why on earth would he do that?'

Carlotta said simply, 'To show his power. Women belong to men. They look after us so they must also control us.'

Jess was appalled. 'That's outrageous!' Although she and Alex had exchanged rings at the registry office, they never wore them. A ring was a symbol of commitment, but it was also a manacle. They viewed themselves as individuals who'd entered a partnership; they would not be chained. 'Human beings are equal. No one belongs to anyone else – that would be outright slavery!'

'Yes. I know now that life is different in other places, but here it's very traditional. A wife must do what her husband says. Papa, in the bakery, if you saw him pound the dough, you'd understand what he could do with his fists, the strength he had.'

Women's liberation had not yet reached Sicily; Jess was aware of this, but Carlotta's casual reference to domestic violence disturbed her. 'Did he used to hit you?'

'Who?'

'Your father?'

Carlotta shook her head. 'There was no need. My father was a blacksmith. Nobody argues with a man who works with hot iron.'

'Hang on a minute! You said he was a baker.'

'I was speaking of Papa Galetti, my father-in-law. My own father died many years ago, when I was a girl. There was only me and my mother.'

'Oh.' Jess was bewildered, her thought processes blunted by the heat and the wine. Carlotta's story didn't make sense in the light of what they'd heard from Agnese Fantoni and why wouldn't the old woman be telling the truth?

Carlotta continued, 'My father I don't remember well, but my daughter I remember precisely. The folds and creases of her little plump legs, her skin so soft and perfect. Her lovely milky scent and the way she laughed. If I close my eyes I try to hear the laugh. The smell, the touch, they are gone, but I have the pictures in my head and, sometimes, the sounds. I miss her. I will always miss her.' She removed her sunglasses, unveiling her nut-brown eyes, her sweeping lashes. 'I lost everything. How could I stay in Belice? My mother nursed me while I was in the coma. One of her brothers works for Fiat in Turin. When I got better we went to live with him.'

Still perplexed, Jess said, 'Your mother wasn't killed when the bakery collapsed?'

'Not then, but our tragedy was too much for her. After we come to Turin, she have heart attack. You see how unlucky I am! One good thing is they give me passport. I have another uncle who lives in Brooklyn. He sponsored me for two years so I can work in his restaurant.'

Donna fugata, Dolly had called her: the woman who fled. And she had been running further away each time. 'So you went to America?'

'I thought I was brave to do this, but really I was too scared to come home. I was very young, just twenty-one. I dreamed of a new life with a new family.' Her head drooped and her mouth curved downwards. 'I was wrong. My boyfriend, Ricky, and I, we planned to marry, but something happened that made it impossible... And then I have news of my daughter. That she may be alive.'

'For the first time, you mean? You'd heard nothing before?'

'Nothing.' She lifted her chin defiantly. 'A mother always knows her child, but it was not me who identified her body. At the time they said it was good that I didn't see her injuries, they were so terrible. I should not have listened to them.'

A few yards away, in sweltering sunshine, the festivities were boisterous and carefree, but the traumatic detail of Carlotta's story chilled Jess's blood. She ventured, 'If you didn't identify your husband either…'

Carlotta said, 'They gave me the wedding ring from his finger. I have it still. They found my baby's shawl, but it was buried with her so I have no memento. Not even a curl from her hair.' She tugged at a lock of her own as if it could anchor her. 'Can you imagine how it feels to be given suddenly some hope? To learn, after all, there could be some mistake. Do you understand, I *had* to come back to Sicily, I *had* to see if it was truly her. But it was no good. I was too late. She was gone away.'

Jess reminded herself that Carlotta had been severely concussed. Her memories were bound to be confused. Was that why she said her father was a baker one minute and a blacksmith the next? Was it possible she'd spent so much time taking care of her brother's baby she thought of it as her own? Or was she suffering survivor's guilt? That was more or less the conclusion she and Alex had come to, after speaking to Agnese. 'She'll be looking for reassurance,' Alex had said. 'Why would she choose to be saddled with a child she hasn't seen for nearly a decade? Even if she could prove a relationship. Keep your cool, Jess.'

She clasped her arms around her knees and said, very gently, 'Our little girl loves being here for the summer holidays, but she has plenty of friends, plenty going on, at home. We will never know exactly where she came from, but the main thing is she's happy now. That's what matters and we wouldn't want to jeopardise it. And I'm sure you wouldn't either. So I hope you don't mind me saying, but there's really no need for you to pretend to be someone you're not.'

Carlotta blanched.

Although Jess tried hard not to be judgemental (that was the preserve of her sisters) she couldn't help blurting, 'Oh, my God! You *were* trying to fool us! Why? Why would you lie about who you are when what we care about most – and you should too – is what's good for Lily herself? I mean, how *could* you?'

Carlotta said humbly, 'Is not my fault. My marriage certificate, my ID papers were destroyed, but I gave correct information. The error was not mine.'

'What d'you mean? What error? Whose fault was it, then?'

It was bad timing. Lily came running towards them, her face streaked as if she had been crying. Jess was instantly alert to distress. She unfolded herself and rose. 'Darling, what's the matter? Are you all right?'

'Yes, I'm all right… But I hurt my hand.' She held it out, palm upwards.

Jess couldn't see anything wrong but she took it anyway and brought it to her lips. 'There, I've kissed it better.' She held onto it, keeping Lily close. 'Shall we find Harry and see what Dolly is up to? I'm sure she'll have some nice snacks ready by now.'

She didn't want to hear any more of Carlotta's excuses. She wanted her to see that the McKenzies, like the Campiones, like myriad Sicilian families, could not be broken up.

9

The night after Ferragosto, Jess, Alex and Gerald sat drinking under the vine-covered trellis, surrounded by candles flickering in glass jars and aromatic cones smouldering to keep mosquitoes at bay. They had moved from white wine to red and on to rich sweet Marsala. The children and Dolly, early risers, were in bed asleep. Jess had spent all day trying to analyse her conversation with Carlotta, her mind beetling around in circles. Alex and Gerald were discussing Toby's imminent arrival. He was flying into Palermo on his way to help catalogue some new finds on Mozia.

'Said I'd pick him up tomorrow, bring him here for a night.' Gerald spoke with the deliberation of a man trying not to slur his words. 'He doesn't want the bother of a car, it's no good to him on the island and he's important enough these days for other people to drive him around.'

Gerald's tone made Jess wonder whether he was jealous. He had taken pains to create his classical idyll and scholarly persona – a life that wouldn't have been possible outside western Sicily – but he was always complaining about it: the heat, the inefficiency, the chaos, the bloody Church, the bloody Mafia, that bloody woman (Dolly).

Alex was drumming his fingers on the table top. 'We'll get him, if you like.'

Jess sat up. 'Will we? What about the children?'

'Kind of you, dear chap,' said Gerald. 'Traffic round Palermo is always a blasted nightmare and you know how my engine overheats. But I wouldn't want to let the boy down and it will be good to see him.'

'We can take the kids with us,' said Alex. 'We usually do. They like seeing Toby too. Also…'

'Also what?'

'We could do a bit of detective work.'

Jess said, 'Is that a good idea?'

'It might lay things to rest.'

'You're talking in riddles,' said Gerald. He poured another slug of Marsala; in the half-light it had given his teeth a purplish stain. 'Aah… is this about the Polaroid woman?'

'We've been given conflicting stories,' said Jess. 'We don't know what to believe, though I'd rather let the whole thing drop.'

Alex disagreed. 'There's a way we could check her out. Agnese Fantoni couldn't tell us what happened to the baker's wife, but she gave us an address in Palermo for his sister. If we go there we might be able to find out if Carlotta Galetti's the person she says she is.'

'Galetti is a very common name,' said Gerald. 'It wouldn't be surprising if there were several Carlottas too.'

'According to Agnese she's married and has a different surname now anyway. Though our Carlotta told Jess she lives in Rome, which adds to the confusion. We could be barking up the wrong tree altogether.'

Jess wished he wouldn't say 'our' Carlotta.

'Agnese's information might be out of date,' said Gerald. 'The girl could have separated from the husband and gone to Rome off her own bat, which is why she's after money… Just playing devil's advocate, my dears.'

'But we don't know she's after money!'

'I thought she'd said something?'

'Well, she hinted about wanting her own boutique… Oh my God, what are you suggesting?' Was Carlotta constructing a subtle form of blackmail, layer by layer? 'Good grief! We don't look rich, do we?'

'To a Sicilian,' said Gerald, 'yes. They think I'm Croesus.'

'Then if we go to Palermo, it will help us know where we stand,' said Alex firmly. 'Clear things up.'

'You really think,' said Jess, 'we should visit that address?'

'What's to lose?'

There came a distant rustle of wildlife in the undergrowth beyond the terrace – a snake perhaps? She tensed but she wasn't going to let it frighten her. 'Okay, you win... There probably won't be anyone home anyway, because she's here, isn't she, in Roccamare? But I'm not sure we should take the kids.'

'It's a long drive right enough,' said Alex. 'And there'll be a lot of hanging around one way and another... If they can stay here with you and Dolly, I reckon they'd prefer that.'

'No problem,' said Gerald, glad to be relieved of the chauffeuring.

'They mustn't go to the beach by themselves,' said Jess.

'Of course not. I'll take them over to Turi's and they can have a ride on his donkey. Bit of a treat.'

'That's very good of you, thanks.' Jess moved her chair closer to Alex's, for the security of his touch. He put his arm around her and she rested her head on his shoulder.

'It will be fine,' he said. 'Don't fret, Jessa-mine, this isn't like you.'

'No,' she agreed. 'Sorry, darling.' The nearest candle guttered out and in the sudden gloom she raised her head and kissed him full on the mouth, without inhibition, because Gerald wouldn't care anyway and she wanted to quash the turmoil in her brain.

*

Although Toby's a flight didn't arrive until the afternoon, they planned an early start and for the first time they set the alarm clock. Gerald was still sleeping, they could hear the snores from his bedroom. Dolly, up and active as usual, looked surprised to see them both dressed and ready to go. 'We're fetching Toby from the airport,' Alex explained.

Harry was spreading hunk of bread lavishly with strawberry jam. 'Can we come?' he asked, an automatic reflex.

'We thought you might get bored. Gerald has offered to take you for a donkey ride instead.'

'Okay,' said Harry, sticking the knife in his mouth and licking the jam off it.

Alex murmured to Dolly, 'But don't let the man drive if he's not up to it.'

'You know I will keep them safe!' she protested.

Jess felt the need to elaborate. 'And I'm going to be taking photos of mosaics and icons and so on, to get inspiration for patterns. You wouldn't want to be inside a musty old church on a day like this.'

'Dolly says we can help her candy the almonds,' said Lily.

On a tray at the far end of the table lay a pile of shelled almonds, milky white because their skins had been rubbed off. 'Hey,' said Jess, 'that sounds great. Be careful though because caramel gets terribly hot. You don't want to burn yourself. And, Harry, put that knife down!'

'Well, you've got the wind up for sure,' observed Alex as they puttered away in the car.

'Yeah, I know. I've visions of Lily falling into a vat of molten sugar and Gerald driving them all into a ditch. And of us not getting home till tomorrow because of Toby's plane landing hours late…'

'And?'

'And of the woman we're going to see, if she exists and it isn't all a wild goose chase, telling us: "Yes, my poor deceased brother's wife now lives in Rome and yes, she is also called Carlotta. And yes, she is a manipulative piece of work who's doubtless trying to blackmail you."'

'That's my girl!' said Alex. 'Keep your expectations low.'

'That wouldn't even be the worst thing! She's no grounds for blackmail, has she? It's not like we stole Lily. No, what would be worse is if she demands her back.'

'That can't happen, Jess. We've done everything legally. Lily is ours and no one can take her away.'

'But there's a moral dimension to this, isn't there? I mean, whether or not a child should be with their biological parent.'

'The evidence of biology,' he said, 'is purely circumstantial. We're not obliged to follow up any contact with the Galetti family. Poor Carlotta suffered a traumatic loss. It's not surprising she's clutching at straws.'

'We should have ignored her. You shouldn't have agreed to meet her.'

'What about when she turned up at Ferragosto? It was you who talked to her then.'

'She buttonholed me! I didn't have much choice.'

She could see he was struggling, as she was, to keep his equilibrium. 'It won't matter what we hear if we can get answers. Sort the facts from the fiction. It's the not knowing that's the problem.'

'I wish I could believe that.' She wound down her window, rested her elbow on the ledge, and tried to settle into the rhythm of the journey as warm air streamed past.

An hour and a half later they reached the outskirts of Palermo. The city's current reputation was unsavoury. Gerald told stories of men being gunned down in the streets and macabre funeral processions: black horses decked with plumes of black feathers pulling a gilded hearse, menacing phalanxes of mourners, every house along the route shuttered as a mark of respect. But Jess and Alex had visited before and they found Palermo exciting. They loved its anarchy and exuberance, the vibrant street markets, the legacy of fine palaces and fountains and rococo churches. And the setting, between soaring mountains and sparkling sea, was spectacular.

Today, however, all these glories passed them by. And after the quiet country roads the traffic mayhem was like an assault. Cars, lorries and scooters shot across each other's paths, horns blaring, exhausts pumping fumes. Drivers slowed to a crawl to hail friends or stopped randomly as if unaware they were causing an obstruction. Obeying traffic lights was voluntary. Pedestrians took their lives in their hands. A truck careered alongside, almost scraping their bumper, forcing them to change lanes. Alex gripped the steering wheel and Jess rotated the map to work out where they were going.

'Turn left,' she said.

'Here? Are you sure?'

'And then right.'

'But it's a one-way street.'

'That Fiat's turning into it.'

Alex stamped on the brake. 'Let me have a look.'

They had marked their destination on the map with a cross but they couldn't take into account the one-way system. Or the no-through roads. Or the blind alleys that ended abruptly at the top of a flight of steps. Reversing was difficult, turning round even more so. Swearing got them nowhere. When they finally escaped the warren of picturesque streets that had trapped them, they abandoned the car on a piece of waste ground. Alex gave a pair of young boys a few hundred lire to keep an eye on it – though they were less worried about its fate than whether they'd be able to find it again. Progress was better on foot, though Jess could feel the sweat running down her spine, and not just from the merciless heat. Alex, with the map in his fist, had taken over the navigation. 'Nearly there,' he said.

The apartment block they sought was large, bland, anonymous, decorated with daubs of graffiti. It reared up from the pavement, casting a shadow across the street. They passed through an archway into a courtyard. Laundry fluttered above their heads. Set out in the sunshine were gaudily painted tins, once containing olive oil and now planted with geraniums. From the gloomier corners came a smell of mould and rotting vegetation. Each side of the courtyard had external staircases leading to the upper floors. Alex checked the address they'd been given and tried to work out the numbering, which was not, they discovered after several false ascents and descents, the least bit logical.

When they eventually identified apartment number 32 there was no reply. Jess wasn't surprised. It seemed altogether too much to expect an actual person to exist at the end of their search. 'We've no way of knowing if it's the right address,' she said. 'She was a bit mad, wasn't she, Agnese? And you admitted you didn't understand everything she was saying. I don't know why Dolly didn't offer to come along to help translate. I can't see her here, can you?'

'Who, Agnese or Dolly?'

'Neither! Carlotta. She's too…'

'Elegant? Pretty?'

'Oh, do you think she's pretty?'

'Don't you?'

'Yes, of course. Gorgeous. That's why… I don't believe she lives in an ordinary place like this.'

He rang the doorbell again and knocked loudly. 'She once lived in cramped quarters above a bakery in a small farming town.'

'If what she says is true.'

Voices floated through the courtyard. Two women with plastic bags full of shopping entered beneath the arch. One turned to scold a child who was lagging behind. The other called up to a high window and a wicker basket was lowered to the ground on a piece of string. Jess was watching the basket being filled with a lettuce, two onions, a lemon, half a loaf of coarse bread when, behind her, she heard a door open. It wasn't their door, no 32, but the one adjacent.

A woman in an overall and slippers peered out. '*Sono andati via,*' she said.

'*In vacanze?*' said Alex.

The woman was distracted by the basket of food swaying and bumping on the opposite side of the building as it was hauled to the top floor. Then, as if the high spot of her day was over, she nodded and confirmed that her next-door neighbours were Carlotta, a nurse, and her husband, Guido Roselli, who worked on the railways. A very good job with many perks if you liked to travel. And yes, this was August, was it not? They were on holiday.

Jess said, 'Ask her where they've gone.'

'Vacanze in Sicilia?' he said. *'Al mare?'*

'Potrebbe.' Possibly they could have gone to the seaside. It was where most people went. She had a faintly exhausted air, as if she could do with a break herself, and from the depths of her apartment Jess caught the wail of a baby.

'Ask her if they have any children.'

But Alex went one better. He took his wallet from his pocket and a Polaroid photograph from the wallet. After muttering, 'God, this is ridiculous, I feel like I'm a fucking PI,' he said, *'Questa donna, lei cognosce?'*

The woman took the photograph and examined it. Then she stepped forward into the light and examined them, as if it had suddenly occurred to her that this was an unusual situation: two foreigners enquiring about her neighbour for no apparent reason. *'Perchè?'* she said.

Alex tried to explain they were looking, for personal reasons, for a woman known as Carlotta Galetti, and they had been given this address.

The woman, now suspicious if not actively hostile, said, *'Si chiama Carlotta Roselli.'*

'Her married name, yes,' said Alex. 'But before, *la sua cognome era Galetti, no?'*

She returned the photograph with a shake of her head. '*Non è questa,*' she said and shut the door.

'So that's all we get,' said Jess. Disappointment weighed her down, her shoulders sagged in defeat.

'It's not bad news,' he said. 'We've learned something.'

'Carlotta Galetti doesn't live here?'

'Aye.'

'How is that not bad news? If it means she isn't the baker's sister, after all?'

'It's early days,' he said. 'I'm more used to following up stories than you are. You can't – are you listening to me, Jess? – You *can't* jump to conclusions. Not yet.'

'I didn't even want to come in the first place. This was your idea!'

She was trembling. They shouldn't quarrel. They *never* quarrelled. He took her hand and led her down the stairs. They crossed the courtyard, and retraced their steps until they came to a shabby bar at the corner of a piazza. He ordered two bottles of cheap fizzy Birra Messina. Neither of them felt like eating. 'Let's forget it,' he said. 'Why would we want to open a can of worms? All we have to do is stay out of the woman's way. We're going home at the end of the week. We can put it behind us.'

'I'm not being a wimp,' said Jess.

'I didn't say you were.'

'And I understand your curiosity.'

'Well, it's a bit more than curiosity.'

'I know…' She'd always been proud of the fact that their views were so much in tune, but perhaps she'd lazily followed his lead because she'd had no reason to disagree until now. Until his instinct to uncover the facts and hers to preserve their family unit were at loggerheads.

Alex said lightly, 'Drink up. Or we'll be late for Toby.'

It was a relief to have something else to focus on, even if it did mean negotiating more pandemonium getting to the motorway and the airport. And waiting longer than necessary at the arrivals gate because, although Toby's plane had landed on time, there was a delay at the baggage carousel. He emerged at last, looking endearingly familiar to them and quite different from everyone around him – Toby's perpetual dishevelment made even Alex's frayed jeans and limp tee shirt appear to be worn with casual grace.

'How good of you to come!' he said, hugging them in turn. 'Hope it wasn't too much of an ordeal.'

'An ordeal?' Jess grimaced.

'Gerald throwing a wobbler, was he?'

'We'll fill you in later,' said Alex, picking up one of Toby's bags.

'Nothing to do with the news, then?'

'What news?'

'It was all anyone was talking about on the plane. And whether to believe it. Elvis is dead.'

'Elvis!'

'Happened last night, though it was still afternoon for him. Found on the bog floor. Overdose of some kind, apparently. What a way to go.'

'It passed us by,' said Alex. 'We've been a mite preoccupied.'

'Oh, Lord,' said Jess. 'How awful.' Elvis Presley had been the idol of her teenage years, until the Beatles replaced him, much to the incomprehension of her parents. His importance had long since faded so, although the details were shocking, she listened to them with detachment rather than distress. It wasn't until afterwards, and for other reasons, that the date she learned of his death was drilled into her memory.

10

Lily dragged a chair over to the stove so she could watch the sugar melt and the caramel crackle. When Dolly judged the stage was right (by sniffing and scrutinising) she tipped in her pile of shelled almonds. Harry wanted to join in so he and Lily took turns to stand on the chair and stir the mixture. They had to change places quickly, to keep the almonds moving so they wouldn't catch and burn. Lily was in charge when the caramel changed consistency and the almonds, instead of being a gloopy mass, took on their individual candy coats. 'They're ready!' she called.

Dolly switched off the flame and because the pan was too heavy for Lily she lifted it by both handles and emptied it onto the tray on the table, spreading the nuts in a single layer with her spoon. The result was very satisfactory, Lily thought. Harry reached out to try one and Dolly slapped his hand away. *'Fa caldo!'* she warned. 'It's too hot. You must wait.'

'It won't be long, will it?' he said hopefully.

But Dolly flapped her apron at him and said, *'Pazienza!* Your tongue will burn.'

Since the entire process had taken little over half an hour, the rest of the day stretched vacantly ahead. They weren't allowed to go to the beach without their parents and Gerald was yet to rouse himself – they knew better than to disturb him. Dolly's next preserving job (Ferragosto signified the start of the harvest) was podding the dried beans but this wasn't as much fun as candying. The children wandered outside: spotting and chasing lizards was a favourite game of Harry's. Once, he'd managed to catch one; as he'd held his prize gloatingly between finger and thumb its tail had dropped off. He'd thrown the body away in disgust. 'I don't want half a lizard!' he'd shrieked. Then Gerald had explained it was a defence mechanism and the lizard could grow another tail. Harry had been trying to repeat his capture ever since.

They were spared from boredom by the jangle of a bicycle bell. They couldn't see over the wall but moments later, barefoot and bare-chested, wearing a pair of yellow shorts, Marcello freewheeled through the open gate and bumped down the drive. He didn't alight. He veered past them into the orchard and wove a route through the trees. At one point he put his feet on the handlebars. On another circuit he heaved the front wheel upwards to jump over an irrigation channel, whooping as he cleared it.

'I want to have a go,' said Harry. At home, he had recently learned to ride a bike, just as he'd recently learned to swim. But the bikes at Villa Ercole were cumbersome and he had difficulty reaching the pedals, though Lily could cope well enough. She hoisted herself into the saddle and pursued Marcello, pretending they were cowboys and Indians riding on horseback.

Dolly came to the door to see why they were making so much noise and rolled her eyes.

'I need something to ride too!' Harry pleaded.

Dolly held out her broomstick and laughed at the disgust on his face.

'Have you got any other bikes at your house?' Lily asked Marcello.

'There's my old one,' he said. 'That I've grown out of. Harry can borrow, if he wants.'

'Can we go and collect it?' Lily asked Dolly. 'Please!'

'How will you get there?'

'On this bike. Harry can sit on the seat and I'll stand on the pedals.'

Dolly considered the rusty handlebars and worn saddle. 'Is not safe.'

'We're only going to Marcello's. It isn't far.' Besides, lots of children rode that way in Roccamare. And plenty of teenagers crowded onto scooters. They knew three at a time was against the law but it didn't stop them doing it.

Harry said, with simple logic, 'And we need to go with him to fetch another bike because he can't ride two by himself.'

'Mamma will give us lunch,' said Marcello.

'*Va bene.* But you must be good or you know what I'll do to you!' She made jabbing motions with her broom as Harry clambered behind Lily and the trio set off down the track.

It was hard work pedalling with the weight of another person on board. Marcello shot ahead and Lily couldn't keep up. The track was bumpy and stony, sending jolts up her legs and spine. It will get easier when we go downhill, she thought, but to her surprise it seemed to get harder.

When they reached the tarmac road Marcello was waiting for them. 'If he's too heavy for you,' he said to Lily, 'I'll take him.'

'I can manage,' she insisted. Gerald described the bikes as old bone-shakers and she could see why. Dust had spurted up into her face and clogged her nose and parched her throat. 'But I need to rest for a bit.'

Marcello pointed at her back wheel. 'Look at that,' he said.

Lily looked. 'Get off a minute, Harry. You're weighing it down.'

'No, I'm not.' But he got off anyway and sat cross-legged at the roadside.

The tyre didn't bounce upwards, it remained flat.

'*Una foratura,*' said Marcello. A puncture.

'Oh…' She latched onto the expletive she heard most often. '*Porca miseria!*' She didn't know what to do. They

111

were nearer to Villa Ercole than the Campiones' holiday home. She supposed she'd have to wheel the bike back up the hill with Harry traipsing gloomily alongside. Marcello could give one of them a lift on his crossbar, but not both, and as a loyal older sister she couldn't abandon Harry.

'We could see if Gerald can mend it,' she said.

'Oh, I can mend it,' said Marcello. 'I have a kit.'

'Do you have it with you?'

'No, but I could go and find it. I'm very speedy.'

Lily considered. They weren't in any hurry and she could tell from the position of the sun in the sky that it would be a while before lunch. 'Okay,' she said. 'Don't be too long.'

He raced away until he was a tiny blob in the distance. Harry tried splitting a coarse blade of grass to make a whistle, without success. 'We've been waiting ages,' he said, after about ten minutes.

'No, we haven't. It just seems like ages.'

'I'm thirsty.'

'So am I. We should have brought drinks with us. How about this? If Marcello doesn't get back by the time I count to a hundred we'll give up, go home and get one off Dolly.'

'I'll count,' said Harry. He started steadily but wavered when he got to the forties.

'You can't stop,' said Lily.

'I'm not stopping. I'm saying them in my head.'

An ineffectual scarecrow had been planted in the field opposite, birds roosted on its outstretched arm. This gave Lily the idea of hitch-hiking, though the road was quiet and, so far, only a couple of cars and a *camionetta* carrying a load of gas cylinders had trundled past. No one would see them sitting down so she stood up while Harry continued to mutter the numbers under his breath. When a vehicle took shape in the distance she stuck out her thumb in an exploratory way. She hadn't even decided whether she wanted to be taken on to Marcello's or up to Villa Ercole, when the car stopped.

She was astonished at the ease of conjuring a lift, but less astonished when the driver got out of the car: it was common for the same faces to reappear in Roccamare. Although Carlotta Galetti's hair was tucked away under a scarf, her pointed chin and big dark glasses were immediately familiar. It was the same car as before, too, but this time she was alone in it.

Carlotta tilted her head to one side, taking in the children, the battered bike, the flat tyre. 'What are you doing?' she said.

Harry jumped up, delighted to see her, and explained in a jumbled way how they'd been going to join Marcello's family and borrow a bike that was the right size for him when they discovered the puncture. He forgot to say Marcello was fetching a repair kit but it didn't matter because Carlotta said, 'I can take you there if you like.'

'What shall we do about the bike?' said Lily.

They discussed whether it might fit in the passenger seat or the boot, but reckoned in the end that it wouldn't. Lily was worried about leaving it on the verge for someone to steal, even if it wasn't roadworthy, so she was grateful for the suggestion they camouflage it with tufts of grass and stems of wild fennel. It was visible if you knew where to look, but not noticeable to the casual eye. Carlotta was laughing as she broke off the fennel stalks. 'This is a little bit crazy, isn't it?'

When they had finished, Harry said, 'Can I sit in the front?'

Carlotta said, 'Yes, if you want.' She gave Lily a long sombre look as if she feared she might object, but Lily climbed equably into the back seat, glad to have been rescued.

'Do you like to ride a bike?' Carlotta asked Harry as she turned the key in the ignition.

Harry said woefully, 'I keep falling off. We're supposed to be visiting the donkey today. Because they've gone to Palermo to get Toby.'

'Who?'

'Our parents.

'And that's what you prefer to do?' said Carlotta. 'Ride a donkey?'

'Actually,' confided Harry, 'I'd rather go fishing.' The promised fishing trip had still not materialised, but he was the person going on about it; Lily didn't much mind.

Carlotta began to motor slowly along the empty road. 'Your parents are in Palermo all day?'

'Yes.'

'And you would like to go fishing?'

Harry's eyes glowed. 'Can we? Do you know a fisherman?'

She hesitated. 'I do, but not here. In Marsala.'

'Can we go there?' said Harry.

'I think it is too far.'

Lily had a hazy idea where Marsala was because they'd been through it on the way to Mozia; she knew it was closer than Palermo. 'Are you very busy today?'

'As it happens,' said Carlotta, taking one hand from the steering wheel and flapping it, 'I am free as a bird.'

'You don't have to meet your *amico*?' Usually her boyfriend was somewhere nearby.

'No,' she said with a hint of bitterness. 'Claudio is not my friend at this moment.'

'Oh.'

'We are not speaking,' said Carlotta, without giving any further details.

'But you've got the car?'

'This is true.'

'Then you can take us!' said Harry with impeccable logic.

'You want to have an adventure?'

115

'Oh, yes! Can we? Please! Can we? Please!'

Harry's insistence was noisy and infectious and Lily wasn't surprised when Carlotta gave in.

'*Va bene,*' she said with a little mock sigh. 'You win.'

It was lucky that she was still driving slowly enough for Lily to spot Marcello in his yellow shorts pedalling towards them. She called 'Stop!' and Carlotta braked. Lily rolled down the window and poked her head through. 'Did you find it?' she said.

'No. I looked everywhere!'

'It doesn't matter. We don't need it after all.'

'Why not? Where are you going?'

'Fishing!' squawked Harry.

Lily wondered whether to ask if Marcello could join them, but Carlotta's mouth was set in its turned-down position. Also, she couldn't risk her changing her mind. Harry would never forgive her. He was the most obstinate of the McKenzies and, having finally got his way, he wouldn't let this chance pass him by.

Carlotta revved the engine. Lily said, '*Ci vediamo*, Marcello. See you later.'

Marcello waved them off without protest. All summer their arrangements had been easy-come, easy-go so this was no exception. And Lily suspected he was showing off anyway, that all he wanted to do was scoot around on his shiny new bike until sundown.

She left her window open so when Carlotta put her foot down the air whistled past and she could pretend they were flying (which was what cruising downhill on the bike should have felt like). In the front seat Harry was prattling away as if the two of them had known each other for years, whereas Lily found Carlotta disturbing. When she wasn't wearing her dark glasses (which wasn't often), her gaze had an unsettling intensity that made Lily think she must have done something wrong.

'Are you okay, Lily?' she asked. 'You are very quiet.'

'I'm thirsty, that's all.'

Harry said, 'Me too!'

Carlotta had taken the main road, which led inland and skirted Castelvetrano. Villa Ercole was now several kilometres distant. She said, 'Then we must buy you a drink. Also, I have been thinking. You need to get permission to come on this trip with me. When we stop for the drinks you should make telephone call.'

First, they had to find a bar with the black and yellow *telefono* sign hanging outside. By the time they located one they were nearly in Mazara del Vallo and Marsala wasn't much further away. Carlotta bought *gettoni* so Lily could feed the telephone slot, and a can of Pepsi each. Harry sat at one of the cane tables and pulled the square napkins from their dispenser, folding them into paper darts. Lily held the clammy receiver in one hand and the can of cola against her cheek with the other, to cool her face. She worried about how much to tell Dolly, who wouldn't be happy to hear of the fishing idea. She'd throw a panic about Harry falling overboard and drowning, even if he was wearing a life-jacket. And if she vetoed it, Lily would have to face his acute disappointment, his wails of, 'Spoilsport!' She'd be sandwiched between the two of them. Fortunately it wasn't Dolly who answered, but Gerald.

'How goes it?' he said. 'We're not expecting you back to eat, are we?'

'No,' said Lily. 'But we had a problem with the bike and Marcello couldn't find his repair kit…'

'Oh, don't worry. I'll get one of the boys to look at it some time. I'm sure you'll have more fun with the Campiones than old fogeys like us.'

'Actually…' Lily faltered. 'We're on a sort of expedition…'

'Well, I hope you enjoy yourselves! The main thing is to make sure you get home before your parents or they'll have my guts for garters.' His voice was jokey because both Jess and Alex would go out of their way to appease Gerald. He was much more likely to sulk than they were.

So Lily giggled because he was clearly in a good mood today, and said, 'Of course we will,' and put the phone down.

'Everything is okay?' said Carlotta. 'You have the permission?'

Lily nodded and drank her cola. Carlotta squeezed her shoulder and let her hand rest on it for a moment. Lily assumed she was trying to be reassuring so she didn't like to shake her off.

'Can we go now?' said Harry. He'd finished his drink and was tired of firing his paper darts.

'You are both ready? *Andiamo!*'

Carlotta drove straight to the quayside in Marsala. Rows of fishing boats bobbed along the harbour wall. The sound of their masts creaking and the sea slapping at their sides, the stench of oil and salt and fish guts, were the same as Roccamare but on a much bigger scale.

'I will know the boat when I see it,' she said.

'Is that it?' asked Harry, whose fancy had been taken by one painted cream and crimson. It stood out like a bowl of cherries amidst all the blue.

'I'm sorry, no. The person I'm looking for, Peppe, is a cousin of my mother's, but I haven't seen him for a long time.'

'So he might not be here?' said Lily. 'He might have got another job.'

'No, *carina*. A fisherman is always a fisherman. I will ask.'

Holding onto Harry, she approached a knot of men who were gathered around a freshwater tap, rinsing out their crates. They welcomed the excuse to stop their work, but they couldn't help. They indicated another man, further along the dock, who reputedly knew everyone. Lily followed at a distance. Carlotta had an animated discussion with the man who knew everyone and told them, 'Peppe is in Favignana.'

'What does that mean?'

She pointed towards the horizon where a hump rose from the surface of the sea. 'Favignana is an island. We often call it the butterfly because of its shape, like a body with two wings. Peppe went there to help with the *mattanza* and has stayed for the summer because the fishing is good. He's probably sleeping on his boat.' She wrinkled her nose, as if the boat might not smell very nice.

'How can we get there?'

'There is a ferry.'

'Oh, wow!' said Harry. 'Can we go on a ferry?'

'Is this what you want?' She was beginning to look uneasy. 'Or should I take you back to Roccamare?'

But Harry began his begging chant again: 'Can we? Please!' and this time Lily joined in. She was curious to see a butterfly-shaped island and if they went home now, without doing anything interesting, they might as well have been sitting in the car all the way to the airport.

Once they had boarded the ferry and were churning across the water, they couldn't help being excited and running from side to side to look at the white trail they were leaving behind. Carlotta kept telling them anxiously to keep away from the edge, though she relaxed when they began to approach the harbour. She pointed out the big brick sheds of the *tonnara* where the

120

tuna were processed, where enormous fish, bigger than a man, would be divided up and squashed into tins. She told them that in the *mattanza* shoals of tuna were driven through a series of nets, decreasing in size, until they were trapped in the death chamber. Then the fisherman, brave warriors rocking in their dinghies, would spear them with their harpoons until they were slaughtered and the sea was red with blood.

The sound of this intrigued Harry. 'Will it happen today?'

'No,' said Carlotta. 'It's too late in the season. Do you really want to see so much dying?' He squirmed and she went on. 'Peppe will be fishing for sea bream and sardines and red mullet.'

Lily said, 'Can we look for him after we've had lunch?'

Before Harry could object, Carlotta said, 'That's a good idea. We should eat.'

A trattoria in the piazza had tables outside, the paper tablecloths held on with clips. It wasn't very different from the places they ate in with their parents, but it had a distinctly novel appeal: here they were on an island in the middle of the sea with a lady who was taking them on a magical excursion, like Mary Poppins. Cartoon penguins might start singing any minute.

'You eat fish?' said Carlotta, scanning the menu. 'Else why would you want to catch it?' They both nodded, but Harry confessed he would rather have pasta and Lily joined him so he wouldn't feel left out. Carlotta chose mussels, picking them deftly from the dish with her sharp red nails. She noticed Lily was staring at her. 'Is there a problem?'

Lily said, 'Why do you wear sunglasses all the time, even when you don't need to?' It was shady under the awning.

'Oh, I'm sorry!' She took them off and Lily at once felt guilty. It was obvious she'd been hiding behind the glasses because she'd been crying over the boyfriend, but she put on a cheery smile. 'I hope we can get to know each other better this afternoon. I want you to have a nice time. You must tell me the things you like to do.'

'We're going on a boat, aren't we?' That was one thing about Harry, he never gave up.

'*Certo*, as long as we can find Peppe.'

'If we can't, could somebody else take us?'

'*Dio mio!* I couldn't hand you over to a stranger, it wouldn't be safe.' By accident, Lily made a snorting noise as she set down her drink and Carlotta added quickly, 'I hope you don't think of *me* as a stranger?'

Lily deliberated. They had seen Carlotta a few times now and she had always been friendly. They wouldn't have got into her car otherwise. 'No,' she said. 'Not exactly.' She wanted to be fair and was surprised when Carlotta seemed upset.

After lunch she promised them ice cream. They chose two flavours each from the *gelateria* to eat in a cone on their way to the harbour. This time their search was more successful. Carlotta found an acquaintance of Peppe's who gave them directions. Further along the shore they spotted a man sitting by himself, mending a net even faster than the widows in Santa Margherita at their crochet. Greying hair curled onto his neck beneath his cap, his trousers were rolled up and his skin was brown like old leather. Carlotta held herself very still and took a deep breath.

'Is that Peppe?' said Harry.

'Yes, we're in luck.' She led them both over to the fisherman. 'Peppe! *Come stai?*'

At first, concentrating on his shuttle, Peppe didn't register their arrival and she had to repeat herself. Then, carefully, he coiled his net away and got to his feet. He tipped back his hat. His eyes were black as currants in his lean lined face. He would have been handsome, thought Lily, if he hadn't looked so *old*.

'*Buon giorno,*' he said. He wiped his hand on the end of his shirt and held it out.

Carlotta took it between both of hers and tossed her hair from her face. '*Non mi cognosce*, Peppe?' To the children she murmured, 'He hasn't seen me for many years. I didn't think I had changed so much, but maybe I am wrong.'

'*Matre santa!*' he exclaimed. '*Che sorpresa!*'

'*Una sorpresa buona?*' A nice surprise.

'*Sei tu Concetta? Ritornata qui? La mia piccola Concetta...*'

'I'm not little any more, am I?' she said gaily to Lily, though actually she was quite small compared to Jess.

'Why did he call you Concetta?'

'Ouf... Who knows?' Then she said, although it wasn't a proper explanation, 'Concetta is what he cares about most of all. It's the name of his boat.'

11

On the way back in the car they found a radio station that was playing Elvis tributes. Alex and Jess and Toby sang along to 'Hound Dog' and 'Don't Be Cruel' and 'Suspicious Minds', giddy with the pleasure of reunion. Jess was transported back to the early days when Alex, barnstorming and gregarious, had introduced her to his diffident friend and she had marvelled at their contrasting personalities and the strength of their attachment. After school, Alex had gone to the LSE (History) and Toby to Leeds (Archaeology), but it hadn't affected their friendship. After graduation, flitting between research and temporary lectureships, Toby had squatted on their sofa and the three of them had done everything together – a bit like *Jules et Jim*, with Jess as Jeanne Moreau. (In the glorious early scenes, of course.)

'Toby's madly in love with you, you know,' Alex had told Jess casually.

'God, that's awkward.'

'Not really.'

'You don't think so?'

'It's fine, I don't get jealous. I'm not the possessive type.'

Alex would give you the coat off his back, he'd share his last crust, his last penny, but wasn't this going too far? 'Are you saying what I think you're saying? You wouldn't care if I slept with your best friend? Are you so sure of me?' As she recalled, things hadn't turned out well for *Jules et Jim*.

'If we're strong together, nothing can beat us. Whatever you do, it won't alter how I feel about you. I'd still love you.'

'I'm glad to hear it. But, as it happens, I don't want to sleep with anyone else.'

'Fair enough,' he'd said, pinning her arms behind her back with one hand and tickling her ribs with the other, as if the conversation had been a mighty joke.

Toby Forrester was the kind of person who grew on you. Initially Jess had thought him nondescript – he was slight and bony, his features unremarkable – but he had a warm mellifluous voice and a cheerful presence. The very fact that he was in the car, tapping out a rhythm and performing his Elvis pastiche, helped her worries subside. Why was she being so selfish over Lily? Genuine love bred generosity. It didn't follow, even if Carlotta Galetti *was* Lily's biological mother, that they couldn't come to an arrangement. It was a challenge they ought to be able to meet.

When the radio programme ended, Alex said to Toby, with a hint of mockery, 'We hear you're the great Phoenician authority now. Gerald can't decide whether to be pleased or miffed.'

'Is that why he didn't want to pick me up?'

'Och, no, we volunteered. Though he has got disgracefully lazy in his old age.'

'I couldn't resist the summons,' said Toby. 'We want to cross-reference the new discoveries at Mozia with the ones they're making at Carthage. The Tophet they're excavating there is much bigger but they're unearthing the same sort of funerary urns.'

'What's a Tophet?' said Jess.

'It's a sacred burial ground, used for the remains of very young children. In fact, when the contents of the urns are analysed, we're finding the bones of small animals in there too, mixed up with the babies. Only scraps of bone, mind you, after cremation. The jury's out on whether it adds up to ritual sacrifice.'

His tone was matter-of-fact, but Jess shivered in horror. 'Of babies?'

'Lots of ancient cultures practised child sacrifice,' said Toby.

'Oh, my God, that's gross!'

'The Phoenicians had a particularly bad reputation, although there isn't any direct evidence. We know the Greeks and Romans accused them of it but there's a strong whiff of propaganda.' He noticed his pen was leaking in the breast pocket of his shirt, took it out and contemplated it. 'Another possibility, if the babies in the crematorium didn't die naturally, is that they were seen as not-yet-human – the way we might consider a foetus.'

'Is that because they couldn't survive without their mothers?'

Toby put the pen back in his pocket; his fingers were now inky too. 'Precisely. But I shan't poke my head above the parapet until I've done more investigation.'

'Go for it, man,' said Alex speeding along an empty stretch of road. 'Never accept the status quo.'

Jess said, 'Please can we stop talking about killing children? It's making me feel queasy.'

*

On their return, Villa Ercole lay basking in the late afternoon sun like a sleeping cat and there was a general sense of torpor. Toby was staying in a guest room in the main house, rather than in the annexe the McKenzies were renting. The three of them strolled into the hallway and were puzzled by the silence that greeted them.

'Did they forget I was coming?'

'Gerald!' called Alex.

Gerald tottered out of his study and into his nephew's embrace. 'So sorry,' he said. 'Must have nodded off. But it's good to see you, as ever.'

'Where are the others?' said Jess.

'Oh, Dolly's outside harvesting something. Beans, I think. Now, what will you have to drink? I've a couple of bottles of Pinot Bianco in the fridge. We're used to sweltering here but the temperature must be a bit of a shock to you, old chap.'

'Where are the kids? Are they still at Turi's?'

'No, we didn't go in the end. They went off with Marcello Campione instead.' He rubbed his eyes, inspected his watch and tapped the glass. 'This humidity's a pest. I told them to be back before you were. I'm sorry, my dear, we lost track…'

'I'll go and fetch them,' said Jess, reluctantly deferring the treat of chilled white wine. 'You've been driving all day, Alex.' She was surprised they'd stayed out for so long, but the Campiones were a hospitable family and a couple of additional children would easily have been absorbed.

She climbed into the car and drove towards Roccamare. The day's heat was trapped in the furrows of the land and the stone of the buildings but the light had taken on a softer quality. The rays of the dipping sun burnished everything they touched: the fronds of the palm trees, the whitewashed cottages hugging the shore, the long ripples on the sand and the sea. The Campiones had a newly built single-storey villa on the outskirts of the town. Marcello's sisters were sitting on the doorstep braiding each other's hair.

Jess said, 'I've come for Lily and Harry. Do you know where I can find them?'

Giovanna said, 'They are not here.'

'Are they at the beach?' When both girls shrugged, she said, 'I'd better speak to Marcello. Or your mamma? Is she in?'

As Giovanna stood aside to let her knock, Marcello rounded the corner on his bike.

'*Ciao,*' said Jess. 'Aren't Lily and Harry with you?' He shook his head and she began to be alarmed. She wondered if she could have missed them on her way down, if there was some mysterious alternative route to Villa Ercole that she didn't know about. It was a ridiculous line of thought, but the brain clutches at straws when it doesn't want to accept the unpalatable.

'When did you last see them?'

Marcello frowned, thinking. *'Sta mattina.'*

'This morning! But that's impossible…'

He pointed at the wheel of his bike and said, *'Aveva una foratura.'*

Jess didn't know what he meant but she was determined not to show signs of panic. Not yet anyway. She thanked him and drove back slowly the way she had come, looking for clues. How could she have failed to spot the bike discarded by the side of the road? She pulled over to take a closer look at it. She could see the flat tyre. She could also see the crude attempts to cover it with shreds of vegetation. Why would anyone do that?

What were they trying to hide? With mounting dread, she returned to the Campiones. The girls had now disappeared but Marcello was still riding up and down. She hailed him.

'I've found the bike,' she said. 'Do you know what happened? Why did they leave it? Where did they go?'

'They go in the car,' said Marcello. 'With the lady.'

She knew who 'the lady' was, the only person it could possibly be. 'What for?' she asked and the words came out like a strangled yowl.

'For fishing,' he said.

'Fishing! Oh, for heaven's sake!' She tried to smile and look grateful as she got back into the driving seat for the third time, and sped off.

There was such a disjunction between Jess's wild imaginings and the affable mood of the three men sitting out on the terrace, they might have inhabited two different stratospheres. She felt as if she were mouthing silent screams and hammering on an invisible wall and the others neither noticed nor cared. Toby was the first to become aware of her.

'Good grief, Jessamy,' he said. 'You look stricken. What is it?'

'They aren't there.'

Alex swivelled his head. 'What do you mean?' He pulled out a chair for her. She didn't sit, but gripped the top of it so hard the wrought iron bit into her palms.

'You promised to look after them!' she accused Gerald.

'The kids? But I did,' he protested. 'I mean, Dolly did. And she rang me.'

'Who?'

'Lily.'

'Where from?'

'Lord knows. Some bar somewhere. She told me they'd had a problem with the bike and they were spending the day with the Campiones. I told her to make sure they came back in good time. I regret, my dear, they didn't stick to their side of the bargain.'

'Regret! Gerald, what were you playing at? They've been kidnapped on your watch.'

'Oh, no…' His face deepened to an unhappy purple. 'Surely not…'

Alex rose and stood behind Jess. 'Don't rush to conclusions, sweetheart.' He wrapped his arms around her like a cloak and she didn't struggle. She allowed herself to be seated, to be given a glass of wine, which tasted like ashes on her tongue. Dolly was tracked down and fetched from the vegetable plot, but she wasn't much help. She threw her apron over her face and sobbed wildly behind it, chastising herself and imploring intervention from the saints and conveniently forgetting a single word of English.

Toby, who was a believer in the value of method and patient deduction, took a pad of paper and a pen from his bag. 'Let's analyse this rationally,' he said, and began writing things down. 'They left with Marcello on the bike? And then they got a puncture? They were picked up by a woman they clearly knew. She agreed to take them fishing. Marcello went home. Lily rang to tell Gerald about the bike and he told her not to be late. She didn't sound scared, did she, Gerald?'

'No.'

'And she didn't say who she was with?'

'She mentioned an expedition of some kind. I presumed with the Campiones... My mistake.'

'So who is this mysterious woman?' said Toby. 'And what makes you think she's a kidnapper?'

Alex was sitting next to Jess, clasping her hand, not letting go. He said, 'Her name – at least the name she gives – is Carlotta Galetti. It's hard to see how it could be anyone else. She's been hanging about the past few weeks, shadowing us. She used to live in Santa Margherita and she's told us she lost her baby daughter in the earthquake.'

Toby put down his pen. 'Am I following your drift correctly?'

'You remember the chaos?' said Alex.

'Of course I do. So where's she been all these years?'

'You may well ask!' said Jess fiercely. Carlotta had forfeited all her previous sympathy. 'And now she's taken – stolen – both of them.'

'They must have gone willingly,' said Toby. 'Or the boy, Marcello, would have said something.'

'Oh, Lord!' said Jess, as the significance struck her. 'Remember how Harry's been nagging us about a fishing trip? And we never got around to organising one. That must be how she persuaded them.'

Toby said, 'Isn't it possible that's what they're doing? It's probably taken longer than expected to catch something, but the pair of them the door any could walk through minute.'

'There you have it,' said Gerald. 'A sensible suggestion at last.'

Alex said, 'You only drove as far as the Campiones'. You didn't go into Roccamare. If we head off to the harbour the lads there are bound to know whether the kids went out in a boat.'

'With Carlotta?' Jess was unable to picture her fishing with either a line or a net.

'She'll know somebody, won't she? Or press-gang that boyfriend of hers to take them aboard. What do you think, Doll?'

Dolly, red-eyed and puffed up like a turkey, gave a little bleat and crossed herself. Despite living close to the sea, few locals ever learnt to swim: drowning was a perpetual fear.

Jess refused to envisage a boat capsizing. She was more concerned that Carlotta was going to make some outrageous demand, holding the children to ransom in the middle of the Mediterranean. And how could they negotiate anything with her, with a person they didn't trust? 'Oh, my God, what might she do to them?'

Alex said, 'She won't harm them.'

'What makes you so sure?' She lurched to her feet. 'Come on. We'll both go this time.'

They headed directly for the harbour. Some mornings they would go with Dolly to the fish auctions held there – all theatre and clamour as crates stuffed with shining silver booty were slapped down and auctioned off. Now, in the early evening, a strong breeze was getting up and the boats tied to their berths were straining restlessly, like horses, in the scurry of the wind.

Alex approached Gaspare, whom he knew from games of table football in the Jolly Bar. Gaspare consulted Renzo, who was sluicing out his cabin. Neither of them had seen the children; they weren't aware of a woman trying to arrange a fishing trip, but Benito could have taken some extra crew. That was his boat in the distance. It might be worth waiting for him to dock.

What choice did they have? The speck on the horizon crept forward at an infinitesimal pace, rolling with the swell of the sea. The wait was agonising, but as long as they could make out the chunky little craft getting closer they couldn't think of leaving. The wind blew Jess's hair into her eyes and made them smart, but it was a warm wind from Africa – not vicious, she told herself, not destructive, but, sweet Jesus, why was the damn boat so slow?

It was still some yards away when it became clear that Benito carried no passengers. Lily and Harry would have been gambolling about on deck, eager to land. Jess recalled Harry that morning, the mischievous twinkle as he licked jam from the knife, the strawberry tip of his tongue. Her own tongue was welded to the roof of her mouth; her throat was too dry to swallow.

'They're not there,' said Alex. 'We've wasted enough time as it is.' He grabbed Jess, pulling her away from the edge of the harbour wall, and ran with her towards the car.

'Shouldn't we wait for Benito? Ask if he knows anything?'

'I'm not making any more fucking useless enquiries.'

It was as if a switch had flipped. Rarely unleashed, Alex's temper was a wild and volatile thing. He thundered back up the hill to Villa Ercole and Jess clutched her seat-belt thinking: Wherever they are, we're six hours behind them, at least; whatever chance have we got? She didn't speak aloud.

It was hard to keep pace with Alex when he was in a rage and he stormed ahead of her into the villa. The others were waiting in the hallway and she was afraid that her husband, looming over Gerald, was going to pick up their host like a puppet and throttle him.

'Alex,' said Toby, trying to intercede from the wings.

'They're not in Roccamare,' Alex yelled at Gerald. 'They've not gone on any fucking fishing trip. You promised us you would look after those wee kiddies, but did you, fuck. All you are is a drunken sodomite who fools himself he's got a brain superior to other people's. So fucking superior you can't sell a single bloody thing you've written... let alone manage normal human interaction.'

'Alex, don't!' pleaded Jess.

'It must be fucking brilliant up there in your ivory tower,' went on Alex remorselessly. 'So blindingly brilliant you never have to bother dealing with anything so tiresome as a six-year old.' Dolly was standing open-mouthed and he wheeled round to her. 'We should have known better than to trust Gerald,' he said. 'But *you*, Dolly. What the hell were you thinking—?'

Toby interrupted again. 'Now, listen, Alex.'

'Fuck off, will you? I haven't finished.'

'No,' said Toby. 'You fuck off. You can't just come in and lambast people.'

'In a situation like this, I've every bloody right to lambast who I want.'

'Gerald has something to tell you.'

'Does he now? It's a bit too goddam late for apologies.'

Toby said, 'Tell them anyway, Gerald, if you can get a word in.'

Gerald coughed and squared his shoulders nervously, although he was always going to look weak and crumbling next to the avenging Alex. 'While you were out, there was another phone call,' he said.

'Who from?'

'Um, Lily, as it happens.'

<u>12</u>

As it turned out, Carlotta wouldn't have been able to identify Peppe's boat because it had a fresh coat of paint and a new name. It was painted a glossy forest green with a white line running around the bow, and in black lettering on the white line was written, not *Concetta*, but *Donnafugata*.

'Is this it?' said Harry, jumping up and down on the spot and flapping his hands in anticipation the way he used to when he was three or four.

'Oh, Peppe…' said Carlotta sadly.

The two of them talked together at some length in Sicilian, which Lily found difficult to follow. She didn't see any cause for dismay, she'd seen boats that were far scruffier and stinkier, but she could sense an undercurrent as their argument escalated. She'd thought Carlotta was pleased to find Peppe, but what had started out as a nice idea now seemed fraught with disaster. She and Harry stood to one side to let them get on with it – that was what they did when Dolly was in full flow, until the row, like a storm, had blown through.

Carlotta called them over to her. 'I'm sorry you will be disappointed,' she said.

'Why, what's the matter?'

'Peppe and I...' The muscles of her throat quivered as she swallowed. 'I mean, it's not a good idea for me to go on his boat.'

'You don't have to,' Harry pointed out. 'It's me who wants to go fishing. Me and Lily.'

'I don't mind,' said Lily. 'I'm not that keen.'

'Well, *I* am.' He glowered at Carlotta. She didn't really know Harry, that was the problem. 'You promised!'

'I'm sorry. I thought it would be fine, that Peppe would be glad to see me after so long. But, instead, he is angry.'

'Why's he angry?'

'He says I don't care about family any more, as a good Sicilian should, but, on the soul of my mother, this is not true!'

Harry nudged Lily. 'Ask him if he'll take me anyway.'

'Ask him yourself.'

'Okay, then, I will.' Harry marched up to the fisherman and began to speak in slow, oddly accented Italian. Lily was proud of him for trying and Peppe's mouth twitched into a smile.

Carlotta, somewhat calmer, said, 'For this afternoon, Lily, what do you prefer? Do you like to walk to the other side of the island or to the fort on the top of the hill? Or do you prefer the beach?'

The hill rose on the butterfly's spine, and the fortress was perched at the top, dominating the view. Lily didn't fancy such a trudge in the heat. 'I like the beach,' she said. 'But I haven't got my swimsuit.'

'Maybe we can find a secret place,' said Carlotta. 'With no other people. Would you like that?'

When Lily nodded she stalked over to Peppe and Harry. Her demeanour changed. She caressed each of them on the upper arm, in that intimate, cajoling way she had, and neither shook her off. Lily could see Peppe begin to soften. After a while, Carlotta called out, 'We have a deal!'

The deal was that Peppe would take Lily and Carlotta for a brief ride on the *Donnafugata* until they found a quiet cove. He would drop them off there and motor further out to sea with Harry to lay his nets; whatever they caught they would be able to take home for supper.

Peppe couldn't be as old as he looked. His movements were agile as a young man's and he swung Harry over his head and deposited him on the deck as easily as if he were a kitten. He held Lily by the elbows and lifted her aboard and then stretched his hand out to Carlotta, but she waved away his help. Peppe cast off the mooring and started the engine with Harry attentive beside him. The two of them were developing their own personal sign language.

'They become friends,' said Carlotta. 'This is good.' She played with one of Lily's curls. 'We become friends too, no?'

'If you like,' said Lily.

The boat couldn't get up to the shore because the water was too shallow. They had to climb out onto some rocks and take off their sandals and paddle through the final few inches. Peppe and Harry cruised merrily away with the gulls circling their wake, on the lookout for pickings.

The cove was one of the prettiest Lily had seen, protected by a low outcrop of lustrous rock and flanked at the rear by a cliff that looked like the curtain wall of a castle. The sea was crystal deepening to turquoise and the sand it lapped was soft as silk – much finer than the gritty golden grains of Roccamare. High up the cliff wall were darker gaps and hollows. Carlotta told her these were caves; bats hung upside down in them and came out at night. Lily tried not to let the creepy prospect of bats frighten her: she would be gone before nightfall. Of more concern was her lack of a swimming costume.

'We have no towel either,' said Carlotta.

'I don't mind. I can dry in the sun.' Grown-ups in general made too much fuss about the things you needed on a beach. She whipped off her tee shirt and wriggled out of her shorts but when she was standing in her knickers, she felt she was being examined, like undressing in front of the doctor.

'Look how pale your tummy is,' Carlotta said. 'Compared to the rest of you, your lovely tanned arms and legs.' She reached out as if she couldn't stop herself and laid her palm lightly against it.

Lily's tummy always grew rounder and fuller during the month in Sicily. She didn't mind its plumpness, but she didn't like the way the extra girth exaggerated her belly button. She was ashamed of the way it protruded, it was so ugly – unlike everybody else who had a nice little dent. Carlotta's thumb grazed the edge of the small blunt knob and Lily pushed her angrily away. Carlotta blushed and whispered, 'Please don't be upset.'

'I hate it,' Lily declared, much as she had done in the past, to Jess. 'I hate the way it sticks out. I don't see why people have to have belly buttons anyway. After you're born, they're pointless, they're no use at all.'

'Tesora,' said Carlotta. 'This is a precious part of you and you should not be ashamed.'

Jess had told Lily that a small percentage of babies was born with the same problem and it usually went away as you got bigger and your stomach got flatter and the muscles stronger. It was rare, but it didn't make her a freak.

'I bet you've got a normal one,' said Lily. She didn't know why she was being so truculent.

Carlotta said softly, 'I'm sorry, you are right. It's not fair for me to inspect you like this.'

She was wearing a sleeveless dress, which flared to the knee. It was a rosy pink, fastened down the front with pearly buttons. She stood up and undid them all, shrugging off the dress like a coat. She had a fancy lacy bra to hold her breasts up (Jess often didn't wear one at all) and, yes, much as Lily suspected, her navel was a neat dimple.

'It used to stick out when I was younger,' Carlotta said. 'Truly, *carina*, you must believe me.'

Then she took off the bra because she didn't want to spoil it in salt water. She said it was expensive because she couldn't afford to buy cheap things (which didn't make sense to Lily). She, too, had pale patches left behind by her bikini top.

'Are you going to swim with me?' said Lily.

'I have to make confession,' said Carlotta. 'I'm not a very good swimmer. I tried to learn in America. My boyfriend, Ricky, was supposed to teach me, but he yelled so much and I yelled at him. He was Sicilian too and we are not like the English. We can't bite our tongues.'

'I can help you,' said Lily. 'My dad says I'm as nimble as a porpoise and I won't shout at you.'

They held hands and ran together across the sand into the warm translucent water. Once they were up to their waists, Lily demonstrated the different strokes but she soon decided to abandon crawl in favour of breaststroke. This was easier because you could pretend you were a frog and Carlotta's hair, slick and straight now it was wet, would be less likely to get in her way. In the beginning she floundered and splashed too much and Lily said, 'You mustn't panic, the salt will help you float. Do you want me to support your middle while you practise with your arms and legs?'

Carlotta said, 'Yes, please.'

When she was brave enough to strike out on her own, Lily stayed close by and if she began to sink too low, Lily would thrust her arm beneath her waist to lift her up. Once, her head went under and she thrashed about as if she were afraid of drowning, although she wasn't out of her depth. Lily rescued her that time too. They reached a rock that had a flat surface to sit on and they pulled themselves onto it to rest. They sat side by side and Carlotta twisted her hair into a rope and wrung out the water. 'If anyone sees us they will think we are mermaids,' she said. She looked very young without her sunglasses and with her make-up washed off.

'Mermaid sisters,' said Lily.

Carlotta put her arm around her and nearly squeezed the breath out of her. 'Thank you so much.'

'What for?'

'Teaching me to swim like this in the sea.'

'It's easier to learn in a pool,' said Lily. 'My dad taught me.'

'You have a special relationship with your father, I think?'

Lily considered. Alex was a source of stories, of treats, of wild ideas for practical jokes; he was also a climbing frame, a chauffeur, a magician and a hero. 'I expect that's because he saved my life,' she said. 'He saved my mother's too, the same year. She was going to be trampled to bits by a horse and he whisked her to safety just in time.' In Lily's imagination the horse's hooves were flailing in the air like great iron clubs, even though she knew that most police horses were steady and docile.

'But with your mother not so much?' said Carlotta.

'Not so much what?'

'A special relationship.'

'Oh, no! That's not right...'

Quickly Carlotta changed the subject. 'If we are mermaids, we should sing. This is what they do, is it not? The sirens sit on their rocks and comb their hair and sing songs that will capture hearts.' She began to hum some notes and her voice flowed into a yearning melody. This was followed by a brighter catchy tune, then another that was slow and sweet. She sang in Sicilian dialect and the rhythms and cadences reminded Lily of folk songs or playground rhymes or mothers lulling their babies to sleep.

Carlotta broke off. 'You want to join in?'

'I don't know the words.'

'You don't recognise any of these songs?'

There had been music in the convent. Lily could remember lining up with the other children, the sweeping movements of Sister Imelda's arms as she conducted the choir, but mostly they chanted. 'Not really,' she said.

'Not one song?' persisted Carlotta.

'I know plenty of English songs.'

'Would you like me to teach you something?'

'Okay,' said Lily.

'This one is very simple,' said Carlotta. 'Listen carefully.' She folded her arms into the shape of a cradle and swayed as if she were rocking a baby to sleep. She sang, *'Fa la ninna, fa la nanna/ Nella braccia della mamma/ Fa la ninna bel bambin/ Fa la nanna bambin bel/ Fa la ninna, fa la nanna/ Nella braccia della mamma.'*

The words were easy for Lily to understand *(Go to sleep, beautiful baby, in the arms of your mother)* and the tune wasn't difficult either. She enjoyed harmonising with Carlotta and cuddling her make-believe infant and she soon mastered the lullaby. There were other versions of *Ninna Nanna* and Carlotta taught her some of these too, until Lily began to muddle the lyrics. Then Carlotta said abruptly, 'This rock is hard! And now you learn the song and I learn to swim and so we are quits. Shall we go back in the water?'

They fooled around for a while, splashing each other's faces and diving for shells, which they pretended were coral or pearls. Then they struck out to shore and Lily noticed Carlotta's swimming was much stronger and more confident than it had been before. This nagged her and when they were lying on their fronts on the beach, toasting in the sun, she said, 'Why did you tell me you couldn't swim?'

'What do you mean?'

'When we were going out to the rock you were a bit hopeless. I had to show you how. But on the way back you were faster than me.'

Carlotta rolled onto her side, propping herself on her elbow. 'I have not much practice,' she said. 'You have helped me, Lily. You have made me a much better swimmer. I cannot do it without you.'

'Are you sure?' said Lily.

'Don't you believe me? New skills are not so easy when you are an adult. If I was not in America I would have no chance at all. How old were you when you learned?'

So Lily told her and Carlotta asked lots more questions about her life in England, about her friends and her school, and whereabouts she lived and what she liked to do and how well she got on with Harry. Lily did her best to answer and to talk about her favourite books and board games and TV shows and sports, but most of these topics came to a dead end because they were so foreign to Carlotta. She hadn't even heard of rounders, which Lily was quite good at, so Lily started asking her questions instead. 'Why did you quarrel with Peppe?'

'Ouf…' said Carlotta, wriggling. 'The men in this country, you wouldn't believe. They always have to be in charge.'

'How could Peppe be in charge of you if he was a cousin?'

'A very distant cousin,' she said with emphasis. 'He wanted to marry me.'

Lily's eyes widened. 'Wasn't he much too old?'

'It is customary for the man to be mature. Some people think it is better. And ten years ago, if you can believe it, he was more of a catch.' She scooped up a handful of sand and let it cascade through her fingers like silver rain. 'I was too young to know what I was looking for. Also I was a country girl. I wasn't sure if I wanted to live by the sea. Besides, there was somebody else.'

'Who?' Lily was alert to romance.

'Francesco. His family were not very kind to me but if you don't know any different you put up with things. And, of the two, I chose to marry Francesco.'

'Why did you have to marry anybody?'

'A baby has to have a father,' said Carlotta. 'And it was right that he should be Francesco.' She smiled ruefully. 'After I lost him, Peppe again expected to be my protector.'

Lily remembered how tearful Carlotta had been when she'd first spoken of the horrendous consequences of the earthquake. She didn't want her to start crying now; it

149

would spoil things. Carlotta said, 'I was like an animal who struggles to get out of a trap.' Lily pictured a soft brown rabbit with a white bib and fluffy bobtail, but Carlotta said, 'A fox, I think. You know, if a fox is caught it will bite off its own leg to escape?' She sat up and squinted out to sea. 'Peppe was cross with me for running away. To be rejected twice is not good. But he should know how hard it is for me to come back to my homeland. How it takes much courage.'

My homeland too, thought Lily, though Carlotta wouldn't know this.

'They are coming now,' said Carlotta, spying the boat. 'We should dress.'

Hurriedly they scrambled into their clothes and Lily, who was quicker, helped Carlotta with all her tiny buttons. Because they were preoccupied with the buttoning, they didn't see the *Donnafugata* drop anchor.

Lily hadn't been concerned about Harry; she hadn't expected him to come to any harm in the company of an experienced fisherman like Peppe the protector. But when it came down to it, she had messed up. She hadn't been a responsible sister, she hadn't taken good care of her brother or let her parents know where they were. And this failure struck her forcibly – like being knocked down by a wave – when she saw Peppe jump off the deck with Harry limp in his arms.

13

Peppe stumbled as he came towards them but he didn't let go of Harry until he reached the shallows. Then he lowered him into the water; Harry had vomit all down his front. Carlotta shouted and Peppe shouted back and soon they were at it again, hammer and tongs. Lily ran to her brother, who was sitting up feebly. 'Take off your tee shirt,' she said. 'It's disgusting.' She tugged it over his head and swirled it about until the vomit was rinsed off and sinking into the sand. Then she plunged him into the water too, to get rid of the stench. 'What happened?'

'I was sick.'

'I can see that!'

Harry revived a little. 'We caught some sardines,' he said. 'I helped to pull up the net.'

'Before you threw up?'

'Yes. But it took a long time to catch anything. I don't think I should go fishing if it makes me sick.' He said this so solemnly that Lily laughed, although her laugh came out as a high-pitched giggle. Harry was like a drowned rat, with his hair cleaving to his skull and his thin bare chest trembling with an agitation he couldn't control.

Carlotta joined them. 'He should wear a hat,' she said. 'What?'

'When you out at sea there is too much sun all around. There is too much exposure. He should wear a hat.'

'That's not my fault!' said Lily, who didn't think it was fair for Carlotta to criticise her.

'No, *carina*, I am explaining, is all. Your brother has sunstroke and maybe also the waves get wild where there is more wind, so he is seasick. Is he clean?'

'Are you clean, Harry?'

Harry staggered to his feet. 'I think so.'

'Oh, dear,' said Carlotta. 'This is not a good outcome. You must sit in the shade and rest before we leave. You are very weak.'

'That's because I've nothing in my tummy,' he said.

Peppe and Carlotta conferred again. Lily borrowed Carlotta's comb and tidied her own hair and her brother's. She found some sweets in Carlotta's handbag and gave them to Harry to suck. She also found the Polaroid photograph taken three weeks ago in Villa Ercole: the one of herself and Carlotta with their arms entwined as if they were good friends although she'd scarcely known her then.

When Harry finished the sweets, he announced he felt better and should be able to walk normally. They set off in a cautious procession to the boat: Peppe leading, Lily following with Harry at her side, and Carlotta at the rear, bunching her skirt in one hand and her wedge sandals in the other. Peppe helped the three of them clamber on deck and motored round to the harbour. He chugged slowly but there was no doubt the wind was increasing. Harry clutched the rail as the boat tilted and tipped and his face took on a greenish tinge. Fortunately, they docked before he could vomit. He was still soaking wet, so anyone who saw him might think he'd fallen overboard, but otherwise he didn't look too peculiar. Lily reckoned he'd have dried off by the time they got home.

But they had failed to take into account the ferry timetable. When they got to the landing stage the ship was already on its way to Marsala, visible, but no use. 'When's the next one?' said Lily, annoyed they would have to hang about. (All because of Harry and his stubborn refusal all summer to wear a hat.)

'Tomorrow morning,' said Carlotta. 'There isn't another today.'

'What are we going to do? Can't Peppe take us?'

'No!' said Harry vehemently.

'Why not? It's the same as a ferry.'

'No, it isn't. The ferry was much bigger and I wasn't sick.'

'Also, I don't want to ask him,' said Carlotta. 'I have made him too much trouble today.'

Lily was aghast. 'But the morning is hours away. Where will we sleep? And Jess and Alex will be worried.'

Carlotta said, 'There is a *pensione* in the piazza, next to the *gelateria*. Did you see it when you chose your ice cream? We can stay there. And we can go to the restaurant and ask them to cook Harry's sardines. I know it's difficult because we have no spare clothes with us, but we will pretend it's all part of our adventure. We will make the best of our circumstances. And you must telephone your parents to explain.'

From the bar, Lily spoke to Gerald again. 'You've given us the most tremendous fright,' he said. 'We thought you were with the Campiones. Your parents have gone down to the harbour to look for you.'

'The harbour in Roccamare?'

'Yes.'

'We aren't there. We're on an island.'

'What island?' said Gerald faintly.

'It's the butterfly island,' said Lily. 'We came here to go fishing with Peppe but Harry didn't feel well so we missed the ferry. We're going to stay the night and get the first one in the morning. Carlotta's car is in Marsala and she will bring us back.'

'Get me Carlotta,' barked Gerald. Lily held out the receiver but Carlotta was negotiating with the lady behind the bar, who owned the *pensione*, and by the time she came over the line was dead.

Lily rang later from the restaurant, with another *gettone*, while the sardines were being flipped on their skewers. Harry's colour had returned and he was looking forward to peeling the charred flesh off the fishes' backbones and popping it into his mouth. He was starving, he said. This time Lily spoke to Jess. She could tell she had been crying so she tried to comfort her. 'It's all right,' she said. 'Harry's better now. You mustn't worry about him.'

'Darling,' said Jess and her voice sounded like wood creaking. 'You shouldn't go off without telling anyone.'

'But we didn't. We told Dolly we were going with Marcello and we told Marcello we were going fishing and we told Gerald…' Here she hesitated because she knew she hadn't been frank with him. 'It was a bit of a mix-up,' she said. 'We didn't mean to miss the ferry.'

'Is she… is Carlotta Galetti looking after you?'

'Yes, she bought us lunch and *gelato* and now we're having the fish Harry caught for our supper.'

'Does she want to speak to me?'

Lily glanced over at Carlotta, who appeared to be listening intently to whatever Harry was telling her. 'I don't think so, not especially.'

'Right,' said Jess. 'We're going to come for you.'

'You can't come now,' said Lily. 'You won't be able to get here.' She felt very sensible and grown-up as she said, 'We'll be okay. We'll see you in the morning.'

The room in the *pensione* had a red tiled floor and white painted walls. The wardrobe, chest and bedstead were made of heavy oak. The landlady put in an extra bed but it was only big enough for Harry, so Lily and Carlotta shared the double. The room was hot and stuffy, from baking in the sun all day, so they had to sleep with the windows and shutters open for fresh air. Lily was restless; she kept thinking about the bats in the caves and how they came out after dark. She imagined them circling and swooping through the window and sucking her blood – which was ridiculous because she was far more likely to be targeted by mosquitoes. Carlotta tried to reassure her and two or three times during the night Lily found she had snuggled herself into her arms and Carlotta's lacy bra was pressed into her back and their hair was mingled on the pillows.

When she was woken early the next morning by the delicate pink sunrise, Carlotta was washed and dressed and wearing lipstick. She was sitting at the end of the bed, on the coverlet, watching Lily yawn and stretch and come to life. Harry had yet to stir.

'I didn't sleep much,' confessed Carlotta with a wry smile. 'Besides, we cannot be late on this occasion. It would be inexcusable.'

They roused Harry and the landlady gave them bread and jam for breakfast and they arrived promptly to catch the first ferry of the day. Lily had assumed Carlotta would drive them home to Roccamare, but Jess and Alex were already at the dockside in Marsala, waiting for them. Even though Carlotta was wearing yesterday's clothes, her parents looked ten times more crumpled. Jess had piled her hair into a topknot, which gave her added height, and the pair of them looked gaunt as scarecrows. And angrier than she had ever seen them, quivering with a fury that was terrifyingly polite.

'You know abduction is a crime?' said Alex.

'I thought Lily had explained on the telephone…'

'You can't blame the child.'

'I don't! I meant that there has been a misunderstanding. I would like to make some explanation. If I can talk to you or see you another time…'

Alex said, 'I think you have burned your boats.'

Jess said simply, 'No.'

Carlotta said in desperation, 'Let me give you my address in Rome.' She scrawled on a piece of paper and held it out beseechingly. 'Please take it.'

Alex ignored her, placing one hand on Lily's shoulder and the other on Harry's. 'Come along now, kiddies.' And they were marched to the car without being able to say goodbye properly.

In later years when Lily conjured up Favignana, their visit to it took on a mystical surreal quality. The boat trip, the swimming, the singing, the hot night in the *pensione*, even dunking Harry underwater to wash away the vomit, might have been part of a dream sequence, something that had never really happened. She knew it *had* happened, of course, that day on the butterfly island, because it was the reason the McKenzies never went on holiday to Villa Ercole again.

Part Two

1979 – 1982

14

1979

Carlotta Galetti unlocked the metal grille and raised it with a clang. Clangs reverberated along the street as other shutters were thrown up and shops opened. She went inside and adjusted the window display. The rising January sun illuminated every fleck of dust. She wiped a cloth over kidskin and hide, buffed a chrome clasp, some brass buckles. She liked polishing handbags, the warm tactile nature of the leather, the satisfaction of burnishing it to a sheen.

Claudio had gone. After two years and four months they'd unleashed their final quarrel. It hadn't been vitriolic: they'd snapped at each other like bad-tempered terriers and admitted, with a sense of release, that their relationship was over. At least it should have been a sense of release – a new year, a new beginning – but Carlotta felt weighed down by anti-climax and, if she was honest, fear. After all, she was nearly thirty and, oh, the horror of it!

The morning trade was desultory. A couple, arm-in-arm, paused to look in the window. When they entered, her hopes rose. They meandered from one side of the shop to the other, picking up bags and putting them down again, leaving fingerprints. Carlotta smiled and waited with her hands folded. They ignored her and left. She called the nearest bar and ordered coffee for herself and Iacopo, who was sorting through the order books in the stock room. The boy delivering the coffee was the only person she saw in the next hour. The day weighed heavy on her. The shop was on a side street off Corso Vittorio Emanuele and footfall was erratic. Then a middle-aged man came in and her spirits lifted again.

This was the easiest of all targets. He would have money. He would have a wife or a daughter or a mistress he wanted to appease. He'd enjoy a bit of banter and demure eye-rolling. He'd watch her calf muscles tense as she stood on tiptoe to hook down a bag from one of the highest shelves (they always wanted a bag from the top shelf). She would spread out his selection and they would be surrounded by the soft flutter of tissue paper and the ripe earthy animal scent of the leather and his hand would accidentally brush against hers as she showed him how clever the clasp was. He would take much longer than necessary to make up his mind. She would take advantage of this by foisting the most expensive choice on him, but she'd reward him with praise as he counted over his lire. Cash was always preferred.

The new customer was burly and thick-set, with an arrogant air. He wanted a briefcase. He was carrying a folder bulging with papers and was impatient to find something more suitable. Carlotta fetched him a couple to compare and placed them on top of the glass counter. 'I think the antique brown is a lovely colour,' she said brightly.

'Oh, do you?' His tone was condescending and he barely raised his heavy-lidded eyes.

Carlotta bit back her temper. She wasn't going to challenge a client and lose a sale. She flashed a charming smile. 'It's a Fendi, so we know the quality is reliable,' she said. 'And it's very capacious. Let me show you.'

He put down his folder at the same time as she opened up the briefcase. As the one knocked into the other, his papers went flying. He swore at her. 'Stupid bitch.'

'I'm so sorry,' said Carlotta. 'I'll help you pick them up.'

She dropped to her knees and began gathering them off the floor. He stood watching, muttering, telling her to be careful. She could feel his contempt. She could also feel his eyes on her legs as she reached into awkward spaces and her skirt rode up. She became flustered. Papers slipped from her grasp, wouldn't stack neatly and the whole operation took longer than it should. When she finished, he didn't thank her. He pointed to the top shelf. 'Get that one down, will you? I want to look at it.'

'Which one do you mean?'

It was in the furthest corner. 'And I'm in a hurry. I haven't got any more time to waste.'

Any other day she might have ridden out this contretemps with a disagreeable customer, but today her heart was squeezed into a ball of pain and her spine was crumbling. It had nothing to do with Claudio. Today was the anniversary of the Belice earthquake. Her ears were full of the clamour of falling masonry; her legs wouldn't move.

'What in God's name are you waiting for?' said the man.

Carlotta fumbled beneath the counter and rang the bell to summon Iacopo. He shuffled in, smoothing the weft of hair that he combed carefully into position on top of his head. He dressed in sober suits, but wore a vividly patterned tie to cheer the world. 'Is there a problem?' he said.

'The gentleman wants to see that briefcase up there,' said Carlotta. 'But I couldn't find the pole to hook it down.'

The pole was resting at an angle, in full view. 'It's here,' said Iacopo.

'Oh, how stupid of me not to spot it.'

He understood. 'Are you feeling poorly?'

She pressed her hands to her abdomen. 'Actually I have a stomach ache.'

Iacopo didn't know the significance of this date, but he was a kind man. The di Monzas had no children of their own and she'd been grateful when they'd taken her under their wing. She didn't dwell on the uncongenial jobs she'd had before she'd spotted their advertisement for a sales assistant who could speak English. They'd even helped her find a cheap apartment nearby (albeit a single room with a bed curtained in one alcove and a kitchen in another).

'I'll relieve you,' Iacopo said now. 'Take some chamomile tea and you'll soon feel better.'

'Thank you.'

She left without reference to the customer, who was grunting irritably, and went into the stock room. She opened the ledger Iacopo had been working through and checked the accounts. She picked up the phone and thought about cancelling her lunch with Eva. 'I want you to give me every grisly detail,' Eva had said when she'd rung last night to tell her about Claudio. 'That man was never worthy of you.'

She was still holding the receiver, inert, when Iacopo came in and said, 'He's gone.'

'Did he buy?'

'No.' He looked at her anxiously. 'You're very pale.'

'Am I?' In truth, Iacopo and his wife, Silvana, fussed over her too much, worrying about her health and her diet. They didn't raise her wages often but they liked to treat her to delicacies that might remind her of Sicily: a jar of sun-dried tomatoes, a box of crystallised orange segments or an embroidered tea towel they'd picked up in the Porta Portese Sunday market. She had a drawer full of tea towels. They kept hoping, Silvana admitted, that one day she would have a full-size kitchen to use them in, because she would have her own family to feed.

'Perhaps you should rest,' he said.

'Oh, no, I'm meeting a friend.'

She put down the phone; she wouldn't cancel. Lying on her bed, staring up at the ceiling, who knew what thoughts from the past would haunt her? What could she remember of Francesco? Thick straight eyebrows; one tooth that overlapped another and gave him a lop-sided smile. A slim waist and deft hands; hungry kisses. A bag of flour bursting and covering him with a white film, through which his eyes smouldered like black coals. At the time, they had laughed and joked that he looked like a ghost. And for eleven years, that was what he'd been: a ghost.

She blinked back the image. 'I'm fine,' she said. 'The man was aggressive but I shouldn't have let him intimidate me.'

Iacopo consulted his watch. Like his tie it was gaudy, the type of watch a child would pick. 'Very well. I'll mind the counter and you can do the stocktaking until we close for lunch. You're sure you'll be all right?'

'Yes, perfectly.'

The bell jangled and he left her. At five to one she shut the ledger and took a postcard from a small selection kept in the drawer of the desk, along with business cards and headed notepaper. She chose a picture of the *Fontana di Trevi* because everyone knew that if you threw in a coin you would be sure to come back to Rome, so, in a way, it was an invitation. She scrawled '*Auguri*' (greetings) and then, more carefully, she wrote the address. She needed to buy a stamp – that was if she sent it at all. Sometimes she would leave a card creasing at the bottom of her handbag, gathering fluff and smudges of lipstick until it became too dirty to post. It depended how reckless she felt.

*

Eva was waiting in the osteria where they'd arranged to meet, at the edge of Campo de' Fiori. She hadn't had far to come; she was apprenticed to her uncle, a tailor who rented a workshop in the warren of side streets that snaked away from the piazza. He'd been reluctant to take on a female: tailoring was a man's job – practically precision engineering. Besides, all his clients were men so how could she take their measurements with decency? But Eva had persuaded him to teach her the skills of cutting and shaping and stitching so she could operate her own business as a dressmaker. Women's clothing would give her scope to experiment – though her interest in fashion was purely technical. She was skinny and sallow like someone who didn't get enough daylight and she always wore baggy shirts over jeans or dungarees so she'd have plenty of useful pockets.

Carlotta knew they made an incongruous pair when they were together: she in her tight skirts and high heels and full make-up and Eva dressed like a garage mechanic. But Eva, as she pointed out, was kept busy in the back room, she didn't have to woo customers. And if any men were to cast inviting looks in their direction she would soon curb them with a scowl. She waved as Carlotta approached, jumped up and embraced her. '*Cara* Carli!' Then she tipped her head on one side, studying her, and said, 'What's the matter? I thought we were going to celebrate. Have you had a bad day?'

Carlotta shrugged off her jacket. Eva must have seen the unhappiness in her eyes. 'It's been a shitty morning,' she said. 'I lost control for a bit.'

'What happened?'

'Oh, I misread a customer. I thought I could flirt with him to get a sale, you know, exchange a bit of banter, but it backfired. He was a real bastard, but I've got over it now.'

Eva indicated the blackboard on the wall. '*Pasta e fagioli* is the special today,' she said. 'You need feeding up.'

Carlotta lit a cigarette. 'Let me calm my nerves first.'

167

'Just so long as you don't regret ditching Claudio. Haven't I been telling you to get rid of him for ages?'

Eva had a very casual attitude to the opposite sex, but she was still cushioned by her large extended family. Gaggles of brothers and cousins. Always a christening or an anniversary or a birthday to celebrate. She'd never had to cross the Atlantic bereft and alone – or fly back again with a second disaster behind her. 'I seem to be lousy at picking men,' Carlotta said.

The owner of the osteria deposited a carafe of white wine on their table and a basket of bread. He was stout and affable, the large belly beneath his apron a tribute to his wife's cooking. She was in the kitchen, juggling saucepans. There were only the two of them so the menu was limited, but it was a cheap place to eat. Most of the clientele were either stallholders from the market or artisans from the hive of nearby workshops.

Eva gave their order, poured the wine into their tumblers and then observed, 'I don't see why you need a man at all. What did Claudio ever do for you, apart from demand all of your attention all of the time? And maybe even that wouldn't have mattered—' here she rolled her eyes, screwed up her nose and sucked in her cheeks before blowing an explosive raspberry '—if he wasn't so fucking boring. Did he ever give you a good time? Be honest.'

Carlotta smiled. 'He was a good dancer. You know I like to go dancing.'

'And in bed, I suppose?'

'Actually, I think the reason we lasted so long was because of the break-ups. It was so romantic when we got together again, it would unite us for a while.'

'I kept warning you not to take him back,' said Eva. 'And every time you ignored me.'

'You were right.' She stubbed out her cigarette. 'We should have split ages ago, after the visit to Roccamare. His behaviour there was impossible, even though he knew how painful it all was for me. It was crazy to have hoped he might give me some support... But I promise we really are finished now.'

Two dishes of pasta and beans were set in front of them, glistening with warm olive oil and pungent with garlic. Carlotta dipped in her spoon. Eva sloshed more wine into her glass and said, very soberly, 'You know, Carli, I think you should leave the past where it is.'

'But I do!' Her voice faltered. 'I can't help that today is the anniversary.'

'Of what?'

'The earthquake.'

Eva looked stricken. 'Oh, my darling, how dreadful! Why didn't you let me know? We could have met tomorrow instead.'

Carlotta said, 'I don't think that would make any difference.'

Eva laid her hand on her arm; her fingers were scarred with tiny nicks and pinpricks. 'I know it's hard for you

169

to take advice, but I'm your friend and I want you to be happy. That's all.'

They talked often of the things that would make them happy. How Carlotta would take over the business when the di Monzas retired and build up the most exclusive selection of leather goods in the whole of Rome. And how Eva, in an elegant atelier, would develop a clientele that was both distinguished and adventurous, how her designs would feature in the pages of glossy magazines. They listed the luxuries they would buy if they had the money: jewellery, cars, holidays, extravagant bed linen. And then they would laugh at their fantasies and go back to work.

They ate for a few minutes in silence. Carlotta, pausing to break off a chunk of bread, noticed a woman with two children enter the restaurant. Shabby and careworn, she spoke in an agitated way to a group of men seated at a table in the corner. They all shook their heads.

Eva followed her gaze. 'I bet,' she whispered, 'she wants to find her husband and they know where he is but they won't tell her.'

Carlotta wasn't interested in the errant husband. She was captivated by the children: a curly-haired baby in a buggy and an older girl, clinging onto the handles, her eyes roving the room, a sweet patient expression on her face. It was the combination of their ages, Carlotta supposed, that attracted her: the baby, a little under a year, like her own, not quite walking. And the girl, Lily's age, with something of Lily's innocent demeanour.

Eva was embroidering her story. 'So the husband has a mistress and these guys have promised to cover for him. Younger than the wife, maybe still in her teens and easy to impress. They're probably only around the corner, bouncing on the bed in a room above the *tabacchaio*. She's defying her father because the silly man insists she comes home every night by nine and this is her revenge.' She giggled. 'What does he know?'

Voices rose and subsided, as the men protested their ignorance. In exasperation, the woman wheeled the buggy around and out of the door, the girl tagging behind. The men went back to their beers.

'It's a year and a half,' said Carlotta, pushing her plate away. 'Since I saw her.'

Eva sighed. 'Carli, I'm sorry, really, but, as you say, it was a while ago and you can't even be certain...'

'Yes, I can. I am absolutely certain.'

'But there's nothing you can do about it.'

'I did try.' She struck a match and watched the flame flare and die, leaving an acrid trace of sulphur. 'I wrote to them afterwards. I begged them to let me see her.'

Eva had been Carlotta's confidante for some time; her tone was soothing. 'I know.'

'They didn't even reply,' she said bitterly – though she'd no way of knowing if her letter had arrived, if she'd used the correct address. 'I'm not asking for much.

Of course it would be wrong to break up the family and she is close to her brother, who is also very cute. But… I can't get her out of my mind… I want her to know that I'm thinking about her, that I haven't forgotten her.' She took the postcard from her handbag and turned the image of the fountain between her fingers.

'How many so far?' demanded Eva.

'Not many, only three or four.'

'You must not do this to yourself.' In a sudden swift movement, like a bird darting to a berry, she plucked the card from Carlotta's grasp and tore it in half.

'What's the point of that?' said Carlotta. 'I've got other cards I can send.'

'You're wasting your time,' said Eva. 'You can't go on tossing words into a void. If you are really serious, if you absolutely refuse to give up this fixation of yours, then there is only one thing you can do, no? You should go to England.'

15

Lily was lying humped under the bedclothes, holding her breath, counting to two hundred. Surely a person who'd once been trapped underground for two whole days should be able to manage without air for a bit. She had heard that if you could count beyond two hundred, if you held your breath for long enough, your body would start to close down and you would faint. And that scared people. Teachers and bullies alike. They'd think they'd done something awful, life-threatening, they might even call an ambulance. They would realise they had gone too far.

'You have to stand up to bullies,' Alex said airily as if it were the easiest thing in the world. Lily was pretty certain he'd never actually been bothered by them. She'd tried to hint, when she'd started secondary school, that things weren't great. But when she mentioned, as casually as she could, how much she'd enjoyed her happy period of home-teaching, her parents didn't register the connection. In any case Jess was lecturing part-time at her old art college so she could access the design equipment. There was no space for a studio at home now that Lily and Harry had their own bedrooms. Lily couldn't expect Jess to give up paid work just because she was having a hard time getting used to the terrifying impersonal warehouse that was her new school, where she never seemed to be able to do anything *right*.

Things had improved in the summer term when Andrea had started to show interest in her. Andrea preferred to be called Andi, which she wrote with a circle rather than a dot over the i. She was tall and sporty and disruptive and even the teachers were a little wary of her. At the time Lily was flattered to be chosen as her friend; she hadn't realised that Andi was the kind of girl who dropped people, for no good reason, after she had winkled out all their secrets. Or that she would use this information to taunt a person once they were in the wilderness again.

Andi had new soulmates now, who picked on Lily because she was an Eyetie and everyone knew Eyeties were cowards. The girls liked to devise little tests to see if Lily could prove otherwise. Which made her current situation in Year 8 even worse than it had been in Year 7. Which was why she was teaching herself how to faint. Fainting wasn't feeble like sniffling or whimpering; it was silent and powerful.

Jess came into the room and drew the curtains. She addressed the hump. 'Better get a move on, darling, or you'll be late.'

Lily didn't answer. She'd reached 129, counting too quickly for it to be a valid exercise.

Jess said, 'Are you feeling all right?'

She should grab this lifeline. 'I've got dreadful cramps. And a migraine.'

'Oh, sweetheart, not again!'

Lily's periods had started not long after her twelfth birthday. The frequency and severity of them took everyone by surprise. Jess had been much older when hers began, nearly sixteen, but she agreed it was a horrible penance to have to go through every month. She'd been sympathetic, but Lily was aware she couldn't over-egg things. She had to keep her suffering at a plausible level.

'You've missed so much school already this term.'

'We don't learn anything anyway.'

'Take some paracetamol,' coaxed Jess. 'And I'll make you a chocolate milkshake for breakfast.'

'Harry will want one too.'

'Then you shall both have one! Right away.'

Another thing Alex always said was: 'Pick your battles.' Lily, sliding her feet from the bed to the floor, abandoned the argument. Maybe this would turn out to be an okay day. The gang wasn't predictable. They didn't always lie in wait, tripping her up to see if she'd cry or getting her blamed for misbehaviour in class. Sometimes they simply ignored her. Besides, Andi often bunked off. She might even have forgotten about the money.

The term before, when Lily thought they were friends, Andi had lent her a belt to help keep her skirt up when the zip broke after PE. It was a leather belt, but quite old and scruffy, and Andi said she could keep it. Now, however, she wanted it back and Lily couldn't find it, couldn't remember what she'd done with it. Suddenly it had become precious and expensive and Andi was nagging her. 'Pay me back, yeah?' she'd said. 'Or I'll tell Miss Wright you stole it.'

Lily could have explained all this to Jess, of course, but Jess still assumed Andi was her friend so it wouldn't solve anything – more likely make things worse. As she struggled into her uniform, she decided to save up the period cramps for another day, but she'd see if she could filch a bit of cash to take as insurance.

In the kitchen Jess was pouring thick brown gloop from the liquidiser into two tumblers. Harry was eating Rice Krispies. Jess's bag was open on the dresser. Neither noticed Lily slide her fingers into the wallet, tweezer them around a pound note and withdraw it. Silently, behind her back, she folded the note up very small and stuffed it into her pocket.

Jess spun around so fast Lily was startled, but she was beaming with the frothy success of the milkshakes. Alex loped into the kitchen, beating his chest with his fists and pulling gorilla faces to make Harry laugh; Harry was always serious in the mornings. After breakfast, he would walk him to school because Harry was still at the juniors. This was in the opposite direction to Lily's comprehensive, which was a pity because if they could all walk along together she wouldn't get that awful growling pain in her stomach, which had no known cause, but wouldn't go away.

Toast popped from the toaster. The kettle whistled. Alex made himself some coffee. Lily and Harry drank their milkshakes. The long hand of the big wall clock jerked through the minutes. Jess said, 'Shouldn't you get going, darling?'

Lily scraped back her chair, swung her satchel over her shoulder, shot Harry a look of lingering envy. As she grabbed her coat from its hook in the hall she heard Alex say, 'You haven't any spare cash, have you, Jess? Just till I get to the bank. I'll pay you back.'

'A few quid, I think, if you want to take a look.'

'I won't clean you out.' His footsteps were crossing the tiled kitchen floor towards the dresser.

Lily fled.

*

Jess could see that Lily was unhappy but she hadn't been able to work out why. She tried to remember her own adolescence, the shock of boarding school. But the loneliness had passed soon enough and anyhow Lily wasn't at boarding school. She was with her loving family and neither Jess nor Alex had put any pressure on her. Alex, in particular, had a healthy disrespect for authority. None of the teachers at last term's parents' evening seemed to have any complaints or concerns (though she did wonder if they'd noticed Lily at all).

She opened her wallet and counted the money again. Alex had taken a fiver. He'd fluttered it at her as he'd escorted Harry through the door and into the street. He'd left her a pound note, but she was certain there'd been another one as well. Jess wasn't good at confrontation. She didn't like to think of her children stealing from her; she couldn't bring herself to accuse them.

This wasn't one of her teaching days so she didn't have to keep to a timetable – but she did need to get to work. There was the chance of a commission from Liberty's and she was anxious to impress. 'The bastion of bourgeois imperialism!' Alex had mocked, while Jess had fantasised about the thrill of mounting the broad central staircase and seeing rolls of her own fabric displayed in the gallery. But instead of getting ready to leave here she was, in Lily's room, eyes raking the bookshelves, the knick-knacks, the shoebox of pens and crayons, the posters of Abba, John Travolta and the Fonz.

Could Lily be squirrelling money away somewhere? Saving up for something? Could Jess bring herself to look? Well, she could check under the bed – something she'd do automatically when hoovering, so as not to clog the nozzle with dirty socks. She straightened the duvet and lifted the corner of the valance. She knelt down and peered. Nothing. She straightened a pile of books on the desk. She opened the top drawer. Then the phone rang and, guiltily, she jumped.

She answered it in the sitting room, perched on the end of the sofa, twisting the curly plastic wire through her fingers.

'Jess?'

'Dinah? Is something the matter?'

Her sister's voice was sombre. 'Daddy's had a stroke.'

'Oh, no! When?'

'He toppled over in the garden yesterday. The dogs found him.'

Jess toppled too, from the sofa's arm to its cushions, her mouth too dry at first for speech. She had a vision of two golden retrievers sniffing at a body on the lawn. 'How bad is it?'

'He's in hospital and they're running some tests, so we don't know yet.'

'Do you want me to come? How's Mother taken it?'

Dinah said, 'There's no rush, but I think she could do with some company. She doesn't like being alone in the house and she'll need driving to the hospital every day.' A long drawn-out sigh. 'I'm used to everything falling on my shoulders and I do what I can, but I have commitments of my own. Rosalind, as always, is too far away to be any use. So, yes, I'd appreciate a helping hand.'

'I'll have to look at my schedule,' said Jess. 'Rearrange some classes. Check what the children are doing.'

'Isn't Alex there?'

'Yes, but… Dinah, I can't just drop everything.'

'You'd have to,' said Dinah, 'if I wasn't holding it all together.'

Jess bridled. Her sister, thirteen years older, had never had to earn a living, or even look after her own children. Her existence rolled along the same measured tracks as their parents', under a comfort blanket of tradition. She was loyal and steadfast, but completely unable to see any perspective but her own.

'I'm not making excuses,' Jess said. 'Obviously I'm worried about Dad and I'll come as soon as I can. When I mentioned the children, it was because… well, I think Lily may be having problems at school and I wanted to check—'

'I'm not surprised,' said Dinah. 'I don't know how anyone can bring up children properly in London. I've said before now that you'd be better off moving down here, closer to family. Everyone knows how frightful those comprehensive schools are.'

'Do they?'

'There's that television programme, what's it called, *Grange Hill*?'

'You watch *Grange Hill*?' said Jess, astonished.

'No, of course I don't watch it. But I've read about it in the paper. I know what goes on. I'm surprised you don't. I suppose your problem, Jessamy, is that you're far too trusting.'

Jess thought of the missing pound note. She'd have to find some way of dealing with it, of teasing out Lily's troubles, which were probably much greater in her eyes than anyone else's. She tried to sound firm. 'Can I get back to you? And will you let me know the results of the tests as soon as you hear them?'

'I'll ring you tomorrow,' said Dinah.

Jess hung up, not much reassured. Dinah's information was sketchy, so there was no way of knowing how disabled her father would become or how her mother would cope, whether her own time would be eaten up by frequent train journeys to Wiltshire, helping to care for them.

She rose from the sofa and was putting on her coat when she remembered she'd left open the drawer in Lily's room. She went back, intending to close it, but the first thing she saw was a diary with a basket of puppies on the cover. There was no lock on it, no fierce message saying 'Private Keep Out', but looking under the bed was one thing; snooping was absolutely against the rules – the McKenzies all agreed on that. Jess's fingers moved faster than her conscience and opened a page at random. It was blank. She flicked through the earlier months.

They were blank too; Lily wasn't keeping a diary or confessing her secrets in code. There was nothing in this room to give cause for alarm and Jess was relieved. She didn't plan to ferret any further.

When she tried to shut the drawer, it caught on something stiff. She tugged to release it and found herself holding a postcard, a photograph of the *Bocca della Verità*. Jess had only seen the Mouth of Truth in the film, *Roman Holiday*, but she regarded the disc of marble with its holes and fissures as creepy and disturbing; sinister even. She could have sworn she'd thrown the card out, along with the others. When Carlotta's first letter had arrived, two years ago now, she and Alex had taken the decision to ignore it. It was harmless enough, an apology, a plea for understanding, typed carefully in stilted English, but it troubled them that she knew where they lived.

'However did she get our address?'

'Fucking Gerald,' Alex had said. 'He's the only person who could have given it to her.'

'Oh, God. What are we going to do? Accept the apology?'

'Risks being an invitation, don't you think? Better to do nothing. That way she won't know whether we've got it, whether we even live here…'

Jess hadn't reminded him that it would have been better to have done nothing in the first place. But after their experience in Roccamare, the instinct to pull up the

182

drawbridge was only natural. They reckoned if they didn't reply they would be safe: one-way communication couldn't go on forever. They ignored the second letter too and then, at irregular intervals, came the occasional postcard. The messages on these were brief – *tanti cari saluti* – because, apparently, they were cheaper to mail. More than five words and the cost of the stamps would go up. It had been a while since the last one and she'd hoped that meant Carlotta was finally defeated.

She had no way of knowing whether Lily had come across this postcard by accident – perhaps she'd needed a bookmark and chose the picture because it reminded her of Italy? Jess hoped she hadn't recognised the signature, but, in any case, she wasn't going to leave it in the drawer. Or in the flat. She banged the front door behind her and shredded it into the litter bin in the street.

16

Carlotta sat on a stool in front of the wardrobe mirror with a towel around her shoulders. Eva stood behind her with the scissors, slicing tresses to the floor. They had discussed going to a hairdresser, but it would have been an extra cost on a tight budget. It had taken months to save enough money to make this trip. Eva, who claimed the idea as her own, had masterminded the details. She'd pointed out that if they went to England in August while the shop was closed, the McKenzies might be on holiday too. So they'd waited until October, until Iacopo could find a temporary assistant to take Carlotta's place, and Eva could get a good deal on a room in a budget hotel in Victoria, owned by a cousin of her father's.

Carlotta was grateful for this. The hotel and the general locality – with its trattorias and cafés and sandwich shops run by fellow Italians, its atmosphere of bustle and fizz – was like a little piece of home, protecting the two of them from the vast bewildering indifference of London. The size and spread of the city was daunting, but they were learning to decipher the Tube map. Eva was enormously excited by the department stores on Oxford Street (one of their easier journeys). These were as grand as palaces, with their marble pillars and chandeliers, and sold such an extraordinary range of products; Selfridges, in particular, enthralled her.

'The quality is not so good,' she said, fingering a skirt in the Miss Selfridge boutique. 'But I like the way they display the clothes on the mannequins. Don't you? There are some useful ideas to take home.'

Eva was full of ideas. Like cutting Carlotta's hair. 'You don't want to be recognised,' she'd said. 'Not at first, at least. This is the quickest and easiest way to change your appearance.'

'Do I have to cut it all off? Can't I wear it up? Or hidden in a hat?'

'We must do things thoroughly.' By this stage they had been in London for three days, getting their bearings. Although Eva claimed her main purpose was to see the famous sights – Buckingham Palace, Madame Tussauds, the Tower of London – she was clearly excited by the nature of Carlotta's quest. 'And you must be prepared to trust me. You know I'm a wizard with the scissors. I'll do a good job.'

Carlotta had agreed with some reluctance. 'Not too short, then. I don't want to look like a boy.'

'Tesora mia,' said Eva. 'No one will ever mistake you for a boy. We should change the colour too.'

'Dye it?'

'Bleach it. Haven't you ever wanted to be blonde?'

Of course she had. Blue eyes and blonde hair gave Jessamy McKenzie a queenly look; she would never be mistaken for a peasant. 'But what about when we get back to Rome? What will people think?'

'Don't worry about it. They'll think you went mad on holiday. Or that the English hairdresser didn't understand your instructions. Anyway, you can dye your hair dark again and it will soon grow if you don't like it this way.'

She had moved in front of Carlotta, blocking her reflection, so she could tackle her fringe. Now she stood aside to let her see. Carlotta had to admit the result was professional, even if she barely recognised the person staring at her from the mirror. She wasn't used to having a fringe, it changed the structure of her face. Her eyes were bigger; her cheekbones more pronounced.

Eva opened the packet she'd bought from the chemist and mixed powder and cream into a paste in a bowl she'd borrowed from the breakfast table. (They were both flummoxed by the English breakfasts. What was the purpose of half a grapefruit and why was the coffee watered down?) 'And another thing,' she said. 'You shouldn't wear make-up.'

'But I always wear make-up! I feel naked without it.'

'If you want to appear incognito, I'm afraid that's what you must do.'

'Not even lipstick?'

'Especially not lipstick.'

'You're trying to make me look like you.'

'Exactly!' They both laughed, though Carlotta's was uneasy. Eva went on. 'We will be a pair of nondescript sisters. That's how you become an observer, Carli. Not by waggling your bottom so that all the men around start whistling at you.' She began dabbing the peroxide mixture over her scalp.

'I'm not trying to attract men. Not that sort anyway – though it would be nice to have someone to take care of me.'

'Ouf, don't sound so mournful! I've told you before, you don't need a husband to make you complete. Things are different now.' This was one of Eva's favourite hobby-horses. 'We are the new generation. We aren't trapped like our mothers. We can get divorced if we want to. We don't have to churn out children to provide fodder for the Church. We don't have to die young.'

Carlotta gave a sharp intake of breath and Eva's brush hovered in mid-air. 'Oh, God, I didn't mean it to come out like that. I meant, you know, that childbirth – stop looking as though I'm torturing you! – is much safer these days. Medically speaking. Besides, there are methods of prevention.'

'I know,' said Carlotta. 'Which is why I can't have another baby.'

'No, you mustn't talk like that!'

187

'Well, I think the Church is right not to approve of the coil.'

There had been many bleak moments in Carlotta's life. Concussion had blotted out the worst of the earthquake; for much of its aftermath she was too numb to feel. But her collapse in her uncle's Brooklyn restaurant was still vivid and accompanied by a recollection of searing pain. She'd been eaten up with it, unable to afford treatment. She had staggered into a table busy with diners and the armful of pizzas she'd been carrying had soared and smashed. There'd been horrified screams. She'd been bundled into a darkened room and diagnosed with pelvic inflammatory disease; the fever had raged for days. Ricky had brought her flowers, but asked her to return his ring.

Eva said, 'The American doctor might have been wrong.'

'The infection was severe. He said it was very unlikely I would become pregnant again... No one wants a barren wife.'

'Unlikely is not the same as never.'

Carlotta shrugged and her towel slipped. Eva knelt to adjust it. She put her arms around Carlotta and pressed her cheek against hers. 'You're very brave,' she said. 'And I understand why you're doing this, searching for your daughter, and naturally I want to help you succeed. But you have a future as well as a past, whatever any doctor says. *Magari*, we're both still young, aren't we?

We have the whole world before us. And it's exciting, isn't it, this adventure?'

'If you don't move away from me this minute,' Carlotta said, 'you're going to have a white streak like a badger.'

Eva squealed and ran to the basin to rinse off the paste that was sticking to her. Then, following the instructions in the pack, she wrapped Carlotta's head in a swathe of plastic and set the alarm on her watch so they would know when the dye had taken.

*

The next morning, they took the Victoria line Tube to Highbury and Islington station and opened up the A–Z street atlas they'd bought. They were too nervous to catch one of the wonderful red buses in case it carried them in the wrong direction, but they were prepared to tramp the streets. Carlotta hadn't quite recovered from the shock of her straw-coloured hair. American white-trash, she thought, familiar from the movies, but highly disturbing when it framed her own face. 'You'll get used to it,' Eva consoled her. 'I think you look like Mia Farrow. Terrific.'

The plan was for the two of them to saunter down the McKenzies' street, chatting, pausing every now and again, or pretending to search for something they'd lost. A contact lens, they'd explain, if anyone tried to help, because it was the kind of thing you could hunt for hours without success. Carlotta had initially intended to do her own research, but Eva had pointed out that a single person loitering would look highly suspicious. 'You don't want anyone to think you're a prostitute.'

'At eight o'clock in the morning, when people are going to work? Who would I solicit?'

'As two women together,' said Eva, 'we won't stand out. In any case, this isn't something you ought to cope with alone. You'd do the same for me.'

'I've had to cope with many things alone,' said Carlotta.

'Precisely!'

The print in the A–Z was small and the distances further than they expected. Carlotta worried it was taking too long to locate the street. Besides, they all looked the same; the houses too. They all had stone steps running up to their front entrances, which gave the illusion of grandeur, though most had been divided into flats and the paintwork was shabby. Leaves were turning colour on the trees and rustling on the pavements along with sweet wrappers and cigarette ends. Dustbins lolled against railings, pictures of a missing cat were plastered to lamp posts. 'A cat!' exclaimed Eva. 'Somebody is worried about losing a cat!'

Finally they reached their goal. 'It's the red door, I think,' said Carlotta, counting down the numbers. Her throat felt constricted, her stomach sick with anticipation.

'Shall I ring the bell? I'll make some excuse about who I am and then you can join me.'

'No! We should cross over so we don't get too close and watch to see who comes out. They may not even live there anymore.'

What could be more frustrating than staring at a door, willing it to open? It was another cool grey London morning, busy enough with commuters and shop workers and school children, but quiet and restrained by Italian standards. No horns, no sirens, no explosions of temper or shrieks of laughter. It didn't feel normal. Carlotta worried the pair of them would be lurking too obviously, contact lens hunt notwithstanding.

A man emerged from a house on their side of the street, swinging his car keys. 'Can I help you?' he said pleasantly, when he noticed the A–Z gripped in Carlotta's hand. 'Are you lost?'

'Oh,' she said, pointing randomly at the map. 'We are looking for this road.'

'Let me see. Oh, yes, left at the end here, then second right for about two hundred yards till you get to this junction… Actually, you might need to ask again. It's a bit of a walk. I'd offer you a lift if I wasn't running late.'

'No, please, is not necessary,' said Carlotta, dragging Eva after her.

The man continued to his car, unconcerned. The women didn't look back until they had reached the corner, turned and waited. Once they'd checked he had driven off, they retraced their steps, feeling foolish. No one else accosted them.

'Why doesn't the door open?' complained Eva. 'Don't the children have to go to school? Maybe it's the wrong address, after all.'

'Or we came too late and they had gone already. Or we missed them while we were walking away.'

'That would be very unlucky.'

'But it's possible.'

Eva threw up her hands. 'Oh, Carli, I'm sorry for all these troubles!'

'You want me to give up, don't you? You think this is a stupid idea and we should leave?'

'I think we should enjoy our holiday, that's all.'

'So I've dyed my hair for nothing?'

'No! For fun.'

'Fun? How can you say that? This is *not* fun. Not for me anyway.'

'Are you the only person on this trip? The only one who matters? I've spent money coming here too, you know!'

For a few seconds they glared at each other; then they embraced. Friends shouldn't quarrel, especially when they're a long way from home. It was ironic, Carlotta thought that although she was the one who had crossed continents and Eva had scarcely ever left the family base in Monteverde Nuovo, her friend was the more confident traveller.

They were still embracing and Eva was gazing over Carlotta's shoulder, directly at the red door. 'Don't move,' she said. 'Don't get excited, but I think someone is coming out.'

Carlotta stiffened. 'Is it Lily?' She had shown Eva the Polaroid photograph, but that was now two years out of date. The girl would be maturing, developing into a woman, displaying those markers of adolescence, which, like her childhood, Carlotta had missed.

'No,' said Eva. 'It's a boy.'

'Harry? By himself?' She turned slowly. She needed to see and she didn't think Harry would recognise her. For a moment she didn't recognise him either: his hair was ridiculously long. Then a second person came through the door, tall and fair, wearing a swirling coat and carrying a small suitcase. 'That's the mother,' she said in an undertone. 'Oh, my God, it *is* the right house.'

'Why does she have a suitcase?'

'I don't know.' Fortunately, neither Harry nor Jess noticed them. They walked along the opposite pavement together, Jess switching her suitcase from hand to hand to ease the weight of it, Harry running ahead and then back again as if attached to an invisible piece of elastic. Carlotta and Eva watched until they were out of sight. 'And I don't know why Lily isn't with them.'

'She could still be inside,' said Eva. 'Shall we knock and find out?'

This was tempting, but Carlotta resisted. If Lily had already left, she might find herself face to face with Alex. She would never forget how angry the McKenzies had been on the quayside in Marsala. 'I'm not ready to do that. I have to be careful or everything will go wrong again like it did before. And it's late to go to school, isn't it? We should come again tomorrow, but make sure we set off earlier so there's no danger of missing them.'

She expected Eva to groan, but her sparrow eyes were bright, the pupils dilated. They had traced their quarry – which was a success in itself – and who knew where it might lead?

17

They were waiting for her at the bus stop: Andi and Michelle and Beverley and Faye. Lily dragged her feet; she wasn't ready to deal with them. Fellow pupils streamed past in ribbons of maroon and grey, twining into knots and untangling again, surging into freedom, but she didn't feel the least bit liberated. The girls ahead were nudging each other, craning their necks to seek her out, their faces smug. She swerved down a side street. She told herself she didn't need to take the bus today; she would walk. If it took longer to get home than usual, it wouldn't matter. Jess was the person most likely to worry and she wasn't there. She'd gone to visit her parents because her father was in hospital. Alex had a more relaxed attitude to time-keeping.

Within moments of turning the corner, she knew she'd made a mistake. On the bus she'd be surrounded by other passengers, the conductor would be patrolling the aisle. Andi and her friends would be all talk and taunts but they couldn't put pressure on her. Here she was on her own and she could hear footsteps catching up. Andi was tall, with a long stride; she wore chunky heels the school disapproved of, which thudded on the pavement. Lily couldn't possibly show she was frightened, so she carried on walking. She knew they were closing in, but she kept her eyes fixed ahead. She pretended she hadn't noticed them until the arm landed on the back of her neck.

'Hey,' said Andi. 'Why are you avoiding me? Why'd you rush off like that?'

'I'm not rushing. Didn't fancy the bus, that's all.'

The other girls hung back, whispering among themselves. Andi left her arm draped across Lily's shoulders; her voice was warm. 'Look, you paid up for the belt, right? So why don't we let bygones be bygones?'

'Really?'

'Yeah, you've shown willing and that's a start. How d'you feel about being friends again?'

Oh, the delicious sensation of being welcomed back into the fold! But Lily was suspicious. Although Andi's behaviour suggested reconciliation, she'd learnt from last term how she could blow hot and cold so you never knew where you stood.

She tried to sound non-committal. 'If that's what you want.'

Andi took a packet of Chiclets from her pocket and offered one to Lily. 'Fab! There's just one more test you have to do to join us.'

Lily's stomach contracted. 'Is there?'

'Honestly, it's a cinch. You'll pass with flying colours.' Andi's hair was drawn tightly from her face in a high ponytail, exposing the mocking lines around her eyes and mouth. She distributed further pieces of gum among her friends. Their smiles also looked false and untrustworthy, but Lily was trapped. She couldn't hope for a passer-by to come to the rescue, there was hardly anyone about: a figure or two in the distance, some younger children playing, the odd car gliding past. The girls linked arms and swept Lily along between them.

'Do you know the shortcut through the estate?'

'No.'

'Come on, then, we'll show you.'

The estate was built in a design that was absurdly confusing, with roads that curled pointlessly or led into cul-de-sacs. Lily generally avoided it for fear of getting lost. 'There are pedestrian passageways,' Andi said, as they passed two identical blocks of flats. 'Can save you a bit of time if you know which to take. Shell lives here, doncha?' Michelle nodded. 'See over there?'

Behind a row of maisonettes was a broad strip of tarmac with hopscotch squares chalked onto it. Facing them were a dozen single-storey garages with up-and-over doors of corrugated aluminium. Lily couldn't imagine Andi wanted to play hopscotch – that was a kids' game. 'See what?'

'Them garages.'

'Oh, yes.'

'Do you know how to pick a lock?'

Lily's eyes widened; she shook her head.

'Then we'll teach you.' Andi grabbed her arm and pulled her along to the end garage. 'Right, Shell. Do your stuff.'

'You're not going to steal something?' said Lily. It was a silly thing to say because Andi did steal. Her locker was crammed with random objects, and once last summer she'd shown Lily her collection of nail varnish from Woolworths: the bottles lined up on her bedroom window sill, far more colours than one person could ever wear.

'No. You are.'

Michelle was advancing on the handle of the garage door with a piece of wire.

'It's a doddle,' said Andi. 'A basic twist and turn mechanism. Watch carefully and you'll see how it's done.'

But Michelle was having problems, frowning and swearing. 'It's a bugger, this one. Must be rusted or something.' She moved on to the next garage, where she had more success. Lily couldn't see properly what she was doing, but she heard a click and saw the handle spin. They only raised the door a few inches because they didn't want to attract attention.

'Now, Lily,' said Andi. 'What we're asking you to do is wriggle inside and nick something. Quick as you can.'

'What sort of thing?' said Lily. 'And why?'

'Because that's the deal if you want to be in our gang.'

'Doesn't matter *what*,' Shell said. 'Don't have to be a bike or anything big. A dried-up old paintbrush will do. No one's going to send you to jail for a paintbrush.'

'Why would you want one anyway?'

'We don't,' said Andi with exaggerated patience. 'It's the initiation. To prove you're one of us.'

Lily looked miserably at the six inches of black space where the door had cranked open. 'What if I say no?'

Bev said, 'I told you, didn't I, she'd be scared of the dark?'

'I'm not scared.'

'Course you're not,' said Andi.

She needed to show she was brave – that was the point of this ordeal. She couldn't make a run for it because she didn't know how to find her way out of the estate; besides, there were four of them and one of her. And Shell was right, who would be bothered about a dirty paintbrush? Faye delivered a little kick to her shin; Lily flinched and said in a last-ditch attempt: 'What if it's empty and there's nothing for me to steal?'

'There'll be something. We don't care what it is, that's up to you. But you should hurry, time's running out.'

Would this be the moment to faint? She took a deep breath but couldn't hold it in for long enough: since she wasn't making a move, Bev and Faye got impatient and pushed her to the ground so all the air wheezed out. On her knees, her cheek against the tarmac, she could see into the dim space but she couldn't see what it contained.

Bev hissed at her. 'Get a move on!'

The quicker it was over, the better. Lily crawled through the gap and waited for her eyes to adjust to the gloom. On the other side of the door, in fading daylight, she could see the girls' shoes and their ankles in ribbed grey tights, but little else. Then, suddenly, she couldn't see their shoes any more. She couldn't see anything because the garage door had clanked shut.

'Hey! What happened?' Her protest sounded squeaky and panicked. She could hear giggling.

'What's it like in there?' came Andi's voice. 'Is it like being in a cave? Or stuck underground like when you were a baby?'

'Let me out!'

'We can't,' called Shell. 'The lock's snapped.' More giggling.

'Never mind,' said Andi. 'You've had practice, haven't you? How long was it last time? Two days?'

Lily thumped on the metal slats till they rattled. 'You can't do this!' She'd told Andi about the earthquake when they'd been swapping confidences and Andi had admitted that her dad wasn't her real dad either. 'You've got to let me out.'

'Only if you stop making a fuss and being such a scaredy-cat. If you shut up, we'll get onto it.'

'You'll go for help?'

'Yeah.'

She knew they'd run off because of the silence they left behind. The silence and then the horrible realisation that they wouldn't be coming back. Why would they confess to anyone that they'd picked a lock? Cause trouble for themselves? Much easier to go on home and pretend nothing had happened. That was why they'd told her to be quiet, so they could make their getaway. This wasn't an initiation test: they'd devised the whole scenario so they could laugh at her.

At first she was rigid with shock at the trick they had played. When she could move her limbs, she pushed at the base of the door on the off-chance the bolt hadn't connected and she'd be able to shift it. It didn't budge. She hammered on the slats again and yelled for help. Surely somebody would hear? There'd be children playing ball or drivers returning home, putting away their cars. She didn't know how on earth she would explain her presence to the owner of the garage, but that seemed a trivial dilemma compared with making her escape.

Her chest felt so tight there was no room for her lungs to expand: no need to practise holding her breath if she couldn't breathe anyway. Would that be the next thing, losing consciousness? She subsided onto the concrete floor, hugged her knees, and wept. But the floor was too cold to sit on for long, so she rose, still tearful, and began to feel her way around the walls. A thread hanging from the ceiling tickled her face and she shrieked, thinking it was a cobweb. (Even though she wasn't actually afraid of spiders.) She reached her hand up and tugged what turned out to be the cord of a strip light that ran the length of the garage.

She wasn't in a chilly claustrophobic cavern any more, but somebody's workshop: shelves stacked with tools well-oiled and cared for, not a stiff old paintbrush in sight. She picked up a mallet. She could make a lot of noise with a mallet. She launched its iron head against the garage door with a satisfying, thunderous crash.

Lily didn't wear a watch. She had no way of telling how swiftly or slowly the minutes were passing. She couldn't understand why no one was coming, why no one had heard her assault with the mallet; her own ears were ringing. She picked it up and swung it a few more times, venting her frustration and fury. But the mallet was heavy and in the brief respite she allowed herself, there came a tentative rap of knuckles on the door.

'You are in difficulty?' said a soft female voice with a foreign accent.

At last! 'I've been locked in,' said Lily. 'Can you get me out?'

'You can tell me what to do?'

Release wasn't going to be as straightforward as she'd thought. 'I don't know!' she wailed. 'I don't know who owns this garage or who has the key. Couldn't you call the fire brigade? Or maybe my dad...' She supposed

Alex would discover what had happened at some point; it would be difficult to keep an incident like this secret, however humiliating. 'Will you ring him if I give you the number? I'm sure he'll know the best thing to do.'

The person on the other side of the door was quiet, as if using a public telephone was something she might find tricky and complicated.

'Or knock at all the flats nearby,' said Lily in desperation. 'Till you get an answer.'

'I am finding my pen,' said the foreign woman. 'I will write down the telephone number. Please don't cry. Don't be upset. I will bring you help.'

<u>18</u>

The windows of the café were steamed up; it wasn't possible to see passers-by splashing through puddles or umbrellas battling the rain. Inside, in contrast, the walls were painted a sunny yellow and pinned with posters of Mediterranean scenes. Carlotta perched at a small table dropping sugar lumps into her double espresso. She had arrived twenty minutes early; she wouldn't risk being late. She'd forbidden Eva to accompany her. 'This is all so delicate,' she'd said.

'I can't believe you don't want me to support you.'

'But you have, *tesora*, in every way! This is something I must do by myself.' She could picture Eva becoming agitated on her behalf, making demands that would never be met, scuppering the entire process. 'I couldn't have done without you up to now,' she'd added – which was true.

Her fingers had been shaking so much when they were in the phone box she hadn't been able to dial the McKenzies' number. Eva had been obliged to take over. She'd fed the coins into the slot too and pressed the button when the call was answered. Carlotta hadn't introduced herself. Clinging to the receiver, she'd rushed into an account of Lily's predicament. Her voice faltered initially, but grew stronger as she described the location of the garages and the name of the road, all the details she'd carefully noted down.

'Is this some kind of a hoax?'

'No, no. I saw it happen. She has asked me to call you.'

And then Alex McKenzie, altogether bewildered by the curious situation, said: 'Do I recognise your voice? *Who* is this? Who am I talking to?'

'I am a visitor.'

'Where from?'

Carlotta said, 'I think perhaps you can guess.'

'Jesus wept!' There was a long grim silence.

Carlotta said, 'Lily is very distressed. Those girls were not nice. I saw them laugh when they ran away. It's important for you to go to her.'

'Of course I'll go to her!' His tone was menacing. 'Whereas you should make yourself scarce. Has she seen you?'

'No.' Carlotta had kept her distance while following Lily to school and attempting to follow her home again, her heart lurching at the sight of Lily's wild curls pulled back, her developing figure in the unflattering uniform, the troubled way she had scuffed her feet along the pavement. 'I spoke to her only through the door of the garage.'

'You'd better not go back there.'

'This is not fair to me!'

'Tough shit.'

She told herself he was worried, he wanted her to get off the phone so he could go to Lily's rescue. 'Can we have a meeting, you and I?' she begged.

'What for?'

'Just to talk. Please.'

In the background, crammed into the corner of the kiosk, Eva murmured, 'He won't refuse you. You know where they live. And now their telephone number.'

'Alone?' he said. 'Jess is away and I don't want her to get the wind up again because of you. And there's no way I'm bringing the kids, so don't even ask.'

She didn't. He suggested the café – 'The owner's Turkish, but he's installed an Italian coffee machine.' – and rang off.

Despite Alex's warning, Carlotta and Eva returned to the site of the garages. They wanted to reassure Lily that he was on his way, but she had already been freed. The door was raised and she trying to explain herself to a stocky man, who was leaning against a green Triumph Herald and scratching his bald head.

'I can't let her see me,' said Carlotta. 'You speak to her, Eva.'

'I don't know how to say the words.'

'It's simple. You say: "I have telephoned. Your father is coming." But don't hang around. We need to leave before he gets here or I'm in trouble again.'

From a distance, her fingernails biting into the flesh of her palms, Carlotta watched Eva deliver her message. When she scurried back, she asked, 'Did she try to find out who you were?'

'I said I didn't understand English.'

'She wasn't curious?'

'I think she was glad to be outside.'

'The man wasn't shouting at her?'

'Carli, stop firing all the questions. You should have gone yourself!'

'You know I couldn't. I'm sorry...'

As they returned to the Tube, Eva observed, 'She looks quite like you, actually.'

'Oh, do you think so?'

'Her complexion is paler, but that'll be because she's grown up in this country.'

'I wish I could have seen her close-up. I wish I could have touched her.' She recalled the warmth of Lily's young body in the bed they had shared on Favignana, how she had watched over her most of the night: the rise and fall of her chest, the tremble of lashes on her cheek, the flail of her legs kicking away the sheet. How frustrating it had been to speak through a barrier, to hear her voice swamped in misery and yet be unable to touch or console her. To have to pretend to be a passing stranger.

She stirred the sugar into her coffee and sipped it. Two men pushed through the door, calling out to the owner, cursing the weather, establishing a noisy presence. One of them winked at Carlotta. It made her feel welcome, as if she were back in Italy instead of this cold city where the inhabitants strove to ignore you, looking through you as if you weren't there. She smiled in acknowledgement (not encouragement, she would have insisted to Eva) and nearly missed Alex's arrival moments later, damp from the rain. He shook the drops from his wet jacket and looped it over his finger as he surveyed the room.

It took him a while to register Carlotta and, when he finally approached, the first thing he said was, 'What the hell have you done to your hair?'

She lifted her hands to ruffle its unaccustomed length. 'I cut it.'

'And some! I wouldn't have recognised you.' Alex was little changed: he still had a scruffy careless air, though the planes and angles of his face were sharp, his expression stern. He narrowed his eyes and banged his fist on the table. 'I suppose that was the whole fucking point. I'm going to order a coffee. Do you want another?'

She shook her head. He dumped a battered briefcase onto a spare seat and went over to the counter. She drew a cigarette from the pack in her handbag, lit it and inhaled the welcome hit of nicotine. At least he had come, he hadn't let her down. She recalled their first discussion, sitting on wobbly cane chairs in the corner of the Jolly Bar, accompanied by a percussion of squeals and jangles from the pinball machine. Then he had been gentle with her, they had circled each other like cats, exchanging snippets of information, neither wanting to give too much away. This was bound to be different.

He came back with his cup, some liquid slopped into the saucer, and sat opposite her. 'The coffee's not bad here. And I thought the surroundings might help you feel at home.' His tone was less aggressive, he was beginning to relax, she thought.

'Thank you.'

'As far as Lily's concerned,' he said, 'there's been some unpleasant stuff with her schoolmates. You could call it a prank if you were being generous, but I'm not feeling very generous today. I'm feeling harassed, which I don't much like. I shall be handling the school business, but meanwhile I've taken time off work to meet you, so let's not mess it up.' He delved into his briefcase and set a small rectangular device beside his cup and saucer.

'What's that?'

'I'm a journalist,' Alex reminded her. 'Haven't you ever seen a tape recorder before?'

'You are going to record our conversation?'

'A sensible precaution, don't you think? A way of keeping everything clear and above board.'

'What will you do with the tape?'

'I haven't decided yet. But I want to make sure there are no more misunderstandings. Does it bother you?' She eyed the cassette suspiciously. He added, 'You've chosen a good spot by the window. Not too much background noise so it should pick our voices up fine.' He was enjoying her discomfiture, his mouth crinkling into a smile. He switched on the instrument. 'Why don't we start with who you are? Why don't you introduce yourself?'

'You know who I am!'

'I'm not sure that I do. And not just because of your new hairstyle.'

'I am Carlotta Galetti.'

'You're certain about that, are you? Because it doesn't tally with my information.' He leaned back with his arms folded, watching her expression carefully.

She told herself she had nothing to lose; she should take the opportunity to put things right. 'Carlotta was the name of my sister-in-law.'

'*Was?*' He frowned. 'D'you mean you've stolen the identity of a dead woman?'

An electric jolt ran through her. 'No! How can you say such a thing? We have no contact, that's all.' Francesco's family had always been cool towards her. They didn't believe her pregnancy was accidental, and her mother's preference for Peppe, pushing her to marry him instead, hadn't been helpful. 'I haven't seen her since the disaster.'

'Is that how you got away with it?' demanded Alex. 'Because you fell out and lost touch? My God, you're devious.'

'Please, you don't understand! It was a simple error. When I applied for the new paperwork, the office in Palermo made a mistake with my first name. My date of birth, everything else, was correct but they were processing so many applications...'

'You could have rectified it.'

She bowed her head. 'I didn't want to send back the passport. I wanted so badly to get away. I thought this new name was like a special gift – one I could use to become a different person. I could forget all the terrible things that had happened and be reborn.' Collecting her shiny new passport had been a diamond flash in a dark period. 'I did *not* tell you lies and you are not being fair. If you wanted to know more about me, why didn't you reply to my letters?'

'I'd have thought that was obvious. We couldn't possibly trust you after what happened in Roccamare.'

'I took good care of your children,' she said defensively. 'They asked to go fishing and Favignana was a little excursion for them. Harry became seasick, that's all.'

'Harry getting seasick was hardly the fucking point!' The volume indicator on the tape recorder shot to the end of the scale. At nearby tables, heads turned. She gazed past them, at the poster on the wall: a picturesque

211

harbour, boats bobbing on a brilliant blue sea. A reminder of another time, another place. 'What on earth were you planning to do with the pair of them?'

'I had no plans. I wanted merely to get a little closer. When I went to Roccamare it was because I heard about the English family who come for holiday every year, with their children who are so different...' Alex rocked back in his chair, one eyebrow cocked; she rushed on. 'Please try to imagine my feelings! My husband is dead, my baby is dead. My old life, it's finished. Then I hear news of a little girl in the orphanage who is from Santa Margherita. They say no one has claimed her, but when I arrive from America she's gone. Then I meet you and you tell me how you found the baby and gave her to the nuns, and they are the same nuns I went to see...' She lit another cigarette, adding to the fug of smoke and steam which made her eyes prickle. 'You must understand. You have a child yourself...'

His voice was steely. 'I have two.'

'Of course, I'm sorry.'

'And, for Christ's sake, if what you did two years ago hadn't been bad enough, here you are, at it again! I could have you arrested for stalking.'

'I just wanted to see her,' pleaded Carlotta. 'To see how she has grown.'

'You haven't approached Lily, have you? She'd no idea you were watching her.'

'You have asked her this?'

'She was more interested in being released, frankly, than why a random tourist had come along. She's probably forgotten about your intervention.'

'You see, I have been very discreet.' But she was cut by his dismissive attitude. 'You should be grateful to me, in fact, for making sure she was safe.'

'I don't think you can lecture me on bringing up kids.' Then, unexpectedly, he switched off the cassette recorder. 'How about another coffee?'

'Yes, please.'

He hailed a waitress and ordered refills. At one end of the table was a large red plastic tomato containing ketchup. Alex picked it up, squeezed it, tossed it from hand to hand as if it were a grenade and said ruminatively, 'I suppose things weren't easy for you, back in Santa Margherita? Before the earthquake, I mean.'

'We were so poor even the Mafia didn't trouble us. Until afterwards.'

He became animated. 'When the funding got misappropriated, you mean? We hit an example of that on one of our trips: a road going nowhere. It was built on stilts above fields of poppies and sheep. We were driving along admiring the view, when suddenly there was a plastic barrier and no more tarmac. We nearly went over the edge, head first into the sheep.'

'This is what we must put up with in Sicily.'

He replaced the plastic tomato and pressed the record button. The tape began to spool again. 'Why don't you take me through it?' he said. 'What life was like for you there.'

'You mean you want to hear how I ran around barefoot, how we fetched water from the pump in the piazza and kept chickens? This will make a good story for your newspaper?'

'Don't worry, it won't be for public consumption.' He sighed. 'It's too personal. I'd prefer the truth, whatever it is.'

'Well, then, I can tell you I was well cared for because I was an only child. The problems came after my father died. We couldn't stay on in the forge, so we lived with my mother's brothers and sisters, one after another.' Sleeping in the corners of rooms, trying to keep out of the way. Wanting to please her mother, but sneaking off for trysts with Francesco all the same... 'Why are you looking at me like that?'

'Sorry. It's because I can't help thinking you'd be a dead ringer for Angelica. Before you went blonde, of course.'

'Who is Angelica?'

'The sultry young woman in *The Leopard*. *Il Gattopardo?* You must know it. Or be aware of it at least. The author, Tomasi di Lampedusa, was the duke who owned the palace in Santa Margherita. Did you never meet him?'

'No, how could I? I was a peasant girl.'

'You were the blacksmith's daughter. Your father might have been called to the palace sometimes, to shoe the horses or fix the railings or whatever. Didn't you get a peek inside some of the rooms before everything collapsed?'

'I think you are making fun of me,' said Carlotta.

'I'm trying to picture you living there.'

'Because you don't believe me?'

'Is there any reason I shouldn't?'

'No!'

He knitted his hands together and rested his chin on them, leaning forward as if to study her more closely. 'It seems to me you've come a long way from the life you might have led. If there'd been no earthquake, I mean. Here you are, independent, emancipated, well-travelled —'

She couldn't tell whether he was being sympathetic or provocative, but his words riled her. 'How can you possibly understand what I have endured? Do you think it is easy to leave your home and everything you know? To live in strange cities? For years, I have difficulties. Some bad relationships. Some terrible jobs. When I was a cleaner, my hands, they swelled and grew red like, what do you say, a lobster? I had no money… Also, I am all alone because I have no family. Do you know how unusual this is, for an Italian?' Sometimes, morbidly, she wondered what it was that set her apart – were all the

215

losses in her life the result of an internal fault-line, a seismic crack in her construction?

Alex said, 'That doesn't mean you can simply pick a kid you like the look of.'

'This is what you did, when you took my baby to England.'

'Oh, no, I'm not letting that pass! When we adopted Lily, it was because we were aiming to do the best we could. It was all above board. What makes you think the nuns would have given her to you, anyway? How could you have proved she was yours?'

'There are the dates,' said Carlotta.

'There were other missing children.'

'And other... signs.' Her fingers twitched at the memory of touching the smooth stub of Lily's belly button when they were on Favignana. 'And she looks like me, you must admit. Especially the hair.' She tugged angrily at her bleached cap, wishing she'd resisted Eva's crazy suggestion.

'Circumstantial evidence can seem overwhelming.' Alex was speaking calmly, secure in his position. 'But it's not enough. It doesn't mean people will accept it for the truth, whatever the balance of probabilities.'

'Which people?'

'People with vested interests, for instance.'

'Like you and your wife?'

'It wouldn't stand up in a court of law either. I'm afraid there's no case to answer.'

Nothing would stop Carlotta holding steadfast to her convictions. 'When she grows up…' she began.

'When she's an adult, Lily can do what she wants. In the meantime, she has a right to a happy, carefree youth.'

'But she is not happy.'

The muscles in his jaw tightened. 'Adolescence isn't easy for anyone. She needs stability and I won't let you threaten that, Carlotta… or whatever your name is.'

'You want to see my passport?' she said, brandishing it.

'Yeah, show me.' He opened the page with her photograph and snorted. 'Let's hope you don't have too much trouble explaining who you are when you get back home! What *were* you called originally, anyway?'

'Concetta. It's a very old-fashioned name. I prefer my new one.'

He returned the passport and said casually, 'And your daughter?'

'She was named after my mother, Serafina. That's old-fashioned too.'

'Serafina?' he said. 'Strewth! Lily should be grateful to the nuns.'

She felt a quiet surge of satisfaction when this slipped out, but before she could challenge him Alex had moved on. 'So now, Carlotta-Concetta,' he said. 'What will it take to persuade you to leave us alone?'

'What do you mean?'

'I hope it's not money, because we don't have masses to spare and I don't give in to blackmail.'

'Money! You think I would sell my daughter!'

'She's *our* daughter,' said Alex. 'You have no claim, no parental rights. But I know you've been through a lot and I'm not vindictive, even to stalkers or would-be abductors. But I also want to protect Lily and I want to protect my wife, who's under a lot of family pressure at the minute. So I'll ask again: what would it take for you to go quietly back to Italy and stop writing or sending messages – at least until Lily is eighteen and chooses to get in touch with any potential relatives?'

It had taken Carlotta months to save up for this trip; the prospect of going back to Rome with nothing to show for it was devastating. 'I can't see her again?'

'Certainly not. What kind of havoc would that create for the poor kid?'

'But I have waited so long!'

He was heartless. 'Then a few more years won't make any difference, will they?'

'Will you send me photographs? So I can see her growing up.'

This time he nodded. 'Aye. That seems reasonable, I suppose. Twice a year?'

'More often. Every two months. In colour.' How pathetic she was!

'Are you sure this won't make it harder for you?'

That was what Eva was always saying to her: Forget the past. But her daughter wasn't among the dead, she was among the living. Why would she want to forget her? 'No.'

He looked at his watch. 'I need to get going. Right, then, I'll send you regular photos and in return you promise not to contact any of us. Ever. Is that a deal?'

Her hands shook as she wrote out her address for him. This time he accepted it.

'It's a deal.'

19

Andi came back to school with her arm in a sling. She and Michelle had been suspended for two days; Beverley and Faye had been given detention. No one was speaking to Lily. It was the worst of all possible worlds. Alex had caused a fine rumpus, marching into the head's study and demanding action, and the head had given a long lecture in assembly about how the school would not tolerate bullying.

Alex was always telling Lily about the power of words, about how the pen was mightier than the sword and how he was a warrior for justice. What about when there were no words? Lily wondered. When you'd been sent to Coventry and were met at every turn with silence? What was the power of words worth then? She wished Alex hadn't got involved. The man who owned the garage had been perplexed but not aggressive. She could have pretended she'd got trapped giving chase to a cat, any excuse would have done. Andi might even have admired her initiative. Instead of which, Alex had come crusading along and Lily had suffered the consequences.

'That's what happens,' he said. 'To people who stand up to the mob. It's not an excuse for letting them get away with it. The school has to be informed. You have to do the right thing.'

She should have guessed he'd react like this. If only she'd been more patient, if only she hadn't been stupid and given out their telephone number. Already she nursed a steady hatred for the annoying little foreign woman who had alerted him, the one who'd bobbed up when she wasn't needed any more to say Alex was on his way. She had stared at Lily curiously. 'What did you expect to see?' Lily had wanted to ask her. 'Didn't I sound like a schoolgirl?' But the woman hadn't said anything more. She'd screwed up her face and scuttled off again as if she'd realised she'd caused almost as much bother as Andi. Now that Lily's misery was magnified, the foreign woman was a handy scapegoat.

Andi winced if anyone touched her and compressed her lips in a brave smile, but she was very mysterious about her injury. She claimed she'd fallen downstairs in such an evasive way that no one knew what to believe. It was rumoured that her stepfather had a cruel streak: he'd lashed out to punish her and *that* was how she'd fallen. Which meant it was really Lily's fault – and yet another reason for her to be shunned. More than anything else in the world she longed for her mother to come home.

*

'Whatever's the matter, sweetheart?' said Jess, when Lily slammed into the flat, kicking her bag under the hall table, ready to fight Harry for the television. She didn't care what he was watching. Even if it was *Rentaghost*, his favourite programme, she'd demand he change channel.

'Oh!' She stopped in her tracks. 'I didn't know you were back.'

Jess enfolded her in her arms. 'I'm sorry. It's been a tough week.'

'Is Grandpa still in hospital?'

'Yes. But they think he's making progress.' Jess smiled wanly.

Lily said, 'It's been tough here too. Did Alex tell you?'

'No, what happened?'

'Perhaps he didn't want to worry you,' said Lily, trying to be generous. 'He probably thought he'd sorted it.'

'Sorted what?'

There was no point in covering up. Jess would find out everything eventually and the damage was done. So she launched into her account, dwelling less on being locked in the garage than on the recent fallout, partly because this could be a torment without end. Jess interrupted only once: 'But I thought Andrea was your friend!' When she'd finished, she stroked Lily's hair back

222

from her face and said gently, 'Oh, my goodness, kids can be so cruel. But it won't last, darling. Those silly girls may not be talking to you but you don't want to have anything to do with people like that anyway; everybody else will forget soon enough. You're strong and you have a family who love you; you aren't a victim.' Then, after a pause, 'Did Andi's stepfather really break her arm?'

'It's not broken. Sprained or dislocated or something. She has to keep it strapped up for weeks.'

'Poor thing. She must have a very troubled background.'

It was typical of Jess to sympathise with the perceived underdog and Lily found it exasperating, though while her mother was in this frame of mind – warmly empathetic but a little bit guilty too – it was worth pushing harder for what she really wanted.

'Do I have to stay there?'

'Where?'

'At that school. I mean, they hate me and I hate them and…' Her voice wobbled. 'Please don't tell me it's all in my head because it isn't and it's never going to get any better!'

'Oh, my darling,' Jess cuddled her again. 'Actually, you know, I have an idea.'

'You do?' Was she going to offer home-schooling again? Would it be allowed now she was older?

223

Jess said, 'Come on, help me get the dinner ready and I'll run it past Alex when he comes in.'

Lily didn't ask why Harry was being let off the chores. She peeled potatoes and carrots conscientiously; she wanted to keep Jess on her side.

Alex breezed into the flat as if there was no problem he couldn't handle. He greeted Lily and Harry with a hug and enveloped Jess in a lingering embrace, kissing her for so long that Lily had to look away. 'Thank God you're back,' he said. 'We missed you, didn't we, kiddies? What's the prognosis?'

'Let's eat first,' said Jess, as if she knew you couldn't have a serious discussion on an empty stomach.

Afterwards, when Harry slid off his chair, impatient to get back to his *Blue Peter* construction of cardboard and tinfoil, Jess didn't stop him or ask him to clear the plates. The three of them sat amongst the debris of dirty dishes, of crusted mash and congealed gravy and empty Ski yoghurt pots. She reached for Lily's hand and said, 'I hear there's been a little local difficulty.'

Most parents would have debated Lily's situation in her absence, but hers had always stressed the importance of being upfront. She was often included in their discussions – even if they sometimes made her squirm. On this occasion, it was Alex who squirmed. 'What do you know about it?' he said gruffly.

'What Lily has told me. In fact, I think I'm more up to date than you are. Did you know those girls are still making her life a misery?'

'Oh, Christ, I'm sorry, love.' He looked more relieved than apologetic. 'But it will blow over.'

'That's what I've told her,' said Jess. 'But as it happens, while I've been away, I've been thinking…'

'That sounds ominous.'

'Yes, well, you're probably not going to like what I suggest. I think we should move out of London.'

Lily hadn't expected this. She understood now why Jess was still squeezing her hand and not letting go: she was to be her ally. Sitting opposite, Alex was gripping the edges of the table; Lily could see his arm muscles tense beneath his shirtsleeves, his knuckles rise in white peaks. 'Why?'

'I think Dinah's right – I know I don't often say that – but I think the kids would do a lot better at school in Wiltshire. I'm not talking about boarding,' she added quickly. 'God forbid. Just ordinary uncontentious state schools.'

'I suppose the need to earn a living isn't a factor when you're as well-heeled as Dinah.'

'Johnnie commutes. It's perfectly possible.'

'Why are you going over to the dark side, Jess? We don't belong in the fucking pony club.'

'Not everyone who lives in the country is landed gentry,' she flashed. 'And we don't have to be like Dinah and Johnnie. Up in the big house, cutting ourselves off from the locals. That's not our way of doing stuff.'

'No,' Alex said. 'But we'll be isolated from all the things we believe in and the people who might be on our wavelength. As soon as you move there the tribe will pressurise you to become like them. Or take advantage of you. You lose either way.'

'My father's probably going to need a wheelchair.' She blinked away tears. 'And my mother's too frail to push him around.'

'Marjorie's as much of a battle-axe as Dinah. You'll end up being at everyone's beck and call.' His tone softened. 'I'm sorry, Jess, but you haven't thought this through. How could we afford it? Where would we live? Hope to God you're not planning to move in with your parents.'

Over the years Lily's grandparents had been shrinking and their living quarters had shrunk too. They occupied a fraction of their large house and many of their rooms had a pickled quality. The attics had long been abandoned and Lily and Harry liked to charge about in them, disturbing the dust and hunting for relics.

'There's the cottage,' said Jess.

'What cottage?'

'The one that was rented out to the gardener, but he's retired now so—'

'I am not going to be responsible,' Alex declared, 'for evicting some old retainer because he's past his sell-by date.'

'No, no,' said Jess. 'He's gone to Torbay to be near his daughter – he's always wanted to live by the sea. The place is empty. It needs work but there's plenty of room for the four of us and I could turn the outbuildings into a studio. And it wouldn't cost much to live there, so we could probably afford to keep on the flat for a while.'

'What about your job?'

'I'll find something locally. I don't do much teaching anyway. It's only to get access to equipment. You know how I've longed for a studio of my own. I could be more productive too.'

'There's a lot of wishful thinking here,' he observed.

The remark sounded sarcastic to Lily's ears, but Jess was flushed with inspiration. 'I've had a week, haven't I, to work it all out? Originally, I was concerned about being around to help Dad when he comes out of hospital – but since I've heard what Lily's had to put up with, it all sort of fell into place.'

Alex expelled a long breath. 'I could do with a beer.' He rose. 'Any in the fridge?'

'I doubt it. It didn't look like you stocked up on anything while I was gone. I had to pop over to Norman's to get stuff for supper because the cupboard was bare.'

This was true. The previous day Alex had taken Lily and Harry out for burgers – as a treat, he'd said, but they'd reckoned he didn't fancy cooking. 'Whisky, then,' he said. 'A wee dram. What about you?'

Jess shook her head. Alex poured a generous slug of Johnnie Walker into a tumbler. He addressed Lily, who had been listening in silence up to now. 'How about we give it six months?'

'Give what six months?'

'School.'

Six months – a term and a half of being cold-shouldered. What could be more crushing? While Jess had been talking, Lily had been imagining herself in a new, happier life, roaming through woods and meadows with real friends, not fake ones; riding bicycles along country lanes, like they used to at Villa Ercole. 'Oh, please,' she said. 'Can't we go sooner?'

Jess intervened. 'Not really, because there are quite a lot of things to sort out. I'd have to give notice and we'd have to fix up the cottage and find the right school for you and it will all take time. But by next summer...'

Alex swirled his whisky and took another gulp. 'This is a big decision, Jessa-mine,' he said. 'And you've tossed it in my face like it's a trip to the flicks. For a film I don't even want to see. I can grit my teeth for a couple of hours, sure, but what you're suggesting is major upheaval... it will unsettle the dynamic. You must appreciate that. Everything will change.'

'It will be worth it,' insisted Jess. 'Lily's been through enough. It's not fair to make her go on struggling.'

'You can't load the weight onto the child's shoulders.'

'I'm not! The move will benefit all of us, as a family. I promise you won't regret it.'

*

For Lily, it was as though a pressure valve had been tapped. She felt buoyant. And the thing about feeling buoyant was that it showed in your demeanour, so other people treated you differently. Her classmates began to speak to her again and include her in their activities. And it was only a few days later that she wandered into the cloakroom and spotted Andi snogging one of the boys from the year above – which wouldn't have been remarkable if she hadn't had both her arms clasped tightly around him; her sling draped over a coat hook. Lily tried to summon a sense of outrage, but failed.

Oh, the relief of not caring anymore!

*

For Jess, the move that had seemed such an obvious solution at the time became more conflicted as their preparations advanced. On the surface, Alex appeared tolerant of the process – dealing with plumbers and electricians, hiring removers. But it had been dangerous to promise no regrets. She couldn't get out of her head the notion of a rip in the fabric of their relationship and she didn't know how to repair it or stop it splitting further. Once they had exulted in honesty, transparency – so why was she afraid he was hiding something from her?

20

1982

Carlotta and Eva were sitting on a bench in the gardens of Villa Sciarra, sharing a bar of chocolate. The park wasn't far from Eva's new premises in Monteverde, which they'd been to view, and Carlotta had suggested they go for a breath of fresh air, away from traffic fumes and the annoying buzz of *motorini*. The afternoon was fine and sunny, a fresh spring light illuminating Rome at its loveliest, and there was over an hour before she needed to get back to work.

Eva was no longer working for anybody. She had finished her apprenticeship and was ready to set up on her own. 'My family think I'm mad,' she'd said, as she'd shown Carlotta the space she was leasing. 'My mother thinks I should squeeze my sewing machine into a corner of the apartment to cut down overheads, but she's always interfering. Besides, clients need to be treated with discretion. You have to make them feel special.' She'd skipped around the dingy room flourishing a retractable tape measure. 'I'm going to have partitions constructed so there'll be a changing cubicle and a toilet with a shower. And there'll be shelves all along the far wall to display fabrics. And a big table for cutting and mannequins in the window wearing beautiful dresses. Like in the shops we saw in London.'

They didn't often refer to their trip to London. Eva had enjoyed it hugely, but she knew Carlotta regarded it as a failure, so the subject was seldom broached except like this, in passing.

'That sounds so exciting! Will it be expensive?'

'Not too bad. My brother will do the joinery and the landlord's agreed to pay for the plumbing and the lovely big window is here already. What do you think?'

'I think you could write messages on it.' Carlotta had traced her finger through the grime: Come inside. Let me inspire you.

'It's a bit of a dump right now. You have to use your imagination.'

'You have a knack, Eva. I know you'll make a success of it. And women always need dresses made.'

'You'd come to me, wouldn't you?'

'If I could afford to! And I wish Iacopo and Silvana were as enterprising as you are. We've got some really fine craftsmen on our books but we keep missing opportunities because the pair of them are so cautious.' She was still trying to persuade the di Monzas to shift

232

their wares upmarket, to be bold enough to move to a more glamorous address.

Eva had grabbed her hands and whirled her in a waltz around the dusty interior. 'They're bound to retire soon and when you're in charge you can do what you want. You'll get your heart's desire, Carli. We both shall.'

It was in this giddy mood that they had bought the chocolate and mounted the incline to Villa Sciarra, taking the route that led to the summit of the park to drink in the view. The city lay spread before them in a voluptuous vision of copper and rose, gold and ivory, all curves and columns, diamonds and sparkle.

'See,' said Eva. 'We have the world at our feet.'

'I hope you're right, *tesora*.'

They descended the steps beneath a canopy of budding wisteria and sat companionably on a cast-iron bench. Nearby, fat marble cherubs sprayed water like glitter into the ornate fountain and silky petals of narcissi rippled in the breeze; behind them, tall cypresses swayed and creaked. Carlotta had a particular affection for Villa Sciarra because its baroque architecture and palm-lined avenues echoed the grand decaying villas of her homeland and helped her to feel less of an exile. She crumpled the chocolate wrapper and focussed on Eva's assurances. Her friend was right: the two of them had ambitions to fulfil, a capital city to conquer. She tipped her face to the warmth of the sun.

The peace of the afternoon was broken by a gang of teenagers. They gathered at the intersection of the paths, a stone's throw from the fountain, and started racing their remote-control cars. They shouted insults and called out challenges and whooped from time to time in triumph. Eva put her hands over her ears. A much younger boy, only about six or seven, broke away from them and hoisted himself onto the bench beside Carlotta. He was wearing a football shirt she didn't recognise, the point of its collar grazing his chin. Elbows on knees, he leaned forward with an intent expression, watching the racing. One of the cars overturned, its wheels spinning, and he blurted in dismay, 'It's not fair. I could do better than that but they won't let me play. And the Ferrari is *mine*.'

Carlotta said, '*Madonna!* If they go on making that much noise they'll frighten the peacocks.'

The boy said, 'What peacocks?'

'You don't know about the white peacocks of Villa Sciarra?'

'I don't know Rome,' he said, a little petulantly. 'We only just moved here so my *nonna* could help look after me.'

Carlotta glanced around for a grandmother. 'Is she with you?'

'No, I'm with my cousin, Paolo. He was supposed to let me join in.' He pointed at the youth manoeuvring the blue Ferrari.

'I don't come from Rome either,' said Carlotta, 'but I know about the famous peacocks. They used to be bred here before the villa was given to the *comune* and nowadays they live wild – if the chicks can survive the cats, that is.'

'Are they really white?'

'Oh, yes, completely. Like snow. And very beautiful.'

'Have you ever seen one?'

'They're quite shy but, yes, I have.' It had been like stumbling upon a fantasy creature from another world, a winged angel in front of her on the path, stately and ethereal. A sight that made you blink and disbelieve your eyes. 'They're supposed to bring good luck.'

The boy slid off the seat. 'Would I find one if I looked in those bushes over there?'

'You could try.'

As he ran off Carlotta remarked, more wistfully than she intended, 'You know what they remind me of? A bride in her wedding dress, with a tiara on top of her head and a long white trailing train...'

'Very fanciful,' said Eva. 'But you've given me an idea. When you get married, Carli, that's what I shall do. I'll design you a bridal gown and tiara so that you can arrive at your wedding looking exactly like a white peacock!'

'That sounds marvellous.' Carlotta tossed back her hair, which had grown dark and abundant again (the gamine look had definitely not suited her) and waggled her fingers above her head like a peacock's crown. Then she became more serious. 'Why are you always trying to marry me off, Eva?'

'Because it's what you want for yourself.'

'You mean you don't?'

'No, not particularly. But you're so restless, like somebody who's endlessly searching.'

'Oh, well…' She gave a rueful smile. 'That's because I am. I'm searching for love, aren't I? Like most people. I just haven't found it yet.'

'Hey, Luca!' There was a shrill whistle. 'You can have your turn now.'

The bushes parted and the little boy emerged, reaching eagerly for the hand-held controls. But the blue Ferrari wasn't going as well as before; it stumbled and stuttered along the path and was slow to respond to Luca's commands.

'The batteries are running out,' said a youth in an AS Roma tee shirt. 'You'll have to get some more.'

'I haven't any money, said Luca woefully. 'Paolo's been playing with it. He should get them.'

The boys huddled together in discussion. Luca hovered on the edge of the group, patently the young kid they didn't want to be bothered with. Carlotta opened her bag; she was tempted to offer to buy the child some batteries herself, but the gang moved off, still arguing. She tapped a cigarette from the pack and hunted for her lighter.

Eva said, 'That's because you won't let go of the past.'

'What is?'

'Not finding love.'

'Oh, Eva, stop lecturing me. You're like a stuck record.' She lit her cigarette and dropped the lighter back into her handbag.

Eva had spotted the letter, waiting to be posted. 'You're the one who's stuck, Carli. You could have a whole new family if only you'd give up your ghosts.'

'Lily is *not* a ghost.' She'd never admitted to Eva how much she looked forward to the photos coming every other month – a tenuous link to the girl she wasn't allowed to know. Some of them were outdoor shots: Lily on a bike or balancing on her hands or linking arms with Harry on a hilltop. Some gave hints of her home life: there she was icing a cake, hanging decorations on a Christmas tree, practising the flute at her music stand. There were never any accompanying messages or explanations. Carlotta had to build her own picture of Lily's activities. They were so different from hers at the same age, it was hard to believe they were less than twenty years apart.

Without warning, the photos had stopped. 'I haven't had one since last November,' she said, in an attempt to justify herself. 'There should have been two more by now and I'm worried. Anything could have happened.'

Eva said, 'I don't see that writing another letter will help.'

'She might be sick in hospital! She might have had a terrible accident.'

'Or her father could have broken his camera or lost your address or plain forgotten about you.'

'We had a deal,' said Carlotta. 'You're supposed to stick to a deal, but he didn't.'

'*Porca Madonna!* You had no power in that arrangement. It was in his hands. If he doesn't send you pictures, it's too bad. There's nothing you can do.'

'I can write,' said Carlotta, waving her envelope. 'I can at least ask him why he's not keeping his side of the bargain, if there's anything I ought to know.'

'If he doesn't reply,' said Eva, 'once and for all, will you promise me you'll let it go?'

'What d'you mean?'

'It will be the end of it. Chapter closed. And maybe that will set you free.'

'Free for what?'

'To begin again.' She gazed earnestly into Carlotta's eyes. 'The next time you meet someone and it starts to get serious, you'll say nothing about this hopeless hankering – which is probably all in your head anyhow. No man wants to compete with an illusion.'

'Lily isn't an illusion!'

'No, but your connection is. She barely knows you exist. Post the letter if you must and leave it at that. Then swear to me, Carli, that you won't let this mess up any new relationship.'

Carlotta didn't believe such a relationship would ever develop. She couldn't see herself making any long-term commitment, though she dated regularly enough. She often went dancing with Eva and other friends, and if she liked a man on the dance floor she might meet him a second time for a meal or a drink or a trip to the cinema. Sometimes she would take him back to her apartment (or go to his, if he had no ties) and let him undress her. Sometimes the sex would be hectic enough to transport her elsewhere; sometimes she would feel detached, as if she were watching through a mirror and the body cavorting on the bed didn't belong to her. Living each day as it came, absorbed in present sensation – that was the Sicilian way. The future was a risk that might never arrive. At least she didn't have to worry about getting pregnant.

'You're impossible, Eva!' she said. 'But I understand what you mean. So, if it makes you happy...'

'It's not to make *me* happy,' objected Eva. 'For the love of Jesus, Mary and all the saints, just make the promise!'

Carlotta glanced at her watch; it was time to be heading back to work anyway. 'Fine. I promise.' Eva was the nearest thing she had to a sister and as Eva herself had only brothers they were mutually dependent; she would never fall out with her.

Eva jumped up from the bench and pulled Carlotta to her feet. They embraced tightly, as if to seal the pact, and then strolled together to the park gates where they parted: Eva to go home to Monteverde and Carlotta towards viale Trastevere to catch a bus across the river. She hadn't gone far when she was accosted by a boy waving a long feather, a dirty shade of ivory.

'Look, I found this!' said Luca. 'Do you think it could be from the peacock's tail?'

Carlotta didn't like to say she had no idea. 'Yes, I expect so. Well done.'

'It will bring me luck, won't it?'

'Of course!'

He fumbled in his trouser pocket and brought out another, much smaller. 'Do you want this one? Then you'll be lucky too.'

He gave her a winning gap-toothed smile and she couldn't help but be touched by his gift. 'Thank you, that's lovely! I could do with some good luck.' She accepted the feather and stowed it carefully in her bag. 'Where are the others? Your cousin and his friends? They haven't left you alone, have they?'

'They went to get batteries.' He pointed to the junction, though Carlotta couldn't see anyone.

'I'd better take you to find them,' she said. 'You shouldn't be by yourself. But first I must post this letter.'

There was a red post-box, plastered with old flyers, on the wall opposite. 'I'll do it for you,' said Luca, keen to impress, though she wondered if he would be tall enough. He ran across the cobbles and stood on tiptoe.

She followed at a slower pace. The street was narrow, one-way only, so they were both surprised to see a pair of scooters bolt illegally around the corner.

'Those damn *motorini*,' said Carlotta, reaching instinctively for Luca, who slipped his small hand into hers, warm and trusting.

At the other end of the street, a grey Alfa Romeo, entering quite lawfully, swerved to avoid a collision. Carlotta and Luca were facing the wrong direction, their attention captured by the scooters. Neither of them saw the car coming.

21

Lily had taken the phone call. Jess had been in her studio – which was rather a grand term for an unheated dilapidated outbuilding at the end of the garden. Lately she'd avoided answering the phone, letting Lily and Harry step in on her behalf. The demands of her relatives were escalating and she was feeling beleaguered. Her father was confined to a wheelchair, her mother couldn't drive and her brother-in-law had managed to lose a large amount of money on the stock exchange.

'The bloody idiot,' Dinah had cursed. 'He knows nothing about these things. He's a civil servant, not a stockbroker or a merchant banker. Agriculture, Fisheries and Food. A farmer basically! We're in debt with the farm too and interest rates are horrendous. I've no idea how we'll get by.'

'I know—' Jess began.

'You can't possibly,' snapped Dinah.

Jess had been going to say she knew what it was like to struggle for cash. Instead, she'd murmured,

'Everybody's capable of making poor choices. It's easily done.'

Two and a half years ago, she had tried to calibrate her own decision with a list of pros and cons. It had been quite clear, on paper, that moving to the country would be better for the children, Lily in particular. (She hadn't even needed to write down: no threat from Carlotta.) But they'd agreed to keep the lease on the flat and maintaining two places was complicated as well as costly. She was increasingly aware of the damage to her marriage. 'Alex doesn't want to,' had headed the cons list and they weren't spending enough time together. When she remonstrated that he was spreading himself too thinly, he countered that she was the one who'd wanted to relocate. He needed to go where the work was.

When Lily thumped on the studio door and fetched her to the phone, it was a relief to discover the call was not family related. It was from a factory in the East End who were processing a new design for her. Due to a technical error, one of the colours hadn't printed as intended; the manager suggested this was an improvement and offered to post her a sample. Jess latched onto the excuse for a change of scene. 'No,' she insisted. 'It will be quicker if I come to you.' If she wasn't around, she could escape chauffeuring duties; she wouldn't have to listen to Dinah complaining about Johnnie; Alex would have to be at home for the children.

At the factory, the manager invited her into his office where orders fluttered on spikes and fabric swatches were pinned all over the walls. He gave her a cup of tea and spread out the template and instructions she had given him and a section of the printed cloth. In Jess's original design the colour had been more muted. What she had conceived as a sage green had developed the strong tint of ivy. The material was a glazed cotton and the glaze worked well on the dark green. The new shade gave an unexpected slant to her quirky patterning, but it didn't clash; it wasn't better or worse, merely different. And Jess was accommodating by nature.

'You're right,' she said. 'It's distinctive, isn't it? Let's leave it as it is.'

The manager beamed and offered her lunch in the canteen. She accepted. Afterwards, she could easily have gone straight back to the country but she was enjoying her freedom too much – it was a rare day when nobody knew where she was – so she took the Tube to Highbury. In the corridor leading to the station exit a busker in a fedora was playing 'A Hard Rain's Gonna Fall'. A crossbreed, part spaniel was curled at his feet, beside another fedora containing coins. Jess recognised them both. She ferreted for a handful of change and dropped it into the hat. 'How are you, Barney?' she said.

Barney strummed a final chord, tipped back his brim and peered at her through bloodshot eyes. 'Hiya, Jess, where'ya been?'

Several years ago, Alex had found Barney and his dog sleeping rough in a doorway and offered the pair their sofa for a few nights. He'd since moved into what he described as 'an okay squat' and taken up different pitches around North London. Jess hadn't seen him for some time. She petted the spaniel's silky ears. 'Is this your regular gig now?'

'Yeah, has been for months. Where d'you get to?'

'Oh, we're living in Wiltshire mainly, for the kids' schooling, but I still come back quite often.' (Though maybe not as often as she had thought.) She glanced at his takings. 'You both doing all right?'

'We get by.' Another train disgorged and passengers emerging from underground flooded past, anxious to reach daylight. He plucked a guitar string; she was eating into his earning time. 'Sorry about you and your man,' he said.

'What? What d'you mean?'

He shook his head mournfully. 'You guys were so solid. Never thought you'd split.'

'We haven't split! We just aren't in each other's pockets quite so much because...' But the problems that came with two homes would always sound crass to a man who had none. Wiser not to go into detail. 'We're still solid,' she said.

'Grand.' He grinned and blew a long strident note on the harmonica hanging from his neck.

'See you around, then.'

245

'Yeah, see ya.'

Jess moved off jauntily but she was disconcerted, as if her world had tilted. How could Barney have got such an impression? Buskers stood for long periods, watching people. They were observant. Alex was gregarious and sociable, but surely Barney would be able to tell the difference between a colleague and a more intimate relationship? Had he really seen Alex with another woman? Her head was spinning and she didn't know how to settle it, who to ask for information. She decided to call into Norman's shop on her way to the flat.

Norman was the McKenzies' first port of call whenever they ran out of anything. His family had sold fruit and vegetables on the same premises for a century. 'Greengrocers and Poulterers' was spelt out in glossy Victorian tiles above the frontage. A list of bargain offers was chalked onto the window – all in pounds and ounces, no misleading metrics. The poultry side had gone and been replaced by shelves of staples: tea and sugar, ketchup and vinegar, dairy products in a chiller cabinet. In the rest of the shop, old-fashioned British vegetables were still king: cabbage and beetroot, parsnips, carrots and potatoes.

Norman wore a tobacco-brown overall and kept brown paper bags on a loop of string. He was an admirer of Margaret Thatcher because she knew what it was like to be a grocer and he was often generous to the children, slipping extra items into the paper bags. 'Good try,' Alex would tease. 'But you can't convert us renegades. Bribery isn't allowed.'

Norman was pleased to have found a way of outwitting the Common Market. 'Better for the little ones to have a bit extra than add to all them wasteful lakes and mountains.'

Politics aside, he was an ally. If his reaction to Jess was the same as Barney's, she might have something to worry about. In the shop his overall hung on the back of the door, but an unfamiliar teenager manned the till. Jess filled a wire basket with bread and eggs, apples and tomatoes and milk. 'Is Norman around?' she asked as the fruit was weighed.

'He's having time off. Because of the op.'

'Oh, dear.' She wondered what kind of op: heart bypass, lumpectomy, prostate, but the boy didn't say and she didn't press him. Norman was of the generation who kept their personal lives very private.

She left with her purchases and let herself into the flat. They'd transferred most of their possessions to the cottage, so it seemed more spacious these days, but forlorn and impermanent too. It was difficult to get the balance right. She had hoped that moving to the country, back to her roots, would shore up family life; instead she could see it was fragmenting and she missed their old unity, the time when they weren't all sprouting in different directions.

She put down her bags and wandered about, flicking light switches on and off, making a cursory sweep of the rooms for evidence of a female visitor: an unfamiliar scent, make-up remover pads, a lost earring. She didn't find anything. But since the notion that Alex had deceived her was distressing enough, she didn't look very hard. She lit the gas fire and turned on the radio and thought about ringing home, but what would she say? Best to sleep on it.

The next morning, she took her address book into the kitchen and flicked through it over a cup of coffee, debating who to catch up with and wishing she'd kept in closer contact with friends and neighbours. When she heard the snap of the letter box she went into the hallway, mug in hand.

A single letter lay on the mat. A proper letter, handwritten. Not an invoice or a bank statement. She bent to pick it up. The hand-writing was familiar and she knew with chill clarity where she had seen it before. She hadn't forgotten the postcards from Rome. She didn't need to turn over the envelope to see the name of the sender on the back flap. This time, however, Carlotta Galetti had addressed her letter solely to Alex.

Although she was fully dressed, Jess returned to the bedroom and climbed back into bed. She abandoned her coffee mug and pulled the blankets around her. She rested the letter on her knees and stared at it. Why after all this time had the correspondence started again? Did Alex know about it and, if so, why hadn't he told her?

She longed to open the envelope, though she wouldn't be so devious as to hold it over the steam from a boiling kettle – or rip into it with a fingernail and claim it was an accident. She reached for the phone beside the bed. The children would be at school; Alex should be in his study, working on a feature. There was no more reason to delay. He'd be expecting her to ring him, to tell him how the factory visit had gone. He answered on the fifth ring.

'Alex?'

'Hey, what's the matter?'

She couldn't fool him for a minute, could she? He'd heard the quiver in her voice. 'Why didn't you tell me about Norman?'

'Norman?'

'He wasn't in the shop. Because he had to have an operation. Was it for something serious?'

'How would I know?'

'You must see him regularly. Didn't he say?'

'Och, I think he was complaining of varicose veins, from all the standing around. Why are you so concerned about Norman? Didn't things go well yesterday?'

'They went fine.' She nestled the receiver in the crook of her shoulder and rotated the envelope in both hands. She couldn't hold it back. 'I have to tell you, Carlotta Galetti's written another letter.'

He must have been startled too: there was silence at the other end of the phone. Then a groan, 'Oh, Christ, Carlotta.'

'Yes. We thought she'd given up, didn't we?'

'What does she want?'

'I don't know. It's addressed to you.'

'Oh.'

'Can you think why?'

'Haven't a clue.' He spoke with a false lightness, which disturbed her.

'I could open it,' she said. 'I could read it to you.'

Did he hesitate or did she imagine it? Was it because Barney's remarks had spooked her that her mind was flying down dark paths?

A hundred miles away Alex said, 'Go ahead, then.'

'Are you sure?'

He was speaking very close to the mouthpiece, his tone soft and seductive. 'Ah, Jessa-mine, what terrible things can she possibly have written?'

She steeled herself. 'Okay, I will. Hang on a minute.'

She slit the envelope carefully, not wanting to damage the contents. A sheet of paper fell out, the squared graph paper favoured by Italians over plain or lined. The previous letters had been typed but this was written in a hand so similar to Lily's it was uncanny – though didn't want to think about that. She held it at a distance and brought it closer as her eyes tried to focus. She picked up the phone again. 'I can't read it,' she said. 'I mean, before she wrote to us in English, didn't she? But this one's in Italian. She's assumed you'd be able to understand it. But I don't.'

'Oh, shit, this is my fault.'

'Why, what did you do?'

'I can explain, Jess, but not on the phone. If you can wait till you get home...'

'Explain what?'

'What happened when I saw her.'

'You saw her! Without telling me! How could you?' But they had spent so much time apart lately anything was possible. 'What else have you been keeping quiet?'

'What d'you mean?'

'Maybe I should ask Barney.'

'Barney?'

'The busker. He thought we'd broken up, Alex. Whatever could have given him that idea?'

'Oh, for fuck's sake! Why would I hide anything from you?'

'You already have,' Jess pointed out unhappily. She looked to see how Carlotta had signed off – whether there was any suggestion of intimacy – but she dropped the receiver as she did so, cutting off the call. Would Alex think this was deliberate, would it make him angry? Surely *she* was the one who had the right to be angry? She was the one who'd been misled. She delayed ringing him back. If their telepathy was as strong as it

251

ought to be, then he'd contact her. He'd know what she needed to hear.

She waited. One minute. Two. The end of the letter read, *'Saluti, Carlotta-Concetta'*, which was odd but told her nothing. Her resolve broke and she dialled the cottage number. It was engaged. He was calling her, of course. The trill didn't come at once, but a few moments after she'd replaced the receiver. She lifted it.

'Hello?' said a voice that was not Alex's.

'Toby!'

'Jess? You're in London! In support of what great cause have the pair of you come up this time?'

'Actually, I'm on my own. Alex is with the kids.'

'Ah, right...'

'And I did the stuff I came to do yesterday.' She paused. 'Are you busy?'

'What, now? Today?'

'Yes.'

'I've a couple of tutorials this morning, and then this evening—'

'But nothing in between? I'm a free agent. I could easily get the train to Cambridge. I haven't seen you for ages.'

'Well...'

'Please?'

22

Jess walked out of the flat without trying Alex again. She'd wanted a change of scene and here was her opportunity; she'd be mad not to take it. Toby had arranged to meet her in a pub called the Eagle, a half-timbered former coaching inn with outdoor seating in the courtyard and three inter-connecting rooms. She searched them all before ordering a drink. She took a bench seat by the window in the main bar and tried to decipher the squiggles of graffiti on the nicotine-stained ceiling.

Toby arrived, full of apologies. 'God, I'm sorry I'm late!' Either he had spruced himself up or, in Cambridge, his dishevelment was less out of place. His clothes were sober and respectable: no rips or spills, no unravelling holes in his jumper. Even his tousled hair had flecks of grey at the temples, which made him look distinguished. His scrawny frame had filled out too, giving him gravitas. He kissed her warmly. 'Have you been waiting long?'

'I just got here.' She pointed to her brimming half of Abbot Ale. 'Honest. Let me buy you a pint. I've imposed myself on you.'

'You're never an imposition, Jess.' His words and tone were genuine, but there was something unreadable in his eyes – though that could have been the result of her own paranoia.

'The buffet lunch is rather basic,' he said. 'But I've got a formal dinner in hall this evening, so I hope you don't mind...'

'Not at all. The aim was to see you.'

The main components of the lunch were veal and ham pie, coleslaw and baked potato. Toby ate methodically, cutting his pie into squares, amusing her with college gossip, but all the time she suspected he was holding something back. Me too, she thought. How could she criticise? Carlotta Galetti's letter was in her bag. At some point – she hadn't decided when – she was going to ask Toby if he could help her translate it. Meanwhile they fell into their usual, casual camaraderie.

'Did you know the secret of life was announced here?' he said. 'One day, nearly thirty years ago, Crick and Watson came in for lunch and told everyone they'd found how the construction of DNA worked, how molecular information was passed on through our genes. They celebrated the beauty of the double helix over a pint, a few yards from where we're sitting.'

'The secret of life?' The concept was too enormous to contemplate. 'Can anyone really know that?'

'In a scientific sense, Jess, not a spiritual one.'

254

'Sorry, that was dumb of me.'

He carried on, 'The significance of their discovery was recognised straight away, but nothing happens overnight. It's taken until now to get the ball properly rolling. There's fantastic potential for capturing information if we can learn how to get at it.'

'Like what?'

'Well, in the field of archaeology for instance…'

'Ah.' She smiled, pushing away her empty plate, raising her glass. 'I bet that's what Crick and Watson had in mind, the benefits for archaeologists.'

'It's a shame there isn't more respect for the past,' said Toby. 'We could learn a lot.'

'Don't you think people need to make their own mistakes? Isn't getting where you want to be through trial and error part of the secret of life too?'

'That presupposes you get where you want to be,' he said.

There was a pipe smoker at the adjacent table. His tobacco was pungent and the fug was thickening. Jess began to cough; Toby thumped her back. 'Are you all right? Do you want another drink? Or are you ready to go?'

'Fresh air would be good.' The pipe smoker puffed on, oblivious.

They left the pub, crossed Kings Parade and headed down Senate House Passage towards the river. The day was by turns overcast and startlingly vivid, the clouds chased by squally gusts of wind. On Clare Bridge they stopped to watch the punts passing through the arches below. A swan gliding regally along the river suddenly flapped its wings and put a punter off his stroke. The student staggered and wobbled and looked about to lose his footing. There came a splash as he steadied himself at the expense of the pole, which drifted out of reach. The swan floated on, stately and unruffled.

Something cold struck Jess's cheek. 'What was that?'

'Rain,' said Toby. 'It's going to pour. We'd better run for it.' He grabbed her hand as they raced through the Backs. Although the sky had deepened to slate, fringes of light cast halos around the college buildings so they looked unreal, like hyper-illuminated engravings. The first heavy drops spattered at random intervals and they sped up, thinking they could avoid the worst of the deluge. They were wrong. By the time they reached the shelter of Toby's staircase, they were drenched.

His rooms were on the first floor, overlooking a quadrangle of immaculate green grass, currently being pounded by the rain. 'You're soaked,' he said. 'Let me get you a towel.'

'My goodness, you have your own bathroom and everything. You have come up in the world.'

'If you get responsibilities, you get perks. I've been made a Moral Tutor, in addition to teaching, I mean. Imagine!' He hung up his wet jacket. 'Luckily I keep a change of clothes here. Are you sure you're okay?'

256

'Sure.' She peeled off her coat and her boots and her socks and took a tour of his room. Arched alcoves on either side of the fireplace held shelves of books. Invitations inscribed on thick white card were propped on the mantelpiece. An elaborate cornice ran around the ceiling. There was a fine oak desk, a drinks cabinet with a decanter and glasses on the top, three faded easy chairs and a large sofa with plump rounded arms covered in a linen union fabric designed by William Morris.

When Toby came out of the bathroom in another respectable jumper, Jess threw a cushion at him. 'Such a traditionalist!' she said. 'Why didn't you choose one of mine?'

He plucked at his sleeve, puzzled, until he realised she was talking about the sofa. 'I hadn't really noticed. Most of this stuff was bequeathed by my predecessor. I'm afraid I live in a bit of a time warp.'

'That must be what we love about you! Centuries of perspective.'

He tossed the cushion onto the nearest chair. 'You know I've bought my own house now? A two-up two-down terrace in the Kite, easy pedalling distance. I'm still sorting out the furniture, but, rest assured, you will make your mark on it. Material for curtains at the very least. I was toying with taking you to see it but I think the weather's against us.'

'Next time, then.'

He said, in a rush, 'It's good to have you here, Jess.' There was a pause. 'Now, what can I get you? A drink?'

'No, I'm fine.'

'I'll light the fire and make you some tea.'

'Please don't bother. I don't want any tea.'

'You're shivering, you need to warm up.' He struck a match and the gas roared in the pipes. 'Why don't I give your hair a good rub with the towel? Sorry I don't have a dryer here.'

He sat beside her on the sofa and she bent her head forward as he instructed. She rarely went to the hairdresser so she wasn't used to the sensation of someone else massaging her head. She enjoyed it and didn't want him to stop.

'How's that?' he said, after a while. 'Dry enough yet?'

She scrunched a damp handful. 'That felt really good. I bet it looks a sight though.'

'Would you like me to brush it for you?'

'Oh… go on, then… yes, please.'

She fetched her hairbrush from her bag and turned her back to him. The bristles tingled against her scalp but the slow rhythmic motion of the brush strokes was as soothing as the hiss of the gas fire and the thud of the rain on the window panes. 'That's nice,' she said. 'Very nice.'

He lifted her hair from her nape in a single sweep and smoothed it forward over her shoulder. This left a portion of her neck exposed and he dropped a light kiss on it. Jess was startled and swung to face him; impulsively she fixed her mouth to his. Toby responded as if this was the most natural thing in the world. When they broke away for air, he said, 'I've always wanted to do that.'

'I know,' said Jess, attempting to laugh it off. A kiss between long-standing friends – was that so unusual?

'Did I make myself so obvious?'

'Not at all. I hope you don't mind, but Alex told me.'

Something in her voice must have alerted him. 'Ah… Alex… Things not going well?'

'It's since the move. You said to give it time, do you remember? I thought he'd adjust. But it's been over two years and he hasn't; he's not happy.'

'I'm sorry.'

The need for his touch had taken her by surprise; so, now, did her tears. She wiped her eyes, swallowed and said, 'Whereas you've really fallen on your feet, haven't you? Prestigious position and all of this. Don't get me wrong. I think it's terrific. You deserve every bit of it. You've worked hard and you're clever and thorough and dedicated and—'

'Stop it, Jess.' He caressed her cheek. 'Nobody ever has everything they want.'

She was tempted to take the hand that was being so tender with her and bite it, with the ferocity of an animal in pain. Instead, her words came out muffled and miserable. 'Looking back, I can see that Alex and I have been drifting apart. And now he's keeping something from me. We never had secrets before.'

Toby chose his words with caution. 'You mean an affair? Didn't you both believe you were above a bit of infidelity? You used to say it wouldn't faze you.'

'That was cocky, wasn't it? Thinking we could keep our options open without losing what we'd found together. But actually, up to now, neither of us ever put it into practice.'

'Nor would I. If I could get you into my bed, Jess, I wouldn't share you with anyone else.'

'Oh, Toby, that's sweet! But the point is…' she shifted position so her head was resting against his shoulder, her legs curled under her and her bare feet digging into the sofa cushions '… we undertook to be absolutely honest about everything. If Alex was seeing anyone else, he should have told me. Straight up. Instead I have this horrible sense of betrayal. I know he's lied to me.'

Toby said with an awkward laugh, 'Before we go any further, I need to come clean too. I'm expecting a visitor any minute.'

She bolted upright and swung her feet to the floor. 'What visitor?'

He looked uncomfortable. It must be a woman. Toby was nearly forty, it was about time he settled into a serious relationship. Perhaps that was why he was now more smartly dressed and better organised. She was pleased for him. He'd admitted he'd always wanted to kiss her and there was no reason for it to affect their friendship. She still loved her husband, didn't she, whatever he might have done? She wasn't looking for new romance – although this afternoon, especially since the rain storm, had a fragile enchanted quality like a bubble before it burst.

She was about to ask, 'Who is she?' when Toby, rather sheepishly, said, 'Gerald.'

'Gerald! Your uncle?'

'Yes. You haven't seen him, have you, since you were last in Sicily?'

'No, we haven't.'

'I didn't say anything earlier because I didn't know how you'd take it.'

'How is he?'

'Oh, much the same. He's visiting because I pulled a few strings for him. You know, he's been doing all this research into Stesichorus? Well, he finally got enough material for a book. He's giving a lecture tonight to promote it and he's my guest at dinner. He's over the moon about it, which is how I manged to get rid of him and meet you. Packed him off with a friend from the Classics faculty. But I didn't know this was how our day would turn out.'

She said, 'Do you want me to go?'

'No, that would be ridiculous. Unless you'd prefer to…'

The McKenzies had left Villa Ercole abruptly. The day after they'd rescued the children from Carlotta, they'd driven north and booked rooms in a hotel in San Vito lo Capo, making the excuse that it was more convenient for the airport. There had been a brief correspondence with Gerald immediately afterwards, apologies on both sides, civil rather than sincere. Jess might have forgiven him by now, but for Carlotta's letter crackling in her handbag.

'The summer of 1977,' she said. 'It doesn't want to go away.'

'What does that mean, exactly?'

'Oh, it's complicated...' She wished she could have stayed snug in Toby's embrace, petted and pacified, but that would have been greedy. She went to sit at the far end of the sofa, just in time: after the briefest of knocks, Gerald waltzed in. Waltzed was a fair description. He skimmed over the carpet on the balls of his feet, gaunt and white-haired, but buoyed with new importance.

'Wonderful fellow, Crispin,' he said to Toby. 'Had a fascinating afternoon.' He made straight for the sherry decanter and was holding it aloft when he noticed Jess. 'Sorry, didn't see you had a guest.'

Jess rose, determined to be polite. 'Hello, Gerald.'

'Jessamy! Good Lord! How lovely to see you. How are you? And the family?'

'I've been escaping them,' she said. 'I was in London yesterday and I hadn't seen Toby for God knows how long so…'

'Did he tell you about my book?'

'Yes. Well done.'

'You must have a copy,' he said, putting down the sherry and unlocking his briefcase.

She said cautiously, 'Is this what you were working on when we last saw you? You were putting a lot of effort into it.'

'Soaked in my blood, sweat and tears,' he said, passing her a slim volume.

The binding was crimson, good quality, smooth to the touch. She opened it and riffled through the pages. There was an index, a glossary, a plethora of notes, but no acknowledgements.

'I had it published privately,' said Gerald, as if he knew what she was looking for. 'At my own expense. One has to keep the page count down.'

'Alex helped you quite a lot, didn't he?'

'To a limited extent, my dear. I dare say he thinks he's an authority on many things but perhaps none of us are quite the experts our egos would have us believe.'

'Why don't you pour some drinks, Gerald?' said Toby, trying to change the subject.

He's still hurt, thought Jess, noting the tremor in Gerald's hand as she took the dainty sherry glass from him.

He said, 'Does he continue to charge about in his shining armour, your husband? Attending to the distress of all and sundry, seeking dragons to slay?'

'That's not fair,' said Jess, her loyalty roused. 'There's good reason for Alex to be the way he is. People can't help being influenced by their circumstances, whether they're aware of it or not. His father made the ultimate sacrifice, didn't he, dying for his country? It's a lot for a boy to live up to. He believes it's his duty to make the world his father fought for a better place and I admire him for trying.'

'Naturally you defend him,' said Gerald. 'And I am a lazy jaundiced cynic. And yes, Jessamy, you're right. I did run some of my writing past him for advice. But the fact is, Alex couldn't help with the translation because he doesn't know any Greek. However, I shall be delighted to inscribe the flyleaf to the two of you with my compliments.'

'It's not that we bear a grudge,' she began, as he uncapped his pen. 'But after what happened that summer, why on earth did you think giving our home address to Carlotta Galetti would be remotely helpful?'

The fountain pen paused, mid-flourish. 'Dear girl, I did no such thing.'

'You didn't?' He had sounded genuinely shocked. 'Then who did?'

'I haven't the faintest idea.' He completed his signature and handed her the book. 'Do you mean to say the woman's been writing to you in London?'

264

'Yes. In fact…' Did it matter how Carlotta had discovered where they lived? A new thought swirled into her brain. Gerald wanted to make amends. He might have spent years translating classical texts, but a sheet of Italian would only take him a couple of minutes.

23

Lily and Harry were now at the same school. This had drawbacks – when he was being an annoying year 7, for instance – but advantages too, when she wanted to play hard to get. No, she told Drew, she couldn't go to the café in town for a Coke because she had to make sure her kid brother got home safely on the bus. This was a gamble, because she had fancied Drew for ages, but when it resulted in a date arranged for Saturday, her spirits soared.

She was feeling both excited and mellow as she and Harry walked home from the bus-stop. Sometimes it was frustrating to be living in the middle of nowhere, but she loved the cosiness of the cottage, which Alex had christened the 'Whispering Pines' because of the towering Leylandii planted by the gate. The front garden was a tangle of rose bushes, the porch was full of Wellington boots and old umbrellas and the front door opened directly into the living room, which had bright rugs on the floor and a wood-burning stove and a surfeit of cushions covered in Jess's off-cuts.

Today it felt less welcoming than usual, though both their parents were in. A line of light crept beneath the study door and Jess's bag was dropped beside the staircase. Lily was puzzled that Jess hadn't rushed to hug them after two days away, but she supposed she must be busy in her workshop. She and Harry shouted out that they were home and went up to their rooms to change. Lily loosened her hair from its scrunchie so it fell around her shoulders and searched her wardrobe for something to wear on Saturday. She picked out a new top with a slash neck and batwing sleeves and tried it on to see if it looked sexy enough. She slicked on some lip gloss and pouted at the mirror. She was struggling with the zip of her jeans when Harry poked his head around the door and whistled.

'Piss off,' she said. 'What d'you want?'

'They're having a row,' he said.

'They can't be!'

'Come and listen.'

Harry's bedroom was over the study and sounds floated up through the chimney breast. Usually this would be Alex at his electric typewriter, the tap of the keys like birds pecking at a frozen puddle. Not today. Today there were agitated voices, which was unheard of. Their parents' fight was always against external forces, never with each other.

'What's the matter with them these days?' said Harry, in a tone of grown-up exasperation.

Jess and Alex were no longer in their old stroking/cuddling/brushing against each other routine – the routine where they communicated instinctively with quick smiles and tiny gestures. In fact, they hadn't been for a while; there was a tension between them. Lily didn't understand why her parents, who had once been so different from everyone else's – so much more relaxed, so much more fun – had become restless and dissatisfied; why the atmosphere sometimes felt stifling, as if the air was trapped and couldn't circulate; why Alex was so often absent. She worried that it was her fault because she'd been the prime cause of their move, but that was ages ago now and this afternoon, in her present glow of contentment, it wasn't something she wanted to dwell on.

'There's someone with them,' she said.

'You mean it's someone else who's arguing?'

'I don't know, but every now and again you can hear another voice. Female, but not Grandma or Dinah.'

'We should see who it is,' said Harry. 'They can't *ignore* us. They know we're home. Come on.'

Intrigued, Lily followed him. The cottage stairs were steep and narrow and thinly carpeted. They tried not to make too much noise, clattering down. 'Shhh, wait,' said Lily, putting her ear to the panel of the closed door.

An angry voice said, 'How can you possibly understand what I have endured? Do you think it is easy

268

to leave your home and everything you know? To live in strange cities… bad relationships… terrible jobs…'

'Who's that?' said Harry.

'Let's find out.' She knocked first, as a warning, and then, sensing a dramatic entrance was required, flung open the study door.

Alex fumbled with something on his desk. Jess gaped as if she didn't recognise her. 'Lily?'

'Why are you staring at me like that?'

'Are you wearing lipstick?'

'What's wrong with lipstick? Anyway, it's gloss.' She looked around the room, perplexed. 'Where is she?'

'Who?'

'The woman you're arguing with.'

'There's no one else here.'

This was irrefutable. The room contained a wall of bookcases, a studio couch, which doubled as a spare bed for visitors, a large desk and a chair. Harry might have hidden in the kneehole of the desk or under the couch but no adult was likely to crawl there.

'But we heard her!'

A quick, desperate look passed from Jess to Alex. He reached out and pulled Lily towards him. She came up to his shoulder and knew she wasn't likely to grow any taller. On the desk behind him was a sheet of graph paper covered in blue ink. At first she thought it might have been torn from one of her rough books where she sometimes scribbled private confidences, but she realised it was a letter when she saw the envelope with the foreign stamps. Then she spotted the tape recorder.

'Is that where the voice came from?'

Jess sank onto the studio couch and buried her face in her hands. Alex said, 'Yes.'

'And the letter? Is that from the same person too?'

'Yes.'

'What's this all about? Who is she?'

Alex said, 'I don't know if you remember Carlotta Galetti?'

Harry said, 'No. Who's Carlotta Galetti?'

'Oh, Harry!' said Lily. 'You're hopeless! She was the woman with the Polaroid camera in Roccamare, the one who took us to Favignana.'

'Oh, yeah. She was okay. Apart from the fishing. I am never going fishing again.'

Alex said, 'Jess is upset because I've been in touch with her.'

'No,' said Jess. 'I'm upset because you didn't tell me.'

'I was trying to protect you.'

'That's so bloody patronising! Thinking you can play God. It's not what we're about.' She corrected herself. 'What we used to be about.'

Lily wriggled away from Alex and went to sit beside Jess. She put her arm around her, anxious to placate her. 'Why does it matter?' she said. 'She doesn't tell the truth, you know.'

Jess's head jerked up. 'Carlotta lies? How would you know that?'

'When we were on the island,' said Lily, 'She pretended she couldn't swim when she could. It was odd because it's usually the other way around: people claiming they're good at stuff and then making excuses not to do it.'

'How do you mean? Did she fake drowning?'

'No, she asked me to teach her. I had to help her learn to float and practise strokes.' She could still see Carlotta's golden body splashing through the water and perching on the rock like a mermaid. 'She wanted me to hold her.'

Jess said softly, 'There was probably a reason for that.' Then she said to Alex. 'You went along with her scheme, you encouraged her. You've a lot of explaining to do, so you'd better make a start.'

Harry planted himself against the door. 'You're not going to send me away. I want to hear this.'

'Yes, you should stay,' said Jess. 'It affects us all. But try not to interrupt.'

Alex stood with his back to the window and his face in shadow. He said to Lily, 'I expect Carlotta wanted to get close to you because she believes – and I have to stress we can never be certain of this – that you are her daughter.'

The words fell like stones into a pond. Outside, birds were singing, spring flowers danced in pools of sunshine.

Saturday, the date with Drew, seemed a long way off, like a mirage. Lily felt curiously detached. 'Am I? She told us she lost her husband in the earthquake. She didn't say anything about any children.'

Then she remembered: a baby must have a father, Carlotta had said when they were on Favignana, and she had taught Lily the lullaby she'd since forgotten. The simple melody now spun in her brain, along with the image of a mother singing to her new-born, rocking the infant to sleep at her warm milky bosom. Was that what Carlotta had done? Had she been trying to suggest a connection, which Lily had missed? How could she have been so stupid? Detachment gave way to rage. She yelled, 'You've known this all along and you never said anything! Why didn't you tell me before?'

Alex tried to keep his tone steady. 'Because it might have been total fantasy. We'd no idea if it was true. We still don't, although there are... indications that it's likely. We wouldn't have deprived you of contact if she'd gone about things the right way, but after she ran off with you both we simply couldn't trust her. You said yourself that she lies. I couldn't let her mess you around.'

'So what's changed?'

'She didn't give up. Somehow she got hold of our address in London. She wrote to us, though we didn't reply. She also sent the odd postcard, which you may have seen.'

272

'Oh, yes,' said Lily vaguely. Postcards often arrived from family friends; she didn't pay them much attention.

'And then she came to find you.'

This was shocking. 'When?'

'A while ago. You remember that business with the girls and the garage?'

It was an episode Lily preferred to suppress. She shuddered. 'That wasn't her!'

'She'd tried to disguise herself,' said Alex.

Lily's mental picture of the little foreign woman was hazy but it didn't fit her knowledge of Carlotta. 'What sort of disguise?'

'She cut off all her hair and bleached it. Drastic to say the least.' He added sharply, 'She told me you hadn't seen her.'

'I don't know who I saw,' said Lily. 'But I know I wished she hadn't got involved. She made everything worse.' Then a handful of words in a soft Italian accent swam through her memory. *Please don't cry. Don't be upset. I will bring you help.*

Alex switched on the tape recorder and the same low voice was saying, '... Try to imagine my feelings! My husband is dead, my baby is dead. My old life, it's finished. Then I hear news of a little girl in the orphanage who is from Santa Margherita. They say no one has claimed her, but when I arrive from America she's gone. Then I meet you and you tell me how you found the baby and gave her to the nuns, and they are

273

the same nuns I went to see…' There was the scrape of a match being struck, the tiny clatter of a teaspoon against china, a background buzz.

Lily whispered, 'Did she really come all the way to London to look for me?'

'She had a bee in her bonnet. What she didn't have was any proof.'

Glamorous, slippery, duplicitous Carlotta. 'My actual mother? My real mother?'

'I'm your real mother,' said Jess, cradling her. 'I'm sorry, darling, this is a dreadful thing to have sprung on you. It should never have happened this way.'

Alex said, 'It was a total shock to me when she turned up. Out of the fucking blue. She basically blackmailed me into having a meeting and I made the tape as a precaution. Jess hasn't heard it before, that's why I was playing it. To explain…' He massaged his jaw, pulling his mouth downwards, etching deep grooves. 'The last thing I wanted was for you to be hassled, so we struck a deal. I agreed to send Carlotta photographs if she agreed to keep out of the frame. I slipped up, I'm afraid. I was busy with other stuff, let a couple of months drift by. And she's come down on me like a ton of bricks.'

Lily thought back to Alex's new-found interest in photography, how he would sometimes sneak up on her, twisting his lens, making a joke of it. She had been duped. Disgustingly. Resentment burst out of her. 'You make it sound like it's nothing. But it isn't, it's horrible.

D'you really think that because you were the person who saved me you have the right to treat me like this? Like I'm some kind of object! A bargaining chip!'

Jess said, 'It's always worse to find out stuff when you're not properly prepared, but you have to remember, darling: *you* are the same person. *We* are the same people. Maybe when you're older, when you're an adult, which isn't long to wait, you can go to Italy and make your own investigations. We've talked about this before, haven't we, about seeing if you can trace any relatives in Santa Margherita? In the meantime, nothing needs to change.'

But everything *had* changed. Irrevocably. Her very identity, her whole life – from the babyhood that was a blank to their final holiday in Roccamare, from the scene in the garage she'd rather forget to this tense showdown – was thrown into turmoil. She longed to crawl under a pile of blankets and blot out the world until she could make sense of it again.

Over the top of Lily's head, Jess said to Alex, 'Look what you've done! There's so much we're going to have to get sorted. You can't leave yet.'

Alex said, 'I thought it was what you wanted.'

'No, that's not fair, it's what *you* wanted. I just said that if you were so unhappy here, if you felt things weren't working, I wasn't going to stand in your way—'

Lily was adrift in a turbulent sea, tossed from one wave of emotion to another. Currently being buffeted on livid – why had she been kept in such ignorance? She sat up and snarled, 'Are you kicking him out?'

'I'm giving him space,' said Jess. 'If he wants to take it. A lot of things have gone wrong. There's been a lack of trust and we need to take some time out and find a new approach...'

'That is such crap,' said Lily furiously. As if there could be any chance of replicating their old family conferences in these circumstances!

'You're not to blame Jess for anything, d'you hear?' said Alex. 'If you feel the urge to have a go at anyone, pick on me. I thought I was doing the right thing, but, hell, I cocked up. Misfired. Good intentions don't always produce good results. I'm not making excuses, but I guess there comes a point in every kid's life when they discover their father has feet of clay.'

Harry, wide-eyed and silent until this point, said with deliberate provocation, 'Not yours though.'

Alex made a general swipe in his direction, which Harry easily dodged. 'You little shit!'

'Are you splitting up?' Lily persisted. 'Yes or no?'

'Of course not,' said Alex and Jess in unison.

She didn't believe them. Carlotta wasn't the only person who told lies. She sat, shivering in her fancy batwing top, unable to stop her teeth chattering. She wished her parents could scoop her up the way they used to when she was little, holding her tightly to the twin thump of their heartbeats, raining down kisses and telling her she was their precious miracle. But it was too late: no one could love an awkward disgruntled teenager who didn't fit into her skin. The charmed existence the McKenzies had created for themselves was dissolving and Lily had no idea where she belonged any more.

Part Three

1988

24

Eva had such a knack with her window display that passers-by might think they had stumbled on a party. She'd clothed her mannequins in vivid cocktail dresses and satin boleros and manoeuvred them into realistic poses, champagne glasses cleverly balanced between their fingers. Sometimes she played her favourite jazz records too, notes from trumpet and saxophone snaking into the street. But if you looked closely, you'd see her incongruous figure bent over a sewing machine in the centre of the room: a little brown sparrow surrounded by birds of exotic plumage.

Carlotta rang the bell. Eva let her in, ribbons fluttering around her neck, a chalk pencil behind her ear. 'I always knew this day would come,' she said, embracing her happily. 'Are you sure you won't change your mind?'

'About Nicolo?'

'No! The dress.'

Carlotta knew Eva was disappointed not to be making the peacock dress. In her imagination it was fully fledged. 'I was planning to sew white feathers on your train and make a headpiece too, with sequins for extra sparkle!'

'No,' laughed Carlotta. 'That's too much for a civil ceremony.' The wedding was to be a quiet affair, as it was the second for both of them. The date had been fixed a few weeks hence, at the beginning of August. No wild celebrations with hordes of stray relatives, but a meal in select company at a fine restaurant. Some dancing afterwards. 'I want an outfit that's elegant and classy. This is Rome, not Sicily.'

They spent a pleasant twenty minutes discussing the style and the fabric and settled on a lustrous silk in pale gold, which Eva described as the colour of sunrise. Then Carlotta undressed in a cubicle so Eva could check her measurements. 'I might need to make adjustments later,' she said. 'Honestly, you'd be surprised how many brides lose weight before their wedding day.'

'That's because they want to look their best.'

'It's not always deliberate. Some of them get so wound up they don't eat properly.'

'I'm too old to be nervous,' said Carlotta.

'Age has nothing to do with it,' said Eva. 'But I am very content for you, Carli. I told you everything would work out if you'd only take my advice. I'm very glad you kept your promise and you ought to be too.'

'I didn't have any choice!' It was a fact she had become used to: Lily was lost to her. There had been no more photographs. Five years ago, she'd received a cool note from Alex McKenzie saying he was no longer living with his family, so there was no point in her writing again.

'I don't know why it's taken you and Nicolo so long to legalise everything,' said Eva. 'But it's good to have the security, isn't it? The final commitment.' Carlotta nodded. Eva removed the tape measure from her waist and jotted in her notebook. 'Right, I've got all the figures down. Do you want to come back in a fortnight for the first fitting? You can leave work early again?'

'Now that I'm the manager,' said Carlotta, 'I can do what I like.' She had overseen the move to larger premises near via del Corso and had two sales assistants beneath her.

'Perfect! Just don't do anything silly in the next few weeks.'

'What, like lose too much weight?'

Eva's lapels were stuffed with round-headed pins, which glittered as she tossed back her head. 'You know what I mean, Carli. Things have been going well for you. Don't spoil your luck.'

The Belice earthquake was twenty years past; her life had turned around. 'Don't you think, *tesora*, I know that better than most people?'

*

It was extraordinary how luck could change – from one extreme to the other and back again. It was a story she liked to tell at social gatherings, with Nicolo close by and Luca interjecting. Luca said it was his story really, because he was the one who'd found the peacock feathers. Also, because he was the one who'd been hit by the Alfa during its frantic swerve. Carlotta had rushed to catch his small body as it was flung skywards and she had broken his fall. As they'd tumbled together to the side of the road, she'd been transported back to Santa Margherita, to the ground cracking and jarring beneath her feet, to the crash of walls collapsing and roof tiles flying, to the infinity of lost consciousness.

The driver had leapt from his car, swearing angrily, justifying himself; the miscreant scooters had disappeared. Luca had lain in Carlotta's arms, his face ghostly pale. The noise of squealing tyres had alerted his cousin, Paolo, and his friends who'd come pouring around the corner.

Carlotta was winded and bruised, but she didn't think anything was broken; there didn't seem to be any blood. She was more worried about Luca, who was lying, warm and solid but inert, across her lap. When he opened his eyes, the irises rolled around the whites, unfocussed, which scared her. Then they fixed on her own. She said gently, 'How are you, Luca?'

'I feel dizzy,' he said. 'Where's my feather?'

She was immeasurably relieved to hear him speak. 'Don't worry about that now. Does your back hurt? Your legs? Can you move them?'

'I think so.'

'We need to get him to hospital,' she said to Paolo.

The car driver said, 'San Camillo's the nearest. I'll take you. You should be checked out also, *signora*.'

Paolo stuttered, 'That's where Luca's father works.'

'Right, you'd better come with us too.'

Carlotta's first encounter with Nicolo Morandi had not been auspicious. She could still replay the fear on his face when she'd stumbled into the hospital emergency department with Luca and he'd heard the convoluted explanations of the driver. The afternoon had dragged into evening and when she'd been discharged she hadn't expected to see either Morandi again. But the following weekend father and son had come to the shop. She hadn't recognised Nicolo at first, in his casual clothes, but Luca she'd known instantly. All pallor gone, he had been bursting with good spirits. He had cocked his head on one side and beamed as he'd whisked a dazzling bouquet from behind his back.

'He chose the flowers himself,' Nicolo said. 'To thank you.'

'I didn't really do anything.'

'You were my cushion!' said Luca and they all laughed.

'He wants to take you out for lunch,' said Nicolo. 'If you are free.'

That was the beginning of the good luck. They had bereavement in common: Nicolo was a widower who'd relocated from Bologna to Rome so Luca could keep in contact with his mother's family. Sometimes Carlotta would help out with the child-care too. She loved having Luca round to her flat, creating dens and playing hide-and-seek in its nooks and crannies. She taught him Sicilian card games and amassed a collection of Lego. When, after these visits, she came across stray plastic bricks, they seemed tiny symbols of hope and renewal.

Nicolo and Luca had been living in a rented apartment in need of a woman's touch. Carlotta had hung pictures and arranged plants and sewn cushions and helped to make it homely. She'd bought toys and ironed shirts and spent much of her spare time there. Their relationship had blossomed by degrees – like Carlotta, Nicolo was chary of commitment. He hadn't proposed until he'd saved enough for a deposit to buy their own place. She'd insisted on pooling their resources and the three of them had taken possession six months ago.

This apartment was in a newly built block not far from the hospital where Nicolo worked as an anaesthetist. (And she only a blacksmith's daughter!) It had a balcony and a car parking space and airy spacious rooms. Carlotta liked to walk around in her bare feet, stroking the walls and the window sills and the modern kitchen appliances, holding her breath at the shine on the cooker hood and the chrome handles on the cupboard doors – afraid that if she let out too much air at once everything else, and not just her lungs, would deflate. Because her contribution had been less than his, they joked that the bathroom (with a full-size bath!) was the space she had bought. She stored all her beauty paraphernalia on its shelves and kept the tiles scrubbed white and spotless. Luca had a smart bedroom with a grand new desk for his homework. And she and Nicolo had an enormous bed, for which she'd chosen a set of sheets with English words scribbled over them: *I love you I love you I love you.*

After leaving Eva's studio, Carlotta called into the butchers to buy veal escalopes for supper and the greengrocer's for spinach and calabrese and a punnet of pink flushed apricots. She didn't even hesitate over the cost of the veal. She was aware Eva hadn't yet given her a precise quote for the dress, but lack of money was no longer a worry. She didn't have to flirt or bargain to get what she wanted – and, oh, this was liberating! Arriving home, she shifted her shopping bag into the crook of her elbow, collected the post from their box in the lobby and let herself into the empty flat. This evening there was no Luca, diligently pretending to study. He'd gone straight from school, as he often did, to visit his *nonna* and *nonno*, Maria's parents.

She didn't look at the mail until she'd put the food away and opened the shutters to let in the light; the heat of the day was fading. She poured a glass of mineral water, ice cold from the fridge, and sat down to flick through it. The envelope that caught her eye had been forwarded from her old address and had an English stamp. She opened it in a mixture of trepidation and incredulity. Her heart somersaulted, her throat closed. It was not from Alex – why would it be? – but from Lily.

Carlotta shook her head in disbelief. After so long, could this really be happening? She'd once hoped Lily might make contact when she became eighteen, but that date had passed three years ago. She'd taken the silence as confirmation the McKenzies thought her a fantasist. Besides, she had fallen in love with Nicolo; the trajectory of her life was altered and she needed to concentrate on the future.

Lily expressed herself in a manner that was blunt and unadorned. (English was such a functional language, lacking the delicacy and grace of Italian.) She stated simply that she would soon be travelling through Italy. She was with a group researching classical Renaissance gardens because she was studying garden design. They would be visiting Villa d'Este and, as Tivoli was near Rome, she hoped they could meet. There were issues they might discuss.

Carlotta smoothed the piece of paper, tracing Lily's signature with her forefinger. Then she noticed the date:

the letter had been sent weeks earlier. It must have been sitting in the postbox in her old building, or in the sorting office itself, where nothing was done in haste. Lily would already have begun her trip. There was no way of contacting her. If she didn't know Carlotta's new address, she couldn't call by. And Carlotta could hardly take a day off from the shop to go to Tivoli on the off-chance of finding her wandering through the gardens. This was crushing news – how could the timing be so horribly wrong? – but once she'd digested it, a second problem arose: what, if anything, should she say to Nicolo? Her brain turned to sludge; she couldn't think properly. Lily's words danced about on the page, taunting her.

She was sitting at the table, with her face in her hands, when Nicolo strolled in. He had an air of authority, of trustworthiness. You knew this was a person who would not let you down. She loved the way his eyes lit up behind his glasses whenever he saw her, as if – even after six years – she was an undiscovered treasure. He came over to massage her shoulders and drop a kiss on her head.

'You look tired. Was it a tough day?'

'No, it was fine. Really. I went to see Eva about the dress. We've picked the fabric and the design but I can't tell you anything about it.'

'I'm guessing this is one of your superstitions?'

'Yes! It's bad luck for the groom to see the outfit in advance because then you won't be dazzled when I appear in it.'

'I'm always dazzled by you, *amore*.'

'Ouf, you're flattering me because you're hungry. I was waiting for you to get in before I started cooking. Luca's with Nonna, she'll bring him back later.'

'I'm on call,' he said. 'So I'd better stoke up on caffeine. It could be a long night.'

He crossed to the kitchen counter. All his movements were deft and measured; he was meticulous. She remained at the table, watching as he filled the basket of the espresso pot and put it on the stove. He set the cup on its saucer, counted out the spoons of sugar. When the coffee was ready he took it through to the living room where she could hear him changing the TV channels with his latest toy, a remote control that let you pick what you wanted to watch without moving from your chair. To Carlotta, who'd grown up without a television, this was magic indeed.

He hadn't noticed the letter. Forcing herself to rise, she put it in a drawer where she kept recipes and calling cards and random telephone numbers. Mechanically, she began to prepare their meal, rinsing the spinach and dipping the escalopes into breadcrumbs. Her life had transformed that day in Villa Sciarra when she'd made her promise to Eva. Fate had granted her the chance to parent a child and she was superstitious enough not to jeopardise it. But this was a new dilemma.

She couldn't decide which was more damaging: the fact that her daughter might still be alive or her own lack of candour. She loved Luca as she loved his father; she was trusted by them both and couldn't bear them to feel betrayed. Nicolo was aware of her tragic losses, of course. He knew how painful the subject was for her so they rarely mentioned it. But if she didn't know how he would react to this information – would he be shocked? Appalled? Incredulous? – should she be marrying him in the first place? She laid down the meat and bent over the sink, to combat a wave of nausea.

The voices in the sitting room stopped abruptly as Nicolo switched off the TV set. She heard the squeak of his soles on the tiled floor as he re-entered the kitchen and came to stand close behind her. If she leaned backwards she could topple into his arms. Explain the whole situation. It would be all right. He'd have a thousand questions but she would answer them with total honesty; their family unit would not be affected. She turned, quickly, before she could change her mind.

'Listen, *amore*,' she began.

'What is it?'

She pressed herself against his chest and felt a curious vibration thudding against her own. It wasn't his heart.

'*Managgia la miseria!*' he exclaimed. 'Not even time for a bite.' He pulled his pager from his pocket and kissed her cheek regretfully. Carlotta's news would have to wait.

<u>25</u>

Lily didn't know the date of her birthday, although this hadn't troubled her in the past. In the past she'd happily celebrated fourteenth April, elected for her by the nuns. The year she came to them it was Easter Day and therefore a good omen. But ever since that awful night in the Whispering Pines, when her world had fallen apart, their choice seemed more like a cruel deception. How old was she really? Might Carlotta Galetti be the only person who knew for sure? Jess insisted there was still a question mark over Carlotta.

It was Toby who'd told her about the breakthrough in DNA testing, in 1986, the year she became nineteen. Her parents had denied their separation for ages, but by then it was obvious and Jess would join Toby for the summer holidays. Harry often stayed with Alex in London, but Lily found the city constraining. She preferred to work outdoors and enrolled on a series of horticultural courses – Alex called her a creature of the soil because she could never get the dirt out of her fingernails.

Her visits to Cambridge were brief because Toby's place was too intimate for comfort, a two-person dolls' house. She'd known him forever and he seemed to make her mother happy but she couldn't help finding the situation *weird*. She couldn't understand why they dipped in and out of each other's lives in this intermittent way. If they ever lived together permanently she hoped they'd get somewhere bigger so she wouldn't feel such a gooseberry; on the other hand, she was convinced that as a pair they didn't quite *fit*. When Alex and Jess had been together, they had glided in harmony, moving to the same rhythm, whereas Jess was too tall for Toby and they were always slightly out of step.

It was a late summer's day, muggy and torpid. Jess was making something called damson cheese, although cheese had nothing to do with it. It was actually a thick jam. Jess was stooping over the preserving pan in the dolls' house kitchen, her face flushed from the rising steam, sifting out the damson stones with a slotted spoon. It was a painstaking task because there were a lot of stones. Toby suggested they got out of Jess's hair and went for a walk. Lily glanced at her mother, who said, 'Yes, that's a good idea. Get some fresh air and I'll be all done by the time you come back.'

They crossed Midsummer Common and headed down to the river. They turned away from the town and followed the towpath through the water meadows. The boathouses were shut up, the barges moored to the bank squatted like sluggish black beetles, clouds of midges hovered between the trees, the willow leaves drooped.

They talked a little about the flora and fauna they passed – Lily was much better at identifying wild flowers than Toby – but she couldn't have guessed where the conversation was leading.

Then Toby said, 'How much do you know about genetics?'

Lily shrugged. She had two hard-won A-levels in Geography and Art. Academic study wasn't her strong point. 'Not much.'

'But you've been looking at plant breeding, haven't you? And you must be aware of the characteristics children can inherit from their parents.'

'Yes, of course.' Fair, slender Harry was clearly Jess and Alex's son; Lily didn't resemble them in the least but she'd got used to that ages ago.

'Have you ever heard of DNA?'

'I don't think so.'

'It stands for deoxyribonucleic acid,' said Toby. 'But I'm not going to go all technical on you. It's a code we carry in our genes, which passes on the instructions that influence our development and makes each of us unique.'

She stared at him. She presumed he couldn't help sounding like a lecturer even on a Saturday afternoon stroll.

Unperturbed, he held her gaze. 'Everyone has individual fingerprints, right? Well, when you break down the structure of a cell to get at the DNA, that gives you another kind of fingerprint. I thought you might have read about it in the papers. It's been used in immigration cases, to prove family membership. And it's beginning to be used by forensics to identify criminals. A murderer, for example, will often leave behind evidence such as blood or saliva or semen. Bodily fluids. And even if he can't be caught, then at least other suspects can be eliminated.' He paused; she waited. 'There may yet be further advances, when DNA can be extracted from hair or teeth or bones. The possibilities could be limitless!'

'Why are you telling me this?' As she spoke, she stubbed her toe on a loose stone on the path and stumbled. He kicked the stone into the river and they both stopped to watch the ripples spread.

He said mildly, 'I thought you might like to draw your own conclusions.'

'My own conclusions?'

'There's a lot of guesswork in my research,' he said. 'Opinion and hypothesis is all we can come up with most of the time. But in your case, Lily, you can kiss the guesswork goodbye. If you wanted to, you could find out who you are.'

'How?' she demanded. 'How would I do that?'

'Well, the process is a bit cumbersome so you'd need to be patient. But basically you, and any possible relative, would both provide blood samples to a lab to see if they matched.'

'And if they matched, there'd be no doubt?'

'No doubt at all.'

Lily started walking again, briskly, with her head down, her mind churning. She could hardly ignore this discovery, but it was a mixed blessing. 'When you say "possible relative" do you really mean mother?'

Toby kept pace. 'I suppose so, yes. That is, if you know how to get in touch with her. Do you?'

'Carlotta? Yeah, Alex gave me her address in Rome last year when I was eighteen. I thought I might ask when I'd really been born.'

(Jess had pointed out that she couldn't change the date because it was on her adoption certificate and her passport, which were legally valid documents, but Harry suggested she could have two birthdays: one of her own and one official. If it was good enough for the Queen of England, it ought to be good enough for Lily McKenzie.)

'Did you write to her?'

'It seemed a weird thing to put in a letter… so, no.'

'Well, it's a tricky subject. It needs a sensitive approach. I don't suppose it'll be simple to ask for a blood test in writing either.'

'Does Jess know you're telling me this?'

'Yes. That's why she packed us off. She thought it would be easier for you to hear it from me. She was worried about being able to explain the science properly – not that I've done that – but mainly, she didn't want to inhibit your reactions. In case you felt obliged to protect her feelings.'

'Reactions, like what?'

He gave her a rueful grin. 'Oh, I don't know... Like jumping for joy?'

*

Lily hadn't jumped for joy, but she'd tucked the information away for future reference. Over the next eighteen months she went to libraries and consulted the back editions of newspapers, looking for stories where DNA sampling had proved indispensable, but she made no move to contact Carlotta. Then came the chance to go on the garden design tour and suddenly her attitude changed.

The prospect of visiting Italy again drove her to a pitch of excitement. She bought language tapes and listened to them morning and night on the tape recorder, practising her pronunciation. She bought records of Italian songs to sing along to. Childhood memories, buried deep, began to surface. Vocabulary used for beach games in Roccamare wouldn't be much use in the gardens of Lombardy, Tuscany and Lazio, but the rhythm and the cadences of the language came back to her. She would be returning to her homeland and she wanted to sound like a native.

It had taken several drafts to compose her letter – she didn't want it to sound either too eager or too impersonal – so it was a major setback to receive no reply. Perhaps her message had been too subtle? But really, how could Carlotta have misunderstood? Lily was coming to Rome; Carlotta had sought her out in the past so why would they not meet now? Once the student group had flown from Gatwick there was nothing more she could do, but she kept alive a glimmer of hope. Jess and Harry knew the phone numbers of the *pensiones* she'd be staying in and promised to ring her if any post arrived. By the time she reached Villa d'Este, at the end of their itinerary, she'd reconciled herself to the silence. She would have to take matters into her own hands.

All the classical gardens they'd visited had been magnificent, but the fountains and springs of Villa d'Este were another experience altogether. Lily stood at the lowest point of the site, watching the water cascade from one pool to the next, shimmering the air with crystal. She stood in full sun, with a bandana tied around her head so sweat wouldn't get in her eyes, absorbing the power and beauty of the spectacle. She should have been sketching or taking pictures with her pocket Canon or, at the very least, taking notes and working out how you could apply this drama to a garden on a smaller scale. Instead she was mesmerised. The grace and the extravagance of the statuary, the hundred lions' heads spouting into mossy green basins, the playing of the magical organ fountain, the burble and splash of the endlessly flowing water enthralled her.

'Quite something, isn't it?' The group's tutor, known by his students as Call-me-Howard, arrived at her side. 'Unique in Europe.'

'I want to drink it in,' said Lily. 'I don't think I'd be able to capture it in a photograph.'

'You can never over-estimate the effect of water in a landscape,' said Call-me-Howard. 'The Japanese are masters at using it to create a calm contemplative atmosphere – and I'm sorry that Japan was out of our league, budget-wise, more's the pity – but you know what I mean?'

Minimalist Japanese design was very fashionable because most of the effort went into the initial composition and structure and high maintenance wasn't required. Clients liked this. The notion that Lily might one day have 'clients' of her own gave her goose pimples.

He went on, 'Whereas the Renaissance princes, or the Cardinal in this case, wanted to show off. It's operatic in a way, isn't it, indulging in all that superb melodrama the Italians love so much?'

Operatic perfectly described the display in front of them, the fountains swelling and sighing in a cycle of crescendo and diminuendo. 'Actually,' said Lily, rapt and enchanted by this showmanship, 'I'm Italian myself.'

'You are? Fancy that!' He called out to the only other group member who was in earshot. 'Louise! Did you know that our young friend here is a local?'

Louise was a mature student, closer to Howard's age than Lily's. She smiled kindly and said, 'That explains why you've tanned so well.'

Lily said, 'I'm not local exactly…' It had slipped out because she was proud to associate with something so splendid. 'I was born in Sicily but I grew up in England.'

She expected they would gang up and press her for details, but the information wasn't nearly as significant to them as to herself. Louise resumed her sketching and Call-me-Howard pulled his panama hat low over his brow. He was suffering from a hangover. They had arrived in Tivoli the previous evening and celebrated their final stop with too much Frascati. However, he did ask: 'Is that why you wanted to stay on?'

They were scheduled to spend the night in Rome and fly from Fiumicino the following evening. Lily had already asked if she could defer her flight a couple of days, because it seemed a shame to get as far as Rome and not see any of it. Call-me-Howard had explained that it was a group booking and couldn't be amended.

Now she said, 'Yes, in a way.'

'So it wasn't because you wanted to go sightseeing?'

'Not really. I've been trying to meet up with a family friend, but I'm having trouble making contact.'

'You think you'll have success tomorrow?'

'I don't know… But couldn't we say I'll make my own way to the airport? And if I don't get there for check-in you're not to worry about me?'

He looked at her doubtfully. His eyes were bloodshot. 'You're an adult, Lily McKenzie, I'm not in charge of you and there's nothing to stop you buying another ticket home if you choose to. But I do think you should let me know your plans sooner than an hour before take-off.'

'Please,' she begged. 'It's not going to make any difference to the rest of you. I don't expect you to wait for me so I won't make you late.'

'You know we've booked a transfer leaving from the hotel at 3.30? You won't have long with this friend.'

'I could get a taxi,' she said recklessly. 'Anyway, if I can't find her there's no reason I wouldn't join you in good time.'

'Five p.m. tomorrow at Fiumicino,' he said. 'And not a minute later.'

'Understood. Thank you, Howard.'

*

Their Roman hotel was near the station. The group breakfasted together and ambled over to Villa Borghese for the morning. Lily went along with them for a while and then sneaked off. She descended from the Pincio to Trinità dei Monti and the Spanish Steps. She was aiming for the address she had written to, and she'd worked out how to get there on foot. She'd done a lot of walking in the past ten days; she was used to it.

She crossed via del Corso and entered a patchwork of streets barely the width of a Cinquecento. The area was busy with tourists but the buildings were run-down and shabby, pockmarked with graffiti and fly posters and missing clumps of stucco. The summer sun was at its most relentless so she kept to the shade. She followed her map, twisting and turning until she reached a road wide enough to have a pavement. Here was a tobacconist with a revolving stand of postcards, a barber's, a shop selling religious artefacts, rosaries and sacred hearts, and another offering a motley assortment of luggage and hats, walking sticks and umbrellas, wallets and wicker baskets. Further along was a scarred double door and a row of bell-pushes with a name beside each.

She studied the handwritten names. Apartment number four, which should have been Carlotta's, announced GORDONE, A. in capitals. It didn't stop her pressing the bell, but there was no answer. Why hadn't she thought of this? If Carlotta had moved house, it would explain why she hadn't responded to her letter. It wasn't because she didn't want to meet her!

Lily felt re-energised. It would be silly to come so far and not make an effort to track Carlotta down, even if she wasn't expected. Hadn't Alex also mentioned that the apartment was close to her workplace? She barely hesitated before entering the shop with luggage piled in the window. She said in her best Italian, 'Excuse me, do you sell handbags?' The man behind the counter tried to interest her in a satchel, but Lily shook her head. 'Bags for women,' she said. 'Is there another shop around here that sells leather goods?'

'There was di Monza,' he said and Lily caught her breath. 'But they closed.'

From behind the curtain at his back, a disembodied voice called, 'No, Luigi. They moved.'

Lily was on a see-saw: down-up/down-up. She tried to say calmly, 'Do you know where?'

He conferred through the curtain and, after several minutes, a woman materialised, holding a cardboard shoe box. She rummaged in it with no sense of urgency. *'Eccola!'* She produced a small white card with a name – *Borse Artiginali di Monza* – and location stamped in a clean elegant typeface. Lily unfolded her map so she could show her where to find it.

'Thank you so much!'

It was the best chance she had – there was no reason not to take it. She retraced her steps towards via del Corso, looking out for window displays of handbags en route, diving down side streets and criss-crossing piazzas. A couple of times she spotted a likely contender and entered the shop with her ready-prepared question: *'Per favore, Carlotta Galetti lavora qui?'*

She wasn't surprised when the answer was no, but she wanted to be thorough. She wouldn't give up until she reached her destination: the one printed so stylishly on the card growing sticky in her hand. But the closer she got, the more her feet dragged – a flock of what-ifs? wrestled for space in her brain. And when she finally located it, she hit a discouraging sight: her own reflection facing her in the shining expanse of plate glass. She was wearing shorts and trainers, a baggy tee shirt and a bandana. She was carrying a canvas rucksack with frayed straps and misshapen buckles. She didn't look like the type of person who would buy anything from an exclusive boutique.

Lily had to be stern with herself. If she was prepared to risk jacking in her plane ticket and incurring extra expenses, she shouldn't let a fancy shop front put her off. She should be bold. The bell tinkled when she walked through the door to face a row of kid and calf and snakeskin bags with enormous price tags, ludicrously large in fact – hundreds of thousands – because they were all in lire. She circled the central display table three times, not daring to touch anything in case she left a dirty mark on the leather. After her third circuit, a skinny girl dressed in black approached her with the poise of a ballerina and asked if she needed help.

26

Carlotta wasn't often sick. She couldn't afford to be. Managing the shop was a full-time affair and when she wasn't on the premises, it was because she was visiting one of the artisans who supplied them. Apart from some designer labels, most of their handbags were sourced from individual craftsmen. She loved being involved from conception and was a strict monitor of style and quality, inspecting every stitch, every clasp, the durability of leather and lining. She wouldn't let anybody cheat her or fob her off with the second rate. And even if she was feeling low, with a cold or a headache or indigestion, it didn't stop her going into work.

Food poisoning was different. She shouldn't have been lazy and ordered takeaways from the *tavola calda*. Nicolo and Luca had both eaten lasagne and been fine, but she'd had the meat loaf, which was a mistake. She'd spent a large proportion of the morning on the floor of her beautiful porcelain bathroom, either vomiting into the lavatory pan or wiping the splashes off the tiles. She'd drunk a quantity of water to rehydrate, but it hadn't improved the way she felt. She kept the shutters closed and lighting low to protect her from the savagery of the day.

Nicolo had promised to come home and check on her if he had a break between operations. 'A half-hour house-call,' he'd said. 'I could spare the time for that.'

When the phone rang, Carlotta assumed it was him. She picked up the receiver and said with a gasp, '*Pronto.*'

The caller was Flavia, one of her sales assistants. Carlotta gasped again, to emphasise her indisposition. 'I hope there aren't any problems?' she said. 'You're coping, yes?'

'Oh, yes,' said Flavia, 'everything's fine, but there's a customer here... Well, she's not really a customer, but an English girl who says she's been looking for you. She's quite agitated about it. Do you want to speak to her?'

The pit of Carlotta's stomach dipped and heaved. She laid down the phone and held a damp linen tea towel to her forehead. It didn't help. Flavia's voice was still babbling; Carlotta restored the handset to her ear and said, 'I'm sorry?'

'*Madonna mia,*' said Flavia. 'You sound terrible. Would you rather I passed on a message?'

No, she thought. I will regret it forever if we don't talk. 'Put her on,' she said.

'Carlotta? Is that you?' The voice was unfamiliar; how could it be otherwise? In Roccamare, she'd been ten years old – younger than Luca; she'd had the high eager tones of a child, full of charm and innocence and wonder. In London, that hopeless botched encounter, they'd barely spoken. Now she was a woman. 'This is Lily McKenzie. You didn't get my letter, did you?'

'Yes, actually I did, a few days ago, but it was too late for me to reply. It came from my old apartment.'

'Miss or Mr Gordone lives there now,' said Lily. 'But no one was in.'

'*Dio mio*, you went there!'

'Where else would I go? It was the only address I had. Then the woman in the luggage shop gave me your new card. That's how I got here.'

'You wished to find me?'

'Yeah, that's why I wrote. I'm glad you got the letter anyway. I hope it wasn't too much of a shock, to hear from me, I mean…'

Carlotta wrapped the telephone cord tightly around her arm as if this might stabilise her and stop her guts lurching. 'I am sorry to be unwell. I should have been at work today…'

'They're about to close for lunch,' said Lily.

'How much longer are you staying in Rome? It's possible I will be better tomorrow.' She was furious about the meat loaf. She would complain to the *tavola calda*. In future she would boycott them.

'I'm booked on a flight that leaves this evening,' said Lily.

'Oh, no, so soon!'

'I could stay on longer if...'

There was a gap in which nothing was said, in which Carlotta could hear the background twitter of shoppers and the ring of the till. She dabbed her face with the tea towel again and said, 'I think maybe you should come here now, but you must understand I am not at my best. Do you have the money for a taxi? Flavia will call you one and she will give you the address of my new apartment.'

She replaced the receiver and hoisted herself out of her chair. She'd been wrapped in her dressing gown all morning and it had taken on a nasty sickly smell. It was essential to keep up appearances, especially for a meeting as momentous as this – though the timing of it was cruel. In front of the bedroom mirror she brushed her hair vigorously, but it refused to shine. She applied her make-up with hands that were less steady than normal. She couldn't use perfume: the slightest whiff revived her nausea. She ate two dry crackers and a handful of grapes, on the basis that it was preferable to have something in her stomach than nothing. She sipped some more water. She dressed in a loose cotton shift so there'd be no restriction at her waist. Her entire body was so sensitive she decided against wearing shoes.

When the bell rang, she padded barefoot to the entry phone to buzz her caller in.

Were they disappointed in each other? What did they expect to see? Carlotta saw a young woman bronzed by the sun, her messy dark hair tied back in a scarf. The canvas bag that she dropped on the floor had left a red welt on her shoulder. Her trainers were discoloured and a knot was coming loose. She looked poor and down on her luck, like a hobo. Carlotta had been much the same age when she went to America. She remembered how carefully she had chosen her outfits, how essential it had been to present herself as a person with prospects. Not one who was running away.

Lily had caught her unawares, at a low and vulnerable ebb. She dreaded to think what she might look like: ageing and fading, with sallow skin and tired lines around her eyes. They stared face to face for a long silent moment. Then Carlotta felt her stomach heave. She covered her mouth and rushed to the bathroom. She shouldn't have eaten the crackers and the grapes. She knelt on the floor with her forehead pressed against the cold tiles, seeking relief. She brushed her teeth with copious amounts of toothpaste, although the mint couldn't mask the taste of bile. When she emerged, Lily was still rooted, aghast, in the hallway.

'Gosh,' she said. 'I shouldn't have bothered you...'

'It's not your fault,' said Carlotta. She managed a faint smile. 'On our excursion there was also vomiting, *non è vero*? But it was your brother.'

The atmosphere lightened a little. 'Yes, poor Harry... You know, he hasn't been fishing since. He goes canoeing though, so it didn't completely put him off boats.'

'I did not think I would ever hear from you.'

'I'm sorry...'

'Please,' said Carlotta. 'Come to sit down.' She yearned to reach out and stroke Lily's cheek, plump with youth and soft and smooth as a nectarine. But she was scared to touch her because of the way her own body was behaving, as if it belonged to somebody else.

They went into the *salone*, where the upholstery matched and the flowers were fresh, not plastic. Carlotta had aimed to create a room that could feature in a magazine; it would contain nothing tawdry or vulgar, nothing of poor taste that would make Nicolo think less of her. But Lily took no notice of her surroundings, not even of the framed photographs that would have given her some hint of Carlotta's new life. She sat on the very edge of her seat, her hands resting on her bare knees, her gaze intense. The thrust of her chin, that small determined point, Carlotta recognised as her own. And then there were her eyebrows... After leaving Santa Margherita, Carlotta had plucked hers into fine arcs and maintained them ever since. Lily's were thicker, straighter, like Francesco's... At which her stomach flipped again. She compressed her lips and gripped the arms of her chair and the sensation passed.

'Would you like something to eat or to drink?'

'Are you having anything?'

Carlotta grimaced. 'My stomach won't let me.'

'Then I'll be fine, really.'

A glass fruit bowl held white-fleshed peaches and the remaining grapes. She saw Lily glance at it hungrily. 'Please, you must have a peach. They need to be eaten.'

'Okay, thanks. I will.'

Carlotta watched her visitor bite into the peach, the sudden spurt of juice. She watched her lick her fingers clean with the tip of her tongue like a cat. Watching was easier than speaking, but she had to make the effort. 'It is a pity you have to travel to England tonight. That there is so little time.'

Lily put the peach stone down on the table and leaned forward, her eyes brightening. 'Oh, I don't *have* to. I mean, the other students are but I've sorted it with the gang-master. I could stay on longer. I've nothing special to get back for and I've money left over from my twenty-first so I can afford to buy a ticket for another flight.'

Lily's expression was transparent; she had nothing to hide. It was clear she hoped for an invitation to stay and it was clear to Carlotta that she couldn't offer one. Where could she put her? If she slept with Lily in her bed, Nicolo would have to share with Luca and it was too much to spring on the pair of them at short notice.

Too much explaining was required. If only she'd been frank with Nicolo earlier, instead of procrastinating. If only she'd still been in her old apartment: one bed and half a bath were not much, but Lily might find it quaint. She imagined her ensconced there while they got to know each other. If only she weren't feeling so ill. If only...

'The thing is,' Lily was saying, 'I sort of need to know for sure.'

'Know what?'

'Whether we're actually related.'

'Whether we're *what?*' She didn't mean to sound hysterical, but hysteria was building inside her, coming out in a harridan's screech.

'It's not like I've got anything to go on,' said Lily. 'Documentary evidence, I mean. Even if I could search parish records or another kind of database, it wouldn't prove who *I* am. And you can't say that just looking like another person is enough. Loads of people look like someone else. Don't get me wrong, I'd *like* to be related to you and I'd like us to spend time together. Become closer. After all, we both come from the same town, we have that much in common. But apparently there's a test you can do now.'

'A test?' Carlotta hadn't had a shred of doubt since the day Lily had undressed on the beach. She wanted to ask: what happened to your navel, Lily? Does it still stick out a little bit? Have you got used to it yet?

But Lily was rambling on about how they would have to have blood samples taken and Carlotta pictured one of Nicolo's colleagues at San Camillo wielding a threatening hypodermic syringe, agog with curiosity. And she didn't know if she could handle it. After all, *she* had all the certainty she needed.

'Is this necessary?' she said. 'I don't think it will make any difference.'

'It will make all the difference!'

'I'm too weak,' said Carlotta, conscious of the shadows beneath her eyes.

'I didn't mean today! I don't want to rush you. It's not urgent. But I feel I'm stumbling about in the dark sometimes. There are things I want to get straight. For example, the date of my birthday... the nuns gave me fourteenth April, but that's not right, is it?'

'My baby,' said Carlotta, 'was born on seventeenth March.'

'I knew it! Oh, my God, I'm a whole month older.'

A neighbour called to another across the courtyard. In the street horns blared and brakes screeched. A shaft of sunlight entered the room through a gap in the shutters and jabbed Carlotta in the eye. English was eluding her and the words did not come out as she intended. 'If you believe you are the same baby,' she said.

Lily jumped up, her body writhing as if she'd been bitten by a snake. 'What do you mean? Why are you playing games with me?'

'I'm not playing games,' said Carlotta, pressing the heel of her palm to her forehead, turning away from the light. 'The doubts are yours, Lily. It seems that nothing I can do will make them disappear.'

Lily didn't sit down again; she strode in a restless diagonal course from wall to window to wall. 'I've done this all wrong,' she said, woebegone. 'Everything's backfired. It's a normal human need to want to know where you've come from. Where you might belong. Who you are. Basic information like that. I realise it's not easy to form a relationship with someone you've hardly met, but you were keen enough to come after me before.'

'Yes,' said Carlotta. 'However, I was forbidden to see or speak to you.'

'Did you know there was a really messy fallout? That it was partly because of you that my parents split?'

'Because of me?' She was startled. The McKenzies had seemed unassailable, a picture-book couple. How could she have had any influence over them? 'I'm sorry to hear that. But your father didn't keep his word to me. That's why I had given up hope of seeing you again.'

'I'm here now, aren't I? I don't understand what the problem is.' She was frowning, perplexed, a little girl again. 'Is it all too harrowing? We don't have to draw it out. I just want to know the truth and I thought you would as well. I'm not asking you to care about me or have anything to do with me afterwards... Oh-h-h... I see!'

She had paused by the shelving unit that displayed books, videos, some Murano glass and framed photographs, mostly of Luca when he was younger: gathering sea urchins at the beach; fooling around at a country picnic; wielding a tennis racquet triumphantly above his head. And then another of Nicolo and Carlotta with Luca between them, holding their hands and grinning at the camera. Lily didn't pick up any of these photos to examine them more closely but the colour drained from her face.

'You must not think—' Carlotta began, but didn't finish her sentence. The sounds and squawks, both inside and outside the building, had diminished and the click of Nicolo's key in the lock was distinctly audible. He was doing what he'd said he would do: dropping home to see how she was.

'A good sign,' he said, as he entered. 'You're dressed.'

Lily was still hovering in the corner by the shelves. He might have felt the presence of another person before he spotted her. He must have wondered why a stranger was visiting his sick *fidanzata*. She came forward nervously, her hands curling and uncurling at her sides as if she didn't know what to do with them.

Carlotta tried to keep the anguish from her voice. 'Nico, this is Lily McKenzie. She is the daughter of an English acquaintance I haven't seen for many years. She's been visiting Rome but, unfortunately, she has to fly home tonight.' It didn't matter if Lily understood what she was saying because she wasn't dissembling; it was all true.

'*Piacere,*' said Nicolo, though she could tell he was perplexed from the way he scratched the back of his neck. 'I wish you a good trip.'

'Don't worry,' said Lily. 'I'm going.' She seized her bag and swung it over her shoulder. Carlotta tried to put her arm around her, to escort her to the door, but Lily stalked ahead.

In English, Carlotta said, 'I have wanted to see you so much, but not like this. This is not a good day for me.'

'Nor for me,' said Lily, quivering with indignation.

'But now you know my new address so, please, we must correspond. And next time...'

'Do you really think there will be another time?'

It must have given Lily satisfaction to pull the door so hard behind her that the walls of the apartment reverberated, but Carlotta felt as if all the breath had been sucked from her body. She'd not even had the chance to shake hands or proffer a fleeting kiss on the cheek. This was an encounter she'd waited years for – and they hadn't once touched each other.

27

Lily stood in the corridor with her forehead pressed against the window. The train was rumbling through the poorer suburbs of Rome and a tangle of overhead pylons. In the deepening dusk the street lamps came on, customers spilled out of sleazy bars into the hot night. In scruffy apartment blocks she caught lighted glimpses of families eating dinner, children going to bed, the flash of a television screen. She could see now, clear-eyed and merciless, how foolish she had been. Why hadn't it occurred to her that Carlotta might reject her? That she'd have another family and no interest in her old one? If Lily hadn't tracked her down, the lost opportunity would have been frustrating, but it wouldn't – *couldn't* – have been more painful. And all she'd wanted to know, for thoroughly valid reasons, was who the fuck she *was*!

The rhythm of the train and the sway of the carriage along the track were soothing. Maybe that knowledge wasn't as important as she'd thought. Maybe what was important was who she was *going* to be. In the future. Carlotta-who-used-to-be-Concetta   Galetti,   had renounced her own beginnings, hadn't she? What mattered was not yesterday, but today. And tomorrow.

Lily had calmed down since leaving Carlotta's apartment. At the time she'd been in such a state of fury and confusion she'd stomped off in completely the wrong direction. Lost and bewildered, she'd been saved by a *tavola calda*. She'd ordered a slice of pizza and, unfolding her map yet again, asked for directions. Then she'd sat on the bus, stalled by traffic, trying to drown out her misery with her Sony Walkman. The taste of the greasy pizza wedge had lingered on her tongue and in her throat, salty like teardrops.

When she arrived at the hotel she found she'd missed the group's airport transfer by less than ten minutes. The desk clerk commiserated, and encouraged her to take the express train to Fiumicino. Stazione Termini was a seething hive, swarming with people, but, apart from the begging children with cardboard labels around their necks, nobody took any notice of Lily. She searched the departures board and was mesmerised by the range of destinations. There were tempting foreign cities like Paris, Vienna and Sarajevo, as well as those criss-crossing the length and breadth of Italy: Milan and Bologna, Ancona and Naples, Bari and Palermo.

A shiver danced up and down her spine. Palermo was in Sicily. It was where they'd flown when they'd gone on holiday to Villa Ercole. The convent of Beata Vergine Maria was also in Sicily. And the towns of Santa

Margherita and Roccamare. Carlotta wasn't the only person with information about her origins.

She joined one of the interminable queues for a ticket booth, but she was no longer in any hurry. In fact, there were hours to kill before departure, which she spent grazing and browsing. The ticket for the sleeper had saved her the cost of a hotel and when she returned to board the train she felt no trepidation. Quite the opposite. The long string of carriages loomed high above the platform, with steep steps up to their doors. The windows were smeared with dust and the corpses of tiny flying insects. The bodywork was dun-coloured, like the parched southern countryside. The train wasn't elegant or streamlined. She knew it would rattle and clunk and the upholstery would be worn and there'd be no air-conditioning. Yet Lily considered it the most exciting piece of apparatus she'd ever seen, taking her on a quixotic leap into the unknown.

She traipsed along the platform searching for her couchette until her progress was blocked by a group of young men. Half of them were wearing the khaki uniforms of military service. The others were casually dressed. The two factions seemed to be arguing, though Lily couldn't tell what their quarrel was about. She muttered, 'Scusi,' and tried to forge her way through. The men weren't physically fighting, but there was a strong undercurrent of aggression, a resounding number of 'vaffanculo's and the smell of alcohol. Not so

318

different from Salisbury, she thought, when the squaddies had a night's leave.

They were jostling each other and she became caught in the fray, in the wrong place at the wrong time. But she was wearing stout footwear; she had sharp elbows and well-developed muscles. There was a brief outburst of wolf-whistles – admiring or insulting, she couldn't tell which – and she held her head high and ignored them. Then, as she was leaving the trouble-makers behind, the strap of her back-pack snagged on someone else's and crashed to the ground, spattering its contents. She lunged towards it protectively. You could never tell whether it might get robbed or used as a football. That used to happen frequently at school and although these boys were older, around her age, their behaviour was equally juvenile.

In fact, the fallen bag broke the tension. The soldiers discharged a volley of raucous comments, probably lewd, linked arms and wandered off. Three of the youths in civilian clothes helped to scoop up her possessions and hand them back. Lily stuffed them into her rucksack, keeping her head down, muttering thank yous. It was a minor incident and she didn't want to see it as an omen of any kind.

The train was now rolling through fields that were empty and dark; the scattering of lights in the hills were out-dazzled by the stars in a clear night sky. In the compartment behind her, her fellow occupants – a quiet couple with a young son and a pair of middle-aged women, one of whom was enormously fat and continually fanning herself – were discussing the sleeping arrangements, who would take which berth. The fat lady declared she couldn't possibly climb to an upper bunk. She roared at the idea; she had to be at the bottom. She fanned her chins with giggles and gales of laughter. Sleep was still far off for Lily so she'd escaped into the corridor.

A young man was approaching from the end of the carriage, and something oddly familiar struck her about his gait and, as he came closer, his intense blue eyes. He had sleek black hair and teeth that were white and even when he smiled. She stood back to give him room to pass, but he didn't. He stopped. Then she realised he was one of the guys who'd rescued her stuff, the one who'd handed over her Walkman and her passport – imagine if that had gone missing! She should thank him again.

But he spoke before she did, saying softly, '*Ancora cammina sulle mani*, Lily McKenzie?'

Do you still walk on your hands? She understood the words instinctively. She didn't even need to translate them in her head. She turned to face him properly. No wonder those blue eyes had seemed familiar. 'Oh, my God! Marcello Campione! It's you, it's really you!'

'*Ciao*, Lily.'

'How on earth... I mean, how did you know it was me?'

He grinned more widely. 'I saw the name on your passport. The date of birth...'

Neither could be expected to recognise the other as a stranger on a railway platform, but once you knew, once you looked closely, the ten-year-old was still there, in them both. He was taller than she was now, suave and clean-shaven. She felt dirty and bedraggled in comparison.

'Well,' he said. 'Can you?'

'Walk on my hands? I don't know. I haven't tried it for ages.'

Those languorous summer holidays, the innocent beach games of her childhood, the freedom of Villa Ercole: the memories welled up inside her and trickled down her cheeks as tears.

Marcello flattened himself, as she had done, as another passenger went past and said curiously, 'Why are you crying?'

'I'm sorry. I'm tired and emotional, I guess. It's been a difficult day but, believe me, it's wonderful to see you again!'

He glanced into her compartment. The fat woman had opened up a cool box and was handing around snacks. Together with the box and her travelling companion she took up a lot of space. 'Come with me,' he said. 'We have a couchette for six, but there are only three of us. If no one joins at Naples, there is plenty of room to share.'

Lily grabbed her bag and followed him, delighted by this change in circumstance. Marcello Campione, who'd have thought it? And he had come to her aid – for a second time. 'Do you remember,' she said, as they lurched along the corridor, 'at Ferragosto when I picked up a prickly pear and you pulled all the spines out of my palm with your teeth?'

His shoulders jerked upwards in a gesture of disbelief. 'No!'

'What about when you came to Villa Ercole on your bike and I got a puncture?'

He nodded. 'That, I remember. It was the last time I saw you.'

His two friends, sprawling across the leatherette seats, she also recognised from the platform scuffle. When she entered, they swung their feet to the floor and rose to shake hands with courteous formality. He introduced them as Fabio and Gilberto, fellow students. Fabio was slight and dapper with a neatly trimmed beard. Gilberto had a chubby face and round glasses; he asked, with some concern, if she was all right.

'I'm fine,' said Lily. 'But those soldiers...' (who must be somewhere along the length of the train) 'Did you know them or something?'

'We never met them before.'

'So why did they have it in for you?

Marcello said, 'There's often bad feeling between the guys who are obliged to do military service and those who escape it. That's why they try to needle us. They want to force us into a fight because they reckon they'll win. It's part showing off, part jealousy.'

'Isn't everyone supposed to do military service in Italy?'

'Everyone is supposed to pay taxes in Italy too,' said Gilberto and the three of them laughed uproariously.

'It depends on your situation,' said Marcello. 'But there are ways to avoid it. You might have a medical condition or be the family breadwinner. Or if you're a student you can defer it.'

'What are you studying? Not English? You speak it really well.'

'Civil engineering. But I spent most of last year working on a project in Malawi. The others came from so many different countries we had to use English as our common language. My accent is okay?'

'Yeah, brilliant!'

Gilberto and Fabio were less fluent. They preferred to stick to Italian, but Lily was pleased to find that she could follow much of what they said. And join in. They had with them a bottle of grappa *alla ruta* which they poured out into paper cups and which helped to loosen her tongue. The atmosphere was festive. They had finished their exams and the summer lay ahead. First they were going to help Marcello's cousins with the tomato harvest and then, in August, they would go to the beach for idle days of soaking up the sun.

Around midnight the train stopped at Naples, but no new passenger interrupted their party. They opened the window to let out the blue fug of cigarette smoke and as the train sped south through the sultry night, Lily felt a transformation taking place. She was relaxing, becoming garrulous and impulsive: she was turning back into a Sicilian! At two o'clock they agreed they should try to snaffle a few hours' sleep before the sea crossing. Marcello and Lily lay across from each other on the lower bunks. She expected to stay awake because her mind was teeming, but the rolling motion of the wheels lulled her into a doze.

She was roused by a cacophony of noise, of clanking and grinding and whistling and a bellow of instructions. Marcello was bending over her. 'You must see this, Lily,' he said.

'Why, where are we?'

'They're putting us on the ferry.'

'The whole train?'

'*Certo*. Come on deck and you can watch the sun rise over Sicily. It is very beautiful.'

This was an understatement. Lily had slept in her clothes; she only had to put on her trainers to leave the carriage and go up to the deck of the ferry, to see Messina rising out of the sea ahead of them, pearly pink and glittering in the new dawn. She fumbled for her camera and angled the lens. She had four or five frames left on her film and didn't know how well she could capture this moment of arrival. But even if the photos were rubbish, simply looking at them could reignite a thrill. She was coming home.

Sadly, Messina at close quarters lacked the miraculous quality of Messina as mirage. The town had been devastated by an earthquake a hundred times worse than Belice, one that killed tens of thousands of inhabitants, and it had been completely rebuilt. It was a port where people passed through and seldom lingered.

'You're not getting off here?' said Marcello, as the ferry manoeuvred into the harbour, lining itself up with the train tracks on dry land.

'No, my ticket's to Palermo.'

'Then you must stay with us.' Gilberto and Fabio nodded in agreement. 'The train will divide for Catania and Siracusa and you don't want to get stuck in the wrong carriage.'

Lily could think of nothing she wanted more than to keep to company she trusted.

'And after we arrive in Palermo, are you going to Villa Ercole again?'

This was the point where her ideas ran out; being hungover and short of sleep didn't help either. 'I haven't made up my mind. They're not expecting me. Actually, I jumped onto this train because...' no, it was too difficult to explain '... because I wanted an adventure.'

'*Brava!*' said Gilberto.

Lily said, 'Do you think your cousins could do with an extra pair of hands to help pick their tomato crop?' When Marcello hesitated, she added quickly, 'I wouldn't be a liability. I know what to do. I've worked for market gardeners in England and I've been studying horticulture. That's why I came to Italy in the first place, to visit famous gardens, but it would be great to get experience of a farm here too. Have you done it before?'

She hoped this might be her trump card, but Marcello said, 'Every summer since I was fourteen.' He flapped a hand in his friends' direction. 'Not these two, *però*. For them it's their second year.'

This was more promising. 'Bed, board and pocket money,' said Lily, recalling the annexe at Villa Ercole, which had been used by seasonal farm workers before Gerald turned it into a holiday let, 'is all I'd want. Is that what you get?'

The boys exchanged glances, nodded. Marcello said, '*Va bene, perchè non?*'

Why not indeed? 'I won't outstay my welcome. But for a few days while I get my bearings… it would be… *favoloso.*'

Things were most definitely looking up. There was just enough time between their arrival at Palermo station and the departure of their bus to Castelvetrano for Lily to buy a postcard, a gaudy montage of tourist sights, and a stamp. She addressed it to Jess (she didn't know where Alex was) and scribbled on the back:

Guess where I am!!!!

28

The original Campione estate had been divided, a generation previously, between two brothers. One owned the olive grove where they celebrated Ferragosto every year; the other had taken on the tomato farm. The Pomodoro Campiones, as Lily thought of them, lived in an old stone farmhouse surrounded by long rows of tomato vines, like a spider in the centre of a web. Here the produce wasn't grown in the polytunnels that were beginning to proliferate in other regions, but cultivated in the traditional way. All the fruit would explode into maturity within the space of a few weeks, hence the urgent, demanding nature of the work. Prime beef tomatoes would go to market, the plum varieties would be sent off for canning, with a proportion kept back for the household, to be bottled into sauce or turned into *strattu*, a luscious thick paste spread onto trays and left to dry in the sun.

When Lily showed up, her hosts were boisterous and welcoming but uncertain what to do with her. The house was occupied by Marcello's cousin, Alfredo, his wife, Daniela, and their one-year-old twins, his parents, who still ran the farm, and an elderly, deaf uncle. The senior Signora Campione was reluctant to let Lily sleep in the barn with the boys (and other random helpers drafted in for the duration); it wouldn't be appropriate. She had to find her a bed in the main house. A small store in the cellar might be suitable, once the boxes had been cleared away to make room for a mattress.

'Please don't go to this trouble for me,' begged Lily.

'There is no window,' said Signora Campione. 'But you will be cool. And you won't be affected by bats.'

'Bats!' She'd been scared of the bats on Favignana and, in the years since, they were still the wildlife she found most threatening, though she couldn't explain why. She didn't plead to be allowed to sleep in the barn after that. However, she did resist the assumption that she would be involved in the cooking: skinning and pulping the fruits, stirring them in the huge copper pans until the mass reached the right consistency. Lily had watched Dolly at these activities and she knew she'd rather be outdoors, however heavy the labour or fierce the sun. She could wear a hat, couldn't she?

'Oh, do let me work outside,' she said. 'I've done lots of gardening and pruning and fruit-picking, but I'm absolutely no good at cooking.'

'You say you are Sicilian,' said Signora Campione. 'But you do not know how to cook!'

'I expect it's because I grew up in England,' she said, reaching for the convenient excuse. Alex's interest in

329

food had been minimal and Jess's was erratic. She and Harry often had to fend for themselves.

'Then we must teach you!'

Lily was saved by Gilberto. With great charm, he explained that, if possible, he would prefer to stay indoors with the two *signoras*. His skin was fair and inclined to burn and he *loved* to cook. They swapped places.

The working days were long. They rose early, before it got too hot, and took a midday siesta. Those were the times Lily felt the most isolated. Alone in her dungeon, with only her Walkman to listen to, she pictured the boys carousing in the barn, propped against the pillows, blowing smoke rings into the rafters, no fear of bats. But then she'd fall asleep with fatigue and Marcello would have to thump on her door to rouse her for the afternoon session.

As she threaded her way along the vines, she liked to imagine a kinship with her ancestors. Most of them would have been agricultural labourers, employed much as she was now, snipping the bunches of tomatoes systematically from the bottom to the top (because the lower fruit ripened first), cradling them carefully into their baskets, emptying them regularly into crates. The only difference would have been the use of donkey and cart rather than the flat-bed truck Alfredo drove.

The repetitive nature of physical activity helped to calm her mind. And on Sunday, Marcello had suggested, they might go to the beach. A return to Roccamare was a treat to look forward to. They could take a picnic of bread and salami, along with a basket of big salad tomatoes that they would munch like apples, dipping them in olive oil and salt to bring out the flavour. And perhaps, after lunch, Lily could stroll up through the scrubland to Villa Ercole, a casual visit, to see if anyone was at home.

The weather was hot and dry – good for the *strattu* – and the first few evenings, after showering off the dust of the day, they all gathered around the trestle table in the yard: Marcello, Fabio, Gilberto and Lily, the twin babies on their parents' knees, Alfredo's father at one end of the table and his deaf uncle at the other. Signora Campione brought out great bowls of pasta and carafes of wine from the neighbouring *azienda*. After the meal, the *signora* and her daughter-in-law took the babies to bed and the men and Lily played cards by candlelight until the symbols blurred before their eyes and they lost their concentration. The old uncle nearly always won.

On the evening of their fourth day, a Thursday, Lily was helping to set out the dishes. The boys sauntered over from the barn, later than usual. It took a few moments for her to work out what was different about them. Fabio, ever the elegant dresser, was wearing a pair of spotless white trousers and a blue shirt in the softest cotton. Marcello's tee shirt had a discreet Armani label, his tasselled leather loafers were brand new. Gilberto had slicked gel onto his hair, which tended to curl, and was doused in a pungent aftershave. 'Why are you all so smart?' she said.

'We're going out after supper.'

'Where?'

It was a nightclub, they said, an unofficial one on the outskirts of town, in defiance of the authorities, populated by word of mouth.

'You mean it's like a rave?' said Lily. 'We have the same sort of thing at home. In old warehouses or places in the middle of nowhere that have been abandoned.' She and her friends would cram into a convoy of cars, follow a muddle of directions and pursue the blast of the music until their ears were popping.

Alfredo and Daniela appeared, gleaming and polished as silver plate. It turned out they were going too, leaving the babies with their *nonna*.

'Am I invited?' said Lily, trying not to sound peeved. 'Will there be dancing?'

Marcello shuffled a two-step in his smart loafers, clicked his fingers.

Signora Campione said, 'They are teasing you, Liliana. Of course they won't leave you behind.'

'Of course not,' echoed Marcello. 'You can change after we eat.'

Change? That was awkward. Lily had been living in shorts. She had a pair of jeans with her, too heavy for the heat, and a couple of dresses. One, a sundress, had a

332

rip at the side seam, the other was comfortable but unflattering. It hadn't seemed so in England, where women wore broad-shouldered dresses that swamped their bodies. But in Italy clothes were shapely; girls flaunted their breasts and hips, they wore high heels to tauten their calves. They wanted you to know they weren't matrons yet. Even Alfredo's wife, despite the twins, had a neatly defined waist.

'I haven't got anything suitable to change into. I was on an educational trip. I wasn't expecting a night-life.'

'You must have something you can wear,' said Marcello. 'I can help you choose.'

'It's okay. I'll manage.'

There wasn't time to mend the sundress so she put on the baggy frock and added a belt, which helped a little. They piled into the farm Land Rover; Alfredo drove. The nightclub had made a home for itself in an old cinema. Layers of tattered film posters were pasted onto its outer walls, too faded to be legible; inside all the seats were gone. The makeshift bar was on a raised platform, framed with a flourish by rotting silk curtains. A light show was being projected onto the screen behind it. The turntables were also in the projection room, the music bubbling from speakers around the walls. But best of all, in Lily's view, the roof of the cinema had been cranked open to let in the air. If she craned her neck and looked up, the constellation of stars was more magnificent than any light show.

Word of mouth was effective: the place was full. It operated from Thursdays to Sundays and no one knew how long it might stay open, so the clubbers were out to enjoy themselves. The Campione party arrived in the middle of a slew of disco hits. Lily whirled herself onto the dance floor to Madonna's 'Causing a Commotion', expecting the others to follow. At first she didn't notice that they hadn't; she was too busy imbibing the music and the drama of the night sky, her head thrown back, feet spinning and arms pumping. Then, as the DJ changed records and she refocussed her gaze, she realised she was the only person dancing alone. This wasn't the free-form free-for-all she was used to in England, where you let your hair down and everyone participated in the rave. Here you were expected to have a partner. She was standing out as a frumpy foreigner and she felt humiliated.

The boys were at the bar watching her. She re-joined them, chastened – and annoyed they hadn't stopped her making a fool of herself. Why was Marcello holding back? Why couldn't he have cut loose and danced with her? Why was it so important for him to preserve his *bella figura*?

'Would you like a drink now?' he said.

'A beer would be great, thanks,' she said stiffly, because she was proud too, and equally determined to keep her dignity.

She sipped her beer and leant against the flaking wall, not caring about the distemper rubbing off onto her shoulders, surrounded by confident vivacious young people transmitting signals she couldn't interpret. At one point Marcello did – almost as an afterthought – lead her onto the dance floor. But when they were halfway through a second number another boy tapped his shoulder and he gave her up, in her view far too readily. She saw him return to the side-lines, to joshing with Fabio and Gilberto; attractive girls with hourglass figures were soon fluttering around them.

Lily couldn't compete. She became convinced Marcello hadn't really wanted her to come. She'd embarrassed him at the start and now she was cramping his style and naturally he'd rather play the field with his friends. So she stayed in the orbit of Alfredo and Daniela and, in spite of the fact that she loved to dance, she made excuses to potential partners: her legs ached, she wasn't wearing suitable shoes, she preferred to watch. She retreated to the edge of conversations, nodding agreement even when she couldn't hear what was being said, absorbing the spectacle and trying to wish away her bitter sense of disappointment. The evening, which should have been so much fun, dragged.

On the way home in the car Marcello observed, to her frustration, 'You looked bored, Lily. I'm sorry you didn't have a good time.'

'Oh, but I did… I was a bit tired, that's all.'

'You didn't dance much.'

She wanted to yell: Whose fault is that? Why did you act as if you were ashamed to be seen with me? Instead, she muttered, 'I don't know, I suppose I felt stupid in this dress, out-of-place, whatever…'

He let the subject drop until they were back at the farmhouse. In the dark, by the door, when the others had gone inside, he rested his hands on her shoulders and said, 'Tomorrow we will go shopping. I will help you to buy a new dress.'

'Oh,' she said. 'Really? But we'd have to take the morning off.'

'I think we have earned it. Everyone will be sleeping late.' Then he leaned forward and kissed her – only once, but lingeringly.

How long does it take to interpret a kiss? Throughout what remained of the night Lily would snap awake remembering the pressure of his lips. Was it an apology for neglecting her that evening? Was it any different from the kiss she had given him in the olive grove a decade earlier? Were they just good friends or was this the start of something new? For the past year or so, she had dated casually. It seemed a long time since she'd had romantic feelings for anyone. Was she drawn to Marcello simply by nostalgia? Oh, come on, Lily McKenzie! she told herself. How can you possibly confuse a kids' friendship with fancying the pants off someone?

Nobody woke her in the morning. When she staggered into the kitchen, where a large portrait of Pope John Paul II presided over the table, Marcello was there already drinking coffee. He didn't greet her any differently, nor did anyone else. But once she too was sipping an espresso, he said to Signora Campione, 'Can I borrow the car to take Lily into town this morning? She wants to go shopping and I don't trust her to do it on her own.'

Gilberto sniggered. Signora Campione said, 'Yes, certainly.'

Lily said, 'I'm not totally incompetent.'

Marcello said, 'Ah, but I'll get you a good deal. There will be sales, too.'

He was treating her as a sister again. She could handle that. She would play it cool, pretend she was shopping with Harry. They took the Fiat Cinquecento that was used for running errands. Marcello was in charge. He led the way into boutiques that had 'SALDI' scrawled across their windows; he pulled the hangers off the rails and held the frocks in front of her for size; he engaged in animated discussion with the assistants (something Harry was unlikely to do). In the first shop nothing appealed to him so she didn't make it into the fitting room. In the second, she tried on a couple of dresses he found fault with and another that was too expensive, despite his advanced negotiating skills. In the third, he waited outside the cubicle until she'd shimmied her way into a close-fitting linen shift. The fabric wasn't printed with the jazzy patterns of the others she'd tried; it was absolutely plain – and bright orange.

'It's perfect,' said Marcello. 'Is that really you inside? You must buy it.'

That wasn't what Harry would say. She could hear him now: 'Fucking hell, Lily, you look like an Orange Maid!'

She said to Marcello, 'You don't think I look like an ice lolly, do you?'

'*Cosa?* Don't be silly!' He steered her closer to the mirror and, without asking, tugged off the scrunchie keeping back her hair, so that it tumbled onto her shoulders.

Oh, God, she thought. I really do look like Carlotta now. She felt a sudden stab in her chest.

Marcello began discussing the price with the sales girl. She offered to include a wide, cinching belt in the purchase to enhance the signorina's figure. Lily wasn't allowed to object; the process had moved beyond her control. Marcello came back to her in triumph. She stood passively as he unzipped the dress so she could slip out of it; she didn't want him to see how the frisson of his touch disarmed her.

Five minutes later, at the counter, the assistant was wrapping the shift in tissue paper. Lily ruffled through the lire in her wallet. 'I haven't got enough money,' she said.

'I can lend you the difference,' said Marcello.

'I'd forgotten I'd bought the train ticket. I don't want to run out of cash.'

'There's a bank on the corner.'

The girl didn't want to lose a sale. 'If you go there right away,' she said, 'I will have this ready for you to collect before we close for lunch.'

'Do you think there's time?' She had queued to draw out cash from a bank a week earlier, in Florence. She knew how tortuous the procedure was.

'You have plenty of time,' said Marcello; he wasn't going to let her backtrack. 'The dress is yours and it will wait for you.'

The bank was a few hundred metres away, a short hop down the street. Marcello took her arm as they walked. There was a bounce in his step and she felt as if she'd grown an extra couple of inches. When they reached the entrance, he bent to murmur: 'You looked very fine in the dress, but all I really wanted to do was take it off.'

'Oh... Marcello!' She flung her arms around his neck and pressed herself so close she could feel the pound of his heart against hers. Then she kissed him passionately, until they were forced to pull apart because they were obstructing passers-by. 'Can we go to the club again?'

she said. 'Now that I'm kitted out for it? Can we dance together all night, under the stars?'

'All night I shall dance with no one else. *Avanti.*' He gave her a gentle shove up the steps to the bank. They stood together in the queue, radiating the kind of joy that drew admiring glances. When she got to the front she presented her cheque and account details and passport and was told to go and wait in another line for her cash. Marcello was starting to fidget. 'I need more cigarettes,' he murmured. 'Shall I meet you outside when you've finished?'

She nodded and they kissed again. She watched him slip away and spent the next ten minutes fantasising about being together on her cellar mattress, getting to know each other's bodies in the quiet dim space. The feel and the taste and the touch of him. Her childhood companion! Who'd have thought it?

When she reached the second window, the cashier said, 'One moment, please.'

'What's the matter? I'm not overdrawn!' Her current account was unusually healthy, partly with her unspent birthday money.

'Please, if you would stand aside,' said the cashier.

'Why? What's going on?' Beyond the glass she could see a man on the phone, with her unmistakable stiff British passport in his hand.

'*Mi dispiace*, the manager will explain.' The cashier beckoned to the person behind her to come forward and

Lily moved reluctantly away.

She couldn't leave without her passport, but she could enlist Marcello's help. She made for the outer doors, but a security guard stopped her. She began to panic. 'I need my friend!' She could see Marcello on the pavement, a newspaper tucked under his arm, grinding out a cigarette. She tried frantically to catch his attention. If he would only raise his head, look up... He unfolded the paper.

Then she saw a police car skid to a halt and two police officers leap out. They entered the bank at the same time as the man who'd been on the phone came towards Lily, still holding her passport. She held out her hand but he didn't give it to her, passing it instead to one of the policemen. 'But that's mine!' she cried.

The policeman said, 'You will come with us, signorina.'

'But why? What have I done?' Had she broken the law by picking tomatoes without a permit?

The security guard held the door open and the policeman guided her through it. This time Marcello did see her and blanched. 'Lily! Why...?'

'I haven't a clue! I don't know what's going on. Can you ask them?'

The policeman said, *'E con lei, quest'uomo?'* Is this man with you?

She nodded. A group was gathering to watch the scene, women weighed down by their grocery shopping, clerks and mechanics taking their lunch break, children and old men at a loose end. Marcello began arguing with the police, the arguing segued into Sicilian and increased in ferocity until they snapped a pair of handcuffs onto his wrists. The two of them were hustled into the back of the car. Fascinated by the arrest, the crowd pushed closer, conjecturing the depraved crimes this young couple might have committed. The driver got into his seat with a superior smile. He switched on the siren and roared down the street to the *Commissariato*.

29

Jess had shut herself up in her studio because she was working on a tender for a commission. The untrained eye would see a mess and a muddle, but she knew exactly where everything was: her paints, her pencils, her pads, her swatches, her silk and cotton threads, the calico she experimented on, the postcards and pictures she used for inspiration. When she closed the door on the outside world, she could lose herself in the act of creation and not mislay so much as a pencil sharpener.

The commission was for a boutique hotel chain seeking a style more streamlined than the recent fashion for swags and bows and ruching. They didn't want every window to be dressed for ballroom dancing. Jess was keen to move in that direction too. You had to stay ahead of the game and she was satisfied with the clean simplicity of her new design. After a few refinements, she might be ready to send it off.

She'd told Harry not to disturb her. He'd finished his end of year exams and although the summer term wasn't officially over, he was wandering in and out of the cottage at unpredictable hours. She wasn't surprised to find, when she went back indoors, that he'd taken over the sitting room. He was listening to The Smiths – for some reason he *loved* The Smiths – 'Stop Me If You've Heard This One Before' and grinding the joystick of the Commodore console that Alex had bought him. He barely looked up from his orgy of destruction to say, 'There was a phone call from Italy. You missed it.'

'Lily? Did she stay on after all?' Lily had been due back two days ago, but had warned that her plans might change. She was old enough to make her own travel arrangements.

'No,' said Harry. 'It was *for* Lily. It was Carlotta Galetti.'

'Christ! Why didn't you come and get me?'

'Because a) you didn't want to be disturbed,' said Harry. 'And b) she didn't ask to speak to you. She wanted Lily.'

'Did she finally get the letter? And just miss her? What a shame.' Actually she was ambivalent about whether it was a shame. She'd been pretty certain, when no reply had come, that Carlotta had moved on, which might prove to be a blessing in disguise.

'No, she saw her.'

Jess felt uneasy, jittery. 'And?'

After a spurt of gunfire and other sound effects, Harry withdrew his attention from the screen. 'I reckon they had a fallout,' he said. 'Reading between the lines.'

'What lines? What did she say?'

Harry sighed, as if to emphasise how patient and obliging he was. 'She said she was sorry she hadn't been feeling well when Lily visited and she was sorry she had to rush back to England so she couldn't see her again. Could I ask Lily to ring her some time? That was it.'

'Do you know where Lily is?'

'No, do you?'

Lacing and unlacing her fingers, Jess noticed they were stained blue. 'Well, she did mention going to London from Gatwick, to meet up with her friend Becky.' Lily's lifestyle was itinerant. She often took short-term digs, depending on where she was working or what course she was on, though the Whispering Pines was still her base. (And a misnomer since the great storm of last October had brought down both conifers.) 'I expect she'll turn up here in a day or so.'

She left Harry to his game and went to scour her hands under the tap, scrubbing away at the lines of blue in the crevices. She didn't want to overdramatise in front of him or make a meal of the call, but she couldn't shake off her suspicion that Carlotta Galetti was dangerous. How come, after such a long silence, the woman had re-emerged and then claimed she wasn't well? To Jess that sounded a lame excuse. She longed to protect and comfort her daughter, but she wasn't an interfering parent and she presumed, if Lily needed succour, Becky would offer a shoulder to cry on. It would be easy enough to find out. She dried her hands and rang her, but Becky had neither seen nor heard from Lily. 'I hope nothing awful's happened,' she said.

'So do I,' said Jess, swallowing her fear. 'I think it's more likely she's upset about something. Gone to ground to lick her wounds. I'll try the flat.' She knew Alex was away, hunting a story in Romania, but Lily had a key. There was no reply so she left a message on the answer phone, as cheery and casual as she could make it.

In the morning, when there was still no response, she scoured the itinerary Lily had posted on the cork board on the kitchen wall and the list of *pensione* numbers to be contacted if any word came from Carlotta. At the bottom of the sheet were the details of the course tutor, Howard Redding: 'Any last-minute queries, don't hesitate to call me.'

Jess dialled. Howard answered. 'Sorry to bother you now the trip's over,' she said. 'I wanted to ask about Lily McKenzie...'

'Who is this?'

'I'm her mother.'

'How can I help?'

'Well, um, we haven't heard from her since she left and I was wondering...'

'Didn't she tell you she was going to stay on in Rome?'

'I knew she might,' said Jess warily.

'She said she wanted to look up an old family friend, asked if she could change her flight booking. It was against my advice, as a matter of fact. Are you worried about her?'

'Someone was trying to get hold of her, that's all. I wanted to make sure... Thanks anyway.' She put the phone down quickly.

If there was any mystery, she told herself, it had been prompted by Carlotta. *She* was the person who was searching for Lily and wanted her to get in touch. But that didn't explain what Lily was doing, all alone in Italy. Unless she wasn't alone: perhaps she'd made friends with other travellers or been suckered into a holiday romance? She was twenty-one, a free agent. But Jess's mind was not so easily quieted; she couldn't stop it leaping to paranoid conclusions.

She went out to the studio, hoping work would soothe her. Usually she could become totally absorbed in the intricacies of design, in the process of stroking colour onto paper or cloth, but she found it impossible to concentrate. She headed back to the house and was only a few yards away when she heard the trill of the phone. She raced through the door and plucked it from its cradle on the wall. 'Lily?' Though, really, why did she think it was Lily? It could have been anybody.

It was Dinah.

'Jessamy,' she said. 'You haven't forgotten it's Tuesday, have you?'

'Oh, God, so it is!'

'Mother's waiting.'

'I'm sorry, I've been a bit distracted… I'll come right away.'

Two years ago, after their father died, Jess had inherited the cottage, the large family home was sold and their mother moved in with Dinah. It was agreed this was the best solution, because Marjorie's funds could reduce the Winthrops' expenses and help maintain outward appearances despite Johnnie's disastrous financial losses. Dinah was praised by her circle for her self-sacrifice and commitment but in fact she had arranged things the way she wanted them: she was in control of the purse strings. Jess was occasional skivvy and errand girl, but her main responsibility was acting once a week as her mother's secretary. Dinah had appointed her to this role because she had the most legible handwriting.

Jess grabbed the car keys, skidded down the drive and arrived, breathless and apologetic, at her sister's house. Marjorie's sitting room was always overheated; even in summer she kept at least one bar of the electric fire glowing. She had also drawn the curtains to keep the sun out of her eyes. Jess took up her place at the bureau, armed with her favourite Italic nib and a pile of Queens' Velvet notepaper, ready for dictation. Marjorie suffered from arthritis and holding a pen was painful. She regarded handwritten letters as essential; anything less would be bad manners and an insult to the recipient. She might have lived through two world wars but chaos was never allowed to interrupt her routine.

Jess sat in the gloom writing two formal responses to invitations, a letter of complaint and another of condolence. When she had finished, she passed over the letters so her mother could scrawl her signature. Dinah poked her head around the door. 'Come on, stir yourself, Ma,' she said. 'Why don't we sit in the garden? It's a nice enough day.'

'I'd never get out of a deckchair,' said Marjorie.

'And I ought to be going,' said Jess.

'Nonsense,' said Dinah. 'I'll put the kettle on.'

They ended up in the kitchen, drinking weak Earl Grey out of Marjorie's fine china teacups.

'You're very twitchy today, Jess,' said her sister. 'What is it?'

'Oh, I have a deadline to get some work finished. And I want to go home in case Lily's been in touch.'

'How is Lily?' asked Marjorie, as if she'd suddenly recollected her existence.

'Actually, I'm not sure. She didn't come back from Italy with the rest of the group.'

Marjorie had breezed indifferently through her three daughters' lives; she'd been more interested in her dogs. 'You're not worried, are you? She didn't get left behind by mistake?'

'No, it was her choice, apparently.'

'She should have let you know,' said Dinah.

Jess was defensive. 'It's not easy to make long-distance calls when you're abroad. It's expensive too. That's why I'm assuming she's still there. She would have rung if she was back in England. It's just that the person she stayed on to see phoned yesterday to find out where she was.'

'What person?'

'The woman I told you about, the one we think might be her mother. I'm sorry now that we encouraged Lily to contact her.'

Dinah said, 'Your job's done, Jess. The girl's twenty-one. Focus on Harry.'

'That doesn't stop me wanting her to be happy. Why should my hopes for her be any different than yours for Amanda?'

'What I'm hoping for Amanda,' said Dinah, 'is that she makes a better marriage than I did. Or you, for that matter.'

'Alex?' said Jess. 'Why pick on Alex?'

'You threw him out, didn't you?'

'No, we agreed to separate.'

'What's the difference? I can't think why you don't get divorced.'

'Because I've no plans to marry again and we share Harry's parenting. It might be different next year when he's eighteen. Anyway, I could say the same to you.'

Dinah twisted her emerald and diamond engagement ring. 'That's easy,' she said. 'I want his bloody pension.

Johnnie's two years off retirement and I'm not letting him walk away with anything.' Marjorie's cup rattled on its saucer. Dinah added, 'However, while he's still working he can have his uses.' Her expression was unusually coy.

'What are you getting at?'

'It's a bit of a puzzle, isn't it, Lily disappearing in Italy?'

'She hasn't *disappeared*,' protested Jess. 'But I think she's still abroad.'

'She could have been mugged. Or kidnapped for the white slave trade.'

'Are you deliberately trying to wind me up?'

'No,' said Dinah. 'But you can't rule out anything... People have to present their ID when they're staying in continental hotels, don't they?'

'Oh, I hadn't thought of that. I could ring the hotel in Rome where she spent last Friday night. Is that what you mean? In case she stayed on there.'

Dinah said, 'She shouldn't make you wait around on tenterhooks. Johnnie has contacts in the Home Office. I'm sure they could flush her out easily enough.'

'It would be peace of mind for you, Jessamy,' said Marjorie, curling her arthritic fingers around Jess's wrist in sympathy.

'What if she doesn't want to be flushed out?'

'Jess,' said Dinah sternly. 'Stop being so bloody wet.'

Jess rose, pushing her cup aside. 'Okay, then,' she said. 'I'll go and get on with the calls. I'll see you both next week.'

She fled the house with a sense of relief, but it didn't last. She rang the Roman hotel and established that Lily had checked out as expected. Since there was still no answer from the Highbury flat and she couldn't think who else to try, she decided to consult Toby. Their affair had run its course. It never really developed into a full-time commitment and had fizzled out the previous year, but he was still a touchstone.

Unlike Dinah, he advised her not to intervene. The problem with Toby was that his approach to time and motion wasn't the same as most people's. He had no sense of urgency. His brain was occupied with a world that was at least three thousand years old, so why would he care about a few missing days?

'You think I should drop it?' said Jess. 'Are you sure?'

'Yes. What does Alex say?'

'I can't get hold of him. He's in Romania. It's because Communism's tottering and there are stories about to break. Did you know women there are forced to have five children each? But they can't feed them so they dump them in orphanages. That's what he's trying to look into.'

'Ah,' said Toby. 'Alex and his orphanages. Anyway, I'm sure there's no need to panic over Lily. Think back to when you were her age. Don't tell me you never had a lost weekend. Give her a bit longer.'

He was right. Jess put the finishing touches to her designs and posted them off. She and Harry cleared away a patch of brambles at the bottom of the garden and he helped her replace some rotten fence panels. She chauffeured him to friends' houses and booked him a course of driving lessons. On Friday morning a postcard popped through the letterbox onto the doormat.

Guess where I am!!!!

30

Eva had cut out the gold silk panels of the actual wedding dress and run up a prototype in cheap cotton to perfect the fit. Carlotta stepped out of her clothes and Eva threw it over her head, but when she tugged at the edges of the central back seam they wouldn't meet. 'You've put on weight!' she said accusingly.

'I can't have done,' said Carlotta, staring at her gaunt face in the mirror while Eva hovered at her elbow. The sickness from the food poisoning had eased at the start of the week but was now worsening again. 'I've hardly been eating. In fact I thought you were going to yell at me for getting too thin, after what you said last time. Are you sure your measurements are right?'

Eva whisked her tape measure around Carlotta's bust. She compared the figures in her notebook. 'Two centimetres more,' she said.

'In two weeks? That's ridiculous! You're exaggerating. You must have written them down wrong.'

Eva denied this. 'Well, thank goodness I allowed plenty of width for the seams. I'll be able to let them out. There isn't much point in continuing this fitting today.

We need to wait until nearer the time or I'll have to alter it again.'

'Are you asking me to go on a diet?' said Carlotta.

Anyone would seem plump beside scrawny Eva. As usual she was swamped in an oversized man's shirt studded with pins, and wearing tight jeans that accentuated her stick-insect legs, but she didn't care what she looked like. All her efforts were on behalf of her clients and they had to do what they were told. She pulled the white cotton from Carlotta's shoulders. 'Now take off your bra,' she said.

Carlotta frowned, but obeyed.

'Look!' exclaimed Eva.

'I've always had full breasts.'

'You don't think the nipples are darker?'

'I can't tell.'

With an air of exasperation, Eva reached forwards. She squeezed one of the exposed breasts between thumb and forefinger. Carlotta yelped with pain. 'And can you tell if they are always so sensitive? *Porca Madonna*, didn't I warn you not to do anything foolish before your wedding day?'

'But I didn't!'

'Carli, I can't believe you're so ignorant!'

To be accused of ignorance was one of Carlotta's greatest fears. She knew how to cajole to get what she wanted and how to present a self-assured face to the world, but that didn't make up for the lack of knowledge in her head. She was aware that her schooling had been sketchy; lessons had been less of a priority than getting the chores done, helping her mother with the laundry. Nowadays she would often sit with Luca while he did his homework, on the basis that she could learn alongside him. Nicolo's level of education was so much higher than hers she was anxious to minimise her deficiencies. 'An accident of birth,' he'd said generously, referring to the fact that they might as well have come from two different nations.

Nicolo didn't believe she was shallow or stupid, so to have her best friend belittling her was the last straw in a bad week. Eyes brimming, she hustled herself into her clothes – it was unbearable to be humiliated when you were nearly naked and the other person fully dressed – and snatched up a large pair of scissors.

'Carli!' cried Eva in alarm. 'What are you doing?'

The prototype dress had fallen onto the floor. Carlotta grabbed it with one hand and sliced the scissor blades towards it with the other. 'You've wasted your efforts,' she said as the tears spilled over. 'This isn't going to be any use for someone as fat and foolish as me.' She cut into the cotton.

Eva wrested the scissors away from her. She took Carlotta's face tenderly between her hands and kissed both cheeks. 'I'm sorry,' she said. 'To have stirred such a passion in you. I didn't mean to insult you, but I can't believe you haven't realised that you're pregnant.'

If Eva hadn't been supporting her, Carlotta would have collapsed to the floor. The door of the changing cubicle was open and, in the room beyond, she was sure she could see the mannequins coming alive, swishing their silks and satins, mincing and strutting.

'You know that's not possible,' she said.

'Why not? You don't sleep with Nicolo?'

'Of course I do, but...'

'You're in shock. Let me make you a coffee.'

In the back room where she had two Calor gas rings Eva lit the flame beneath an espresso pot. Carlotta slumped onto a chair, picked up a magazine and fanned herself.

'Come and sit more comfortably,' insisted Eva, leading her to the couch and moving a pile of pattern books so they could sit down together. She poured out the coffee.

Taking the cup, Carlotta said, 'I can see why you think what you do.'

'You've been sick, yes? Your breasts are swollen and sore. I bet you've missed your period.'

'My periods are irregular.'

Eva rolled her eyes. 'What more evidence do you need?'

'The doctor said...'

'Didn't I always tell you the doctor could be wrong? You know what you should do now? You should go to the pharmacy and buy a pregnancy kit. Use it when you get home and as soon as you find out you must call me.'

'I can't do that,' said Carlotta as a wave of nausea hit her again. Could it be the coffee? How dreadful if she couldn't drink coffee! 'They'll both be there. Nicolo's on a late shift. And I need to know for definite before I tell him.'

'Why? How d'you think he'll react?'

'I've no idea, that's the trouble. We weren't expecting anything like this to happen. We have Luca and we're perfectly settled, the three of us. He wants to focus on his career and so do I – we're not so young any more. Besides, I don't want to look like an idiot if it's a false alarm.' (She could hear voices from her past: silly Concetta, why do you always get everything wrong?)

'It's not a false alarm,' said Eva. 'But I appreciate that you need to be sure. Give me some money and I'll pop round to the pharmacy while you finish your coffee. I'll explain that it's for one of my clients. It won't be the first time. I hear more confessions than the priest!'

Once Eva had spurted through the door, a petite energetic whirlwind, Carlotta abandoned her coffee and gulped a glass of tap water. Pregnancy. A baby. Her mind kept swooping back to the first time, to the bundle of creased flesh she had loved so fiercely. Serafina had been an enchanting, gurgling infant, sunny-natured, responsive, a mischievous smile, a throaty giggle. She tried to recall the heft of her, snuggled on her hip, a plump starfish hand clawing at the front of Carlotta's dress to get at her dinner. The speed of her little knees, the waggle of her bottom when she put her down to crawl. She used to pull herself upright with a triumphant beam, wobble and move around the furniture. 'Soon she'll be taking her first steps unaided,' Carlotta was told, but she had never seen her walk.

When Eva came back with the testing kit, Carlotta took it into the cramped lavatory that had been created from a cupboard. Together, nervously, they waited for the result. Eva was the first to declare, 'You see! I was right!'

Carlotta waited a while longer until there could be no mistake. 'Honestly, I was convinced I could never conceive.'

'We think we have control of our bodies, but I'm not sure that we do. Perhaps God has given you a miracle.'

'I don't know why He'd do that.'

'*Tesora!* That's God's business. Don't ask why.'

'I stopped believing He cared for me,' said Carlotta.

'Well, you were wrong.'

'You think this pregnancy is a good thing?'

'Why not?'

'I don't know if I'll be any use as a mother.'

'What nonsense! You're fantastic with Luca. I mean to say, taking on another woman's child the way you've done—'

359

'He's not another woman's child any more. He's mine.' Carlotta found this line of argument disturbing. Jessamy McKenzie had done precisely the same thing. 'And it's so long since I've had practice with babies.'

'You don't need practice! It's an instinct. You're making excuses. And if you're worried about Nicolo's reaction...' Eva put an arm around her shoulders. 'It's best that you find out now, before the wedding, no?'

*

Approaching the apartment block, Carlotta could see Luca playing football with a group of friends. The memory of their first meeting – his delighted presentation of the peacock feather and then the trauma of his small body somersaulting through the air – was as vivid as ever, but now he was a lithe twelve-year-old who couldn't seem to stop growing, out-stripping her. The ball bounced on the tarmac and against the side of the building and the sign that read *Non Giocare con le Palle*. The low sun lit up the boys' faces, their expressions of glee. Luca, catching sight of her, gave a sporting wave, and then raced towards an opponent. Her spirits generally lifted at his youthful energy and enthusiasm, but today she was in too much turmoil. She fixed a smile on her lips but luckily he wasn't close enough to spot its lack of spontaneity.

Nicolo could tell something was wrong, however. She read the puzzlement on his face as she soon as she walked in. She should have been jubilant, fizzing with details of the dress – hints, rather than a full description. She should have danced into his arms.

'Darling,' he said. 'Are you still feeling sick?'

'Yes, I'm going to lie down. Will you come and talk to me? I have to explain the reason for this sickness.'

'Ah, so you know?'

She nodded and he followed her into the bedroom where she lay on the sheets that proclaimed *I love you, I love you*. He took off her shoes and massaged her feet. 'How does that feel?'

'Lovely, thank you. Nicolo…'

'Yes?'

'I've taken a test. It was Eva's idea, after she measured me again.' She said, as neutrally as possible, 'According to the test, I'm pregnant.'

'I thought that might be the case,' he said. The massage continued. His hands moved to her ankles and along her calves, drawing out the tension from the muscles, the fatigue that came from serving in the shop all day.

'So you're not surprised?'

'Well,' he said. 'You had the symptoms.'

'But you aren't pleased, are you? *Amore*, why can't you be pleased for me?'

'Is it what you want?' he said.

Her mind was reeling, taunting her: It's not what he wants – he already has a child, he doesn't need another. But he can't leave me. We're getting married in three weeks. She said, 'I don't know. I was supposed to be infertile so I never imagined I'd find myself in this condition. What about you? Do you hate the idea?'

'Of course I don't! I love you and I want everything to be right for you.'

This should have been reassuring, so why did it make her uneasy? What was he holding back? Nicolo took off his own shoes and lay down beside her. He leaned over and unbuttoned her shirt and slid his hand beneath the waistband of her skirt, resting it on her abdomen, with the tiny speck of life inside. 'I always wondered,' he said quietly, 'if you were afraid to have another child, after what happened to your first baby. That kind of loss must be very hard to overcome.'

Carlotta swallowed. She should have given a fuller explanation of Lily's visit by now; she'd let the opportunity slip past too often. 'I have something else to tell you,' she said.

His palm was warm on her skin and perfectly still. 'Oh?'

'It's possible there was a mistake with the identification of Serafina.'

'What do you mean?'

'I had some news, years ago, but I couldn't do anything about it. Or rather I tried and failed and had to

362

give up. But I believe my baby may have survived the earthquake after all.'

'*Porca miseria!* She's alive somewhere? You know this for a fact?'

'Actually, she came to see me,' said Carlotta. 'Last week. Do you remember the young woman called Lily McKenzie? You met her as she was leaving.' He was silent, stunned. 'Unfortunately, our meeting didn't go well because I was so sick. She was like a stranger to me. I fed her and clothed her and cuddled her and sang to her when she was little but I played no part in her upbringing. Now I don't know what to think or how to feel.'

Nicolo was looking at her in disbelief. 'You're saying your daughter Serafina has grown up in England with the name of Lily McKenzie? She wasn't killed, as you thought?'

'It seems not. It seems she was rescued and adopted by an English couple.'

'You're positive of this?'

'Yes.'

He whistled in amazement, made an effort to collect himself.

She added timidly, 'I'm sorry. I should have told you before but the information was so uncertain and until this month I couldn't know if I would ever see her again.'

His next suggestion was unexpected. 'Then you should get in touch with her.'

'Oh, I've tried! After she left I telephoned to England, but she hasn't called me back. I'm afraid she's annoyed with me.' She'd handled Lily's request so badly she'd driven her away. What had she been thinking?

'*Stai tranquilla*. You must take things very easy.' He patted her abdomen and then re-fastened her buttons one by one. He was as dextrous as ever but his movements were mechanical – there were no sly tickles or caresses during the buttoning – as if he was distracted by something.

'What is it?' she said.

'Perhaps we should invite her to our wedding?'

'Lily? Do you mean that?'

'Yes, if it would make you happy.'

'Oh, it would! But the journey from England, it's too far… it's too much to ask… She wouldn't accept.' And Carlotta had only herself to blame. She wriggled on the bed, tossed her head on the pillow. 'But why aren't we talking about our new baby, Nico, the one we made together in spite of all the odds? Isn't that the real miracle?'

'All life is a miracle,' he said.

'So why are you reacting like this?'

He took her into his arms and stroked her hair from her brow, but it didn't feel consoling. It felt as if he were trying to protect her from a sudden onslaught and concerned that he wouldn't make a very good job of it. 'Hush,' he said. 'Let's discuss it after you've had a scan.'

'But that's usually at three months, isn't it? Which will be after the wedding... *Dio mio!*' She pushed him away. 'It's because you don't want anyone to know. You're ashamed!'

'*Amore*, please...'

'You think this pregnancy makes us look like grubby teenagers, like kids with no self-control. You think Luca will be embarrassed? Okay, that was true of me the first time – I admit it! But we're already living together, so why wouldn't everyone be happy for us?' She drew down the corners of her mouth. 'Anyway, Eva knows. You can't stop people talking.'

'I don't want you to wait three months for a scan. You must have one as soon as possible. I'll try and make some arrangements when I go in tonight. Maybe you should come with me.'

This was why she was frightened. Nicolo wasn't volatile the way Romans or Sicilians were, but this deliberate calm of his was unnatural, unnerving. 'Why is it so urgent?'

'Your infertility,' he said, 'will be the result of the damage to your fallopian tubes. If they're badly scarred, no egg can pass.'

'So it *is* a miracle?'

'A chance in a million. And it would be amazing if we've beaten those odds. But it's also very risky. If the

365

embryo can't reach the womb, it can't develop and grow. That's why, although you have all the symptoms, I don't want you to build up your hopes before the scan. An ectopic pregnancy wouldn't be viable.'

His message was clear. It was just as well she hadn't conjured up a baby, a little boy similar to Luca, with Nicolo's serious brown eyes and a wicked smile. It wasn't like Serafina: you couldn't mourn what you'd never had. It was merely a prospect that had lived in her head for how long – three hours? – and now dissipated like a puff of wind. Whatever made her think Carlotta Galetti deserved such a piece of fortune? She was guilty of rejecting her living daughter, wasn't she? She was not fit to mother again.

'Sometimes there can be further complications.'

His gaze was searching, as if he were trying to compute and collate every bit of her in his memory. This was what he would have done when nursing Maria through her cancer. Carlotta could see the pain of recollection. She shivered. 'What do you mean?'

He clasped her hands between his. 'I mean, it could be dangerous for you too. That's why we must get you to hospital straight away.'

31

The policemen were drinking coffee, ordered in from the bar, and laughing at each other's jokes. Lily couldn't follow what they were saying but she suspected they were laughing at her too. Marcello was sitting on a metal chair, rubbing his wrist where the handcuffs had chafed it. His jaw was clenched and there was a whitening around the edges of his nose and mouth. At the counter Lily had been given a form to sign.

'I don't understand what it's for,' she said, casting an anguished glance at Marcello, hoping he'd leap up and translate.

'Sign it,' he said, without moving. 'It's to register your arrival in Sicily, that's all. Then they'll give your passport back.'

Her passport was on the counter in a plastic folder. The number had been copied down and the authorities informed. What authorities? she'd wanted to know. '*In Inghilterra,*' they'd told her, because it was quite an event for a provincial police station to be involved in matters of international diplomacy. They were accustomed to dealing with petty theft and road accidents (and taking bribes from the Mafia, Marcello had said contemptuously).

Lily was not much wiser about the reason for her arrest – though they'd explained she was being apprehended, rather than arrested as such. Her details had been flagged up as requiring investigation, but they couldn't tell her why the order had been issued. They were simply doing their job. And now they needed her to answer a few questions: When did she arrive? Where was she staying? Did she have a return ticket? She'd answered truthfully and then worried whether the Campiones would get into trouble, whether she'd be classed as an illegal worker.

On arrival at the police station, she and Marcello had been separated. Lily had been cloistered in a bleak waiting area, but he'd been dragged away, presumably to the cells. They'd been threatening to charge him with insulting a police officer. As the hours passed, she guessed they were deciding whether to make good their threat. Alex had warned her about people who wore uniforms of the sort that conferred high-handed powers. Behind a desk they were tin-pot tyrants, behind a riot shield they became ruthless thugs. He'd had first-hand experience during his days of youthful defiance, which he laughed about now. Marcello wasn't in a mood to see the funny side; he'd been released but he was fuming.

Lily signed the form and passed it back across the counter. A policeman selected a stamp, rolled it over one of many coloured ink pads and smacked each page with relish. Then he returned her passport.

'Is that it? I'm free to go now?'

He grunted.

'Both of us?'

'*Sì, sì.*' He flicked his fingers towards the door. His fellow officers indicated a collection box on the way out as if a donation was expected but, after their ordeal, neither of them was feeling charitable.

The street was deserted, baking in the afternoon heat. The boutique and the bank were both closed. They got into the car and Marcello juddered away from the kerb.

'God,' said Lily. 'That was a nightmare, wasn't it?'

He honked furiously at a truck about to pull out. 'The police are imbeciles.'

'They didn't… mistreat you?' There were no marks on him, apart from the red weal of the handcuffs, but that didn't mean he hadn't been subjected to brutality. Or humiliation.

He said in disgust, 'You know they accused me of abducting you?'

'They didn't! That's ridiculous. I'm a consenting adult.'

He wouldn't look at her; his beautiful blue eyes were frozen chips of ice. 'Absolutely, it's ridiculous! Why would I want to abduct anybody?'

He was smarting from the indignity and Lily wretchedly interpreted this as why would he want to abduct *her*? He was attractive and personable, with an acute sense of honour. To be accused of abduction was an insult. 'Look, I'm really sorry. I don't know what the original problem was, but you shouldn't have had to be involved. It was nothing to do with you...'

'Forget it,' he said, accelerating onto the main road.

Even if his anger was directed at the police and not at her, the incident created a distance between them. In Lily's view their relationship had soured before it had a chance to begin. Why would Marcello want to associate with someone who gave him grief when there were plenty of other willing and less troublesome girls around? She gripped the edges of the hot, clammy car seat and abandoned any notion of inviting him into her cubbyhole.

By the time they returned to the farm, the siesta was over and the workers were in the fields. She joined them in miserable silence. The regulars bantered among themselves, but she hadn't mastered the dialect and, anyway, she needed to figure out what she should do next. By the end of the afternoon, she'd made up her mind. It only took ten minutes or so to stuff her belongings into her holdall and backpack.

At dinner, after the main course but before the fruit and cheese, she said, 'Thank you all so much for having me. I've had a terrific week, but this'll be my last meal. I need to leave tomorrow.' She'd deliberately made her announcement in public so she couldn't be dissuaded.

Marcello was at the other end of the table; she'd avoided sitting near him. He looked up in surprise.

Alfredo said, 'We've been working you too hard?'

Lily was so tired her bones ached but she denied this roundly. 'No, I've enjoyed the work. But I'm afraid I'll cause trouble for you because I don't have a permit. The police said there was a problem with my passport – even though there wasn't – and now they know where I'm staying they might come and hassle you.'

'You are our guest,' said Signora Campione. 'Not our employee.' (This wasn't strictly accurate, but truth was a slippery concept and could be adjusted.)

'I've some friends I promised to visit,' said Lily.

Marcello's voice was sharp. 'The old Englishman in Villa Ercole? Did you telephone him?'

'Yes,' she lied, though he must have known she'd had no opportunity. She planned to leave first thing in the morning and phone from a bar over breakfast. If Gerald or Dolly didn't answer, she'd think of something else.

'How will you get there?'

'I'll get a bus some of the way, I guess. And then I'll hitch.'

Signora Campione said, 'That is not advisable.'

'But people always give each other lifts in the country. I've done it at home and here too, actually.' (Though getting a ride with Carlotta ten years ago probably didn't count.)

'But you are a foreigner,' said Signora Campione.

Lily wanted to argue: No, I'm not! I come from Sicilian peasant stock, like you. The sun had brought out the melanin in her skin, the smell of tomatoes had impregnated her hands, the soil had worked its way between her toes – it was almost impossible to wash her feet properly in the shower. She was not a *straniera*. But that was what the farmer in his beat-up truck or the salesman in his dusty Fiat or the motorbike rider would see when she stuck her thumb out. They'd be able to tell from her clothing, from the way she carried herself, that she wasn't a local.

Identity is more than bloodline, more than ancestry. It's the upbringing and culture you are exposed to, the habits and values you take for granted. Spending a week in Sicily didn't turn her into a Sicilian, not in anyone's view. And, if she was honest, she could see this life had its limitations; there was a lot of drudgery in it. Lily loved to be outside, loved working with plants, but she wanted to be creative too, which would be a luxury here. Growing, cropping, harvesting, that was the priority. Survival.

'I'll take you,' said Marcello.

'You will?'

'Yes, if I can borrow the car again?'

Signora Campione nodded and went to get the cheese.

In the morning, Alfredo paid Lily in cash for the days she'd worked, which was good because it meant she didn't have to risk another trip to the bank. 'You must visit us again,' he said. 'You will be welcome any time.'

Both the Signoras Campione kissed her and made a great fuss of her, causing the twins to grizzle for attention. She took leave of Fabio and Gilberto, who were casually confident they'd see her again: *'Ci vediamo, senz'altro.'* Then she got into the Fiat with Marcello.

Twenty-four hours ago, she thought, we were on our way down this same road. Was he giving her a lift to speed her departure? Out of obligation? Or to make up to her? And if the latter, why didn't he take his hand off the gear-stick and squeeze her thigh, offer some acknowledgement of his feelings? Would she ever get another kiss? Should she make the first move? She'd no idea how to breach the space between them.

Villa Ercole was an hour's drive away and thus, for Marcello, another hour back. 'You didn't have to do this,' she said.

'It's okay. It makes a change from the labouring.'

'But it's Saturday. Don't you have the weekend off?'

She didn't ask what he was doing that evening. She guessed the boys would go to the cinema-nightclub again. They'd be flirting with pretty girls and getting into fights with their boyfriends. That was what people did on Saturday nights and her dreams of dancing with Marcello under the canopy of stars was just that, a dream. Nipped in the bud. She glanced at his profile: set and stubborn. She was stubborn too. The business at the bank wasn't *her* doing. She was as much a victim of random bureaucracy as he was. They both stared straight ahead, casting about for a topic that was neutral.

'It's a long time since you have been to Villa Ercole?' said Marcello, with the detachment of an acquaintance making small talk.

'Yes, though Toby keeps in touch.'

'Who is Toby?'

The question gave her difficulty. Toby was her father's best friend and had for a while been her mother's lover. That was peculiar, wasn't it? 'Very Bloomsbury,' she'd overheard someone say once, in a snide tone. Lily reckoned all three of them would have hated the connotation.

'He's Gerald's nephew,' she said. 'And a friend of my parents.'

'They haven't seen you since you were a child?'

'No.' She was going to add: Nor had you – as a way of reviving the good, fun things about the past week. But it was too pointed a remark, as if she were begging and no way was she going to beg. Instead she said, carelessly, 'They're a strange couple, aren't they, Gerald and Dolly? I wonder why they never married. I suppose it's a class thing, which is a bit mean when you think how hard Dolly works for him.'

Marcello had been crouching over the steering wheel, flooring the accelerator until the Cinquecento gathered speed on a downward slope. He relaxed his foot. 'You're surprised *l'inglese* hasn't married that woman?'

'That *bloody* woman!' she corrected him.

'Is it possible you don't know?' he said.

'Don't know what?'

'That he is *finocchio*? He goes with men.'

'Oh, my goodness.' She squirmed. How stupid she was! But how could she have known? She'd been a child and, even though her parents wouldn't purposely keep anything from her, they didn't waste their energies dissecting other people's sexuality. Any general allusions would have gone over her head. Gerald had often sought the company of young men, but it hadn't seemed noteworthy. He'd gone out to Italy in the sixties when homosexuality was illegal in England, but he'd've had other motives too: the climate, the wealth of art and history, the low cost of living, which meant he could lead a life of hedonism while *that bloody woman* did all the work.

'I'm an idiot,' she said. 'I thought it was one of those situations where she masquerades as the housekeeper. Where she sneaks into his bed at night, but he's too much of a snob to marry her.'

'No,' said Marcello, overtaking a tractor with very little space to spare. 'That's what happened with the priest.'

Lily's eyes popped. 'What priest? Tell me! Did you know this before? I mean, in the days when you came to Villa Ercole to play with me? Because if so, why didn't you say?'

'No,' he admitted. 'Not when we were ten. I discovered later that Addolorata was first the housekeeper for Father Rondini. Did you know him?'

'I think maybe I did once...' Father Rondini was the name of the priest who'd been involved in the process of her adoption. He must have visited the convent; she could picture a long black soutane but she couldn't fill in the features of its wearer.

'The rumours were very strong, about their sexual relationship. The reason he didn't marry her was because he couldn't. Priests don't like to give up their job or lose their power.'

'Poor Dolly,' said Lily.

'It happens a lot,' said Marcello. 'The Church pretends not to see. But if there's too much talk, they have to show an example and punish the sinner. The sinner is Addolorata, naturally, and not Father Rondini, because she tempted him.'

Dolly, with her solid bosom, stout legs and hair like iron filings, a temptress! Lily would have laughed if she wasn't already boiling with resentment on Dolly's account. The hypocrisy of it! 'Is this really true?'

'I don't know. It's what people say.' He went on, 'Father Rondini gave references for her cooking, her cleaning and so on, but there aren't many jobs in this region. She couldn't find anyone to employ her. Also her reputation made it difficult to find a husband. She was going to leave for the mainland, my father said, and then she learnt that Villa Ercole was being renovated and the owner wanted a housekeeper. *L'inglese* employed her when no one else would. I think she's grateful.'

Lily digested this slowly. Gerald and Dolly's relationship wasn't exploitative. They were equal beneficiaries: Gerald, because he had someone to attend to mundane and tiresome tasks while he pretended to be the great intellectual; Dolly, because she had a roof over her head and a bed of her own, an abundance in the garden and total control in the kitchen. Lily understood better now the power play between them. She'd sometimes been a little scared of Gerald, because of his moods and his sarcasm and the way he blew through his moustache, though he'd tried to be kind. Now she saw him as someone who'd done something gallant and principled. There must have been other women queuing up to keep house for him, but he'd chosen the one who was a reprobate. Just like himself.

She'd half hoped Marcello might suggest they stopped at a bar en route for a drink and a game of table football. If they could vent their frustration on the rods of metal players, spinning the handles, walloping the ball, it might unite them again. She could also make an advance phone call to the villa. 'I'll check they're going to be in,' she'd say. But she couldn't bring herself to suggest a break – or confess that neither Gerald nor Dolly had any idea she'd be turning up. She'd have to bluff it out.

And then the road became suddenly familiar: it was the route into Roccamare. When she snapped her head from side to side to take in the view, she was encouraged to see how little it had altered: a mere handful of new villas presiding over half-dug swimming pools and clusters of low-rise apartments blending into the landscape. And there, ahead of them, was the sea, shimmering on the horizon. Marcello circumvented the resort and climbed along the track that led to Villa Ercole.

Lily's stomach was all over the place, struggling to confine a surfeit of butterflies. This was worse than going to meet Carlotta because that would have been a new chapter, whereas this was a place that held memories. Happy memories were delicate and fragile and she didn't want to damage them. 'You can drop me here,' she said to Marcello.

Afterwards she was mortified that she'd been so churlish. He was undertaking a two-hour journey and she was dismissing him without even offering a glass of water. Dolly would have welcomed him, would have linked arms with them both and marched them indoors for lemonade and amaretti. She would have exclaimed over the coincidence of their meeting on the train and finally they'd have been able to laugh over the embarrassing police incident. And then Marcello would have kissed her again. Or Lily would have kissed him.

Except she didn't know if Dolly would be there. She didn't know if she would recognise her, how she would explain everything, including the Carlotta business. After all, her family had left on bad terms eleven years ago. She couldn't be certain Dolly wouldn't bear a grudge.

She got out of the car. Marcello had to get out too, to open the boot so she could fish out her bag – another obstacle between them. If she put it down and tilted up her face, would he get the message? This time yesterday he'd wanted to undress her. Had she become such a nuisance in the interim?

'You've been so good to me,' she said, holding out her hand. 'You've gone out of your way to help and I've been nothing but trouble.'

'You picked many kilos of tomatoes,' he said. 'I'm sure Alfredo will say you earned your keep.'

He took her outstretched hand. If either of them had given a slight tug, over the barrier of the bag, they might have fallen into each other's arms. Instead, after a brief handshake, Marcello dropped back into the driving seat. Shingle spurted beneath the tyres as he reversed. His window was open and he waved goodbye through it – a cheerful, no hard feelings, amicable sort of goodbye.

Lily began to chase after the car. 'When will I see you again?' she yelled.

She thought she heard him say, 'In Roccamare, one day,' but she couldn't be definite about it.

32

The villa, so imposing in the image that Lily had clung to, looked faded and diminished. Its distemper was patchy and the trees around it had grown taller, as she had herself. She knocked at the front door but wasn't surprised to get no response; it was seldom used. She skirted around the side of the house. Would she see Gerald lounging on the terrace with a black Sobranie and a glass of Marsala? Would Dolly be gathering rocket and radicchio for one of her bitter salads? No one was visible, but the door to the kitchen was ajar. She couldn't *not* enter.

The kitchen instantly took her back to childhood: the laden shelves, the deep sink, the stone chimney breast. And the combination of aromas that was Dolly's own: nutty and spicy and fragrant and fruity all at once. She caught her breath. There, on the table – same table, same position, same bench – was a bowl of peaches, the glorious rose-flushed golden peaches of her earliest memory. In addition to the peaches, under a cover to keep off the flies, was a dish of flaky pastries filled with ricotta and raisins and dusted with sugar, just as Lily liked them, just as if Dolly were expecting her. Momentarily she was swept into a fairy tale: Goldilocks in the house of the three bears, or Alice in Wonderland reading a label that said 'Eat Me'.

The fantasy evaporated. Oh, how she regretted sending Marcello away! They could have had such fun reacquainting themselves with the villa and its land. They could have raided the huge old fridge and demolished the plate of pastries in no time. Her treatment of him had been pathetic. As childhood friends they'd fallen out occasionally, but they'd always made up. If it hadn't been for yesterday's kiss, he'd have come in with her, as he used to do. Was that the result of kissing somebody? When you stepped over the boundary, when everything between you became sexually charged, you didn't gain a lover, you lost a friend. How had she managed to make such an unholy mess? She sat down at the table, laid her head on her arms and sobbed.

Her sobs were noisy so she didn't hear a footfall. In any case, he was wearing his favourite rope-soled espadrilles. But she sensed another person and looked up to see an elderly, stooping man in a loose linen shirt with a pair of half-moon glasses balanced on the end of his nose. Why didn't she recognise him sooner? Gerald had always been effete, but there'd been a toughness behind his languor; he used to give the impression of a lion, napping but capable of arousal. This man had an air of vulnerability and she'd need to explain herself without startling him.

He shuffled into the room, blinking and smiling. 'You came, my dear.'

Was his sight poor? Was he expecting someone else? 'I'm sorry,' she said, wiping her eyes. 'I did knock, but I don't think you heard me. I shouldn't have barged in though. It's a bit much to spring myself on you like this. It's Lily, by the way, Lily McKenzie.'

'I know,' he said.

'Oh, gosh.' She rushed forward and took his hand and kissed his cheek. 'I was afraid you wouldn't have a clue who I was.'

He indicated the fruit and the pastries on the table. 'Dolly's been busy. We hoped you would come.'

'It's so lovely to see you! Where is she?'

'She's having her hair done. She'll be back soon.' Dolly patronised Tonella, who operated the oldest of the salons in Roccamare. Other stylists had come along to challenge her and she wasn't especially skilful with her scissors, but she was the best source of gossip. Her regulars wouldn't go anywhere else. 'Why don't you help yourself to a drink? There's wine in the fridge. You can pour me one too.'

When Lily opened the fridge for the wine, she saw it stacked with her favourite treats: a salad of artichoke hearts and sweet marinated onions, baby stuffed peppers, a wedge of snowy pecorino, soft pillows of home-made ravioli ready for boiling. She was overcome. Dolly and Gerald had no quarrel with Harry or herself – they'd been hapless children – and it was silly to have thought she'd be turned away. They weren't like Carlotta; they had missed her!

'Lilianina!' Dolly was in the doorway. 'It's true! You have arrived.' She held out her arms and Lily wished she were small enough to be enfolded into her embrace, like a chick with a mother hen. Dolly's newly styled hair was now more like cotton wool than wire wool, white and fluffy. Her black dress strained at the seams as it had always done and her gold crucifix jiggled up and down on her chest. 'You will be hungry,' she said, and began pulling plates out of the fridge and piling them onto the table. She set out a basket of bread and lit the gas under a pan of minestrone.

'You'll stay with us?' said Gerald. 'There's a Dutch family in your old quarters. I think they've gone down to the beach. Dolly doesn't cook for guests – it's all self-catering these days. But there's spare bedrooms here in the villa and she's made up the beds.'

'Really? But how... I mean, I don't understand how you knew I was coming?'

'Your mother telephoned,' said Gerald.

For one crazy moment, she thought he meant Carlotta. 'But I didn't tell her either.'

'You sent her a postcard. That's how she knew you were in Sicily. She got it yesterday and rang to see if you were here. We hoped you'd turn up. Dolly, as you can see, could hardly wait.'

'I should have called you earlier,' said Lily. 'I'm really sorry. I wasn't sure how I'd be received. I haven't been here for so long.'

'I remember when you were a little thing,' said Dolly huskily. '*Una piccolina*. With all your curls cut off. Your father bring you here and we always eat the peaches. You love the peaches.'

'You ought to ring your mother,' said Gerald.

'Now?'

'It would be a good idea. While the soup heats up. She didn't say, but I got the impression she was worried.'

He wasn't reproaching her, but she felt sheepish all the same. 'Can I use your phone?'

He nodded and she took her glass of wine into the entrance hall where the phone, the familiar two-tone grey plastic, sat on its marble-topped table. In ten years, she thought, nothing has changed here. It was a place frozen in time, but it was becoming down-at-heel: the rug on the tiles was worn thin in places, the mirrors had more rust spots, the china ornaments more chips. Cobwebs drifted in high corners: in earlier days Dolly would have banished them, but they'd escaped her notice.

Lily lifted the receiver. It was such a relief when Jess answered her call that she nearly burst into tears again. Jess's voice was young and girlish, with a faint hint of

West Country that she'd cultivated so as not to sound like her sisters. 'Oh, my darling, I was so worried about you!'

'You didn't need to be. I'm fine.'

'Why did you stay on in Italy? Was it because of Carlotta Galetti?'

'Sort of.' She had to bite back the tears. 'It was awful. I found where she worked and they told me she'd moved to a new flat, but when I got there she couldn't get rid of me fast enough. I think it was because she has another kid now. And a man. She always has a man in tow, doesn't she? And she doesn't want them to know about me.'

'Actually she rang to speak to you,' said Jess. 'That's what alerted us. Harry took the call. I think she wanted to apologise.'

'Apologise for not wanting to find out if she was related to me? Well, tough.'

'Darling, it's not surprising that she has another family. It would be more unusual if she didn't.'

'I know.'

After a beat, Jess said, 'Why did you go to Sicily? Was it on a whim?'

'Yeah, and you'll never guess who I met on the train!' That was when it all came out about Marcello and the tomato picking and the police. And it was when she got onto the police that Jess's soft and tender tone struck an odd note.

'You were arrested?'

'It was nothing *important*. They had to check my passport details for some obscure reason. But it backfired because then I couldn't stay on to work at the farm and Marcello tried to stand up for me so they took it out on him and he got into a sulk... Though it doesn't seem so bad now I'm here and Gerald and Dolly are pleased to see me...'

Jess had gone very quiet at the other end of the phone. Lily heard her murmur, 'I'm so sorry.'

'It wasn't your fault!'

'I shouldn't have said anything to Dinah.'

'Why, what did she do?'

'I'm not sure,' said Jess. 'She didn't consult me. But before I got your postcard she talked about Johnnie having contacts who could find out where you were, through the Home Office or Foreign Office or something. She means well and she was only trying to help but you know how interfering she is.'

'Dinah!' said Lily. 'Bloody Dinah!' She, too, was shocked into silence.

Jess said, 'I'm sorry you had to go through all that hassle, but there weren't any serious consequences, were there?' Lily gave a non-committal grunt. 'Now, listen: we're going to come out and join you.'

'You are? You and Harry?'

'Harry's off to Cornwall with the Robinsons, surfing. But I'm working on Toby because he hasn't seen Gerald for ages. I'll keep checking Teletext for last-minute flights and when a bargain comes up, I'll nab it. When I was talking to Dolly yesterday it seemed ridiculous to have stayed away for so long. I mean, there's rivers of water flowed under the bridge in the past ten years... So, yes, I'm coming.'

*

Lily slept in the bedroom at Villa Ercole as if she hadn't slept for weeks. Salt-laden dreams blew in through the open window, flapping around her like kites trying to become airborne, jerking her awake with sudden strong bursts of emotion. She'd register their sensations of grief or joy, despair or elation and then fall asleep again immediately. She hadn't realised how shattered she was.

She woke in the morning to the pleasure of being cosseted by Dolly, no tomatoes to pick, no men to complicate matters. Then she remembered it was Sunday and that Marcello had talked of going to the beach. Was that what he'd called to her as he'd driven off? Not 'In Roccamare, one day,' but 'In Roccamare, Sunday.'

No doubt she was being fanciful – and what was the likelihood that she'd bump into him anyway? Nevertheless, on the off-chance that coincidence would favour her twice, she dug out her swimsuit and borrowed a towel. Gerald offered to drive her but she said she'd rather walk; it wasn't too far if you didn't have a lot to carry. The beach was busier than it used to be. Sunbathing on the sand, she watched groups and families come and go. She was the only person by herself; everyone else was attached to at least one other companion. When she went to the bar for a drink, a gaggle of young men tried in turn to chat her up. All were lively, some were charming, none was Marcello.

She left the bar to wander along the shoreline. She kept tripping over racquets and balls, rubber armbands and small children. She hadn't given up hope of seeing him but when she reached the end of the beach she didn't turn around to search again. She continued into what, according to a newly erected noticeboard, was now a designated nature reserve. The strip of beach here was thinly populated; why would the day-trippers and holiday-makers leave the familiarity of the crowd? But Lily loved its wildness, the way the plants clung to their habitat. The land was low-lying at the mouth of the river, thick with succulent agaves and the feathery fronds of tamarisk, punctuated by silver poppies and golden buttons of santolina.

This was where she and Marcello had invented their private games. They used to wriggle their way through the bushes so no one could find them and emerge scratched and bitten and triumphant. This was where the old dinghy had been too, though she could see no sign of it. Rotted or burned for firewood, she supposed. If she shut her eyes she could recapture Marcello's ten-year-old head poking from beneath it, like a turtle coming out of his shell. Then the grown, twenty-one-year-old Marcello took over, whispering in her ear: '*Ancora cammina sulle mani*, Lily McKenzie?'

There was no one about. Lily cartwheeled across the sand, relishing the exhilaration of whirling upside down, the whoosh of the air as her body sliced through it. When she had limbered up, she spun onto her hands again, flinging her legs upwards, keeping her back straight and her toes pointing to the sky. She managed six paces and lost her balance. She tried several more times. She was rusty, the knack of it didn't come spontaneously, but she could improve. All it required was practice.

She returned to the villa in a buoyant mood. Over dinner, Dolly tried to establish how she had spent her day, puzzled that she hadn't sought out the myriad people who would have been delighted to see her, nor stayed around long enough for the *passeggiata*.

'But no one would know who I was!' protested Lily.

'This is not true! You don't remember Nuncia, in the bakery, and how she give you little treats? Or Benito, who takes you to find sea urchins? Or Tonella who cuts the hair?' She was away then, recounting the scandals she'd heard when she was in the salon.

Lily half listened, recalling Dolly's own scandalous story. How could she reconcile this busy bossy matron with the sexy siren who had seduced (or been seduced by) a priest? How did the affair begin? Did he break his wrist and need help undressing? Did he stumble across Dolly sponging her ample breasts and find her irresistible? Did he creep into her bed or she into his? Afterwards, did she have to kneel and whisper her sins to him in the Confessional?

Dolly's blackcurrant eyes narrowed, as if she guessed Lily was bursting with unasked questions, though she couldn't possibly have known the slant of them. Then, out of the blue, she proposed a visit to Santa Margherita. She said, 'I make promise to visit my friend Agnese Fantoni and you have opportunity to come also.'

Lily was jolted from her reverie about Father Rondini – did he wear pyjamas or a nightshirt? – to exclaim, 'Agnese Fantoni's still alive!'

'Agnese is strong,' said Dolly. 'She survives more than an earthquake.' There followed a long list of maladies, many of which were a mystery to Lily, but she readily agreed to go. It was one of the reasons she'd travelled to Sicily in the first place.

The excursion was fixed for Wednesday. Over the next couple of days Dolly insisted on taking Lily into Roccamare and parading her to all the locals who'd known her as a little girl and wanted to see her grown into a fine young woman. There were so many encounters they became jumbled in her head. The chief one to make an impression was Nuncia. She described laughingly how Lily and Marcello would run into her shop to beg for crusts of *sfincione* because they were always hungry; then she made a casual remark about the Campiones opening up their villa for the summer holiday.

'Do the family still come every year?' said Lily. But of course they did! How could she have forgotten: Marcello had talked of joining them when he left his cousins. 'When do they arrive?'

'Per Agosto,' said Nuncia. *'Altre due settimane.'*

Another two weeks. Lily didn't know if she could stay that long. She had a sneaking suspicion that part of Jess's mission was to bring her back to England. She must stop thinking about Marcello; she should focus on tomorrow's trip, though it was a daunting prospect. (Not just because of the enormous significance of reconnecting with her roots, but because the image she carried of Agnese Fantoni, the wicked witch, made her shudder.)

She didn't mention this to Gerald or Dolly and was glad she hadn't, because when they arrived and entered Agnese's stuffy little apartment, she was surprised to find a harmless old granny sorting through her Mass cards. There were even a couple of grandchildren, or maybe great-grandchildren, crouched on the floor, helping her. Agnese was swathed in black like a badly wrapped parcel and her hair was drawn into a severe bun, but she was smiling indulgently and humming. The cage hanging from the window held a pair of chirping lovebirds and the view beyond them wasn't as barren as before. There was a lot of scaffolding but there were new buildings and proper roads too. Agnese offered the visitors a drink and they all shared the pastries that Dolly had brought.

Out of politeness for the company, the two women were speaking in Italian and not Sicilian. Lily heard Agnese drop the name, Galetti, into a sentence and stiffened.

'She is here this week?' said Dolly.

'Yes,' said Agnese. 'The aunt of her husband died, they came for the funeral.'

Gerald said, 'Would that be Carlotta? Do you know where we can find her?'

Lily gasped. This was *not* what she'd anticipated. 'Carlotta's here too?'

Gerald patted her knee. 'She's talking about the *real* Carlotta Galetti, my dear,' he said.

33

Jess rose at dawn for the early flight to Palermo, a charter carrying sun-seekers to a large hotel near Cefalu. She stood in the queue for check-in, shuffling her suitcase forward with her toe. She and Toby had arranged their tickets separately, since they were leaving from different locations. She wasn't concerned, initially, when she didn't see him, but once the flight was called and the crowd milled towards the departure gate, she began to panic.

Since most of the passengers were on a package holiday, they were well organised and orderly. The tourist rep was ticking off their names on her clipboard and ushering them into the gangway. A few stragglers came down the turquoise-carpeted corridor. Jess gave a pleading smile to the flight attendant at the desk. 'I'm waiting for someone,' she said.

'We'll make a tannoy announcement,' the girl said. 'If they've checked in. What's the name?'

'Toby Forrester.'

She studied her computer printout. 'There's no Forrester on this list.'

'Are you sure? We got standby tickets. Could that be why? Am I on there? Jessamy McKenzie.'

'Let me see…' She ran her finger down the list again.

Jess, raking the corridor one last time, saw a figure loping towards her, jacket flapping behind him, not running exactly, but moving with quick light-footed leaps. 'Alex!'

'Alexander McKenzie?' said the attendant. 'Yes, his name's here, above yours. Your husband?'

Jess nodded. Even through the girl's mask of make-up, she could see her thinking: So where does Toby Forrester fit in?

'Alex,' she said again, when he was within earshot. 'What are you doing here?'

He pulled a crumpled boarding pass from his pocket and bestowed a charming smile on the confused young woman. 'Did I hold you up…' he flicked a glance at her name badge '… Fiona? Many apologies. It was the queue in the duty free.' He flourished a houndstooth box containing a bottle of Diorissimo.

Jess was surprised; he was not normally a perfume-buyer. 'Who's that for?'

'You don't want it?' He held it out with his boarding pass. 'What about you, Fiona?'

'We can't accept gifts and you have to board in the next three minutes,' she said, though not as primly as she might have done.

'What *is* all this about?' said Jess as they settled into their seats.

'Actually I bought it for Lily,' said Alex, stuffing the scent bottle carelessly into his pocket. 'She's at an age now, isn't she, for that sort of thing? And this one smells of lily-of-the-valley.'

'I know.'

'So what you're really wondering, is why the late substitution? Where's Toby?'

'Yes, I am. Go on, explain yourself. How come you're here?' The plane began to taxi down the runway. The atmosphere was buzzing with anticipation for the good times ahead. Fiona was demonstrating safety procedures, her gaze fixed on a point in the middle distance. 'You've been incommunicado for weeks.'

His face was solemn. 'That's because, in Romania, Ceausescu's closed down all the media outlets and it's a nightmare trying to make a phone call. I tell you, Jess, grinding poverty doesn't begin to describe it. People have to queue for the most basic foodstuffs. Much worse than Russia. The great socialist ideals are lost, totally. It's soul-destroying to see that kind of dictatorship in action.'

'Isn't there any opposition?'

'It's building. Things can't go on the way they are.'

'When did you get back?'

'Sunday. A quick turnaround, but I did manage to wash and change if that's what's bothering you.' A

396

trolley was inching down the aisle dispensing breakfast. Fiona hovered over them with a jug of coffee. 'Right on cue,' he said. 'You're a lifesaver.'

Jess asked for tea. Accepting the plastic tray and the steaming polystyrene cup, she said, 'I hoped it might ease things with Gerald if Toby came along.'

'Whereas I'm persona non grata?'

'How would I know? I also thought it would be nice for Toby to have an actual holiday in Sicily, instead of squatting in the blistering heat, brushing dust from fragments of human remains.'

'What, drag the man from his passion? What did he say?'

'That he was supervising some postgrad students who were up against a deadline, but he'd do his best to get away.' She sighed. 'He was never going to come, was he? But I don't understand why he didn't tell me himself.'

'You know Toby,' said Alex, prodding his scrambled egg and watching it bounce. 'He hates to let people down, but he can't help being a workaholic.'

'And you were fancy-free, nothing else to do?'

'I have to collate my notes and write my article, but I can do that anywhere. And, Christ, Jess, I *wanted* to come with you. She's my daughter too. What's the problem?'

She considered. 'It's because I had no warning. It makes me think you've been cooking up all sorts of plots with no reference to me. Like I don't count.'

'Okay,' he said. 'I confess. I talked Toby into it and asked him not to tell you. I wanted to spring a surprise. But as for not counting, that's the most ridiculous thing I've heard.'

'You bullied him into swapping?'

'Toby's his own man, as you well know. And I'm not a bully.'

This was true; though Alex's persuasiveness was of a kind that was hard to resist. She gave him a sharp look, which he ignored. He pushed his breakfast aside, reclined his seat and shut his eyes. He'd always had an enviable ability to doze in any circumstances and didn't wake until they began the descent to Palermo.

At the airport they hired a Fiat Uno. Alex, refreshed from his nap, was the driver. It was a journey they knew well, the familiar landmarks still in place, but for Jess there was one trip in particular that stood out. 'Oh, God,' she said, 'Do you remember our quest for Carlotta Galetti? Those scary back-streets and suspicious glances: who were we and what were we after? They set my teeth on edge. And that was only the beginning! It was a dreadful day.'

'Do you know what happened when Lily went to see her?'

'Not really. Do you?'

'How could I? Like you said, I've been incommunicado.'

'She told me she wasn't welcomed, which was all the information I got. I worry that we shouldn't have encouraged her – it was too risky a venture.'

'You have to take risks,' he said. 'You can't spend your life avoiding them.'

'Well, then, we should have been on hand to support her.'

'Isn't that what we're doing now?'

When they reached Villa Ercole there was no one at home. They rang the bell and knocked on the windows. They went round to the back of the house to try the French doors, which were rarely locked, but couldn't gain access. They sat on the terrace to wait. Alex strummed his fingers on the table top; Jess turned her face to the sun, feeling drowsy. After a while, he got up and prowled the premises, past the nut trees and down to Dolly's kitchen garden. He peered through a window in the old barn and noted the clothes draped outside on the portable drying rack.

'I think there's a family staying there,' he said. 'But no cars to be seen. I'm guessing everyone's gone out for the day. I don't think we should hang around.'

Jess had been in transit for eight hours; she didn't want to move. 'Where are we going to go?'

'Into Roccamare.' Alex never had any trouble taking decisions. 'We'll book a room.'

'What for?'

'What for, Jessa-mine, what for? So you can get some sleep. You look bushed.'

'I did have an early start...'

'Well, then? We'll come back here after the siesta and you'll be fresh as a daisy.' He chivvied her out of the chair and into the car and she hadn't the energy to object.

Since the holiday season was under way there was pressure on the local accommodation. The better quality hotels were fully booked, but the third *pensione* they tried had a room free. It was at the back of the building, overlooking a yard decked with empty gas cylinders, a desiccated rosemary bush, a three-legged stool, two mangy but four-legged cats, an old pram and a lemon tree in a pot; the lemons glowed with sunny good health amid the detritus. The landlady apologised that there wasn't a sea view available.

'It doesn't matter,' said Alex. 'We want to sleep.'

The room and the double bed were both small. There was a basin, a chest of drawers and not much else. Jess subsided onto the bed. Her original plan, which had involved herself and Toby arriving at Villa Ercole and being greeted affectionately by Gerald and Dolly and Lily, had been hijacked. This was the primitive kind of place she and Alex had stayed in decades ago when they'd first met and gone travelling together. Alex, she reflected, wasn't much concerned with personal comforts. He and his fellow journalists would

400

congregate wherever they could get a drink, setting up camp in the bar and lowering the tone. Toby, on the other hand, was used to the high standards of life as a Cambridge don.

'What are you going to do now?' she said.

'Oh, don't worry about me. I'll go for a walk.'

He fastened the shutters to darken the room and closed the door softly as he left. Jess lay basking in a sensuous heat, permeated with the tang of lemon and the drying spikes of rosemary.

When she woke up she was disorientated. She'd no idea what time of day it was or why Alex was lying beside her, naked. He was on his front, his face hidden so she couldn't tell if he was sleeping. She poked him lightly in the ribs. 'What on earth do you think you're doing?'

He was awake. He raised himself onto his elbows. 'Keeping you company. Stifling, isn't it?'

'I thought you went out.'

'I did. Got myself a beer and a panino and won two free games on the pinball. High score: six and a half million.'

'Why did you get into bed with me?'

'I'm not in bed,' he pointed out. 'I'm on the bed. And I'm here because I want to talk to you.'

'What about?'

'Can't you guess?'

'No, but I've got my suspicions. And I'm not happy about whatever you and Toby have been up to. I'm not a piece of property to be passed between you.'

'We don't believe in ownership,' Alex reminded her. 'That was one of our ground rules.' It was why neither of them had ever worn a wedding ring.

Jess swung her legs to the floor, the tight strip of space by the window. 'Did you touch me?'

'When?'

'When I was asleep and you were lying next to me.'

'Would it matter if I did? Some people would think physical contact was normal, between husband and wife.'

'We don't live together anymore.'

'True. And didn't we only get married in the first place to annoy your parents? Because I wasn't Johnnie Winthrop of the many acres and the hunting fraternity. Or was it because you'd done a deal on those matching suits in the Portobello Road and wanted us to show them off?'

'Stop it, Alex,' said Jess. 'Stop fishing. And for God's sake put your pants on.' She rose and grasped the window sill. 'Hell, did that sound as though I was talking to Harry? I'm sorry. But if you want to have a proper discussion about things now, we should act like grown-ups.'

'I undressed because I was hot,' he said and she heard the snap of elastic at his waist. 'You can turn round,

Jess. Don't act martyred. Anyhow, this is crunch time. To start with, here's some news that might interest you. I'm thinking of buying the flat.'

'What flat?'

'The one in Highbury, of course. You know old Cooper died? His son's planning to emigrate. He wants to sell up and go to Australia.'

'So?'

'We've been rent-controlled for years, but if we get another landlord it could go sky-high. And the son's offered me first refusal. He wants to do a deal and avoid all the hassle with estate agents. I think it's a good opportunity.'

'We don't believe in ownership,' she teased.

'Socialism's taken a beating, but we haven't lost yet. This doesn't make us Thatcherites. I'm being practical. And it would even up any divorce settlement.'

The moist air was suddenly chilly on her skin. 'Now you want to get divorced?'

'Don't you? We can't go on in this kind of limbo.'

She left her spot at the window. He was running the tap in the basin, splashing water on his torso to cool down. They'd fall over each other if they weren't careful. 'I guess not, but what's brought this on all of a sudden?'

'It's hardly sudden.'

In the five years since their parting, which had never quite acquired official status, they'd danced around this conversation on a number of occasions. Then one or other of them would dive away, neither ready to draw a line nor reopen a wound that might otherwise have a chance to heal.

'I suppose there wasn't any point until one of us wanted to marry again... Jesus! Is that why you're here?'

'No, it isn't why I'm here. And nobody's talking about marriage.'

'Oh,' she said, deflated.

He looped a damp towel around his neck. 'So there you have it. What do you think?'

'About divorce? It seems... very final...'

'Look, I never wanted us to split in the first place. But I accept now that I wasn't pulling my weight. I was making things tough, whereas Toby...'

'Toby was a port in a storm, when Lily was going through that difficult patch, partly brought on by what *you* did. And when my father was ill... and you were never around.'

'You asked me to stay away!'

'Only while I was trying to sort out my head. Do we have to hash all this up again? Anyhow, it's more than a question of physical distance. It's a question of trust. The knowledge that somebody is 100 per cent on your side...' She tailed off.

Alex had folded his arms and was gazing at her with almost forensic analysis. His face, his collarbone and the prow of his nose had caught the sun in Romania; the rest of his body, still sinewy and disconcertingly familiar,

404

was pale. 'As it happens, I'm not here because I want a divorce. I'm here because I want us to get back together. Don't you know how much I've missed you?'

She sank onto the bed again because there was nowhere else to sit. She pulled one of the pillows close to her chest and rested her chin on top of it.

He went on, 'You know I genuinely believed that what we had could transcend everything...'

'Oh, Alex, the great deluded romantic!'

'It might be misguided to keep to your ideals, but isn't it better than being a total cynic?'

'We did have something special,' she admitted. 'Losing it was heart-breaking.'

His voice was low and coaxing. 'You don't have to tell me. I know exactly what we threw away. But maybe we can reclaim it. Give it time, you said. Haven't we done that now? Come back to me, Jess. Please. The sights I've seen recently, the grimness of everything...'

'The orphanages?'

'They wouldn't let me in. Officially. But what I found out is frankly horrendous – and it concentrates the mind. I've experienced enough, to know what matters to me, what I value, and I'm not interested in anyone else but you.'

She laughed at this. 'Not your typical mid-life crisis,' she said.

'We're not your typical mid-lifers.'

He joined her on the bed, his restless eyes seeking hers, the corner of his mouth lifting wryly. 'I think you should move out of the Whispering Pines and in with me.'

'But I like my little cottage! Suppose I want to stay in the country?'

'In your sister's pocket? Really? Your opportunities will be much better in London. We spent so many good years in the flat, didn't we? And I thought, if we could buy it, if it was really ours, we could get some of that back.'

'You forget Harry's still at school.'

This was a minor obstacle to Alex. 'He'll leave next year. Not long to wait. The main thing is that we can be comrades again, we can share and support each other as we always used to. So there you have it, Jessa-mine, my cards on the table.'

'Are you serious about this?'

'Look me in the eye,' he said. 'Tell me you haven't missed us. We belong together, don't we, you and I? We always have.' He began to hum, inaccurately, the Bill Withers song, 'Just the Two of Us'.

She didn't look at him. She covered her face with her hands. One of the cats in the yard yowled. They could hear the vegetable seller trundling his cart along the street: *'Carciofi, melanzane, zucchini, pomodori... Carciofi, melanzane, zucchini, pomodori...'*

'I've been too busy,' she said. 'I've been a single parent with demanding relatives, trying to build a career in the poorly paid creative sector, while you've been pursuing your *ideals*. Swanning around forbidden territory – no excuses because you *like* worming your way into dangerous places – glorying in your mission to call the world to attention!'

'I don't travel all that much.'

'That isn't the point...'

'No, the point is, it's all a bit meaningless without you. Can't we give it a go?'

'I don't know if the timing's right.'

'If you wait for the timing to be right,' said Alex, 'you wait forever.' As if he were pulling a rabbit out of a hat, he produced a bottle of Grillo from beside the bed and waved it at her. 'I bought this while I was out. Fancy a lukewarm white wine?'

'Have you got a corkscrew?'

'Sweetheart, have you ever known me to travel without a bottle-opener? Promise me you'll think over what I've said.'

She flipped the pillow she'd been cradling behind her back and leant against it. The range of vegetables in the seller's melancholy cry was expanding: '...*zucchini, pomodori, cipolle, fagiolini*...'

Alex rinsed a dusty glass (there was only one) poured in some wine and offered it to her. They sipped it in turn.

'Okay, I'll think about it,' she said.

34

Lily was following Tina Roselli through a forest of white marble: arches and pillars and domes, angels and virgins and crucifixes. The paths were narrow and the graves very close. People wanted to be interred together, stacked on top of each other for companionship in the afterlife. Fresh flowers adorned recent burials but most of the bouquets were plastic, their colours bleached to pastel by the strength of the sun. Tina stopped and laid a single white rose next to a pot of artificial pink ones. She took a tissue from her bag and rubbed some smudges of dirt from the headstone. She took another tissue and dabbed her eyes. 'My poor mamma,' she said. 'My poor papa. My poor little brother.'

She'd apologised that she had only a couple of formal photographs of her parents, kept in her flat in Palermo, and none at all of Francesco or his daughter. Lily pictured him slim and dark and handsome, a bit like Marcello, but it was impossible to know for sure and the features of Carlotta-known-as-Carlottina Roselli (formerly Galetti) didn't give her much of a clue. Signora Roselli was matronly, like Dolly, but more formidable.

She had a helmet of black permed hair and jangling gold earrings. She was wearing a kingfisher-bright dress because her husband's aunt's funeral was now over. She'd insisted it was no problem to take Lily to the cemetery to pay her respects to the souls of her family.

Lily regarded Catholicism as a fascinating but alien doctrine, a bizarre conspiracy, with its emphasis on ritual and sacrifice, to keep people downtrodden and miserable. Not that the Catholics she'd met in person were particularly miserable – and the Roselli family, despite three days of sitting around a dead person's coffin, had been both cheerful and hospitable to her. She had been received with great warmth and a combination of excitement, disbelief and curiosity. Might she really be their niece?

'Anybody can see she's from *nostro paese*,' Tina's husband, Guido, had declared, meaning specifically their neighbourhood, the Belice valley, rather than the entire island. Guido was a plump avuncular man, with feathery tufts of speckled hair above his ears. He wore glasses with clip-on dark lenses. When he raised them, he looked like an owl.

'*Veramente?*' Lily said, marvelling. 'Really?'

'Even if you are not of our blood,' said Tina graciously, 'you are welcome.'

Gerald was acting as interpreter, explaining Lily's situation, smoothing the way. 'You don't barge in with a demand,' he'd warned. 'That would be crass. You have to build up gradually to what you want. We invite them to take a drink with us. We exchange *complimenti*. We find out who else and what else we have in common. Though it's probably best not to mention the other Carlotta.'

Dolly had stayed with Agnese. Gerald and Lily had gone with the Rosellis to a nearby bar, newly-furbished like their bit of the town, where rows of neat modern houses sat cheek by jowl with the abandoned ruins. They chose a table inside because it was too hot on the pavement, despite the shade of the awning. A fan revolved on the ceiling and another smaller one whirred on the counter without much effect. Lily felt, as usual, under-dressed, but nobody looked critically at her. She ordered a Coke; the older generation chose coffee and grappa.

Carlottina apologised that her own children had left directly after the funeral. 'They would be nearer to your age,' she said. 'Company for you. Sandro, our youngest, is twenty-six.'

Cousins, thought Lily. I could have actual cousins!

And then it turned out that Tina was a nurse, so a blood test was no problem for her and she would be willing to oblige. This result came a good way into the afternoon. Lily had finished her Coke and another round of coffees had been ordered. Gerald had covered a number of topics until he'd found mutual acquaintances. These included a doctor in Palermo, an electrician who turned out to be Guido's cousin, and a con-merchant at whose hands they'd all suffered. Finally, he broached the subject of Francesco – which the Rosellis had been expecting all along, because of the message from Agnese Fantoni.

Tina was enthralled by the idea of acquiring a long-lost niece, who was also *inglese*, and her cheeks flushed. That was why she agreed to the DNA test. She fanned herself with a scarf she kept in her handbag. It was one of the most capacious handbags Lily had ever seen. It was mottled green and shiny, as if it were made out of crocodile skin. She knew it couldn't be, and it wouldn't bear scrutiny among the elegant bags in the di Monza boutique in Rome – though Tina was not the sort of person to be intimidated by glamorous sales girls.

They'd left Guido in the bar, watching sport on the television suspended from the ceiling. Tina had agreed to direct them to the family grave. Gerald's car, unusually for Italy, had a retractable hood, which he had lowered so they could enjoy a breeze. She'd sat regally in the front seat, in her smart clothes, soaking up intrigued glances. 'This is a small town,' she'd said to Lily, with the satisfaction of one who had escaped its boundaries.

Lily's feet were now filmed with white dust from the marble chippings. She was standing six inches from (potentially) the bodies of her grandparents and her biological father. And the pitiful remains of an infant, thought to be Serafina Galetti. She added a white rose of

412

her own to Tina's and stood awkwardly to one side. Her reactions were so muddled and confused she couldn't disentangle them.

Tina was still wiping her eyes and blowing her nose; Sicilians were never afraid to show their emotions. She embraced Lily and said solemnly, 'We can't argue with the will of God.'

'No,' agreed Lily, thinking: Francesco didn't get beyond twenty, younger than I am. He didn't grow old enough to betray or disappoint or fail. The pathos of this hit her hard. She might be the only thing he had left behind – which was a breath-taking responsibility. It must be the same for Alex; he must have the same little voice whispering in his ear: are you up to it?

Tina let Lily go and dropped to a crouch to alter the position of the two white roses. Then she shook her scarf from her green crocodile handbag and tied it over her head and made a sad clucking noise. 'I am going into the chapel to pray,' she said. 'Do you want to come?'

What was the correct answer? Would she be aghast to hear Lily wasn't a practising Catholic? Before she could speak, Tina was flicking invisible grains of dust from her bare shoulders and giving her an affectionate pat. 'But no, you have nothing to cover yourself.'

The chapel would be cool and dark and tranquil. Lily was exposed to the blast of the sun and dazzled by the glitter of the marble, but she said, 'It's okay, I'll stay outside.'

'*Va bene.*'

Gerald had taken refuge by a line of cypress trees; he was smoking a cigarette and keeping his distance. She went to join him.

'How goes it?' he said. 'With the aunt?'

'She's gone inside to pray. I don't know who for. She doesn't seem bothered about Serafina. Whoever she was.'

'Are you?'

'Yes, I am! Poor mite. She must have had family searching for her. They must have been driven wild when they couldn't find her. That's so sad! And what will the Galettis do if the DNA comes back positive for me? Dig her up? Which would be horrific.' She was struggling to cope with the scale of the tragedy, her emotions churning. *She* could have been the one in the grave, instead of the unknown infant who surely deserved her own memorial.

Gerald said, 'They won't dig her up.'

'How d'you know?'

'Because they won't want to disturb the dead. Who knows what fragments the coffin contained anyway?' Lily flinched and he consoled her, 'Mourning goes on a long time in this country and the souls of those who passed on are revered. That child won't be forgotten, wherever her actual remains may lie.'

A prickling sensation ran down Lily's spine. 'You say she won't be forgotten, but look at my case! I'd have been stuck in that orphanage, wouldn't I, if it hadn't been for Jess and Alex?'

'That's not the Rosellis' fault. They'd have had their own kids to look after and no spare cash. It would've been the same for any other relatives – even if they did start to suspect a mix-up.'

'I'm not blaming *them*, but I don't understand why it took Carlotta nearly ten years to show any interest. That's not the way a mother behaves.'

'Why do you say it was ten years?'

'Okay, so I know she told Alex she'd come back from America to find me and didn't get here in time. But that sounds awfully convenient, doesn't it? I don't believe her.'

Gerald lit a fresh cigarette from the tip of the old one. He seemed nervous. 'She may have been telling the truth,' he said.

'I don't think she ever comes clean about anything.'

'Look, I can see that's how it might appear to you, but you shouldn't be too hard on her. I hope you won't be too hard on Dolly either.'

'What's Dolly got to do with it?'

'Quite a lot. Shall we go for a walk while your long-lost aunt is saying her Hail Marys?'

'This is what Toby does,' said Lily.

'What?'

'Takes me for a walk when he has something serious to say so he doesn't have to look at me. It must be a family trait—' She broke off. She hadn't previously been able to claim any family traits of her own, but, if the DNA results were as expected, in future she could compare herself to all the other Galettis. How freaky was that?

Gerald didn't notice her unfinished sentence. 'Dolly was brought up in an orphanage too,' he said. 'She doesn't talk about it much. It was during the war, so conditions would have been harsh.'

'Oh, my goodness,' said Lily. 'It wasn't...?'

'Your convent? No, though she wasn't keen on you going there either. You should know that Alex brought you over to us and she tried to persuade me to take you in. I hope you won't hold this against me, but it wouldn't have been appropriate. A middle-aged man and a little girl... So you were placed with the nuns, but Dolly was determined to get you out. She didn't want you to endure what she'd been through. You'd rather captivated her.'

'She wanted me to be adopted?'

'Not by just anybody, dear girl. I once had a bit of a soft spot for Alex, I'll admit, but the fact is, if it wasn't for him, you wouldn't be here today. Dolly felt the same. And she felt this justified some string-pulling. Do you know much about bureaucratic procedures in Italy?'

'They're slow?'

'Pace is infinitesimal – even back then when adoption regulations weren't so strict. Cases are batted from pillar

416

to post for months; years. And for a foreign one, you can double it. Not yours. Yours was remarkably smooth and swift thanks to the intervention of Father Rondini.'

The priest who had lost Dolly her reputation. Lily didn't see why he should be thanked for anything.

'He's always been very obliging to her,' said Gerald. 'She used to work for him, you know. He was besotted with her *cartocci*.'

Lily supposed this was a sweet treat and not a part of her anatomy, but she couldn't suppress a snort of disgust.

'What is it?'

'I've been told about Father Rondini.'

'Ah… Rumours are pernicious, aren't they? Priests tend to have older housekeepers but at that time Dolly was young. It's a nice job and it must have seemed like heaven to her, but it was an unwise appointment. People were jealous, perhaps? Who knows?'

'So she didn't have an affair with him?'

'It doesn't matter whether or not something is true, the crowd will believe what it wants. And measures have to be seen to be taken. I don't ask about her private life and I don't expect her to meddle in mine. Whatever happened between them, the padre knew she'd been unfairly treated. Perhaps that's why he was prepared to listen to her request and use his influence to speed things up.'

417

Lily noticed that he hadn't once called Dolly 'that bloody woman'.

He went on, 'It's possible the other Carlotta had learned about your placement in the convent and did come back from the States, as she said. She probably thought she'd have plenty of time to get down to Sicily and claim you – though she may have been nervous of her reception by the Galettis.' He chuckled. 'Especially as she'd stolen her sister-in-law's name.'

'Don't make excuses for her,' said Lily.

'But if Dolly got wind of this, she wouldn't have allowed it to scupper the process. She was doing what she thought best and she was convinced you'd have a better life in England with Alex and Jess. That's why, if Carlotta came, she came too late. You'd already gone.'

They had reached the end of the line of cypresses. In the distance Lily saw the door of the chapel open and Tina Roselli emerge, a strong splash of turquoise against the white background. She folded her scarf and fluffed out her perm. She put on her sunglasses, peering around for them, and began to stride towards the parked car.

Lily and Gerald turned back too. 'It's also why she felt guilty,' he added. 'When Carlotta turned up again that summer.'

'And took us on the fishing trip?'

'It was a frightful mess, wasn't it? A catalogue of disasters. Dolly wanted to put things right. I didn't find this out until recently, but she was the one who told

418

Carlotta where you lived in London. Not a wise move. Apparently, she'd said she wanted to write a letter of apology, but I gather she went a bit further than that.'

'Yeah, she caused plenty of trouble.'

'Dolly loves your parents,' Gerald said abruptly. 'Such a shame they're not together anymore.'

'Their split was Carlotta's fault,' said Lily. Then she relented. 'And mine too, I suppose.'

Gerald fingered his nicotine-yellow moustache. 'We have the leading role in our own lives,' he said. 'But not necessarily in other people's. You shouldn't beat yourself up – any more than Dolly should. It seems to me you've had a quite a pleasant existence as a McKenzie. But nice to be in a position to find out about the rest of your heritage too.'

'You didn't have to tell me any of this,' said Lily. 'So why did you?'

He indicated the mass of gravestones, sharply defined against the blue haze of the distant hills, commemorating the generations who had lived and worked and died in the valley. 'You couldn't come this far, to this cemetery, without knowing the beginning of the story. What you do with the information is up to you.'

35

A note had been pushed under the door at Villa Ercole but nobody spotted it until the morning. Dolly came across it when sweeping with her long-handled dustpan and brush and passed it to Lily. 'See! They are arrived!'

The note was written in Jess's firm italic script.

> *Hope you enjoyed your outing! We are staying in Pensione del Sole in Roccamare and will come to see you tomorrow. J xx.*

Lily had slept fitfully because she'd had too much to drink. They had stayed in Santa Margherita to eat with the Rosellis in a pizzeria owned by another of Guido's cousins. Gerald had paid for the pizzas but the wine had been on the house. Her head was throbbing and the discovery that Jess was down the road was a relief. She didn't want to wait for her to come to the villa. She persuaded Dolly that they should go and find her.

'We missed her because we were out for so long yesterday. I don't know why she didn't tell us when she was coming.'

'Pensione del Sole is not very good place for your mother,' tutted Dolly. 'She must sleep here.'

But when they called at the *pensione*, the landlady informed them the occupants of room seven had gone out; she didn't know where. Dolly needed provisions from the *alimentari*; she would go to Nuncia's and stock up on bread too. Did Lily want to come?

'I'll go for a wander,' said Lily. 'You don't need to wait for me. I expect I'll find them somewhere and they can give me a lift back to the villa. Or else I'll walk.'

'As you like.' Dolly seemed mildly put out, but Lily didn't want to go back to Nuncia's and have her exclaim and reminisce about how close she and Marcello used to be in the old days. It grated.

She set off through the town, heading for the main piazza, hoping to spot Toby and Jess taking breakfast – cappuccino and cornetti, at any rate – in one of the bars there. They would be sitting outside; they wouldn't hide away from the sun when they saw so little of it. They would stand out among the Italian holidaymakers; Jess, in particular. First she tried the Caffe Centrale, which she and Harry had always preferred, followed by the Jolly Bar opposite. She had no luck in either.

She noticed, with sudden glee, that the fountain in between the cafés was playing again. The jet was more of a spray than a torrent, but it wasn't competing with Villa d'Este. It had flushed away the dead leaves and, from a certain angle, appeared to cast a shower of rainbows. She was admiring this spectacle when a scooter cruised so close that it almost shaved the back of her leg. She jumped out of the way and collided with a group of boys engaged in dribbling a Pepsi cola can to each other across the cobbles. One of the players stamped on the can; the others howled and threw themselves on top of him in an invigorating brawl. Lily left the piazza.

She mooched along the promenade, checking at the other bars that overlooked the deep enticing blue of the Mediterranean. The sea was especially tempting in the morning, when the sand was raked and litter-free and the sun benign. She crossed the road and stood at the top of the steps that led to the beach. Few swimmers were in the water and she wished she'd brought her costume with her. It would be bliss to plunge in. She took off her sandals and walked down to the water's edge. The ripples felt cool and refreshing between her toes. With her free hand she shaded her eyes to see if she could recognise any of the frolicking bodies. Some young children in a family group were leaping after an inflatable ball. A bald man in goggles was powering himself parallel to the shoreline as if swimming lengths in a pool. Two ladies in vivid floral swimsuits were tentatively preparing themselves for the change in temperature.

Then she saw Jess. She'd risen in spectacular fashion from beneath the surface, like a mermaid, her hair falling in wet sheets down her back. She was splashing water at the man with her and he was splashing back. They both dived out of sight again and the place where they had been boiled and frothed as if they were scuffling under the sea. Lily was puzzled. She didn't think they could be fighting. She hadn't detected any aggression or heard any cry for help, but the behaviour seemed out of character for Toby. More like Harry, in fact. Harry loved to goad.

When Jess's companion rose and shook himself like a dog Lily felt a glow of delight. Harry had come after all, he was here too! They'd be able to revisit their old haunts around Villa Ercole. It wouldn't be the same as being with Marcello, but they'd know how to have fun. And Dolly would smother him to bits. Harry was on typical form, thrashing about again, getting carried away. And Jess must have thought so, because she put her palm against his chest and very deliberately pushed him back under the water. Before he submerged he grabbed her hand and pulled her down with him in a great splash. Moments later they surfaced simultaneously and it was what he did next that threw Lily into a state of total disarray.

He kissed her.

Lily dropped her sandals and rubbed her eyes. She was over a hundred yards away. They had the same height and lanky build, but it wasn't Harry she was watching. She was an idiot! Harry wouldn't have given up surfing with his mates for a holiday with his sister. It was her father. She jumped up and down on the spot, calling out their names, 'Jess! Alex! Over here!'

They both turned to the shore. Then they waved. It was one of those hearty vigorous waves employed by people who wanted to compensate for any possible embarrassment. For what? Fighting in the sea like kids? Not coming directly to Villa Ercole? Being together? She watched them approach, paying close attention to their body language. At one point Jess's footing faltered and Alex grabbed her arm. He didn't immediately let go.

'Lily, my darling!' Jess cried when she reached the shore. 'I hardly recognised you. You look wonderful, so healthy and tanned.'

'What are you doing here?' said Lily.

'You knew I was coming.'

'No, I meant Alex.'

He winked at her. He didn't consider, as Jess would have done, that he was soaking wet and if he cuddled her she'd get wet too. He wrapped his arms around her and raised her off the sand as if she were a child. 'Aren't you pleased to see me?'

'Put me down, first. Then I'll tell you.'

He laughed. Jess had fetched their towels and handed him one. 'We couldn't resist a morning swim,' she said.

'Oh, was that swimming?'

Alex, towelling his chest, lunged for her. He knew how ticklish she was. 'I can throw you in too if you're asking for it.'

Lily squealed. Then she made her face go solemn and said to Jess, 'You never told me you were bringing him.'

'I didn't know myself until yesterday. It was his choice. He wanted to see you.'

Alex said, 'You've had quite a time of it, my flower.'

Lily took a deep breath. 'You won't believe this,' she said. 'Yesterday I met the other one.'

'The other what?'

'The other Carlotta Galetti.'

'Oh, my God!' said Jess, stunned. 'The one who lives in Palermo?'

'She was in Santa Margherita with her husband for a family funeral. She's called Tina Roselli now so luckily it's not too confusing. Anyway, she's going to do the test with me.'

'The DNA test, do you mean?'

'Yes.'

Jess might have been sculpted from ivory. When she took Lily's hand the contrast in their skin tones was striking. 'And if you find out you're related to her, it will mean the Carlotta in Rome was telling the truth, won't it?'

'I suppose it will. But I should go ahead, don't you think? Why wouldn't I? It was your idea in the first place. You got Toby to tell me about it. Didn't you say he was coming too?'

'He couldn't make it after all,' said Jess, wrapping her towel around her like a sarong and starting up the beach.

'So there was a spare plane ticket?'

'Yes.'

'If Alex has come here with you,' persisted Lily, 'does this mean that the two of you have got back together again?'

'No, it doesn't,' they both said in unison.

She didn't believe them.

*

Lily waited outside Pensione del Sole while Jess and Alex went up to their room to change. She propped herself against the whitewashed wall watching a cat toying with a prickly pear, impervious to its spines, batting and rolling it along the dusty path, then pouncing as if it were a live creature. She didn't have to wait long. When they emerged Jess had a suitcase; Alex didn't.

'Aren't you checking out?' Lily asked him.

'I don't know. It might be easier to stay on here. It rather depends on the reception I get.'

'You mean, from Gerald?'

'Do you think he'll want to see me? Especially if I'm not the person he's expecting. Mind you, I'd hope we could be civilised. He can't help being a self-centred bugger but—'

426

'He's very kind,' Lily defended him. 'Kinder than you know. He's even fond of you, for some reason.'

'Really?' His expressive eyebrows danced a little jig on their own, but Lily had no intention of repeating her conversation with Gerald; it was private, between the two of them.

Alex slung Jess's case into the boot of the car and they climbed in, rolling down all the windows. Jess said brightly, 'You must have so much to tell us, darling. Were they fabulous, the gardens?'

'What gardens?'

'The ones you went to visit in Tuscany and so on. You did see them, didn't you?'

'Gosh, I forgot… so much has happened since.' That trip had taken place in another lifetime and been overshadowed by subsequent events. 'Yes, they were amazing. The emphasis is on the structure rather than the planting and it's given me a few ideas. I learnt lots of tricks of perspective that'll come in useful. There were these guys on the course who always had to work out the maths and geometry of everything on their calculators, which I thought was a bit over the top, but —'

Jess broke in, 'That reminds me, someone you met on your travels phoned for you the other day. An Italian, I mean.'

'Oh?'

'I gave him the number of Villa Ercole and told him to try there.'

A man. Lily's heart lurched. Marcello? But why would he ring England when he already knew where she had gone? 'Did he give his name?'

'Oh, yes. Nicolo.'

'But I don't know anyone called Nicolo!' She reviewed her workmates among the tomato vines: Fabio, Gilberto, Alfredo. They wouldn't know her British telephone number either. And she couldn't recall giving it to anyone else during the garden tour.

'Well, whoever he is, you must have made an impression on him.' Jess laughed. 'I expect you'll find out when he rings the villa.'

There was both consternation and joy at the appearance of her parents. Alex hung back, unnaturally subdued, to allow Jess to be feted by Dolly. But Dolly had no inhibitions. She threw her arms around his waist because she couldn't reach much higher and tugged him inside the house. Gerald was more circumspect. He hovered on the threshold between his study and the hallway, with a bemused frown.

Alex held out his hand. 'I don't want to impose on you,' he said. 'But I was worried about Lily – I heard she'd been in trouble with the police – and Toby gallantly let me take his place on the plane.'

Lily had to admire the way he was spinning the incident for his own ends. She murmured to Jess, 'He does know it was all Dinah's fault?' Jess nodded.

Gerald clasped the proffered hand. 'Dear boy, it's been far too long.'

They moved in a group towards the kitchen. On the table lay a good selection of Nuncia's wares. 'In case you are hungry,' said Dolly, setting a pot of coffee on the hob.

Jess and Alex were talking in overlapping sentences, reminiscing, firing questions, explaining their movements, apologising for the years of silence. Lily wondered if really they were conversing with one another. Neither Dolly nor Gerald seemed particularly attentive. In Sicily, you lived in the here and now.

Gerald, absently examining his fingernails, suddenly muttered, 'Good Lord! The present!' and stumbled out of the room. He came back with a stiff paper carrier bag with the word 'SALDI' written on it. 'This was dropped off while you were out, Lily. The young man said it was a present you'd left behind.'

'Marcello?' said Lily faintly.

'Is that who he was, Marcello Campione? Well, fancy!'

'Where is he now?'

'Went down to Roccamare, I believe.'

While she had been in Roccamare, he had come to Villa Ercole. And vice versa. How frustrating!

'As a matter of fact,' said Alex, leaping to his feet, patting his pockets, 'I've brought you a present too.'

'Have you?'

She was aware, when he produced the bottle of perfume – 'Eureka!' – and insisted she try it, that she should have been more grateful. She exclaimed over the lovely floral scent and dabbed it behind her ears and on her wrists, but she couldn't stop her eyes darting to Marcello's gift.

'What's the mystery in the bag?' he said.

Lily drew out the orange dress. Jess and Dolly both leant forward instinctively to feel the fabric.

'Christ, love,' said Alex. 'You're going to look like an ice lolly in that.'

'Shut up,' hissed Jess.

'It's all right,' said Lily. 'I've tried it on. I know it suits me. I couldn't go back to pay for it because of the police business… so Marcello's stepped in. I'll have to go and find him.'

'But you've only just got here.'

'I know.' The coffee was bubbling and Dolly was assembling the cups. Lily turned to Gerald. 'Have you still got those old bikes? Could I borrow one?'

'Dear girl, when do we ever throw anything away?'

'Isn't this a bit of a wild goose chase?' said Alex. 'You've no idea where he is.'

'You spend half your life chasing wild geese! Not getting anywhere.'

'Aye,' he acknowledged. 'But Marcello's bound to come back here, isn't he?'

'Is he?'

'After a gesture like this? He bought the dress, right?'

'Yes.'

'Then I reckon he's going to want some gratitude.'

'That's exactly what I'm going to do,' said Lily. 'I'm going to cycle into town and find him and thank him.'

They didn't argue. Gerald rescued the least rusty bike from the lean-to shed. Alex checked the tyres. Lily rode off. For the second time that morning she cruised the streets of Roccamare, with an eye out for both the Fiat and its driver. She drew a blank with the Cinquecento because they were so many and so often beige and she couldn't remember the registration. Cycling around the piazza and through passageways and up and down the promenade was much quicker than walking and she wasn't going to give up her search, even if it meant dumping the bike and diving into the gloomy back rooms of every café-bar. But before she did that, she would try the beach.

She rode along the front again, slowly, looking for a figure swimming or sunbathing, hoping she wouldn't make another silly mistake like muddling her father with her brother. When she finally spotted Marcello, he was strolling beside the shore with his hands in his pockets and his sunglasses tucked into the neck of his white tee shirt. She made him out easily. They had toiled as a team for a week and she'd become familiar with the rhythm of his movements, his lilting tread, the set of his shoulders, the shape of his head beneath the close-cropped hair.

She bounded down the steps with the bike. The wheels got stuck in the soft sand but she ploughed through it. She intended to hail him when she was within a few yards, but by then he had noticed her. 'Lily!'

She thrust the bike towards him and he caught the handlebars before it fell. 'Watch me!' she said.

She sprang onto her hands, keeping her back and legs straight as a rod, and began to circle him. He lowered the bike and smiled. When she wavered, he caught one of her ankles to steady her and she completed another circuit. She was aware, from her upside-down position, of the interest of small children, many of them dipping their own heads to see what it would feel like. She jumped back onto her feet again and shook the sand from her hair. She was feeling dizzy and breathless and her face would be pink from exertion, but she was too proud of herself to worry about any of that.

'*Bravissima!*' said Marcello, clapping.

'I didn't know if I could do it, but I've been practising. What about you?'

'You want me to make a fool of myself, here, in front of all these kids? Dream on, Liliana.' He came closer. 'You have sand in your eyelashes.'

She blinked and he drew his thumb lightly down her lid, flicking the curl of her lash. The caress continued, outlining her cheek and jaw, the contours of her mouth.

She kept her eyes shut. He slid both his hands around her back so that he was squeezing her tightly again, as he had done in Castelvetrano. Then he bent his head and they repeated the kiss, leisurely and gloriously fulfilling. She didn't want it to stop. She savoured every second, every nerve end tingling. Her insides were dissolving; it didn't seem credible that her outer flesh could stay firm and tangible. His body was reassuringly solid too, muscular and scented with tomatoes. 'That's what I can taste,' she said when they eventually pulled apart. 'Tomatoes.'

Marcello lifted her hair and dropped a procession of kisses on the back of her neck, which made her quiver. 'You smell even more delicious.'

She supposed that wearing expensive French perfume to perform handstands on a beach was a little eccentric. 'It's lily of the valley. A present from my father.' She added hastily, 'I must pay you back for the dress. I can't let you buy it for me.'

'It's not necessary.'

'No, please, I insist.'

'*Come vuoi.* As you like. I hope I see you wearing it.'

'Absolutely! When? How long are you here? Shouldn't you still be picking the tomatoes?'

'They're finished, more or less,' he said. 'We even worked on Sunday to gather the crop. That's why I couldn't come to the beach.'

He hadn't abandoned her. He was always going to come back. Their fallout had been entirely in her own mind. 'So now you're free?'

'Yes.'

'But your family aren't due for another two weeks?'

'Who tells you this?'

'Nuncia in the bakery.'

'Ah, Nuncia! Well, in ten days, I think. But for me, is different. I can go there when I want.'

He'll have a room with a proper bed, thought Lily, not an old mattress on a cellar floor. Comfort as well as passion! 'Does that mean we can go dancing tonight?' The clubs in Roccamare wouldn't have the surreal atmosphere of the derelict cinema, but there would be music and mellow lighting. 'And I can wear the dress.' She didn't say anything about letting him take it off, but that was hardly necessary. A pleasure deferred would have its own appeal.

He must have shared her thoughts. He beamed and kissed her again.

'You should come up to Villa Ercole with me now,' she said. 'They'll all want to see you. Leave the car. Let's walk. We're not in a hurry, are we?'

He picked up the bike for her and carted it off the beach and onto the road. They took turns, one pedalling, the other jogging, interspersed with delays and diversions and flurries of electrifying kisses among the juniper bushes, to make their way to the villa.

Lily couldn't have said how long she'd been absent but she didn't think it was any cause for alarm. Marcello was greeted with enthusiasm; there were especial cries of rapture from Dolly that the two of them had reunited, but Jess couldn't hide her agitation.

She took Lily aside. 'He rang again,' she said.

'Who did?'

'The man called Nicolo, the one I gave this number to. You need to call him back.'

36

In the world Carlotta had grown up in, convalescence was an indulgence. That was why her father had never recovered from the pneumonia that felled him. The giant in the leather apron, master of iron and fire, had become wheezing and grey-faced, but he had wielded his red-hot tongs until the end. Likewise her mother. After every miscarriage she'd had to get back to her chores; no wonder her energy was sapped and her heart overburdened. Even Carlotta's own journey to Turin had been made in reckless haste, given the nature of her injuries.

Now, in contrast, she lay restfully in bed in her own pleasant apartment, attended to by solicitous friends. Washing, cooking and cleaning was taken care of. She didn't have to get dressed and go to work. She could listen to music and watch television and eat grapes. She could open her shutters and hear the sounds of normal life proceeding, outside in the street.

Normal life.

Life.

Was that what she'd had inside her? A bunch of dividing cells, advanced enough to give her pain and vomiting, but incapable of taking human form? Not a miracle baby at all, but a malevolent organism, threatening rupture and internal bleeding, threatening to destroy her. It was her own fault: a punishment because she hadn't looked after her first child properly. Nicolo would tell her this was nonsense, but she knew she had failed as a mother.

Immediately after the surgery, her dreams were distorted and populated by ghosts: her parents, Francesco, her in-laws, her old teacher from elementary school, the priest who had taken her First Communion. Nicolo explained that this was due to the effects of the anaesthetic and the delirium would pass. He would make sure she was getting the correct medication. But among the hauntings was another sequence of images, not so much a dream as a relived experience: walking up the path towards the door of the convent of the Blessed Virgin Mary, her feet hurting because new shoes had given her blisters; waiting in the anteroom to meet the nun she had written to; watching the shadows of the trees in the garden darken and lengthen; being watched by the painted Madonna hanging on the wall, with her chubby curly-haired infant on her lap and her eerily calm composure.

Every time Carlotta had heard a footstep, she'd jumped. She hadn't wanted to be caught off-guard, but impatience had drawn her taut as a violin string. At last Sister Imelda had blown through the door as if there were a gale behind her, wringing her hands, her wimple awry. 'Signora Galetti, I apologise for keeping you waiting so long when you have come to us all the way from *America*.' She'd spoken the word with a mixture of reverence and disdain, as if America were a mythical place, a wonderland of temptations to be resisted.

When Carlotta had written her letter of enquiry, there'd been no point in mentioning Serafina by name. There'd have been nothing to identify the baby the nuns had taken in, but they were used to foundlings, orphans, the general unwanted. The child would have been given a saint's name, a bed and an education of sorts. Embroidery and drawn thread work if they were nimble with their fingers, music lessons if they had an ear and a voice, instruction in laundering, cooking, growing vegetables, scrubbing floors – all for the glory of God.

'The child I'm looking for,' said Carlotta, speaking the words with difficulty, 'would be four years old now. You have a little girl about this age?'

'We have two,' said Sister Imelda, ringing a bell.

A few minutes later they were ushered in and introduced. The first, Federica, was surely too old; she was losing her baby teeth. The other, Teodora, had a slight cast in her eye. Carlotta should have taken more time to interact with them, but she knew instinctively that neither was Serafina.

'My baby was perfect,' she blurted, unable to contain her distress. Every mother's baby was, naturally, but she was sure she would have noticed if Serafina's eyes hadn't been absolutely true.

'God is not concerned with outward appearance. He sees the beauty of the soul.' Then, belatedly catching Carlotta's meaning, she said: '*Your* baby?'

'I'm sorry if I didn't explain properly.'

The nun said stiffly, 'We understood you were an American lady wanting to adopt, like the English couple.'

Carlotta felt a wave of panic. 'What English couple?'

'You are married?'

'Widowed.' It must have been obvious she wasn't a rich widow, though the painful shoes were well polished and her dress from Macy's sale was a good quality cotton.

'And you so young,' said the nun in a show of sympathy. 'Forgive me, *signora*, but I don't think you're in a position to adopt a child.'

She was a newly returned émigré, hoping to find a job as a waitress. How could she be responsible for anyone else? 'It's not a question of adoption,' she said, 'if the child is mine.'

Sister Imelda placed a hand on each of the heads of Federica and Teodora, who twisted their fingers in front of them but otherwise kept completely still. 'But these two are not,' she said.

'Don't you have another little girl?' Carlotta had said in desperation. 'Did the English couple take her? Do you have any pictures?'

The nun tried to be helpful. She shooed the children away and came back with a long photograph, which she unscrolled. It showed a row of orphans sitting on benches, but with their shorn locks and dark overalls they all looked exactly the same. Identification was hopeless and Sister Imelda could give no assistance. She put her palms together. 'I shall pray for you, *signora*.'

Then the painted Madonna raised her hands in prayer too, as Carlotta's mind fractured and her memories took on a hallucinatory quality, turned into a nightmare. The door of the convent was banging shut behind her; she was stumbling on the path in bleeding blistered feet; great black birds were swooping down from the sky, attacking her, pulling out her hair to line their nests. She heard a scream from behind the locked door, the guilty cry of the nun, she supposed, until she realised Nicolo was holding her hand and the scream was her own.

'You are in pain?' he said.

'Yes.'

'Where?'

Her feet hurt, her head hurt, her abdomen hurt. 'Everywhere.'

'You need more rest. You need to be well for the wedding.'

The wedding seemed as remote as a mirage, a point she could never reach.

'I know you're disappointed,' he said tenderly. 'But there could be a good side to this.'

'Really?' She couldn't see it.

'We know you have viable eggs. If it's what you want, we can make a baby another way.'

'In a test tube, you mean?'

'Exactly. So much is possible these days.'

She could hear the laughter of children, pretty and fragile as glass. School holidays had begun and they were everywhere. Skipping and jostling on the pavement, riding bikes, playing ball games. Luca might bound into the apartment at any moment with a friend or two. She knew it was afternoon because the sun had moved around the building, but she was sleeping at odd hours and her days had no shape.

'I didn't expect to get pregnant,' she said. 'But what I find so difficult... is coping with the loss all over again. The failure... I think it's broken me.'

'You aren't broken,' said Nicolo, rational as ever. 'You've had a physical trauma, which is influencing the way you feel, but you'll recover from it. And everyone who loves you is going to help.'

*

He was right; she wasn't short of companions. Silvana and Iacopo came daily. Now they no longer had responsibility for the shop, the di Monzas wanted to look after her again and feed her up – just like the old days. Luca was in and out all the time, dancing around her bed in a show of exuberance, reeling off a terrible selection of jokes he thought funny. Eva often called by in the lunch hour and again in the evenings. She'd brought the bridal dress, which she'd finished according to Carlotta's original measurements. It was now hanging from a hook on the back of the bedroom door, under a sheath of polythene, rustling when anyone entered and catching the light like a beam of early morning sunshine.

Silvana insisted that Carlotta lie down after lunch each day to conserve her energy. She reminded her that Nicolo had suffered too. The fear of losing a woman he loved twice over was more than enough for any man. He was staying strong for her benefit and it would be unreasonable of her to neglect her recovery and jeopardise the wedding. She'd go obediently into her bedroom but she tried to avoid sleep; in the daytime it was shallow and superficial and brought with it the hauntings and bad memories that had troubled her. She was glad when Silvana knocked and called her to the phone.

She padded into the sitting room and picked up the receiver. '*Pronto.*'

'This is Lily,' said the voice at the other end, in English.

Carlotta staggered and reached for something that would support her. Silvana swiftly pushed forward a chair and helped her into it. 'Lily?'

'I didn't know who Nicolo Morandi was,' said Lily. 'But he'd been leaving messages so I rang him back. My Italian isn't as good as I'd like it to be, but I think I understood most of what he was saying. I wasn't aware you weren't already married to him, that the boy in the photos...'

'Luca.'

'Yes, Luca. That he wasn't yours. That you had problems with pregnancy...'

'You are calling from England?'

'No, I didn't go back there after I left you. I'm in Sicily. I came to Roccamare instead. And it's been a good thing to do because I've met up with people I hadn't seen in years. Do you remember the Campiones, who had that big party for Ferragosto? And the boy who was my friend, Marcello?'

'I think so.'

'Well, it's great we got together again because now...' She broke off. The happiness leached from her voice. 'But that's not why I'm ringing. I'm so sorry you lost the baby. It would have been a miracle, Nicolo said.'

'There was only one miracle baby,' said Carlotta, taking a deep breath. 'That was you.'

The silence was so long she was afraid Lily had gone away. She rose from her chair and wandered towards the window. The cord of the telephone snaked behind her. 'For my operation,' she said into the void, 'they used keyhole surgery. What they do, they make tiny cuts in your tummy and they send a camera through your belly button. This is so they can discover the site where they need to operate. Do you remember, on Favignana, you said you didn't see any use for a belly button *after* you'd been born? Well, you see, it's not true.'

'Did I say that?'

'You didn't like the way yours stuck out.'

Lily's tone was peevish, as if she resented Carlotta bringing up childish complaints. 'I was a silly self-conscious kid.'

'But for me this was very important. When I saw it I knew you were mine.' The silence was even longer this time. Carlotta continued, 'However, I will do the test with you. I've had so many blood tests in these days, one more will make no difference.'

'It's okay,' said Lily. 'I met Tina Roselli and she promised to do it too.'

'Carlottina?'

'Yes.'

'Matre santa!'

She wished she could see Lily's face when she said, 'She took me to the cemetery. To Francesco's grave. We gave him a white rose each.'

444

Carlotta would not cry. Her gaze travelled around the *salone*, from one vase of flowers to another, in all the colours of the rainbow; her friends had been generous. 'I carried white roses in my wedding bouquet,' she said. 'But I missed his burial.'

'That must have been awful.'

'When something so terrible happens,' said Carlotta, 'it takes a long time to rebuild trust in the world.'

'But you are getting married again? To Nicolo.'

'Yes, in two weeks. I have been given instructions to get well because it's too late to rearrange everything.' She spoke ruefully. The event, once a source of anticipation and delight, had become tainted.

'He invited me,' said Lily.

'Nicolo did?'

'Yes, but I didn't know whether it was a good idea. I wouldn't want to spoil anything.'

He had followed up his suggestion; he had known what would make her happy! Carlotta said, 'I would love to see you there. And I would love you to meet Nico and Luca properly. I know you will like them both. It's a simple ceremony. Not a big traditional church wedding as in Sicily. We will go first to the Campidoglio to make registration and then to a restaurant. I won't wear white and you don't have to wear black.'

'Surely black is what people wear for funerals?'

'For every big occasion. Black is smart. When only have one good outfit it needs to be black.'

'Actually,' confessed Lily, 'my one good outfit is orange.'

'That will be perfect!' said Carlotta. 'Because when we have the photographs I will be like the sunrise and you will be like the sunset.'

'Are you sure you want a stranger at your wedding?'

'But you are not a stranger...' Warm air breezed through the open window, intensified the scents of all the flowers in the room, the jasmine and stephanotis, the phlox and the lilies. Suddenly it seemed the most important thing in the world that her daughter should join her, that the celebration should be doubly joyful. 'I hope it's not too much to ask? I understand it's a long way for you to travel. And you won't know any of the other guests. If you would like to bring someone, your *fidanzato* perhaps?'

'*Fidanzato?*'

'It means boyfriend.'

'Yes, I know.'

'Is he not... Marcello?'

A small stifled giggle. 'Okay, thanks. I'll ask him. I'll think it over and let you know.'

Carlotta tried to keep the longing out of her voice as she said, 'Oh, Lily... I would love it so much if you come.'

37

Jess took breakfast alone on the terrace at Villa Ercole. Dolly flapped around her, bringing pots of coffee, a jug of warm milk, a bowl of fruit, bread rolls and three kinds of jam. 'This is not right,' she said. 'You should not be by yourself. Where are they? Your husband? Your daughter?'

Last night Lily had gone out dancing with Marcello Campione. Jess hadn't been surprised when she didn't come back to the villa to sleep. Alex had offered to stay on in the *pensione* to give her more time to think over their future. To Dolly, she said, 'Alex didn't want to take Gerald's hospitality for granted. He was being tactful.'

'Tsk!' said Dolly. 'That is not a reason. He must move here today.'

'And I'm sure Lily will be back soon.'

Dolly muttered and grumbled. Gerald sauntered out briefly with a coffee and a greeting and offered Jess a two-day-old English newspaper. She flicked absently through the pages, through news that seemed distant and irrelevant. She pushed it aside and watched the sun climb above the vines and the almond trees. She watched the Dutch family pile out of the annexe and into their estate car to set off on a sightseeing trip. She thought they must have forgotten some essentials when she heard the crunch of tyres returning, ten minutes later. But then Lily and Alex rounded the corner, their faces cheerful, their voices animated. The sight of them revived her, made her heart swell and glow.

'We've come to take you to the beach,' Alex announced. 'Dolly too. She deserves a day off.'

'I'm going to change first,' said Lily, who was looking distinctly crumpled.

'Where's Marcello? Isn't he with you?'

'He had to return the car to the Campiones. Alfredo will give him a lift back. The other guys might come too so there wouldn't be room for an extra passenger. But it doesn't matter because I thought, since you've come all this way for me, I ought to spend the day with you anyhow.'

'Oh, that's good to hear! Did you have a nice time?' Jess was aware of the inadequacy of her question as soon as she asked it. Lily simply grinned and twirled and skipped into the house for a shower.

Alex spread a roll with mulberry jam and munched it. He looked searchingly at Jess; she held his gaze. Neither of them spoke. At length he said, 'I'm going to complete my peace treaty with Gerald. I'll meet you and Dolly by the car in, what, twenty minutes? Half an hour? I know it takes her an age to get stuff ready but we're not leaving her behind.'

Jess underwent uncanny flashes of déjà-vu as Dolly filled two baskets with equipment and provisions. 'Are you sure we need all this?' But Dolly insisted. And Gerald, despite the fact that he had his arm around Alex, gave the distinct impression he couldn't wait for them to go and leave him in peace. The three McKenzies were ready and waiting when Dolly scurried back indoors for the beach umbrella. She opened it up for inspection and the fabric, rotted by salt and sun, fell in tatters from the frame.

Alex leapt out of the car and bundled Dolly onto the back seat beside Lily. 'Stuff your excuses,' he said. 'Forget the umbrella. You're coming with us now. *Capisce?*'

'You're being rather bossy today,' observed Jess.

'Somebody has to take control,' he said, grinding the gears. 'No more dithering.'

'Is that a dig at me?'

'Why would you think that?'

Jess didn't reply, conscious of the audience behind them – although Lily would be too wrapped up in her own new relationship to care about her parents'.

Alex parked on the edge of town and they found a clear spot on the beach to decamp and spread out their towels. Lily and Jess discarded their clothes but Dolly did not undress. She sat on the folding chair Alex had

449

carried down in her black linen blouse and skirt. As a concession to the temperature she'd taken off her stockings and her cardigan, but she didn't look happy.

While Jess creamed her legs, Alex took Lily aside and conferred with her. Then he said, 'Right, Doll, you win. We can't have you uncomfortable. I'm going to buy you a new umbrella. Do you want to come and help me choose it?'

Dolly beamed and took his arm. They made an odd couple as they shuffled through the hot sand, she squat and bustling, he shortening his stride and bending to her ear. Jess wondered if this was a deliberate ruse so that she could talk privately to Lily about her plans and she was impressed that he'd thought of it. Except, it turned out, it was Lily who was the interrogator. She squirted sun lotion onto her palm and massaged it into Jess's shoulders. Jess relaxed and closed her eyes.

'I asked you yesterday,' Lily said, 'if you were getting back together.'

'Mmm, you did.'

'And you denied it.'

'Well, it's early days.'

'So it might happen? You're not seeing anyone else?'

'No.'

'Nor's he.'

'I wouldn't know about that, darling.'

'Yes, you would.' The rubbing stopped. 'He's been upfront. He's told you how he feels.'

'Jesus, Lily!' Jess sat up abruptly. 'Where did this come from?'

'From Alex, of course. We met for breakfast in the Caffe Centrale and then Marcello had to get off and I asked Alex why he'd come out here. Was he really so worried about me because he shouldn't have been, I didn't need rescuing. And he said no, he wasn't worried but he was glad you'd overreacted—'

'I didn't overreact. You'd gone missing and been arrested!'

'Because it gave him the chance to join you. And he said he'd grabbed it at once, because you were the love of his life.'

'Did he really say that?'

'Well, not in those actual words.' A brief, dramatic pause. 'What he told me was that if you walked into a room full of people he simply wouldn't see anyone else. They might as well not be there because you were the one and only person who lit up the room for him.'

Jess burst out laughing.

'I don't see what's so funny,' said Lily. 'I thought it was a wonderfully romantic thing to say.'

'Yes,' agreed Jess. 'I suppose it is. And I was the one who said it.'

'You did?'

'About Alex.'

At which Lily began laughing too, until the pair of them were breathless with giggles and wiping away tears. 'What an operator!' said Jess, recovering herself. 'It was years ago when I was trying to explain the effect he had on me to Toby. Obviously, Toby told him and he squirreled it away for later, when it would suit his purpose. He relied on you to report it back to me this time.'

Lily didn't seem to object to being used as a go-between. She said, 'Seriously though, it's true, isn't it? Neither of you has met anyone else who could hold a candle to the other. You *know* if you love someone, don't you? You just *know*.'

Jess smiled. 'Are you saying this is what you feel about Marcello? So soon?'

'We've been working together,' Lily pointed out. 'We were friends before that. And we had a few near misses before last night.' She blushed deeply beneath her tan at the recollection of whatever had happened last night. Jess felt a surge of warm blood through her own veins at the memory of the first time she and Alex had lain in bed together, embarking on their mutual journey of discovery. Lily continued, 'That's why I don't want to go back to England with you next week. I'm not ready. You don't mind, do you? I'd like to spend the rest of the summer here in Roccamare. Dolly says I can help her with getting the annexe ready for visitors and with the harvesting too, so I'll be pulling my weight.'

'The rest of the summer,' repeated Jess, suddenly afraid that she would lose her daughter, that her native land would reclaim her.

Lily said, 'Don't worry. I'll come home in September and finish my course. Marcello's a student too, so we're not rushing into anything.' Reclining on her towel in her skimpy bikini, one hand tousling her curls, the other resting on the curve of her thigh, she looked like a Renaissance Venus. Her smile was beatific. 'I want to have a good summer.'

'Of course you do, my darling!' She hesitated. She couldn't *not* mention the event. 'Does that include going to Carlotta's wedding?' Lily had relayed the phone conversation with details of the invitation and Jess had tried to keep her own opinion neutral.

'Oh, God, that's a tricky one.' Much trickier, evidently, than her feelings for Marcello Campione. 'I still can't decide…'

Jess rolled over, reached out and grasped Lily's hand. 'She wants you there, doesn't she? Basically, I think you should avoid doing anything that would cause any more pain. Either to yourself, or Carlotta…'

'Or you?'

'*I* know you'd never hurt me deliberately, but for her, I guess, it's different. You've misunderstood each other in the past so you need to be clear now. It wouldn't be fair to keep her dangling. Or let her down.'

'I don't want to be paraded among her new family like a specimen from Lost and Found.'

'Why d'you think that would happen?'

'I don't really. I'm picturing the worst-case scenario.' She bit her lip. 'Which is cruel of me, when she's just lost another baby…'

'You're scared she's got too much invested in you,' said Jess. 'I can see why.'

'Alex says sometimes you have to take the risk.'

'And he's probably right. But we can't tell you what to do. You have to make up your own mind.'

'Yeah, I know.'

'Didn't she suggest you could bring Marcello too?'

Lily nodded.

'Well, that would help, wouldn't it?'

Jess was feeling magnanimous. How could she not, basking under a blue sky, wrapped in the warmth of the day? Carlotta Galetti might have been partially responsible for the fracturing of her family and the break-up with her husband, but, God, the woman had suffered and Jess would never choose to cause further suffering.

A large blue and red umbrella was approaching, swamping the couple beneath it. Alex was holding the handle and keeping Dolly well shaded because she was carrying four ice-creams. Once they'd joined them, he ploughed the umbrella into the sand and she handed round the cones. For a few moments they were all too busy with their tongues, licking the melting flavours of pistachio, nocciola and stracciatella, to make conversation.

Then Jess said, 'It's a lovely umbrella, Dolly. Are you pleased with it?'

Dolly nodded and consulted her watch. 'Is nearly midday,' she said. 'We were long time to find the best one.'

Alex said, 'We had to try practically every brolly in the shop before she was happy.'

'There's no hurry for anything, is there?' murmured Jess, lying back on her elbows with her knees drawn up.

'Midday, you need to check out,' said Dolly.

'What's she talking about?'

Alex glanced at Lily, who gave a quick dip of her head as if answering a question he hadn't asked aloud. He said to Jess, 'About Pensione del Sole. And whether I keep the room or not.'

'You mean whether you come up and stay in Villa Ercole instead?'

'Yes.'

Lily was studiously licking her ice cream, as if it required her full concentration.

Jess had been enjoying idling on the soft sand, but now she rose, slipped on her flip-flops and pulled her sundress over her head. 'Come on, then.'

'Come on, what?'

'Let's get over there and fetch your bag. Stick it in the back of the car.'

Alex scrambled to his feet. 'Does it need the two of us?'

The glare of sunlight in her eyes obliterated the company around them. There might have been no one else on the beach, no swimmers or sunbathers or picnickers, no children, no families, no Dolly, not even Lily. Only Alex, a heartbeat away. 'Yes,' she said. 'I think it does.'

38

After two weeks of false starts Lily and Marcello were impatient. Impatient, inventive and insatiable. They made love in the sand hollows in the nature reserve, in the shallows of the sea after dark, in his bed, in her bed, beneath the branches of an old olive tree, between the beanpoles in the kitchen garden, even in the larder of Villa Ercole one time, when they went in search of Dolly's preserves. The air was laced with spirits and vinegar, honey and spice, as if they were cloistered in a cupboard full of aphrodisiacs. Off they went again: licking and tasting and sampling, unbuttoning their clothes with sticky fingers, eager for the warm jolt of flesh into flesh.

Lily was totally absorbed in her romance, living each delicious moment in the present tense. She pushed Carlotta's invitation to the back of her mind – she needed to mull it over, she told herself – until suddenly Jess and Alex were leaving. As she waved goodbye to their bouncy Fiat Uno, Alex said, 'Let us know how it goes.' And she understood she couldn't defer her decision any longer.

She lay with Marcello in their favourite spot in the nature reserve, shielded by vegetation, but with a splendid view of the sea. 'I have to tell Carlotta whether or not I'm going to her wedding,' she said. 'I can't carry on putting it off.'

She was stretched out on her front; he was trailing a hand between her shoulder blades. 'I don't understand what is the difficulty.'

'Apart from anything else, there isn't time to do the DNA test and get the results. Suppose it turns out later that I'm an imposter?'

'That's Carlotta's problem, isn't it?'

'She didn't think it was necessary in the first place. Because of my belly button, apparently.'

'Your what?' He laughed and rolled her onto her back and they tussled until he was sitting astride her. He scooped up a handful of sand and scattered it over her stomach; some grains fell into her navel and he examined it closely. 'It looks normal to me.'

She pushed him off and sat up. 'Yes, but when I was little it stuck out. It was what you'd call an identifying feature.'

'*Allora!*'

'And then there's the hassle of getting there. To Rome, I mean. It's a long journey.'

'You could take the sleeper, no?'

'Would you come with me? You are invited.'

'I am?' A slow smile spread across his face. 'If we book a couchette for two, imagine the fun we could have!'

She hadn't expected him to be so willing. But the sleeper had brought them together, hadn't it, so how could the prospect of a return trip not be enticing? 'Okay, then,' she said. 'I'll do it. I might regret it forever otherwise. I'll call her tomorrow.'

When she rang the next morning, another woman answered and said Carlotta had gone to the clinic for a check-up. Lily had hoped to speak to her herself. 'Should I try again later?'

'If you like, I can take a message.'

'Oh, all right...' And that was it: she was committed.

The train left Palermo at nine, crossed the straits of Messina at midnight, and was scheduled to arrive in Rome the following morning. Lily and Marcello pulled down the blind between their carriage and the corridor and tested the top bunk and then the bottom. Everything about the trip was thrilling: holed up in their tiny private space as the world rushed past their window, mysterious and invisible in the night. They reached Naples at dawn but remained dozing, her head on his chest, their arms and legs entangled, until the gentle light leaking around the edges of the blind became strident. Then the train jerked to a halt. Roused by the clash of brakes, they unravelled themselves and went in search of coffee.

The attendant in charge of the espresso machine had no idea why they had stopped. No one did. In the buffet car they looked out over a swathe of fields and, in the distance, eroded but majestic, a fine Roman aqueduct. The train remained in the field for an hour. When it lurched forward again it never quite gathered its previous speed.

'Oh, God,' said Lily, beginning to panic. 'What if we're late? We should have come up yesterday.'

'We agreed it would be better to spend time in Rome *after* the ceremony, remember? But it's okay. We won't check into the *pensione*. We'll take a taxi directly from the station to Piazza Venezia. We'll make ourselves ready now, in the carriage.'

And it was fun, if challenging, to wash and change and prepare themselves in such a cramped space. Marcello drew up the zip of her one good dress; he fastened the clasp of her bracelet and brushed her hair into submission. She tied his tie and kissed a fleck of shaving foam from his cheek and shook out the creases in his jacket. When the train chugged into the station and they stepped down onto the platform, a glamorous, head-turning young couple, they felt ready for anything.

*

It was unthinkable that a bride and groom should spend the night before their wedding on the same premises.

460

Nicolo and Luca had gone to the di Monzas' apartment to keep Iacopo company while Silvana had been guarding Carlotta like a lioness. She had fielded phone calls and admitted the hairdresser and the florist and three or four girlfriends and chastised Eva for not arriving sooner. The bevy of women preened and chattered like starlings, exchanging lipsticks and anecdotes, happily contradicting each other. They were keyed up and anxious that everything should go right today.

Carlotta sat among them in her dressing gown, drinking coffee, having her hair done, obeying instructions. She felt as if the arrangements were beyond her control, much as they had been for her first wedding, when Mamma Galetti and her own mother had taken charge. She'd slept restlessly and woken early and although it wouldn't be long before Nicolo was at her side again – the ceremony was scheduled for 11.30 – she missed him and willed the hours to pass. She hoped she could master her nerves.

Flavia, who considered herself an artist, took over her make-up, although Carlotta could do it perfectly well herself. She tipped up her face to have her brows plucked, to receive foundation, blusher and mascara. She flexed her fingers to let her nail varnish dry. When hands and face and hair were ready she stepped into her dress.

Eva had brought her sewing bag in case there was any last-minute mending. She sighed contentedly as the gold silk swished and shimmered. 'You look marvellous, *tesora*.'

'I spoke to Nicolo already this morning,' said Silvana. 'He is very composed, as you would expect. And Luca is looking so handsome!'

Carlotta said, 'Lily didn't ring again?'

'Not since last week.'

Carlotta had been disappointed not to take Lily's second call herself – though why should it make any difference? Lily had told Silvana that she and Marcello would be pleased to come to the ceremony. It was unrealistic to expect any more detail. She had no rights over such a tenuous relationship and it was impossible to explain – even to these close friends, even to Nicolo – how vital it was that Lily should be there, the one link between her past and her future.

A horn sounded in the street and Eva peeked through the shutters. 'Iacopo is here with the car.'

'Oh, my goodness!' exclaimed Carlotta. 'Where are my shoes?'

The women darted around the apartment, searching. Flavia laughed and said, 'They'll be calling you Cinderella!'

'Calm yourself,' said Silvana. 'They are in the box in your closet, remember? The car can wait. The guests can wait. There is no one more important than you today.'

Her friends went ahead in two cabs. Iacopo helped Carlotta into the passenger seat of the hired Mercedes and they made stately progress, giving guests plenty of time to congregate in the anteroom of the Sala Rossa. Carlotta would have to wait in the piazza until she was due to make her entrance on Iacopo's arm. It was impossible to relax. 'How will I know if everyone's arrived?' she said.

'Silvana has the guest list. She'll know.'

Carlotta wasn't reassured. Fortunately, Luca was twitchy too. He left his father's side to come out to see her.

'We're still waiting,' he said.

'What for?'

'For our turn. There's one more group to be done and then it's your go.'

'We are not queuing for a ride at Luna Park,' said Carlotta with a nervous laugh. 'I wonder if she is here yet.'

'The English girl?' said Luca.

'Yes. Will you tell me if you see her?'

She had shown him her one and only snapshot of Lily when telling him the story of her miraculous survival. It had been far harder to explain the circumstances to Luca than to Nicolo. At first he'd been incredulous: 'You're saying you have a grown-up daughter? Who lives in England? It's not possible! I don't believe you!' Then he'd been intrigued. Finally, he'd admitted he was curious to meet her.

Carlotta patted his arm; he was so confident, so mature, she was so proud of him! 'I know you will become friends,' she said. 'And I know you will find her for me. She'll be easy to see. She'll be wearing bright orange.'

'Suppose she doesn't come?' said Luca with a matter-of-fact nonchalance.

'Tsk!' said Iacopo with a frown. 'Don't cause alarm, boy.'

Carlotta gripped her bouquet, trying not to crush the stems. 'She will come.'

*

There was a queue for the taxis or, rather, a shape-shifting throng, which never seemed to diminish. Marcello didn't need to consult his watch because there was a clock on a pole by the taxi rank and they could see the hand inching around it. He decided a bus would be quicker, so they abandoned their places, ran across Piazza dei Cinquecento to the number 60 bus stop and jumped aboard. In via Nazionale traffic was snarled to a standstill. Even Marcello, who had resolutely kept his cool, was beginning to look flustered. He took off his jacket and loosened his tie.

'Do you think the wedding will run to schedule?' said Lily. 'Does anything run to schedule in Italy?'

'They may begin late,' he said.

'But?'

He shrugged. 'The civil ceremony, it's not like the Mass in a church. It's very short.'

'How short?'

'Fifteen minutes?' When he saw her expression, he said quickly, 'Or twenty. It's a legal formality, that's all, though the feasting afterwards will go on forever. Why don't we get off and walk? At least we'll be moving, not like the bus.'

Lily was rarely daunted by walking, but she hadn't wanted to turn up on this occasion with dusty sandals and sweat patches under her arms, trailing her battered rucksack. Marcello, in his shirt sleeves, still managed to look unruffled. 'Come on,' he urged. 'It's not so far, about two kilometres.'

The street was a cacophony of horns blown by irritable motorists. The pavements were busy with shoppers and tourists. Marcello took Lily's hand and threaded a route at speed through the crowds. Her bag bounced against her hip, her hair frizzed in the heat and coiled damply on her neck. Neither of them stopped to draw breath, even though she had a stitch beneath her ribs and her nose and throat were clogged with petrol fumes.

'We will do it,' called Marcello over his shoulder. 'Don't worry.'

Three weeks ago, she hadn't even known about this wedding – but three weeks ago she had been angry with

Carlotta, considering herself abandoned by her twice over. Now she knew differently. She could hear Jess saying, 'You should avoid doing anything that would cause any more pain.' So she clung to Marcello's hand and pounded down via Nazionale, past Trajan's Column and the monstrous white edifice that was the Victor Emmanuel memorial; then they rounded the corner and she stopped in dismay.

'We are nearly there,' he said. 'We can arrive in time.'

They were standing at the bottom of a steep flight of steps that seemed to stretch to infinity. 'We have to climb that?'

He stroked her hair back from her face and kissed her forehead. 'No, not that. The one next to it. It's a very splendid staircase, you know. It was designed by Michelangelo.'

The Cordonata was a broad elegant ramp with a much shallower incline, but so monumental she couldn't see where it led. She was hot and footsore and short of breath; she didn't think she had enough air in her lungs to take another step, let alone tackle a hill. 'Oh, fuck Michelangelo,' she said. But it was inconceivable to give in now, so they linked arms and trudged onwards and upwards.

The vast piazza at the top of the ramp was framed by three magnificent palaces and a view over the ruins of the Forum. Disparate clusters of sightseers, tour groups and wedding parties milled in a surreal spectacle. The tourists were mostly in shorts and trainers and gaudy tee shirts. The wedding guests wore tailored suits, buttonholes, precarious high heels. There was more than one bride, drifting about in a cloud of white candy floss. Almost everybody carried a camera, the shutters whirring and clacking like birds.

Lily was aghast. 'However will I find her?' She shaded her eyes and spun in a circle. She had only seen Carlotta once since the trip to Favignana, and on that occasion she had been pale and drawn and unwell. In fact they had both avoided eye contact. What chance did she have of recognising her in this arena?

Then, from some yards away, a young man hailed them. Lily supposed he was an acquaintance of Marcello's, a fellow student perhaps, surprised to meet him out of context. As he came closer she realised he was more of a boy than a man: he had wavy brown hair and a smooth fresh face, no need yet to shave. The well-cut suit and the flower in his buttonhole had made him look mature.

'*Sono Luca Morandi,*' he said. '*Et tu sei Lily?*'

Of course: the boy in the photographs, Carlotta's stepson. '*Sì, sono Lily McKenzie.*' She clasped his proffered hand and forgot to let go. 'Oh, my God!' she exclaimed in English. 'We have the same initials. D'you think that's an omen?'

He looked at her blankly. Marcello took over, introducing himself and explaining the delays they'd had, the mad dash across the city.

'Did Carlotta think I wouldn't make it?' said Lily. She couldn't help being fascinated by the boy. She couldn't have imagined Harry at the same age showing such poise. A new stepbrother! Her family was expanding daily; it was really quite exciting.

Luca gave a very Roman shrug. 'She is waiting, she will not go into the building. She asked me to look for you.'

'And you found me?'

'*Facilemente.*' Easily.

He began to lead the way across the piazza. He called out and a small elderly man with thin strands of silver hair, spectacles and an unusually garish tie jumped to attention. So did the woman he was escorting. She was carrying a bouquet of roses in shades of apricot and cream; her dress was also the colour of glowing apricot. Her hair had been swept up and styled into a French pleat rather than tumbling over her shoulders, but she was instantly recognisable.

'That's her?' said Marcello.

'Yes! Do you remember now?'

Carlotta was approaching, opening her arms as she did so. Marcello took charge of Lily's bag and gave her a little push forward.

'Oh, Lily!' said Carlotta. 'You came!'

'You were expecting me? I'm sorry I didn't speak to you myself, but...'

'I have hoped,' said Carlotta, 'that Silvana did not make mistake.'

'I was worried we'd be late because the train got stuck and we've had to run all the way here from the station. We haven't missed anything, have we? Where are your guests?'

'They are inside, waiting. I stayed out here because I didn't want to miss you. I didn't want to lose you again. And Luca has helped me to find you. You must also meet Iacopo. He is giving me away.'

The elderly man smiled and kissed Lily's hand.

'Afterwards there will be photographs,' said Carlotta. 'You won't believe how many. And I want you to be in them, with Nicolo and Luca. And then we will go to the restaurant and I hope you are hungry because we will have mountains of food. And there will be dancing and speeches. But you must know this. You have seen it before.'

'No,' said Lily. 'Actually, I've never been to a wedding.'

'What, *never*? Is it possible?'

'This will be my first one.'

'Veramente?' Carlotta seemed quite overcome.

Iacopo said, *'Non deve piangere, cara.'* You shouldn't cry, my dear.

Carlotta buried her face for a moment in her bouquet. When she lifted it, her tears sparkled on the roses like raindrops. 'It's because I am happy,' she said. Then she took Lily's hand and they walked together across the travertine paving, through the haphazard selection of other people's wedding guests, towards the grand open doors of the palazzo and the well-wishers who awaited them.

We hope you enjoyed this book.

Penny Feeny's next book is coming in 2019

Acknowledgements

I am deeply indebted to my agent, Laura Longrigg, for her wisdom, support and encouragement – and for being such excellent company; to my editor, Lucy Gilmour, who has been a pleasure to work with – her guidance always insightful and astute; to the team at Aria for their commitment and attention to detail in producing this book; and to the people of Sicily who inspired it.

Author's Note

The resort of Roccamare is fictional, but all other places mentioned in the novel exist. The Belice earthquake, in 1968, became notorious for the length of time it took to rehouse survivors. Fifty years on, the ruined houses of Santa Margherita can still be seen, cheek by jowl with the new town.

HELLO FROM ARIA

We hope you enjoyed this book! Let us know, we'd love to hear from you.

We are Aria, a dynamic digital-first fiction imprint from award-winning independent publishers Head of Zeus. At heart, we're avid readers committed to publishing exactly the kind of books we love to read — from romance and sagas to crime, thrillers and historical adventures. Visit us online and discover a community of like-minded fiction fans!

We're also on the look out for tomorrow's superstar authors. So, if you're a budding writer looking for a publisher, we'd love to hear from you. You can submit your book online at ariafiction.com/we-want-read-your-book

You can find us at:
Email: aria@headofzeus.com
Website: www.ariafiction.com
Submissions: www.ariafiction.com/we-want-read-your-book
Facebook: @ariafiction
Twitter: @Aria_Fiction
Instagram: @ariafiction

19471359R00271

Printed in Great Britain
by Amazon